Susan E.. Wallace

The Repose in Egypt

a medley and Along the Bosphorus

Susan E.. Wallace

The Repose in Egypt
a medley and Along the Bosphorus

ISBN/EAN: 9783337234829

Printed in Europe, USA, Canada, Australia, Japan

Cover: Foto ©Andreas Hilbeck / pixelio.de

More available books at **www.hansebooks.com**

THE

REPOSE IN EGYPT

A MEDLEY

BY

SUSAN E. WALLACE

AUTHOR OF "THE LAND OF THE PUEBLOS," "THE STORIED SEA,"
"GINEVRA," ETC.

WITH ILLUSTRATIONS

NEW YORK
JOHN B. ALDEN, PUBLISHER
1891

DEDICATION.

TO

The two dear friends with whom I learned that travel is the saddest of pleasures.

S. E. W.

CRAWFORDSVILLE, IND
October, 1888.

LIST OF ILLUSTRATIONS.

An Egyptian Woman.....................Frontispiece

Head of Menephthah, the "Pharaoh" of the Exodus.. 32

On the Banks of the Nile........ 38

Head of Rameses II............................... 52

 "   " Thothmes II........................... 52

The Asp... 60

The Ibis.. 60

Egyptian Standards................................ 64

Forms of Isis..................................... 64

Egyptian Vases and Amphoræ....................... 68

Egyptians Ploughing and Hoeing.................... 76

The Tomb-Chamber of the Third Pyramid........... 80

The Sphinx of the Pyramids....................... 96

View of the Great and Second Pyramids............ 110

Band of Six Musicians............................. 168

Egyptian Systrum.................................. 168

The Twin Colossi of Amenophis III................ 176

Pharaoh "Necho".................................. 178

An Egyptian King destroying His Enemies. 180

Egyptian Columns.................................. 196

Egyptian War Chariot.............................. 206

Crown Prince of the Ottoman Empire............... 389

THE REPOSE IN EGYPT.

CHAPTER		PAGE
I.	The Burden of Egypt, -	9
II.	The Landing, - - -	11
III.	Suez and Sinai, - -	24
IV.	Crossing the Red Sea, - -	30
V.	Alexandria, - - -	35
VI.	Obelisks, - - -	45
VII.	Cleopatra, - - -	59
VIII.	To Cairo, - - -	70
IX.	The Rise of the Nile, -	78
X.	At Heliopolis, - - -	85
XI.	The Flight into Egypt, -	94
XII.	The Return of the Holy Carpet,	106
XIII.	The Pilgrimage to Mecca, -	120
XIV.	Mecca, the Sacred City, -	128
XV.	Pilgrimage, - - -	136
XVI.	The Repose, - - -	142
XVII.	Poetry and Music of the Arabs,	157
XVIII.	The First Cinderella: A Tale of the Red Pyramid, - -	175
XIX.	In the Isle of the Lily: The Story of the Three Kings, -	194

CONTENTS.

CHAPTER   PAGE

XX. In the Isle of the Lily: Thalia's
Story,   -   -   -   212

XXI. Still in the Isle of the Lily: The
Antiquary's Story,   -   223

XXII. Conclusion,   -   -   252

ALONG THE BOSPHORUS.

I. The First Voyage, 1390 B.C., -   263

II. The Second Voyage, A.D., 1884,   288

III. One Woman: A True Romance,   314

IV. In the Harem,   -   -   368

V. Wedding Customs in the East,   377

VI. At Yildiz Palace,   -   -   383

PREFACE.

The papers here collected contain little to reward the lover of useful knowledge, their purpose being to amuse rather than to instruct. Yet when truth is offered it is on high authority or the result of patient investigation, that no mistake of mine may mislead the reader with whom I love to journey. None will find half the pleasure in hearing, that the writer has had in telling her tale.

The Story of *One Woman* is easily identified. A life, somewhat idealized, too well-known to elude recognition, and familiar in the Orient as stories of Lady Hester Stanhope and Lady Mary Montague were to a past generation.

For permission to re-appear in this shape, I must thank the father of the nameless magazine which died young (Peace to its ashes!), the respective editors of *The Independent, Advance, Congregationalist, Youth's Companion, Christian Advocate*, Bacheller Syndicate, *Frank Leslie's Magazine*, and *Sunday-School Times*.

THE REPOSE IN EGYPT.

I

THE BURDEN OF EGYPT.

I DID not think to write it, but petitions have come to me, mainly from readers who pine to sing and soar, and see; whose unsatisfied wishes are strong and numerous, whose salaries are narrow and narrowing. Give us something about the Nile they say. Tell how the Sphinx looks; is the nose really knocked off? and how about the Pyramids, are they equal to their fame? and were you disappointed in Karnak? So I have a message to deliver; which is the mission of the traveller from the times of Caleb the spy, to the days of Livingston the explorer. I cannot tell anything but what has been told a thousand times, and a thousand times better than I can tell it. For in the oldest literary composition we find allusion to the Pyramids. The name is thought to be the same with the Hebrew *chara-both*, rendered in our version, "desolate places." The first sheik of Arabia, the patient man of Uz, knew those wonderful sepulchres; and their purpose is exactly expressed in his words:

> "For now I should have lain still and been quiet,
> I should have slept; then had I been at rest
> With kings and counselors of the earth
> Who built themselves *pyramids*."

In the face of description at least four thousand years old, I dare not hope to offer new facts or fictions, yet, as the Oriental face changes not, but always holds a compelling interest for the stranger, so the scenes of its abiding are forever old, forever new, in spite of countless repetition; attempt to describe the indescribable.

I confess to pleasure in thinking there are readers who believe all has not been sung and said about the Pyramids. To behold those unfabled mountains of stone, had been to me a desire and a despair from childhood to mature years, and when at last I did see them, with these eyes, looking exactly as they should look, I felt like Simeon of old in the Temple.

You who have felt the fascination and mystery of the shrouded land of Sais; the inscrutable divinity over whose face was written, "I am that has been, which is, and which shall be, and no mortal hath lifted my veil," may turn this leaf. You who have read its story, till the country of Mizriam is a twice told tale, need go no further. Not for you I sing. But for *you*, the young and the poor, the lustrous eyes beloved scanning a near horizon, the men and women of scant leisure, whose restless souls are filled with unsatisfied longings for the far-off, the dim, the unattainable, *you* are the reader claimed for these chapters.

II.

THE LANDING.

AFTER a voyage, smooth from Beirout, without incident or accident we landed at Port Said. Four travellers from the land made Holy by the blessed feet of the Man of Nazareth, the Son of God.

We had knocked about so much that sharp American angles had been rounded; the acute had become obtuse. We had learned to accept our portion whatever it might be, asking no question; to manage salads drest with strange oils suggesting petroleum, cucumbers stuffed with abominations, cheese-cakes with pepper, and we gaily saluted a rosebud in the butter and accepted nutmeg in mashed potatoes, though no one pretended to admire the flavor.

Better than this discipline, we had discovered that immediately means in an hour or so, presently means next week, and to-morrow means never. When we missed a train, we did not rave or fume, but silently betook ourselves to sketch, scratch, and other books and calmly bided our time. Western activity is doomed to death, suffocated under the soft, slow feather-bed pressure of Oriental indolence, and we were in a fair way of conversion to *kismet*, and of incoming ills to say, "Allah wills it," and serenely accept destiny.

Long travel had somewhat changed the party

whom I trust the dear reader has not forgotten, for we journeyed together across the Storied Sea. The two, of whom your correspondent is one, looked and felt older by a year than when we parted. Travel enriches memory and lavishes treasure for imagination, but it is a wearing pleasure, and we felt no time was to be lost till we set our faces in return toward the best land the sun shines on.

The Antiquary's crow's feet were a deeper track. His eyebrows mealy, and hair weak and straggling, and he was more helpless than ever without the green goggles. Thalia, the widow, my pretty Thalia, was younger and prettier than last year; this partly because she had laid aside mourning. I suspect the mourner had a struggle with herself over the point, and she broke it to me gently on this wise, one morning in our state-room, when she was trying to brush the dust out of her kilt pleats.

"I think," she began, hesitating, and fiery red, "no dresses are so hard to keep clean as black."

"True," I said, not raising my eyes from my paper, "you know brown is my favorite color."

"Don't you think," embarrassed and doubtful, "I'd better try a plaid of some sort, or get out that old dark merino in the bottom of my trunk?" This from my domineering friend, who in matters of taste ruled us without thought of disobedience! What was going to happen?

I laid down my pen, first wiping it with slow deliberation, and looked straight into the girlish face so eager and timid, the little blue veins in her temples beating a swift pulse. Wistful, anxious, as though life and death were in the coming words, she appeared to regard my judgment about the expediency of the travelling dress as a decree or a sentence. I knew perfectly well what she wished to hear and, with determination to be agreeable said, boldly, "Slate color or gray are much better, they shake out without rusting."

There was dead silence as she went on with the coat brush. She must have known what I suspected; so I added, meaningly, " pardon, dear child, but it *is* time; the day has come to make a change."

She blushed, paled, trembled. " Yes, it *is* time," she said with sharp, unnatural voice; and what did the dear girl do but drop the dress on the floor, and burst into a passion of tears.

Now Thalia had never given me her confidence in words, and I did not feel free to advise, where advice had not been asked, in a matter of deepest moment to her; wherefore I thought best to slip away and let her cry it out alone. For in that implied confession, she snapped the last thread of the bond which had bound her to Willy Benson, her husband, lying two years in dreamless sleep by the blue lake at Chicago.

Maybe she thought we had not noticed the criss-crossed letters, covered with post marks. which came with unvarying regularity, and were shyly read without comment, but with brightening eyes and tell-tale cheeks. Maybe she thought her fellow voyageurs insensible to the fact of her sitting up o' nights, not to jot down notes, nor to abandon herself to the fascinations of the guide-book. I would not wrong my Thalia by such suspicion of search for useless knowledge. Presumably the midnight oil was spent in answering those weighty documents. Maybe she did not know that a generation ago we too learned how to conjugate the first verb taught in the languages of the nations.

There is deep meaning in the custom which makes the wedding blossom a bloomer at all times and seasons, perpetual emblem of happy marriage. Bud, flower, and fruit come on together, and fast as one golden bough is stripped, another as bright and as shining appears. I had watched this second start; a late, summer growth, about which she was bashful as a schoolgirl. At some unwonted beauty of sea or sky, she had ceased to whisper in cherished echo of early feeling, "How Willy would have enjoyed this." Latterly in dreamy abstraction she wore the look which revealed her eyes were with her heart, and that was far away. Love is immortally young, in fact never anything but a boy, and blind at that. There was no good cause why the widow, but little past twenty-eight, should not gather up the broken threads of her life, and weave them again into a tissue of brightness.

Thalia has an April day temperament, and the warm shower of tears went by, leaving no sign save in the freshened roses of her cheek, and

a vivacious lighting of the entire face. After
our greasy breakfast, she came on deck in the
old drab merino. Thalia's dresses never scrape
or rustle; they are the clinging kinds without
starch, as becomes her still and modest presence ;
in harmony with the voice, " ever soft, gentle,
and low." The old merino was wrinkled by
long packing, but borrowed grace from the
girlish shape, and behold, in her straw hat an
ostrich feather! No cloudy apparition, as I at
first thought, but a genuine waving plume, one
of the tender grays, bought never so cheaply
as that day at Port Said. Her abundant hair,
still the golden age, was loosely knotted below
it, low in her neck. I could hardly believe
my eyes, but there it was, blown this way and
that, by the warm land breeze; dancing, fluttering, the modest, yet unmistakable signal
that the old wound had ceased its fevered
throbbing and had healed, not without a scar.
From a dried bouquet which lasted from Jaffa
she had picked out a few carnations not entirely withered, and with a spray of evergreen
made a bright *boutonière.* So the period of
mourning was ended, and it was plain as daylight we could not hope to keep our spoiled
darling abroad much longer, or one more must
be added to our party.

Antiquary gazed at the nodding feather with
undisguised admiration for the wearer. The old
man made no secret of his worship of the most
lovable woman in the world, with whom he had
many rousing debates verging on the fascinating

edge of quarrel. They had great disparity of
years and of tastes. The works, grand and
dry, in which the bachelor revelled, she detested,
and there was a pathetic appeal in his hopeless
and constant obedience to her, when he knew
her smiles were not for him; and by no magic
juice on her eyelids could she admit him to the
realm enchanted, where youth rules forever.

Without words he wanted to show his ap-
proval of Thalia's toilet, and toward evening
came up from below with a sealed paper envelope,
very delicate in tissue, peach-bloom in tint. He
tore open one end of the package, and drew out
and unrolled a large square kerchief of gold and
brown silk, edged with brown and yellow knotted fringes and flossy tassels. "Will you wear
this?" he asked, with quiet directness.

"It is very pretty," said Thalia, evidently delighted with the sheen and texture of the showy
garment, "but do you think it will be suitable
for me?"

"Nothing can be more so. Pardon," he
added, as in slow and painstaking movement, he
lapped one corner bias on another, "but it will
please me to see you in it; in fact will keep me
in good humor a whole day."

Antiquary has the pale, slender hands we
associate with our ideal scholar, and there was
positive grace in the action, when he laid the
folded scarf respectfully, even reverently, on the
shoulders whose taper line the vile fashion of
epaulettes had not deformed. She passed the
ends through a large cornelian ring, bought of a

Meccan trader, a trinket warranted to keep off the evil eye.

"The *kufiyeh* is from Damascus," said the lover of antiquities. "It came by caravan, and by the changeless fashions of the Orient we may safely assume such a head-covering was worn by Job, foremost of Arab sheiks when he was first of all men of the East. The Arabians arrange it in several loose layers, pleats you call them, don't you?" he asked, with a man's helplessness in matters of toilet.

"Folds, you mean," said the smiling Thalia.

"Yes, folds, close down to the eyes, and keep it in place by a silk or camel-hair rope round the head."

"I remember that gallant Bedouin, the Sheik of the Jordan, flaunted such a thing when he escorted us from Jerusalem to Hebron, and thinking how changed he looked when he took it off, under the oak of Mamre."

"Right," said Antiquary, gratified at the allusion, "and it is fitting that the first woman who has entered the Cave of Macpelah, should adopt a portion of the costume of the Abrahamic dispensation. I believe a garment like this shaded the neck of the Friend of Guests, as the Moslems name him, when he sat in his tent in the heat of the day and beckoned the wandering angels in."

"I remember too, this lovely color, in some picture of the Magii."

"Right again, you are improving, Mistress Thalia. In the celebrated Adoration at Ant-

2

werp, Melchion, the Arabian King, wears the
kufiyeh to show his oriental origin.   It becomes
you," he continued, admiringly, "it gives the
sunny look I love.   The colors vary and shift
with the light, like tints in the plumage of
certain feathered throats."

And the vivid changeable dyes did harmonize
with the violet eyes, and the clearness of a complexion whose ivory neither freckle nor tan
could hurt.

" Yes," he continued, encouraged by his successful compliment, "Thalia is one of the Muses,
one of the Graces as well.   "Now,"—with his
antiquated bow—"I see all the Graces in one.
Her namesake of old lived in the Parnassus, and
drank of the Castilian Spring ; her statue in the
Vatican wears ivy leaves and holds a shepherd's
crook.   She presides over comedy."

" You are too kind," said the radiant Thalia ;
" this is really more than I deserve."   And she
had reason to be gratified over such speech from
a dry old bookworm.

" The *kufiyeh* is so graceful and pleasant," he
went on, as if speaking to a large audience, " it
must have been in general use and, not despised
by princes, it may have bound the beautiful
brows of Absalom.   The pale light ones offered
in the Bazars of Smyrna are counterfeits ; only
the brown and gold are the true ones.   They are
woven in the peerless city called by the ancients
Chrysorhoa, or Stream of Gold, beloved by
Naaman of old.   From it come swords of secret
power, and scimitars of matchless temper.   These

silky stuffs are worthy her prime before she fell
into the hands of the fanatic legions of the Desert,
her treasures scattered till but two genuine blades
of Damas steel remain in that oldest of living
cities. The Syrian from whom I bought the
kerchief said, it throws the sun and the moon
into shade, and so it does when worn by Her
Grace Madame Thalia. It has taken six thousand years of æsthetic culture to produce the
perfected ugliness of the Christian stove-pipe hat.
The people we call heathen," he prosed along,
warming with his own eloquence, "and barbarian,
knew how to mix dyes and how to make themselves comfortable."

No one opposed or answered the scholar.
Thalia was gazing with unseeing eyes at the long
low coast line, looking not at it at the past or
the present, but into the future, opening brightly
into Paradise Regained. The undaunted speaker
continued. "More than that, they knew how to
write respectable compositions. When Job
penned the Iliad of his woes, and the shepherd
king sang the Lord is my shepherd, the latter
day poets who insist Adam was a baby man,
and evolution's the thing, may learn something
of musical numbers, that is if vanity and ego-
tism allow;" and the Antiquary gave a grunt,
as is his wont when in disapproval.

He was dying for a discussion, but for once we
let the gentlest of grumblers have the disappointment of his own way without opposition. Thalia
demurely moved her seat, to watch the coming

and going of passengers, and the old man following her with dim eyes, murmured:

> "On her glowing, languid visage
> Lay the magic of the Orient.
> And her garb recalled the splendor
> Of Scheherezade's legends."

My feminine reader who has felt the depressing
effect of long-worn crêpe may recall the feeling
with which it is laid aside. In the beginning,
there is a sort of sad surprise at self, for in the
first dark days of funereal gloom we are sure we
shall never smile again nor put off the trappings
of woe; and we believe that impossible state of
mind must be lifelong. It is a forgetfulness, a
sort of treachery to the one over whose head-
stone we wrote in heartbreak, was ever sorrow
like unto my sorrow? Surprise comes that we
could or would be comforted; in fact, it must be
admitted, are already so. In those days of perpetual anguish how brutal the thought of second
marriage! A whisper of such thing would be
sacrilege.

Thalia's dusty bombazine was in the bottom
of the trunk or the sea, and her spirits rose with
the first elastic rebound from heaviness cast by
memory of the dearly loved, early lost, deeply
mourned, and soon to be replaced husband of
her youth. Her charming *gaîte du coeur* came
back. With sparkling eyes and glittering hair
she was a phantom of delight. Instead of the
afflicting refrain about the returning dead Doug-
las, usually hummed in the twilight, she gave a
bar of the Blue Danube, and a few waltz steps
with her own shadow, moving with airy ease and

buoyant grace. I never knew her so delightful, and we all caught the gay contagion. Later she overflowed in playful pranks and little mischiefs which culminated in the decrepit joke of tickling the back of my neck with a straw, making me jump and brush off a supposed representative of the fourth plague of Pharaoh.

There was no comment on her change of dress or manner, for we try to keep in that small and charming circle of human beings who never ask questions. And we felt sure that in good time the secret would be out.

So our landing at Alexandria was a very different affair from what it had been without the gray ostrich feather!

Strangely enough, the spectator in these familiar dramas sometimes has a lingering pity for the beloved dead, which the main actor does not share. Especially is this the case where the bereaved one is young and the observer old; for the grief of later years though less vehement, is more oppressive than in youth and clings with rooted tenacity to its object.

Thalia had been seven months an idolized wife, two years a faithful widow. Her husband was snatched from her by a violent death and the sharp pang which parted them was the only one then known; hence her first love brought her first sorrow. Not romantic, and too healthful for deep dejection, she did not seek solitude to nurture spectral fancies and drop into the melancholy whose common outlet is sad prose or elegaic verse. Given absolute health, a

cheerful disposition, ample fortune, grief is easier
to bear than where there is the wrestle with two
giants, poverty and indigestion, and nights of
writhing in the fangs of neuralgia. She was
born to trip it on the sunny side of the wall, to
gather the roses and feed among the lilies.
Fainter and fainter come the voices from the
tombs, little by little the daylight of the world
gains on the dreary night of mourning, the stars
have willed it, Destiny foretold it, now it was
gray, now purple, now a blushing gleam, now
full dawn again, and lo! in the golden kerchief,
clad with beauty she is radiant as ever in the
outlook toward second marriage.

There are better players in the world than on
the stage, and we need not seek Jo. Jefferson to
realize how soon our places are filled when we
disappear from the sight of our nearest and
dearest.

Sometimes it seems inexplicable that the grief
of parted lovers is more lasting than the mourning of the married. Is it not because the sentence of Death is final? The black curtain
dropped, that act is ended. The decree accepted,
there is nothing to do but move forward into
other scenes and form new ties and associations
to people the emptiness which at first rules the
universe. The human mind readily adjusts
itself to a certainty, but while this side eternity
the beloved one remains and unwed, the dream
may go on unbroken, there are possibilities of
re-union in the future. Among them, the secret
unconfessed even to self, the hope of a recovery

of the object cruelly missed, renewal of the worship of the ideal unfulfilled and the flowery garland woven in the freshness of morning.

Useless is it to cry out if the soul we thought our very own has passed into the everlasting silence, but while yet it is on the earth come questionings. The quarrel on such slight provocation, the letters, the souvenirs exchanged, the rings returned, have they indeed come back forever? Does he not share this wild yearning? In the hush of some wakeful night will he not feel the old time rush over him and pour out his love and his words, waiting, not quite despairing, to the answering spirit? Or, under the thrill of the old familiar strain sung together in summer eves, will he not long, with longing past all power to endure, for the presence he cannot afford to lose? his guiding light when heart, voice, life itself were blended with another, and separation was—to die?

The thieving years, in passing, rob us of many precious possessions, and not the least of the jewels snatched from our treasure-house by Time is the blind unquestioning faith in the eternity of earthly love. You who write tenderly of reunions after death, tell me not happy spirits revisit their houses of clay. No, no. It would be too sorry a sight to see our places filled, and to listen for, and hear not the faintest echo of the little stir we made on earth.

III.

SUEZ AND SINAI.

SUEZ is a poverty-stricken place, rich in nothing but associations. Its straggling houses of sun-dried bricks, glaring with whitewash, are near the line where the desert begins. A waste of yellow sand, it stretches away to the wilderness, whose silence is like the silence of death, whose desolation is best described in the Arabian phrase, "Out in the desert there is nothing but God." With the best field-glass, not a tree nor a shrub nor any green thing is to be seen on the African side of the Gulf. From the verdureless, wind-swept coast, dotted with mud hovels, the weary eye wanders in delight to the mountains of Sinai, in the dazzling, speckless sapphire, lifting up peaks that appear airy and evanescent as passing drifts of cloud. He is a dull clod of clay who does not thrill in his inmost soul, when first he hears the name of the Mount of the Law, where Moses, the man of God went up, and the trumpet sounded long and waxed louder and louder, and the glory of the Lord came down. Then the rebellious host faltered, "Speak thou with us and we will hear, but let not God speak with us, lest we die."

We knew it was folly to think of making the six days' march into the desert, which brings the traveler to Sinai. The limitation of sex, occasionally mentioned by the strong-minded, is a barrier eter-

nal as the red granite ; old as the world's foundations. Not for my vision was the ruined fort,
said to have been built by Rameses II., whose
daughter drew Moses out of the water and
adopted him as her son. The cartouche with
his name, signifying, Beloved of the Sun, is
carved on the frieze of a ruined temple on the
borders of the wilderness, sharply cut as though
finished yesterday, a temple which historians
tell us was founded centuries before the time of
Abraham. This makes the convent begun by
Justinian in 555, a modern structure, commem-
orating the site of the Burning Bush. We
should have been glad to see the sign-manual
shown there of the false prophet. It was made
by dipping his hand in ink (for he could not
write), and has been the protection of the monks
of St. Catherine and their brethren through centuries. They plaited their straws, and hoed
their onions and joined in prayer at the foot of
Sinai thirteen hundred years before the founder
of Islamism was born. And hard by the convent, at Jebel Mousa, is a high place, where
legends told by the Faithful teach that Mohammed talked with God, as friend with friend. We
women must die without the sight of much that
is dear to the antiquarian heart.

The three thousand years of Suez have
brought nothing but bare existence to a few
Bedouins, and in later times the ten thousand
inhabitants are maintained by the canal and the
railway. It has never held the commercial
importance promised by the canal, and has the

usual lifelessness of Arab towns. Several mosques not imposing, may be visited, and in the bazars inferior stuffs and corals are sold to the unwary traveler for their weight in gold. Steamers run from Suez to Jedda, the seaport of Mecca, the holy city seventy miles inland. Thus the way is made easier than it was formerly to the hundred thousand pilgrims a year, traveling to purchase Paradise by kissing the Black Stone which was brought from heaven by the angels. Their snowy wings still lift and float the *Kiswal,* or covering of that most sacred of shrines.

Glowing dreams cheer the heart and cool the brow of the true believer as he toils, ankle deep in sand, under a sky of heated brass, from which the sun pours a blinding brightness, unshaded by vapor, mist or cloud. He knows that when the angel Israfil shall sound the blast of the resurrection, the Pilgrims shall rise and mount white winged camels, accoutered with saddles of gold, which stand waiting for the elect. From tents of hollow pearls will flock forth black-eyed Houris, and the meanest in Paradise shall have seventy-two of them, the four wives he had on earth, and eighty thousand slaves besides. There will be ceaseless music and enchanting visions, fadeless roses, tufted carpets, green flowered mantles, feasts always ready; and the myriad souls, waiting by the well Zem-zem, with one taste of the elixir of life will be cured of all disease and enter eternal bliss. Winter frost cannot chill them, nothing can harm them further, for the dreamer shall rest under the perfumed tree which springs from the musky banks of the river Al-Cawthor. He will meet the shining legions who have fallen for the glory of Islam. Troops from the burning depths of Sahara, from the Indian Sea, from the wide plains of Sennaar, faithful found among the faithless; followers of the green standard and bearers of the scimiter in whose shadow is Paradise. Peacefully flows the bright river whose sands are jewels, and sweet the final rest on green pillows. Every day will bring glad surprises and night is a twilight of trances which are better than sleep. In poverty unspeakable, in nakedness, and misery, the Pilgrim is the richest of visionaries. Wave your hand to El Hadji, for he is the stuff of which holy martrys are made.

Near Suez is a noted camping-ground for caravans; the camels of which sometimes number thousands. The Western traveler never loses his interest in the caravan; each one brings fresh and endless suggestion, vague imagining out of the voiceless regions traversed by the train which makes a sinuous line like a crawling serpent. To watch their comings and goings is to feel the spirit of the farthest East. The brown bales may be merely cotton, but we fancy them carefully packed freights of rare silks and gauzy tissues, such as are not seen in dull cities where looms are smoky with coal and noisy with steam. The patient brutes, slaves of slaves, bear light robes of rainbow dyes and glimmering pearls sought by the veiled and delicate beauties of the harem. We fancy the route is scented by their rich spices, and sweet perfumes, frankincense and life-giving balm, aromatic powders and costly juices that have been sought by famous women shining in song and story, eternally young and immortally beautiful.

Maybe yon thirsty, withered beast has passed the abandoned cells of the cliff-dwellers of Arabia the stony, the unhappy. Certain it is he has knelt in the plain at the foot of Sinai, where debased Hebrews kindled unhallowed fires on strange altars, and returned to the animal worship of Egypt. His portion has been to toil over mountains of rock and blistering sand-plains, resting only at the wells which mark the few oases. By day a fierce heat like flame; by night a radiance of stars so luminous we do not wonder they are worshiped by devotees in the country of the patriarch Job and the prophet Mohammed.

As we gaze over the shimmering plain, ever present to imagination is Moses the hero of the Old Testament, who made the highest sacrifice possible to humanity, became a slave among slaves that he might deliver his people. He had commanded an army in the Ethiopian expedition, and knew the way as well, beyond the Sea of Reeds or Flags, for he had married the daughter of the chief of a tribe of Ishmaelites, or Arabs, who dwelt at the foot of Mount Sinai. The sterile, burnt-out region beyond the Land of Goshen is strikingly like portions of the Rocky Mountains, fit place for the silent communing of the Hebrew Cromwell, as the still margins of the Black Ouse River were to the preaching soldier, named by his loyal countrymen, the Regicide. Recluses concentered on one thought become what the world calls fanatic. In the desert, Moses was a dreamer of dreams and a seer of visions. It is not easy to think of him as a shepherd or a lover, but he was both in the Plain of Midian.

Half way down the bald and dreary summit of Horeb, under an overhanging rock, is a perpetual spring, the Fountain of Jethro. Moses must have made his midday meal in its shadow beside the cool water, and from the recess he watched the flocks of his father-in-law feeding on the scant herbage below. The stone on which he sat is yet pointed out to the traveler. Tiny ferns with hair-like stems cling to the moist places, and a wee, pink flower, hardy as the Alpine Edelweiss, starts up after the winter snows are melted.

Not a great way from Moses's Seat shown on Horeb, another illustrious shepherd fed his flocks in the plains of Arabia. The great law-giver received, amid thunders and lightnings of fearful brightness, the commandment, "Thou shalt have no other gods before me. Hear, O Israel, the Lord our God is one God." The Arabian shepherd proclaimed to the idolaters of Mecca, "There is no God but God." It seems a reverberation of the outcry on Sinai, spoken two thousand years before; and on those simple words, the Prophet we name false founded a

religion which is something more than imposture and delusion. It has driven from its seat
the commandments given on Sinai and the
gentler teachings on Olivet, and to-day holds
every shrine dear and glorious to the heart of
Jew and Christian.

IV.

CROSSING THE RED SEA.

THE march of the Hebrews under Moses, can
be traced with accuracy from the starting at
Rameses to Heliopolis (where the great leader
had been educated in all the wisdom of the
Egyptians), even into the terrible wilderness.
The deeper the study of history, the more fully
and clearly are the Holy Scriptures confirmed ;
and, tried by the strict test of geography, the
conditions of this region are the same as when
signs and wonders were performed till the last
blow broke the heart of Pharaoh. There is
never any waste of miraculous power. The
plagues were natural calamities, incident to
Egypt, intensified and exaggerated, and the
features of the peninsula are so changeless that
the route of the Israelites may be traced and
camping-places fixed with certainty. To-day
the desert pilgrim finds the same springs of
brackish water; the same groups of stunted
palms, the acacia or shittim-wood, the country
where quails yet abound, and pleasant valleys
where he can reach sweet water, drink and live.

The north end of the Red Sea exhibits the

same conditions as when Jehovah led his people like sheep by the hand of Moses and Aaron. The rise of the tide is from three to six feet, above a long, narrow sand-bank which stretches many miles westward, slightly covered when the tide is out. Before the canal was cut, caravans often crossed the head of the gulf in safety, and on the verge of the great sea when strong east winds blew, the waters were pressed back, sometimes so rapidly that shoals of fish were left dead on the shore; the water was changed to land and an easy path opened through the bed for a host. The Bedouins yet tell of ruins of cities on the eastern shore, where Pi-hahiroth was of old, and other armies besides Pharaoh's, flushed with conquest, have been destroyed by the treacherous winds and waves of *Yam Suph* or the "Sea of Reeds," as the Hebrews named it. In making the way for the ships, a work declared by Darius, the Ptolemies and Pharaohs, to be impossible, M. de Lesseps records he has seen the north end of the sea blown almost dry, when next day the waters were driven far up on the land. When it blows from the south the tide joined to this wind makes a depth to be dreaded, where a few hours before the ford was dry.

As the Israelites, fainting with fear and their hearts dying within them, lifted up their eyes and beheld the Egyptians marching after them, they "cried unto the Lord, and he caused the sea to go back by a strong, east wind all that night, and he made the sea dry land, and the waters were divided. It is a night to be much

observed unto the Lord for bringing them out of
the Land of Egypt; this is that night of the
Lord to be observed of the children of Israel in
their generations." No other migration has
been like that flight of a whole nation. They
had eaten the unleavened bread of the Passover,
with loins girded, with shoes on their feet, staff
in hand; eaten it in haste. They were well
warned and ready to move the day when the
first Passover feast was done. That very night
they were cast out by their enemies, their ren-
dezvous the wilderness, their goal the Promised
Land. The road across the desert was before
them, but God led them not the way of the Land
of the Philistines, though that was near, for
"God said, Lest peradventure the people repent
when they see war, and return to Egypt."

In the roaring tempest, in confusion and alarm,
six hundred thousand men with flocks and herds,
their wives and their little ones huddled by the
coast. These bond-slaves had been used to looking through green forests of reeds on the placid
waters bordering the Plain of Zoan, and the
"great sea" was a sight to fill them with awe
and wonder, had there been no other terror.
Through the cries of anguish and wild prayers
of the fugitives, the reassuring order came to the
bewildered and frightened souls, " Fear ye not,
stand still and see the salvation of the Lord
which he will show to you, for the Egyptians
whom ye have seen to-day, ye shall see them
again no more forever." The strong wind blew,
the waters were gathered together, the floods

HEAD OF MENEPHTHAH, THE "PHARAOH" OF THE EXODUS.

stood upright, a black wall on their right hand
and their left. God's way was in the sea, and
his path in the great waters, and his footsteps
were not known. The ransomed crossed in
safety, the Egyptians followed in close pursuit,
but the wind fell, the tide rose, the sea returned
to his strength, foaming billows drowned the
chariots and the horsemen, and of all the hosts
of Pharaoh that came after them there remained
not so much as one. They sank as lead in the
mighty waters.

It was my good fortune to know an Englishman familiar with the regions round about Suez,
who had crossed the Red Sea ten times. He
sought the route of the Hebrews and says he had
marched in the midst of the sea near Pi-hahiroth
(See Exodus xiv: 2) "The Place of Abysses."
When the waves receded the land became so
solid that sometimes it scarcely took the imprint
of a camel's foot. To experiment on the quality
of the soil, he pressed the end of a cane into the
ground, when "suddenly, at a few inches' depth,
it was swallowed up nearly to the hilt." Precisely the condition as when horses, horsemen
and chariots were sunk. "And it came to pass
in the morning watch the Lord looked unto the
host of the Egyptians through the pillar of fire,
and of the cloud, and troubled the host of the
Egyptians and took off their chariot wheels that
they drave them heavily." It was light to the
pursued, dark to the pursuers. There was no
waste of power in the miracle of destruction, and
Moses knew the doom of the proud, when no

sang, "Thou stretchedst out thy right hand and the earth swallowed them."

It was the beginning of liberty for the enslaved Hebrews, and in the morning watch when Emancipation Day broke over the rock-mountains of Arabia, Israel saw the Egyptians dead on the sea-shore. Looking eastward the desert is bare till the eye reaches a clump of palms, warped and twisted by varying winds, the first oasis marking the watering-place known from immemorial ages as the wells of Moses. A green scum covers the pool, but under it the water boils up freshly as it did when the greatest of caravans encamped by the inexhaustible spring, and Miriam the prophetess and all the women after her went to greet the ransomed host. In this very spot she took up the song of Moses, answering, in chorus, "Sing ye unto the Lord for he has triumphed gloriously, the horse and his rider hath he thrown into the sea."

A few tamarisks cling to life beside the wells, and dried carcasses of camels tell the woeful tale of privation and starvation in the road which runs eastward from Suez. There can be no doubt that this was the first halting-place for the fugitive slaves. Here the painted coffin, inclosing the mummy of Joseph, was rested from men's shoulders, and here the jubilee was sounded.

Strange questions enter the mind of the student. Will the place of Exodus be the open gate of the return of the chosen people? It is still called the Tongue of the Egyptian Sea by the natives, and the miracle of the return will be as great as the Exodus when men shall go dry shod over Egypt's dark sea, and "when the Lord shall set up an ensign for the nations, and shall assemble the outcasts of Israel, and gather together the dispersed of Judah from the four corners of the earth."

Pretty myths hover over the region dear to the lover of Moses and the Prophets, stories of Andromeda and lovely nymphs of the Mediterranean, but there is not time to tell them now. In Mohammedan fables the legend runs that the point where the stiff-necked Pharaoh was whelmed in the hill of waters, there are always breakers, reefs, and dangerous currents, over whose troubled depth, since that awful day, the spirit of the storm has never ceased to flap his sable wings. And the ghosts of the drowned Egyptians may be seen (by him who sees aright) ever moving in sad unrest at the bottom of the Sea. The lost souls are always busy there, recruiting their numbers with shipwrecked mariners, and sometimes hundreds come down at once, when their moanings can be heard like the moaning of the waves when the winds are low

V.

ALEXANDRIA.

It has been said that Cleopatra is the one distinct figure of Egyptian history. This may be true to the tourist coming by way of Italy, but for those who enter from Palestine. it is somewhat in the spirit of the Roman Emperor, who, after visiting the shrines of Holy Land, went to search the Red Sea for the hosts who pursued the Hebrews, (petrified into rocks at the bottom,) and to kiss the footsteps left in the sands by the infant Jesus while He dwelt with his parents, safe from the vengeance of Herod.

We have little time to mark the coral reefs of the Red Sea, which are marvelously beautiful. Their levels are slightly raised above the water and their varied color makes them appear like floating gardens. The flowery meads, not fitted to sustain palms and willows, are full of running vines of scarlet leaves and blooms. Lovely isles such as dreamy poets sing of, rocking with slow rise and fall, wafted by warm winds to happy shores or swinging like freighted vessels idly lying at anchorage.

The waves dash over the surface and keep the basins and pools filled, and birds of swift and tireless wing dart across and circle round the red reefs making the air resound with shrill notes.

At evening the ripples break in rings of iridescent light about them; a fringe beaded with brilliants like the coronation robes of an Indian Prince. The native boatmen note the phosphoric gleam and name the rainbow flashes, "jewels of the deep."

Approaching Alexandria we feel we are entering the oldest domain of history. Here are the most venerable records of the race of man, sculptured before the period when Abraham

drove his herds into Egypt, in quest of fresh
pastures which drought had destroyed in Canaan.

Freshly come to mind the old, old stories which
our mothers (they rest in peace!) taught us with
our cradle hymns. We see the pathetic figure
of Joseph, the darling boy sold as a slave by his
brothers, and afterward set over all the Land of
Egypt. The King's ring (such are found in the
oldest tombs,) on his hand, a gold chain about
his neck, his vesture of fine linen, his chariot
next the jewelled wheels of the demigod who
spoke and said, " I am Pharaoh and without thee
shall no man lift up his hand or foot in all the
land of Egypt." A reality, even at this late
hour of the changed yet unchanged Egypt,
beside which all other kingdoms and empires are
dim and their splendors transitory and fleeting.

The Nile, the sacred, beneficent Nile, is alone
like a god; and like a god the pagans worshiped
and sacrificed to the divinity by which they
existed. For the country was, and is the gift of
the river; and without the overflow would be
nothing but bare rock and sad. It varies from a
width of ten miles to a shrunken strip of verdure.
There is no border of famishing vegetation los-
ing itself in drought. The water limit makes a
dividing line, clean cut as with a sharp knife.
You may lay one hand on the tenderest, most
exquisite herbage in the world and fill the other
with arid, gray sand. Perfected vegetation
against absolute sterility, and all by the bounty
of the blessed river. For fifteen hundred **miles**
he moves solitary.

During that long course, wholly unshaded,
exposed to the evaporation of fierce sunheat,
lowered by thousands of canals, absorbed by
porous banks and thirsty sands, maintaining by
healthful water every living thing.

When the star Sirius, the most adorable light
in the universe of God, rises with the sun he
outshines, the sympathetic stream begins to rise.
Slowly it swells; moving with such fate-like
precision that agriculture is predetermined with
the exactness of mathematics. There are no
rain-clouds to be dreaded, no frosts to blight, no
winds to lay the harvests low. Three months
the Delta is a lake; then the mud houses built
on raised mounds stand like islands in the level
expanse. The water carries a rich deposit of
loam and the grounds needs nothing more, not
even a sabbath-year to lie fallow. From the
unknown ages, Nilus has almost invariably risen
to within a few hours of the same time and to
within a few inches of the same height, year
after year.

When the flood recedes the ooze is scratched
with the crooked stick which has been the Oriental plough through fifty centuries, and three
crops a year of corn, wheat, sugar, cotton may
be raised. The tranquil inundation, placid as
everything is in this land of ceaseless calm,
leaves no mark of violence; nothing is disturbed
by the weight of the waters. Within banks the
Nile carries a tremendous volume, but without
rush or hurry; steadily flowing, majestic as the
serene and stately sculptures on its shore which

look on with stony, sleepless eyes to all eternity, seeming to say while the river runs I stand.

So the years come and go; from the beginning the same, no guessing about the weather, no dread of changes for there will be none. Everything is foreknown and the seasons are arranged as by a Destiny.

You may travel by steamer from Alexandria twelve hundred miles, and afterward in a light sailboat, only the guide-book may tell how far. Away, away, to mythic haunts of the Phœnix, the regions of Chimeras, Flying Serpents, Basalisks, Vampyres and Dragons; where men's feet blister and lions' manes are scorched off by the heat. Of the mysteries and marvels of the Upper Nile, the ancients told many wonderful stories. Not the least among the wonders were the miraculous springs which supply "the life-giving artery of Egypt whose pulse gives one throb a year." They tell us the water of the Nile never becomes impure, whether reserved at home or exported. On board vessels bound for Italy that which remains is good, while what they happen to take in on the voyage is corrupt. It is preserved in jars like wine, and, anciently, with the age of the water was an increase of value, as with wine:—a legend we are disposed to doubt.

Familiar as it was, by story and picture, I was not prepared for the appearance of the Land of Goshen, which lies to-day much the same as when seventeen hundred years before our era, Pharaoh gave it to Joseph. It is very like the

prairies of Illinois; richer, with a lighter green—
the true Nile-green—than the wheat lands of the
Mississippi valley, and a more even level. It
does not "roll" like our prairies, but stretches
flat as a floor; fat with the black loam which
forms the "golden soil." Sowing, ploughing,
reaping go on at the same hour in the mild
December which is sweet as bridal June with us.

The papyrus—which the Greek wrote over
with undying names—the rush on whose frail
bark are records more enduring than marble, has
disappeared; but there are yet rank, aquatic
plants, in the stagnant marshes, left after the
overflow. They lift their graceful, feathery heads
in close, dank masses, and a man in a rush canoe
casting seed upon the waters, reminds us of the
olden promise of bread and the fair child of the
Hebrews saved from the curse of its brethren.

From some such reeds as these was made the
basket-boat, where the sorrowing mother— with
what anguish of soul let other mothers tell—
laid the baby Moses. There was an ancient belief that the papyrus was a protection against
crocodiles, and the tall flags on the river's bank
were like these which shadow the shallow waters
we see. We are very near the spot where the
childless princess came down to bathe in the
sacred river, and seeing the green ark among the
flags she sent her maid to fetch it. The child
wept, and Pharaoh's daughter adopted him with
the name which means, "Saved from the Water."

The tropic luxuriance of the Delta—the garden of the Lord as it is called in the Old Testa-

ment—was a delight to the Israelites. They longed for the fertile valley bearing melons, onions, cucumbers, which were part of their daily rations. They remembered the sycamore and fig trees, the luscious date palms and waving willows. When fainting in the blazing heats of Arabia, among awful fiery peaks and wells of bitter waters, their souls sunk within them. They had, in the grim and vast expanse, prickly thorns, starved weeds, and the stunted acacia of which the Tabernacle was made. They longed with feverish longing for draughts of the cool, abundant, brimming river of the land of captivity and bondage and groaned out, "because there were no graves in Egypt, hast thou taken us away to die in the wilderness?" Not strange that the heart of their meek leader was well-nigh broken in the thankless cause, and he prayed that the burden of the people might be removed, "I am not able to bear all this people alone, because it is too heavy for me. Kill me and let me not see my wretchedness."

After the ceaseless stir and activity of crowded Egypt, the stillness of the desert was like the silence of death. The dwarf mimosa, the outer picket of vegetation, fights for life at the foot of Sinai, but there is no chance for animals there. No bird, bee, insect, sings or hums in the lifeless waste, and the desolation was the more complete from contrast with the green valley left behind. The weird silence of the desert gave full effect to the dread thunders of Sinai, and the orders

under which the encampment was made and
tents struck in the Sand-sea of Sin.

The fertile Delta is the land shadowing with
wings, and swarms with aquatic birds which appear strangely tame. The pigeons are familiar
to us, the nestlings of the belfries in our village
churches. They do not excite our curiosity, nor
do the cormorants, pelicans, or storks on the
reedy margins.

One bird, moving in robes of white, we single
out for our inquiry and interest. The gentle
Ibis; the avatar or living emblem of the god
Thoth or Hermes, the Egyptian deity who answered to the Mercury of the Greek. Its spotless plumage well symbolizes the moon, and its
snowy broad-winged counterpart in the Everglades of Florida is named the White Heron.
Never has the beautiful bird, haunting

" The gloomy moss-hung cypress grove "

been so well described as by our poet, Maurice
Thompson. The long, slender, curving **neck**
is exceedingly graceful, and the snowy feathers
of the Ibis, in the good old times of the gods,
used to scare the crocodile and even kill him.
It appeared in Egypt at the rise, and disappeared
with the inundation of the Nile; and such was
its devotion to the Kingdom of the Pharaohs
that it pined and died of self-starvation if sen-
tenced to banishment from its native land.
Spotless in outward, as well as inner life, it
drank only of the purest water, and the strictest
of the priesthood drank nothing except water

from the pools where the Ibis had been seen. To kill such a divinity was punishable with death.

Besides, the Ibis was the deliverer of Egypt from the winged serpents of Arabia which, since the beginning, have guarded the divine perfume that lives in the frankincense-trees. In the time of Herodotus (and a very good old time it was,) they flew from Arabia, in the spring, through a strait between two mountains which the first of historians and story-tellers visited, and he saw prodigious mounds of serpent bones and ribs piled on heaps of different heights. Supposably the remains left by the avenging Ibis. But let us not smile too broadly at the tale. Hear Isaiah: " The burden of the beasts of the South ; into the land of trouble and anguish, from whence come the young and old lion, the viper, and fiery flying serpent."

One writer affirms the sacred flying-serpent had wings like a grasshopper, and others that animals bred in the slime of the Nile were devoured by the friendly Ibis ; itself incorruptible by death. If incorruptible, we cannot understand why they should be mummied, as we found them at Memphis done up in terra cotta jars, covered with a lid and sealed with lime.

The sacred white bird and the asp are forever recurring in the hieroglyphs, and I was at some pains to find a genuine specimen of the

" Pretty worm of Nilus
That kills and pains not."

It is a vile gray snake, mottled about the head with yellow splashes. The head is large and dilates like a cobra's when the reptile is excited. The bite—a mere prick almost painless—produces gradual lethargy, overcoming the senses like natural sleep. Hence the name, *Aspis somniculosa.* Cleopatra pursued conclusions infinite, of easy ways to die, and boasted

> "—— if knife, drugs, serpents have
> Edge, sting or operation, I am safe."

and after many experiments she chose the death which follows the aspic's bite, to the "imperious show of the full-fortuned Cæsar."

In the Delta, I made diligent inquiry about the Phœnix. It has disappeared from mortal sight, except in lurid chromos which emblazon the walls of insurance offices in the United States. Even good old Herodotus never saw it, except in a picture. Surely the student of accurate knowledge will thank me for copying his account of the bird :—

"It comes to Heliopolis but once in five hundred years and then only at the decease of the parent bird. If it bear any resemblance to its picture the wings are partly of gold and partly of ruby color, and its form and size perfectly like the eagle. They relate one thing of it which surpasses credibility. They say that it comes from Arabia to the Temple of the Sun, bearing the dead body of its parent, enclosed in myrrh, which it buries. It makes a ball of myrrh shaped like an egg, as large as it is able to carry, which it proves by experiment. This done it excavates the mass into which it introduces the body of the dead bird ; it again closes the aperture with myrrh, and the whole becomes the same weight as when composed entirely of myrrh; it then proceeds to Egypt to the Temple of the Sun."

Remembering this tradition, the Phœnecians gave the name Phœnix to the palm-tree, because when burnt down to the ground it springs up again fairer and stronger than ever. A more satisfactory interpretation of the antique myth than any other I have been able to find. The Egyptians supposed the Phœnix to have fifty orifices in his tail, and that after living one thousand years he builds himself a funeral pile, sings a melodious air of different harmonies through his fifty organ pipes, flaps his wings with a velocity which sets fire to the wood and so consumes himself.

I asked, too, about Pygmies. They have vanished into the golden mist overhanging the First Cataract. We may safely presume our own Midgets are the last representatives of this interesting people, who by the help of ladders climbed up the goblet of Hercules to drink from its contents.

VI.

OBELISKS.

Since the pillage of Alexandria, in 1882, it has lain an unburied wreck. There is not much left worth seeing, and you must draw on imagination to fill the empty, dreary spaces. The hackneyed sights are names familiar from school days. A twenty-second revolving light in the harbor has replaced the beacon in the Pharos—whatever that was—dedicated by the King Ptolemy to the Saviour God of those who travel by sea; and in the island of that name Greek traders sought shelter before the days of Homer.

Anciently, two great streets crossed each other at right angles; in their intersected square was the superb mausoleum which held the body of Alexander. It was embalmed in Babylon, brought hither with dazzling pomp, and laid in its resting-place with honors due to a god. The warmest fancy cannot raise from these ashes the city declared the centre of Alexander's world when all was conquered. It was circled with stupendous walls, fifteen miles in circumference. Read Gibbon for accounts of it in the days of its glory, when the revenues of a province were allotted the crown princess for her sandal strings, when idleness was unknown among the people, and even the lame and the blind had industries suited to their condition.

After the Saracenic conquest, the temples of Alexandria were one by one torn to pieces to build Cairo, the "City of Victory," and in one Turkish mosque there are four hundred Greek columns from this fallen star in the East, once a shrine to scholars and the greatest depository of learning in the world. The desolate column known as Pompey's Pillar is the last survivor of the four hundred belonging to the Temple of Serapis, the noblest building then on the face of the globe, except the Capitol at Rome. This shaft was perhaps part of the quadrangular portico, a matchless work, which sheltered marble statues, the best of Grecian genius, and was reached by one hundred steps of purest marble.

Among the columns, shaded from the fierce light and heat, wise philosophers walked and talked, asking then, as their thinking descendants yet ask, the old, unanswerable questions : Whence come I? Where go I? And wearily they worked at the unsolved problem : Given Self to find God.

Here was the lecture-room of Hypatia, the beautiful, crowded with the wealth and fashion of the luxurious Orient. The gilded chariots of effeminate, pleasure-loving youth stopped daily at her door, and her learning and eloquence, her spotless life and tragic death, shed a last illustrious light over the fading myths of Greece. Here was the greatest library of antiquity, " the assembled souls of all which men hold wise," and here Cleopatra wore the holy garment of the goddess Isis and conquered the conquerors. Here Mark Anthony gave the world for love and thought it well lost ; and while he kissed away kingdoms and provinces, she demanded of her royal lover the whole of Judea and Arabia ; but the mailed Bacchus pacified her with the present of two hundred thousand volumes for the Library of the Serapion. No trace of these glories, as we drive through sandy waste and Moslem tombs, beyond the stir of city life, to the site of the despoiled temple which once lifted its proud front and glittering roof, plated with metal, against the rainless blue.

In order to mingle the transient glory of his Egyptian campaign with the abiding fame of the Pharaohs, Napoleon, in 1798, buried the soldiers who fell in the attack on Alexandria at the base of Pompey's Pillar. The whole army assisted at the august ceremony, and the names of the heroes are recorded below the inscription of the Emperor Diocletian, "the Invincible." How well he understood human nature, that young general of twenty-nine years, who with the loss of only thirty men, planted the tri-color on the walls of Alexander's city! Where is the Frenchman who would not do and dare all things for such a record of service rendered?

The great historian will tell you the tale of final ruin of the Serapion by Christians, when the marble walls were a fortress; and how the successor of Mohammed destroyed the library the reader near his school days knows. The books, mainly of papyrus, supplied the four thousand baths with fuel for six months. When the victorious general sent to the Caliph to know his pleasure, said the fanatic Omar: "If the writings of the Greeks agree with the Koran, they are useless, and need not be preserved; if they disagree, they are pernicious, and ought to be destroyed." A strange order for one who habitually quoted the Arabic proverb: "Paradise is as much for him who rightly uses the pen as for him who takes the sword."

Such is the tale taught in our schools; but the earliest and wisest of Egyptologists say that the famous treasures of the Alexandrian Library were stolen, scattered in portions, and sold to Constantinople, long before Caliph Omar invaded Egypt. The accepted story is demonstrably a tribute to the Empire of Fable. Mohammedan heroes, in the fresh inspiration of their new faith, and secure in the sanctity of their cause, demolished the old foundations of many kingdoms, and tried to conquer Egypt in the same way. " Know, O soul," they said, with reverence and solemnity, " that everything in the world that is not of God is doomed to perish."

The fine, susceptible mind of the Arabs, their keen, quick apprehension, enabled them to appropriate rapidly scientific researches of the conquered Egyptians ; and the hoarded treasures of priestly lore were transferred to Cairo, the new city, founded opposite Memphis. Caliph Omar was shrewd enough to see that a restless, maritime capital, often insurrectionary, and rent by bloody religious feuds, was not the best center of the new religion he intended to plant in the Nile valley. The victorious Moslem in Alexandria boasted of having captured a city of four thousand palaces. He dwelt with rapture on the elegance of the Gymnasium, and the space and splendor of the Hippodrome for chariot-races and games ; and such was the store of wheat sent by caravan to Medina, that he declares the first of an unbroken line of camels entered the Holy City of the Prophet before the last camel had left Egypt. This latter declaration we may be permitted to doubt.

Not far from Pompey's Pillar, there were till recently two obelisks of the fine red granite of Syene, engraved with the names of the Pharaohs who placed the frontier of Egypt just where

4

they pleased; the throne-names which appear
often on the sacred beetles in the hearts of mummies. The obelisks (named Cleopatra's needles:
why or when I know not), were symbols of sunbeams, or taper fingers of the sun, ever pointing
upward to the flaming god of Eastern idolatry.
They were from the sacred and learned city of
On—city of the evening sun, seat of solar
worship—where Joseph married the priest's
daughter. They may have seen him and his
bride, with their arms round each other's necks,
posed like the sculptured figures about us, bearing the bland, restful expression of a stately pair,
linked in loving marriage. The continual recurrence of such pictures of husband and wife,
with arms entwined, makes us think those
wedded lovers in old times were of a race not
only affectionate, but demonstrative, and not
ashamed of public stare or criticism. Gazing in
each other's eyes, with quiet admiration, the
strange, sad, half-smile on their lips, which
modern sculptors vainly try to reproduce, thus
they have sat for thousands of years, worship-
ping the one eternally beautiful and beloved.
Among stiff, grim drawings of all possible and
impossible animals and plants, it was always a
refreshment to come on this pleasant picture,
which needs no reader of hieroglyphs to interpret.
It can have but one meaning.

One of the obelisks, which lay prostrate for
centuries in sand and mud by Pompey's Pillar,
now stands alone and gloomy in the murky air
of the Thames, above Waterloo bridge. Its

twin-brother may be seen by the reader, in a remoter country and a stranger environment, in the New York Central Park. The far New World, which comes to learn of the oldest, boasts of this ancient monument, and of the mixed spoils carried away, year by year, by greedy collectors, and rich hunters of curios.

In the year 357, Constantius, son of Constantine, wished to present the Romans some memorial of his gratitude for their munificence. He thought first of offering an equestrian statue, but concluded an obelisk from Heliopolis would be the most kingly present to the most arrogant of his allies. The death of Constantine had suspended the transportation of one of these marvelous pillars, and left it, after floating down the Nile, neglected at Alexandria. Constantius had a special vessel provided to convey the tremendous weight, and it was safely transferred from the Nile to the Tiber, and raised, with great rejoicings and solemn ceremonials, in the Circus Maximus at Rome. Long before, Augustus had embellished the amphitheatre with a similar trophy, and the Emperor doubtless dreamed, as he sat alone in his sacred car, dazzling the sight with robes encrusted with gems, that the obelisk he offered to propitiate the populace would remain till the sun himself should die. Scholars of the nineteenth century are doubtful if it still exists. In what siege of the many Roman sieges, or in what earthquake the shaft was overthrown, is not known. The antiquary vainly seeks its history and its frag-

ments, if they be spared from barbarian fury
and violence.

The Vatican is enriched with obelisks, and
beside the Flaminian gate stands one, in the
Piazza del Popolo, which Moses must have seen
when he was a student in the learning of the
Egyptians. It is the most ancient thing in the
Eternal City, and old Rome is young beside the
hoary antiquity of that granite sunbeam. The
obelisk in front of the Church St. John Lateran,
is the tallest in the world, 105 feet in height.
It is covered with the choicest sculptures. The
tracings of the figures drawn in hieroglyph writing, are delicate as cameos, carefully engraved
as the intaglio of a ring, and bear the appearance of being impressed with seals, instead of
being wrought with chisels into stone that is
hard as adamant.

A history of what it has seen, and what it
has survived, would fill many a volume. The
procession of nations in resistless march passed
by, till four successive empires, drunk with
glory, declined and died, while this consecrated
pillar pointed heavenward in Egypt. A living
interest attaches to it, because it retains the
symbol of the force which first opposed the
power of the living God. For unto that Pharaoh, Thothmes Second, whose cartouche is en-
graven on its side, was the message sent through
Moses, "that thou mayest know that there is
none like Me in all the earth." He was one of
the greatest of the line which ruled for twenty-
three centuries in the boasted purity of unmixed

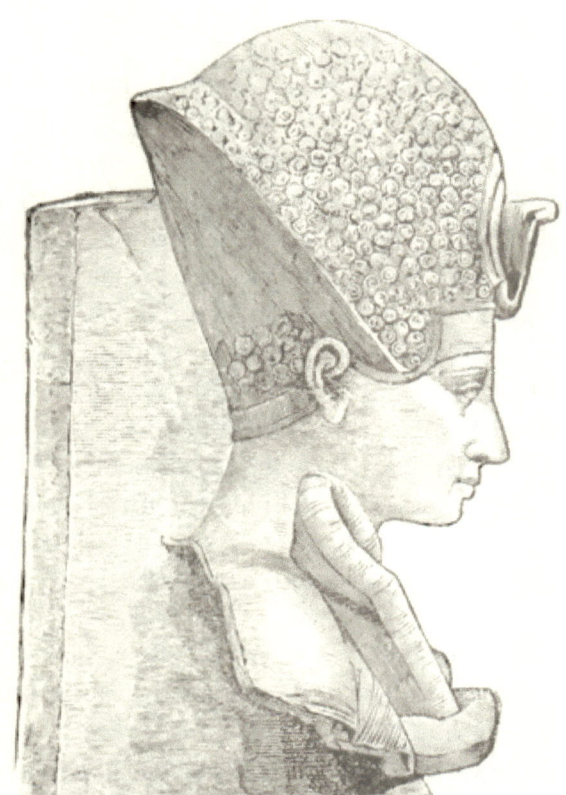

HEAD OF RAMESES II.

HEAD OF THOTHMES II.

royal blood. Our one hundred years dwindle to
a grain of sand in the presence of the records on
these granite shafts. It is doubtful if the careful tracings will long endure foreign atmospheres.
The moist, smoky air of England blackens and
mildews the obelisk set up with rejoicings and
imposing ceremonials; and already the scattered
brethren, banished to life-long exile among alien
races, look dreary and decaying. Farthest out
of place is the lonesome obelisk in gay and
laughing Paris, torn from its home by the sun-
flooded palms, the Nile, and the slow, sad song
of the sakia. At its base the bloody waves of
revolution surged and broke, and some mad
spirits attempted its overthrow; but in vain.

VI.

OBELISKS.

CONSTANTINOPLE holds an obelisk transported
thither when Byzantium was capital of the
Empire of the East, and the legions loyally
raised the new emperors upon their shields. It
stands in the *At-Medan,* or horse market, an open
space in old Stamboul, anciently the Hippodrome,
and has seen " the entire universe pass by between
walls of silk." There, amid shouts of frantic
crowds, the jeweled chariots flew before the
emperors of the Bosphorus. Turn to the pages
of Gibbon for accounts of the unapproachable
splendor of the pearl of two seas, in the centuries
when tributes from every known continent were
wafted into the sacred waters of the Golden

Horn. The city of Constantine was then a museum of priceless treasures from Italy, Greece, Egypt, and Asia Minor. In stately porticos, colossal equestrian statues rose on loftly pedestals in front of theatres and baths. The granite column of Marcius is there still, bearing its marble *cippus*, with the imperial eagles, but the temples and palaces have vanished like visions of the night. Of the spoil from Egypt—the Cleopatra's needles and bronze sphinxes couched on porphyry pedestals—one obelisk only is a final reminder. It looks melancholy and far from home, chilled by mists from the Black Sea and the gray winged vapors flying from the Marmora. The lone sunbeam is dulled in the clouds of Constantinople, pale and shadowy beside the red gold of Egypt.

Under a pitiless destruction, to which the slow decay of time is gentle, the statues of emperors, gods, heroes, have been reduced to lime. The rows of marble seats were torn away by Solyman, the Magnificent, to build his palaces. Eighty exquisite columns, which supported the Emperor's box, are gone forever; and the vast area of the Hippodrome, 900 feet long and 450 feet broad, is largely built over.

Many a trophy won in bloody fight has this obelisk seen. The renowned brass horses, above the entrance of St. Mark's, Venice—the only representative of the famous alloy of copper, gold and silver—were brought here from Chios, by Theodosius. Some day I hope to tell you of the most interesting relic of Grecian antiquity, **to**

which we now give a passing glance, because it
stands near our obelisk. It is a serpent column
of bronze, or copper, with three bodies twisted
spirally. Three heads, spreading outwardly,
once upheld the golden tripod of the Pythia, the
maiden priestess of Apollo, in Delphi, when she
gave the inspired oracle to the poets. Herodotus
writes: "The Greeks, after the victory of Platea,
479 B. C., collected all the money, and put aside
one-tenth of it for the god of Delphi. With this
they made a tripod of gold, which they offered
to the god; it was placed upon the three-headed
copper serpent, which was near to the altar."

The consecrated tripod was carried off by the
Phocians in the Holy War, but the bronze pillar remained till the insatiate and bloody Constantine set it up in his capital. The serpent heads
have been lost, supposably in the siege of Stamboul by the Turks in 1453. It is said one is
among the confused relics in the Church of that
sweet St. Irene, who had her son's eyes put out
with red-hot irons in the porphyry chamber,
where she had borne him; but I failed to find it
there. Mutilated and degraded, the entwined
serpents bear testimony to the religion of the
Greeks and the rapacity of their conquerors.
That nothing may be lacking, it has recently
been "restored" by a coat of fresh green paint.
It is a newly-wrought statue beside the over-
shadowing granite quarried three centuries before
Abraham was driven by famine into Egypt. On
the side of the obelisk may be seen the elliptical
frame, or cartouche of the second Pharaoh, dating

the mystic era when civilization began in the
valley of the Nile, sixteen hundred years before
the star-led Magians sought the caravan-route to
Bethlehem.

A strange doom has brought these two monuments together, symbols of religions long dead
and gone, and planted them near the minaret of
St. Sophia, where the Muezzin proclaims the one
God and calls the followers of Mohammed to
prayer. The Egyptians used to say to the first
Grecian philosophers: "You Greeks are mere
children, talkative and vain, you know nothing
at all of the past." To the beauty-loving
Athenian, the valley of the Nile was a land of
enchantments. The prehistoric life, the labyrinths and pictured tombs, their giant statues
sitting on granite thrones, their sorceries and
mysticism, shrouded it in a veil of illusions and
marvels. Side by side in the Hippodrome, the
representative columns of the strongest race and
the most beautiful race, keep a solitude unbroken,
though in the midst of a stream of tumultuous
life, not far from the pontoon bridge, which one
hundred thousand persons cross daily.

The single block of stone, as its pompous
declaration declares, was lifted by godlike power
on an everlasting pedestal, and overwritten with
a language too holy to be entrusted to the vulgar.
It must have had a sort of mystery even to the
people of its own generation, when first the
colossal mass was placed in front of the Temple
of the Sun, at Heliopolis. Theodosius the Great,
transported it to Constantinople, A. D., 390, a

memorial of his victory over Maximus, usurper of the Empire of the West. The monolith rests on a pedestal seven feet high, which is based on three circular steps. On one side, sculptured in bas-relief, are the Emperor Theodosius, with his wife, enthroned, receiving ambassadors and the homage of barbarians. On another, the same figure, viewing chariot-races and the Olympic games. The third shows the Hippodrome and its adornments, and the machinery by which the obelisk was raised, after it had been thrown down by an earthquake. In the fourth bas-relief, the Emperor appears with the crown princess holding a diadem.

The hieroglyphs engraved on the red granite shaft are of different periods, and belong to several dynasties. The side facing the South is inscribed with the following touching and simple prayer, from one of the greatest of the Pharaonic kings to the life giving deity:

"GOD PHTA SAKARIS.

"Grant power, and cover with the principle of divine wisdom the gentle king, Oh! guardian Sun, vigilant and just Sun, continuator of life.

"Guide his innermost thoughts, so he may show himself active and just in all things.

"Sublime Wisdom, grant to him the principle of thy essence, and the principle of thy light, so that he may collect fruits in the impetuosity of his career.

"Four times he thus distinctly implores thee,

Vigilant Sun of Justice of all times! May the
request which he makes to thee be granted to
him."

Many a scene, revolting to humanity, has this
obelisk looked upon. One of the saddest was
when the conqueror of the Huns, Persians, Afri-
cans, Vandals, and Goths—Belisarius, surnamed
"The Glory of the Greeks"—with eyes blind
and heart-broken, groped his way, begging for
bread at the base of the monuments of antiquity
which his arms had so often defended and saved
from destruction by barbarians. There are grat-
ulation and high ceremonial when the poor, mis-
placed obelisks, scattered to the four winds of
heaven, are set up on foreign shores. To me,
they appear monarchs banished to lifelong exile,
uncrowned, mourning for the cloudless face of the
god of their idolatry.

To rest undisturbed in the dry, dewless air of
Egypt, is earthly immortality. Names idly
scribbled by travelers remain indelible as though
deeply carved; and lotus-wreaths round the
heads of mummies are perfectly kept in the
painted tombs scented yet with strange spicery.
Well might the arrogant Pharaohs name themselves "Lords of the Daybreak," "Children of
the Sun." So unchangeable is this dead-alive
country that modern engineers have adopted a
stone record, forty-five hundred years old, and
from it have exact routes of travel in the Delta—
metes and bounds, oases and wells, given without fault, and relied on by English armies of to-
day. It is to be hoped that England's steady

hand on Egypt may protect her memorials of
the past, and one day lift the glorious statue of
Rameses from the mud, and set the godlike face
once more to the morning sun and the river of
his love.

VII.

CLEOPATRA.

WE must not leave Alexandria without further
mention of Cleopatra. In these tropic airs she
rode on swift camels and floated in gilded barges
with Anthony, and after years of revel, here she
was buried with imperial pomp in his tomb.

You know she was last of the race of Ptolemies
and was of Greek descent. Hers is a melodious
name, through many generations a favorite in the
royal families of Macedonia and Greece, and it
had a sweet meaning for the little girl in her
downy cradle: "The Pride of her Father." No
princess of unmixed Oriental blood was ever so
named, for in the East the pride of fathers is
bound up in their sons and the word is not empty
sound to those who comprehend.

We ask, as thousands have asked before us,
What was the secret of her charm? The historian who lived within her century and had perhaps the testimony of men who had seen the
siren, describes her as rather slight in stature,
not so beautiful in person as bewitching in manner. Her whole aim and study was the art of
pleasing, and her voice was like a musical instrument tuned with many strings. She had at

command seven languages in which she addressed ambassadors at her court, each in his
own tongue; she knew how to adapt herself to
the varying moods of men, governing them by
change with resistless fascination.

In the ruinous roads of Alexandria there is
not one trace of the shining marble pavement
where the capricious witch, yielding to Anthony's
humor, hopped forty paces through the streets;
nor is there sign of the palace where she was
unrolled from the bale of carpet, and tamed with
one glance the mighty Julius. There later she
vainly tried her charm on the cautious and cruel
Octavius Cæsar. Nor is there one stone left on
another of the monument where, close to the
Temple of Isis, she collected treasures, gold, silver, emeralds, pearls, ivory, ebony and cinna-
mon, heaped with quantities of combustibles
ready to consume her misfortunes and herself in
one tremendous flame.

This is the site of the city which saw the
costly shows for the people which almost made
them forget the extravagance that drained the
royal treasury. Here she sat in a chair of jeweled gold on a tribune of silver, wearing the
many colored robe of Isis, calling herself a goddess. Enthroned beside her was Anthony, her
king, in regal diadem and Oriental scimitar,
beneath their feet crimson scarfs on which sat
their twin children named the Sun and Moon,
kings of kings. One little prince in Median
dress, with turban and tiara, the other in long
cloak and slippers, his head circled by a diadem.

THE ASP.

THE IBIS.

In wanton waste they broke alabaster boxes made from the mines east of the Nile and filled the whole palace with the precious perfume. With the masters of the world, the queen feasted; she gamed, she hunted, she drank. The stories of her salt fishing and of the pearl ear-ring need no repetition here. They have been recorded with the undying names of eternal Rome, and accounts of her rambles at night in a soldier's cloak, seeking adventures.

Tricked in her best attire she showed herself to the populace at theaters and in the crowds of the Circus or Hippodrome, where chariot-races were made in power and splendor which Rome could not surpass; and in the Gymnasium with the small white hand familiar to the lips of kings, she crowned the best wrestlers and boxers. In company with Anthony, she fed to the sacred crocodiles, cakes and wine and when the sun, looking over the hills of Arabia, kissed the statue of Memnon, they listened to the wondrous songs without words that answered the warm touch of the Lord of the Daybreak. They moved in state, surrounded by a body-guard of four hundred Gauls—after Cleopatra's death given by Octavius to Herod. And, by way of variety in their pastimes, they made ghastly trials with unknown poisons on slaves and con-demned criminals. Like victims foreseeing their approaching doom, they sought knowledge of the swiftest, surest, most painless death.

The Pharos was a square building of white limestone, laid in several stories, each smaller

than the one below it. A winding road led to
the top, and Cleopatra drove a pair of horses to
the summit and there turned and drove them
down again. Doubtless they consulted the sacred bull, Apis, with small faith in his divinity;
visited Lake Mœris to laugh at the ascetic Jews
on its marshy shore and in their mad pranks
threaded the mazy Labyrinths which after all
were not serpentine, but quadrangular, with
rooms and passages of multiplied doors. Blinding structures for concealing the coffins of their
builders. In their impious daring they must
have entered the Pyramids and wondered at the
mountains of stone piled over the tomb of one
king. Perhaps in mockery they knelt to Serapis, the Sun-god, who ruled the hours and the
seasons, the winds and the storms, king of the
stars—himself an immortal fire.

Plutarch records that his grandfather had accounts from, or, as we might say, had interviewed
the cooks of Alexandria who basted wild-boars
for the suppers whose profusion shamed the delicate banquets of Apicius. Read his quaint
chronicle and for the spirit of the "Serpent of
old Nile," who professed to believe her soul had
once been the soul of a tigress, read the sensuous poem of W. W. Story. Her lament for the
lost existence when she knew no law but the law
of her moods. The tiger blood in her was
roused when she ordered the assassination of her
sister, in the Temple of Diana whither she had
fled for refuge, for it was Cleopatra's pleasure
there should be no other heir near the throne,

and her cruelties might go far to converting one
to the doctrine of metempsychosis.

When present with Anthony she gave him no
time to think, lest reflection and repentance
might come to rob her of her hero. When
absent she sent him love-letters enclosed in onyx
and crystal caskets, and worded with passionate
appeal. Meanwhile the slaves hungered and
thirsted and went starving to untimely graves.
Whole provinces were beggared in order that the
matchless pageantry might not flag.

There is a portrait of Cleopatra at Denderah in
a temple which she built to Ammon, the god
under whose sunny wings Egypt lay basking.
Like the ancient temples everywhere, this has
been a quarry for building-stones and whole
towns have been raised from its fragments. The
Sun-king and his worshipers have passed into
the region of romance and fable and the most
commanding Queen of History is almost a myth
in this degraded spot.

What do the Bedouins care for except backsheesh?

Usually Egyptian temples were open to the
sky but this was roofed. A group of marble
columns rise from the dust and sand-heaps,
swarming with vermin, which surround the
temple. Arab huts are stuck among them ; and
on the adytum of the temple the low born Sheik
of his tribe has set the mud bricks for his house.
It is dirtier than a kennel. A den, a sty for
beings apparently children of the slime and ooze

of the river; creatures sprawling in the sun like
lizards and frogs.

Once this was a court all greenery; blooming
gardens, rushing waters, plashing fountains running like quicksilver in the sunlight and dropping into alabaster basins. Now not a tree, not
a shrub nor blade of grass is in sight. Stoop
under the low door, a small dark stone room, the
boudoir of the peerless queen. It is a sort of
tombs or jail, where government criminals are
confined. It reeks with noisome smells and
filth, and prisoners lie prone in abject wretchedness on the floor.

With a lighted torch in hand the tourist surveys the portrait on the grimy wall, which many
travel far to see. The Arab torches flare wildly
in the drafts, the smoke is stifling. Higher,
Abdullah and Hassan, lift up the lights while
we study the picture: not twice in a life-time
shall we see the face of such a sorceress. The
sculptures are not handsomely cut, and are
crumbling, but we trace the one authentic
portrait. The features are small, and lovers of
Greek lines are compelled to admit the nose is
not correct. In fact it turns up a little the
nose of the all-conquering beauty!—and the lips
are too full for our ideals.

How are the mighty fallen! In an innermost
sanctuary of the resplendent palace dedicated
by the priestess of Love and Beauty to worship
of the sun, the Sheik has chosen to place his cel-
lar, and made it a deposit for refuse which may
only be hinted at. This shrine once sparkled

EGYPTIAN STANDARDS.

FORMS OF ISIS.

with gold and silver, amber and ivory, a recess
veiled by richest curtains fringed with gems
from Ethiopia and India. It was redolent of
musk and rose-oil, and the costly ointments kept
in alabaster boxes made sacred by the offering
of Mary. Purple cushions on soft couches lined
the voluptuous resting-place, and if ghosts are
permitted to haunt the scenes of their earthly
existence, surely Cleopatra might be allowed one
moment of abhorrence in this spot. It would
add to the torment of Hades.

On the capitals of the few spared columns is
the Egyptian Athor, or Venus, bearing a peculiar
majesty and sweetness but remote from the
loveliness of the Greek Aphrodite. Here, too,
are colossal figures of Cæsar's sons in the regal
crown of the Ptolemies. They are not well
drawn and the stone begins to crumble. Let
them go; the poet of all time has given us a
hint of the Queen:

—" For her person,
It beggared all description."—

There is the master's outline, fill up and color
to suit your own ideals. And paint me this
picture, O painter, people the emptiness with
princes, priests, courtiers, a worshipful throng
crowned with garlands and robed in costliest
vestment attended by slaves whose breath is of
no more account than the tenant of one of the
heaped-up ant-hills.

From the gray shifting sand unearth the
painted gateway, guarded by obelisks, the gran-

5

ite sunbeams ever reminding the worshipers of
the supreme of the many gods of Egypt. The
approach through avenues of sphinxes and colossal sculptures in white and red marble. High
flaunting over all, hang out the scarlet and azure
flags with Isis-headed standards. The ponder-
ous red flag-staffs are yet found among fragments
of painted walls and pillars that used to fence
the august sanctuary. In these cities they are
so numerous that when Homer called Thebes
the City of a Hundred Gates, it was not poetic
exaggeration. Add to the glowing picture
what no painter has painted, and no poet can
sing: the ceaseless movement of an overgrown
civilization. The armies, the vast processions,
the strange barbaric music of crashing cymbals
and fishskin drums, the rattle of myriad chariots,
the clang of steel and brazen arms, the noise of
the captains and the shoutings.

Could we wake those wild lovers from the
long sleep where they were laid away surrounded
by familiar objects, so that on rising after a
thousand years of slumber the dead might not
feel estranged, and could we bring them to see
this squalor, they might well ask what power
could destroy their works, built for eternity?
Was it earthquake? I think not. The destruction has been too deliberate and complete for
anything but conquering armies equal in might
to the ones which of old defended them. They
must have labored almost as long to undo, as
their predecessors did to set up the grand, majestic works. The statues seem all-powerful, with

hands resting on their knees in the attitude of repose; and one has the feeling that the giants, serene of aspect, have lost their wish to slay and devour, and now sit, in stony stillness after toils, enjoying the sunshine and ceaseless calm.

The dreaming traveler turns from dreamy statues to the woman who held in check the generals of wars which changed the map of the world, and to the miseries of millions who did awful deeds in the teeming population of Egypt.

How Cleopatra saved herself from degradation by death, and obliged Augustus to content himself with her effigy carried in his triumph; how her sons marched in chains through Rome, is too familiar a story to need repetition here.

When Anthony called her his "Serpent of old Nile," he felt the fascination of her eyes. Hear the gray-haired warrior rushing to suicide; because a Roman might not survive his good fortune: "I am dying, Egypt, dying; only I here importune death awhile, until of many thousand kisses the poor last I lay upon thy lips."

And as the shadows of the last mystery gathered before his sight, the Past with its pomps and glories, by that one woman lost forever, his dying charge was worthy the Anthony of the great triumvirate. He knew himself a poor, fallen man, caught in the strong toil of grace spread for him; the deeper in the debasement from having been a hero. The Roman spirit leaped up and went out in one up-springing flash ·

" The miserable change now at my end
Lament nor sorrow at ; but please your thoughts
In feeding them with those my former fortunes
Wherein I lived the greatest prince o' the world,
The noblest ; and do now not basely die,
Not cowardly, put off my helmet to
My countryman. A Roman by a Roman val-
iantly vanquished."

I suppose they made a mummy of her, the exquisite, the beauty-loving, after the manner described in hideous detail by Herodotus. The professionals filled her veins with subtle medicines, swathed the sinuous limbs in bandages, spicery, and gummed the body with varnish : and the revolting process was called embalming ; as though costly drugs and bitumen from the Dead Sea had been potent to keep the dear dead woman from decay.

The darkness of the prison-house was relieved by gaudy figures on the mummy cases, painted brilliant blue, yellow, vermilion and black. Then they were gilded and the portraits with awful glass eyes follow you, stare at you, as though the sleepers below had waked from fearful nightmare and lay transfixed, unable to move.

Perhaps the triple coffins, shaped to the slight figure of the enchantress, may yet be found, dragged from the alabaster sarcophagus and Cook's Tourists may peer into the coffins and behold the most sweet Queen crowned with lotus-wreaths as she entered the long sleep, decked with jewels as in life, robed in fine vesture her fair belongings at hand ready for her to make an immortal toilet after the repose of almost two thousand years.

EGYPTIAN VASES AND AMPHORÆ

These people did not dread the transition we call death. Soon as the King came to his throne he began to build his tomb and the care given the body was because their religion taught that while it was undecayed the soul hovered about it. When the clay goes to pieces the soul enters some low order of animal and when it has made the circuit of all terrestrial and marine animals and all birds, it again puts on human shape. This circuit they said is accomplished in three thousand years. The reader will remember that Pythagoras was converted to the doctrine and transplanted it into Greece, where it influenced the converts even to their abstaining from animal food.

The inscriptions, which are the state papers of Egypt, throw no light on this religion; since, with the exception of one doubtful carving, thought to represent the return of a sinful soul to earth in the form of a pig, no hint of this belief has been discovered in the ancient monuments.

Many wild and weird tales have been told of seeds found in the hands of embalmed Egyptians being sown and growing into flowers of matchless beauty, but with a deadly perfume which has destroyed the health of the wearers. It is said English gardeners have raised peas and wheat from dried grains found in the hold of mummy hands. I am deeply gratified to see the guide-books unite in testimony. No such gardening has been accomplished, and every such story is false. Notwithstanding the fact travelers buy the small samples of grain offered in tattered rags, by venders, as veritable corn from the granaries of the Pharaoh who was a dreamer of dreams when Joseph was prisoner in the dungeons of the king, and servant to the Captain of the guard.

The custom of burying seed grew out of the ancient idea that the soul carries in its hand, from this life, a few grains of wheat with which to begin anew the life in *Amenti*, or Paradise. After the spirit has raised wheat in the Fields of the Blest, he makes bread and offers it with prayer to God.

VIII.

TO CAIRO.

VERY pleasant was that ride to Cairo, the city called by Orientals the Precious Diamond in the handle of the green Fan of the Delta. It was the retreat of the Fatimate Caliphs, the beloved asylum of the poets, and is famed in flowery prose and voluptuous song.

Our swift train appeared to glide through rather than break the stillness of the drowsy country. The mellow sunshine was like our Indian Summer, balmy and yellow, glorifying all it touched, and made less melancholy the squalid, filthy Arab villages, haunted by hags who are not witches, but wives and daughters of the fellaheen. No transfiguring power can beautify them till they are touched by the sacred finger of Allah, as the Arabs describe the approach of death. The mud houses are like

an outgrowth of Nilotic slime and ooze, and beside them grow lovely acacias and mimosa or
gum-arabic trees, in which pigeons flock and
flutter. About the straw-heaps at the door
chickens cackle, and dirty sheep hunt for food,
and sore-eyed children lie basking, resembling
torpid reptiles.

Women work in the fields with the men,
each wearing one loose garment. There is no
machinery but the *shadoof*, like our old-fashioned
well-sweep, the most primitive of pumps and a
rush-basket. Swinging the water-tight basket,
they move with machine-like precision, these
forever oppressed Egyptians, without recollections of a great past or ambition pointing to a
better future. Their very souls are enslaved by
centuries of grinding tyranny, knowing no change
but a change of taskmasters. The locomotive
gives them no impulses, and they do not lift
their heads as the herald of a new civilization, a
chariot mightier than Pharaoh's, rolls past.
Among the low bending figures we saw the tat-
tooed faces and painted blue lips, forbidden by
Levitical law. In a slow, heart-broken way they
move steadily, swinging the rush-basket in the
hard service of the field named in Deuteronomy,
drawing up water from the river and emptying
it on the fields in the higher levels. Sometimes
the passer-by may hear a dull, groaning sound
from the unpaid toilers, a melancholy chorus
chanted by gangs of boys and girls, degraded
unspeakably, who are set to work together along

the Nile banks. The Arabic scholar tells us
these are the words of the slow, sad song:

GIRLS.

They starve us, they starve us!

BOYS.

They beat us, they beat us!

CHORUS ALL TOGETHER.

But there's some one above,
There's some one above,
Who will punish them well,
Will punish them well.

Another burden in full chorus is.

The chief of the village,
The chief of the village,
May the dogs tear him, tear him, tear
him!

In the oldest of the world's illustrated histories, on the walls of Thebes, are pictures, perfect
as though sculptured yesterday, for which these
waiting human machines might have served as
models. There is little doubt that, this is the
very same cry which went up to heaven from
the enslaved Hebrews, groaning under their taskmasters. An exceeding bitter cry when swelled
in a chorus of multitudes doomed to perform
impossibilities, gazing in despair at their uncon-
querable work.

There is a tomb-painting near Ghizeh supposed
to represent the hard usage of Israelites in Egypt,
an accurate illustration of the house of bondage.
The features of the Jews it is impossible to mistake. They are making brick, their bodies are
splashed with clay, and their service is plainly
exacted " with rigor." In the center of the pic-

ture sits an overseer or taskmaster, with baton
in hand, ready to enforce obedience— an actual
portrait of some Egyptian face, with oblique
eyes, and narrow, receding forehead.

As we journeyed, camels in twos and threes
went by, their Arab drivers seated on horrible
high-posted saddles, taking the motion of the
brute in that tilting perch. The mangy, dreary
creatures did not take fright at the steam-
whistle; they were too far gone for that. They
only turned, and chewing the cud of nothing
particular, surged slowly along unmindful of our
invasion on the sanctity of the past; and mus-
ing, it would seem, on the hard lot of the beast
of burden, the slave of slaves. I thought they
had no spirit left, but when a load too heavy to
be endured was being girded, the kneeling beasts
gave a complaining groan most dismal to hear.
The Scripture word "girded" first has meaning
here. It was a new idea to see two heavy bales
balanced, one on either side, and kept in place
with broad bands, wound round and round the
animal.

" Why do they cry," I asked.

" Because their backs are sore; they all have
sore backs," answered the guide, " but," he
added, reflectively, "they last as long as though
their backs were not sore."

It is not possible to write of Cairo without
mention of the *Arabian Nights.* It is the beaten
track which I have tried to avoid; but there is
no other way. Necessity obliges me to quote
the words of the Caliph: " He who has not

seen Cairo has not seen the world. Its earth is
gold, its women are bewitching and its Nile is a
wonder." And Sultana Scheherezade praises the
City of Pyramids: "As compared with the
sight of this city what is the joy of setting eyes
on your beloved? He who has seen it will confess that there exists for the eye no higher enjoyment, and when one remembers the night on
which the Nile comes to its height, he gives
back the wine-cup to the bearer full, and makes
water flow up to its source again."

There is no more delightful memory than
Cairo. Even the traveler who has visited the
palaces of Europe and the splendors of Asia
must yield to the fascination of its dim bazaars,
and the mysterious, close-barred lattices which
shut in the beauties of the harem—darlings
bought with a great price. Western influence
has been felt in the City of the Caliphs, and
cheap buildings are rising among the massive
piles of stone and marble which belong to the
former centuries. Saracenic carvings are giving
way to commonplace porticos, and arm-chairs
and carriages take the place of the divan and
sedan chairs, made of ebony and inlaid with
pearl, in which ladies formerly moved about.
Houses, streets, people, are suffering a change,
and he who seeks the picturesque, sighs over
the fast coming innovations, the banishment of
gay color and costume, and of the desert minstrels with the mournful two stringed guitar.

A street-car line is projected for Cairo. Venerable and historic monuments are laid low to

make room for glaring hotels, and the dreadful costume of the Christian is adopted, instead of the flowing robes and soft, light fabrics suited to tropic heat. Comfortable, loose slippers are abandoned for leather shoes, and women are forsaking cool draperies for corsets and the many discomforts of Parisian toilet. It is consoling to learn they must keep to the veils which law and religion hold sacred, and which no foreign influence can alter.

Go soon if you would catch the coloring of the Orient, the brilliant "symphonies of shades" which make the blood of the artist tingle as the divine melodies of Beethoven touch the sense of the musician.

Some of these tints, in the fast colors of the Great Master, are unalterable. The hills of the Libyan desert gird the horizon and frame the matchless picture, and the mountain tombs of Ghizeh tower against the sky, blue as when Cleopatra lavished her blandishments on Anthony, as they did when the great Rameses breathed the burning incense offered to him as to a god. They look no older now than when the first patriarch saw them as he went down into Egypt to sojourn there, for the famine was grievous in his land. Not the least charming feature of the landscape is the *dahabeeyah*, a light vessel with one lateen sail, peculiar to the Nile, as the gondola is to Venice and the caique to the Bosphorus.

A morbid desire for originality prevents my saying they skim the water like sea-gulls, speed-

ing before the north wind which blows **steadily**
by day, and dropping northward with **the** current of the river at night.   Away **to the mystic**
regions of chimeras, dragons, flying-serpents
they sail, and from the antique markets bring
precious gums, ebony, sandal-wood and charcoal
of the Numosa, cargoes of ivory, ostrich feathers, gum-arabic and slaves, the black-skinned
tribes of the tropics, who from the beginning
have been branded with the curse which Noah
pronounced on the sons of Ham, hewers of wood
and drawers of water then and now.

Formerly the soft sand of the streets of Cairo
gave back no sound of chariot wheel, hoof, or
footstep; now the paved roadway of the Muski
is a din worthy Regent Street or Broadway.   It
has lost in dignity and quiet, but much gain is
made, in some respects, by the improvements of
Ismail Pasha.   Instead of donkeying to Memphis, or perching on a back-breaking camel, you
ride in an open barouche to the very foot of the
Great Pyramid.   It is a delicious drive, eleven
miles on a raised causeway, under the shady
acacia trees, sacred in our eyes to poetry and
song.   The highway was built for the Prince of
Wales, according to an immemorial compliment
in the East, which orders a new road made for a
guest the king delights to honor.   Verily, Ismail
Pasha builded better than he knew, when he ordered this for the Prince of Wales.   His it is
now.

The Arab proverb runs, "Time mocks all, but
the pyramids mock time."   How the outer cas-

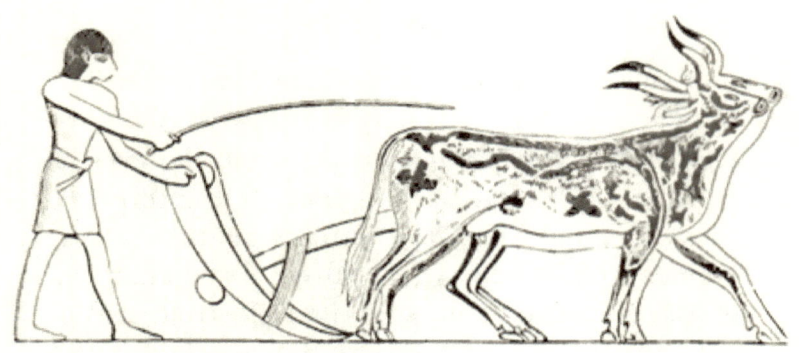

MODE OF PLOUGHING

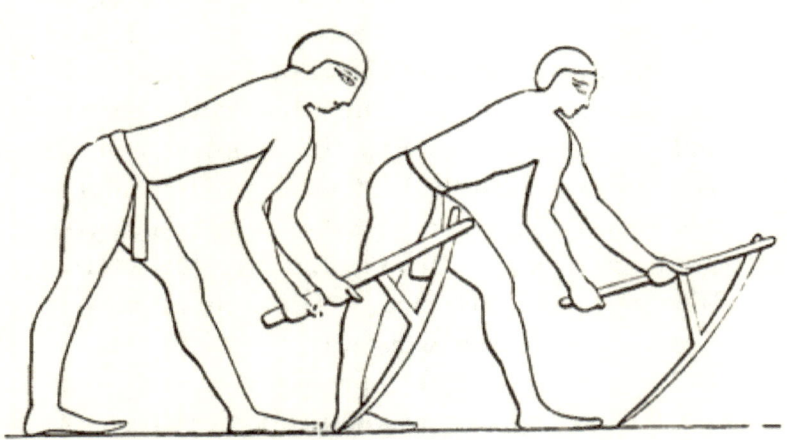

EGYPTIANS HOEING.

ing of Ghizeh has been carried off to found new
towns, and for the upbuilding of Cairo, is an old
tale and often told. The illiterate children of
the desert paid no heed to tablets of hewn stone
which contained precious histories, and the conqueror Amron founded the City of Victory on the
field where the leathern tent of the commander-
in-chief was pitched. When he was to return to
Alexandria, and ordered his tent to be struck for
the march, he was told that a pair of pigeons had
made their nest on its roof. He exclaimed,
"God forbid that a Mohammedan should deny
his shelter to a living being, a creature of Allah
who had confided to the protection of his hospitality. Leave the tent standing. It is an omen
of good."

The pigeons remained unharmed in their nest,
and when Amron returned, flushed with triumph,
from Alexandria, he found it there standing, occupied it again, and made the spot a center for
the new capital, Fostat, *i. e.* the tent. The reader
will remember a similar story told of the Emperor Charles of Spain in Flanders, immortal-
ized, in verse by Longfellow, "Golondrina is my
guest," the Emperor said, "let no hand molest nor
hurt her." And when the army disbanded, the
canvas palace was left standing for the sake of
the swallow's nest.

IX.

THE RISE OF THE NILE.

THE Saracens thoroughly subjugated the Egyptians, and treated them with more mildness than often falls to the portion of the vanquished. It is said the conquerors overran the domains of science as quickly as they overcame the kingdoms of their neighbors, and two centuries after the conquest, the son of Haroun al-Raschid found, in the Valley of the Nile, the rich fruit of a scientific life. The Arabs dismantled Alexandria and Memphis, but they built observatories, and, profiting by the astrology of the Egyptians, studied the stars, and gave them names familiar now to every school-boy. And when the Caliph in 801 sent to Charlemagne, from Bagdad, the keys of our Saviour's sepulchre, as a pledge of esteem from the Commander of the Faithful to the greatest of Christian kings, it was the mingling of sound policy and delicate compliment, which yet marks the crafty and courteous Arab. The invading army found ruins so extensive and colossal, that the Arabic historian concludes the ancient Egyptians were long-lived giants, who were able to move tremendous blocks of stone by the use of magic wands.

In the year 638, Memphis was a dead city, infested by robbers, employed by commercial companies, who searched the fallen temples and sepulchres for hidden treasures. The great un derground vaults, many miles long, escaped destruction, but the movable blocks of marble, the white walls of the fort, the granite temples of the gods, were quarries for the builders of the city, not named Cairo till two hundred years after its foundations were laid. And thus vanished Heliopolis, on the bank of the river opposite the new capital. The stones were easily transported when the Nile was in overflow, and the work was done rapidly and more carelessly than is usual with Arabic artisans.

As I said, the pyramids have been quarries, and have not been blown in air only because danger to Cairo was apprehended from so great an explosion.

The face of the Sphinx has been a target for Mamelukes through centuries. They hurl their spears and level their guns at " the idols," with infinite zest and vigor. Still do these remains of the Pharaohs survive, but it is only because the worshipers of the one God revealed by Mohammed had not the power or machinery to lay them low. Iconoclasm should have its limit, and the later Christian learns that even idols may have their uses. At their feet and on their breasts are traced hieroglyphs invaluable and irreplaceable if lost.

Far up the Nile, near the last rapid, is a curious pagan temple containing stone tablets with the commandments of kings, and the words of hymns sung to the Nile on festival nights, when the overflow commences.

A massive stone table of black granite has

recently been discovered, worked into the foundation of a house of Cairo. It is the record uninjured of a pæan devoted to the honor of Ptolemy Soter, and in the mosque of Amrou, most ancient of Egypt, are numerous pillars, supports of capitals in Greek, Roman and Byzantine workmanship. No visitor can fail to notice the vast number of columns from old heathen temples employed in the construction of Moslem sanctuaries.

The conquerors loved Cairo always, and lavished untold sums on it, besides the rich plunder afforded by the neighboring cities. Amrou in his despatches described the Nile Valley as first a desert, then a sweet water lake, then a blooming garden; the three gradations given the country by the river, without which there is no life.

The night of June 17 is known as the Night of the Drop. From the kingdom of the myths, a traditional belief comes to our times, that during this night a mystic and magical drop from heaven falls into the Nile, and starts its rising. Anciently it was a tear of Isis, the beautiful goddess with ambrosial locks, and it fell near her sacred home, the Isle of Philæ. At once the sympathetic river began to swell, and Sirius looked on with a brilliance which outshone the sun, for the soul of that star was Isis.

The genius or deity of the sacred stream was *Hapi Mou.* He is represented as a fat man, of a blue color, with aquatic plants for hair. The god had two statues at Luxor, and was employed

THE TOMB-CHAMBER OF THE THIRD PYRAMID.

in binding the thrones of the Pharaohs with the lotus and papyrus of Upper Egypt. The Greeks used to say it was easier to find a god than a man on the Nile banks, and we readily imagine idols of the beneficent deity ever present on the shores of Father Nilus. The water was so delicious that the old Sultans transported it to Constantinople. Persian kings carried it with them for their banquets, and a Roman general rebuked his soldiers for demanding wine in its presence.

The rise begins at Syene, and in ancient days the priests, in gorgeous garments, with music and solemn incantation chanted their hymns, and speeded forward the torrent rushing toward the thirsty sands. That solemnity was the grandest event of the year, and was celebrated with incredible pomp. A lovely virgin of noble birth was crowned with garlands, and thrown into the river, the bride of the Nile, to insure a plentiful inundation and generous harvest.

The Arab conqueror abolished the heathen sacrifice, and the river did not rise for three months after the usual time of increase. The people were frightened, and Amrou wrote to Caliph Omar to tell what was done, and of the threatened calamity. Omar returned brief answers, expressing approbation of Amrou's action, and enclosing, in a letter, a note to be thrown into the Nile. It ran as follows: " From Abd-Allah, Prince of the Faithful, to the Nile of Egypt. If thou flowest of thine own accord, then cease to . flow; but if it be God, the

6

Almighty, who causeth thee to flow, then we
implore God, the One, the Mighty, to let thee
flow." Amrou obeyed the command of the
Caliph, and lo! the river rose sixteen cubits the
following night.

In Cairo the breaking of the Nile is still celebrated. The *dahabeeyahs* are illumined with
lanterns and dressed with flags, little boats fly
across the twinkling waters, and the air resounds
with melancholy hymns of women in chorus of
song, ending in wailing anything but festal to
our ears. In the tents on shore are dancers,
musicians, reciters, laughter and feasting, vari-
colored lights, and a dazzle of bright arms and
costume.

At midnight the men begin to work on the
dyke, and at daybreak the Khedive and attendant officials in splendid uniforms, appear in a
tent overlooking the embankment, and testify
that the Nile has reached the height for bursting
the dyke. The testimonial is forwarded to the
Sultan. The Khedive scatters small coin in the
shallow edge of the river, the poor dive for them
in the mud, and evil-minded and malicious tourists say the small coin grows smaller, and fewer
in number, every year.

There are legends that the bride of the
Nile is now represented by a waxen image of a
girl, blooming and decked in bridal robes; but I
could find no foundation in truth for the story.
Nor could I learn when and where it was the
custom to seal a mummy finger in a costly casket,

and fling it an offering to the god of the bursting river.

One remnant of the obsolete ceremony survives in the rigging of a large boat called *Akabeh* by the Arabs. It is painted in brightest colors, and illumined with flaring lamps and streamers. You may leave Cairo in the afternoon on this sacred vessel, and sail to the Isle of Rhoda (or roses), and from its deck watch the night-long pageant. In the rosy glow of morning, rockets and cannon and thunderous shouts of multitudes announce that the Nile has risen.

At Rhoda, the traveler may see the Nilometer or measurer of the overflow—a deep well connected with the river by a subterranean canal, so that the height of the water in the well is precisely that of the Nile. In the centre is an exceedingly slender eight-sided pillar, on which exact markings of the rise are kept. Under twenty-four feet gives a scant harvest; under eighteen feet means famine for thousands. The sixteenth cubit indicated on the Nilometer is called the "Sultan's water," the annual tax being remitted if the river fails of this height. The visitor may go down the steps (I did not), and read for himself the record, and find the water-level. And from this exquisite isle—ah, how that beautiful sight comes back to me now!—he has the finest view of the most imposing of Oriental ceremonials. A miracle-play of night and day, so aflame with shifting color, and alive with movement and resonant minstrelsy, that our wildest festivals in comparison are **poor**, tame and dull.

No words of mine can give an idea of the Babel of language, the tumultuous rejoicing, always within the limits of decency and sobriety. Maskers in formless mantles glide like ghosts through the crowd, and what wild uproar when one is discovered through his disguise, and struggles away again to some shadowy column, which may screen him from the searching blaze of the lanterns! A sense of the superhuman comes to the mind of one for the first time watching the swelling waters, which rise silently and surely, as though predestined by fate, and without rain or storm appear impelled by some magic underswell.

Christian and Mohammedan influences, through centuries, have been unable to make the Fellahs or peasants comprehend that the Nile is anything but the direct gift of God. And the workers in the fields give Him the glory of the indescribable green, and the mellow grain with fat ears, which repay the sower a hundred-fold. At all hours, in all times and places, there is this fearless recognition; a constant reference to the presence of the Omnipresent, which is admitted in our secret hearts, but named, alas, how rarely in audible petition by the Christian!

X.

AT HELIOPOLIS.

FIVE miles away from Cairo are the ruins of *On*, or Heliopolis, on the edge of the overflow or cultivable ground. Irrigation makes the black soil fruitful, and the water-line is the line of division between life and death, arid gray sand and velvet greenness. Above fields rich with corn and rice are causeways raised high over the level of the inundations. On one of these smooth roads you drive in an easy carriage, and alight within a large inclosure of earthen mounds sparingly cultivated with gardens. You look in a pool unkept and dirty—the Spring of the Sun— and survey the oldest of obelisks, and ponder on what it has seen and what it has survived. Bereft of its brethren, it stands alone and sorrowful, the solitary survivor of one hundred columns dedicated to solar worship. Older than Joseph, it is named by the Father of History. Plato may have mused in its shadow, and Pythagoras here may have learned the secret lore of the priesthood, and Hypatia, studying the religion the " finger of the sun " represented, may have thought it ennobling as the degraded Christianity she saw in Alexandria. The Nile floods the country without hinderance, burying deeper and deeper the dead civilization of which the obelisk is the tombstone. The huge pillar is the oldest work in Lower Egypt, a monolith over **one** hundred feet high, erected by Usertisene I. in the year 2803 B.C. By the annual deposit two meters of earth have accumulated at its foot during the two thousand years since the ruin of Heliopolis.

Many a long procession of priests, prophets, saints, brethren, false and faithful, has passed by since first its shaft was lifted to the rainless blue. Heaps of *debris* mark the site of the city, in pagan times crowded with idols. Now there is no stone to point the foundation of the famous Egyptian University, a center of intellectual life, or the Temple of the Sun, a marvel of architectural splendor. Christian churches early sprang up in the wastes of Egypt, founded by outcasts from Judea, persecuted and driven out by the chosen people. And not far from the site of Heliopolis is the village of Matarea, where the Holy Family rested, and for a time dwelt in a grove of sycamores. This circumstance (I am tracking the old legends) gave the sycamore a peculiar and sacred interest in the early Christian era. With loving care and some expense the crusaders imported it into Europe, and, under a religious feeling, Mary Stuart planted one from France in her garden, the first one of its kind to wave its fan-like leaves in the pale grey mists of Scotland.

As usual, when they halted, a miraculous spring appeared for the refreshment of the Holy Family. It still exists, under the name of the Fountain of Mary, and is shown in a neglected place, in a wild garden of oranges and lemons, inclosed by an iron railing, and surrounded with fragrant jessamine. Near by is a patriarchal for-est son of Anak, hoary, venerable, which looks as though it might have upborne the weight of the Flood. Like the lone obelisk, it is last of its kindred, and is carved over with hieroglyphs, the gnarled and knotty trunk made a register for names of tourists. Tradition calls the plane-tree a descendant of the one that sheltered the Holy Family while they were fleeing before out-laws, possibly murderers. They hid in the hol-low of the riven and decaying trunk, and a spider wove her web across the opening, com-pletely veiling the fugitives under a gauzy cur-tain. The same tale is told of Mohammed in the Hegira, and of some other illustrious outcast, I forget whom.

We say this is only a fable invented by super-stition; but we must remember the highways of travel are unchanged, and the well must have made the spot a halting-place. The miracles we may receive or reject. The predecessor of the historic tree, as is shown by actual record, died more than two hundred years ago. Certainly for two centuries this one has kept watch over the spring, called in poetic Arabic phrase, the "Eye of the Sun;" by Christians, the "Virgin's Well." Aquatic plants choke the pool, and the feathery foliage of tamarisks is borne down by horny leaves and prickles of the cactus.

After the fall of Heliopolis, during the French invasion, General Kleber visited, as a pilgrim, the Tree of the Holy Family, and wrote his

name on one of its branches, but it is overgrown
or in some other way has disappeared.

Whether she saw this tree or not, we know
the tender glance of Mary fell on the same yellow desert with its three sand hills, on reedy
margin and rushing river. The divine Child
with calm, eternal eyes looked from her shoulder
(thus Bethlehem women still carry their babies)
and saw the pyramids in sharp profile—mighty
wedges, blue in the distance—mysterious, unknown, then as now. They are unchanged since
the patriarch Job saw them and wrote, "There
they all lie, the kings in their glory, *each in his
own house.*"

Many have questioned how the Holy Family
subsisted in the two years, if two years they
were, near On, or Heliopolis. Tradition tells
that Joseph worked at his trade—but small car-
pentry is demanded in the mud houses of the
poor among whom their lot was cast, and it is
said that Mary did embroideries. Garments of
divers colors and curious needle-work have belonged ever to the Orientals. Blue and scarlet
and the Tyrian purples, which were varied
shades of crimson and blue, were known to the
people called barbarian by dyers who seek in
vain the secrets of their craft.

There is a legend that the Virgin worked
mummy-cloths. They are linen towels about
the size of an ordinary bath-towel, and are discovered in catacombs fresh as though laid there
yesterday. Every thing in Egypt is for eternity,
and the credulous are taxed to believe that a

mummy-case has recently been opened, its tenant found rolled in linen shawls which bear the
initials of Mary, daughter of Joachim and
Anna. The ornamentations had been identified
as Bethlehem work, and they are believed by
devout souls to be the very stitches set by the
hand of the Madonna. Would it not be a strange
sensation to touch a fabric wrought by the
mother of Christ?

I think the poverty of the exiles has been exaggerated. The gifts of kings to a God were
not trifling symbols or mere souvenirs. The
gold of the Magian was for present extremity,
and with the simple wants of a primitive people, unused to luxury, the offerings of the Wise
Men must have lasted a long time. Slight food
and scant raiment sufficed. Nor should we
think that night in the khan at Bethlehem was
a sign of extreme hardship. It was no more to
the family of the taxpayer coming up to Jerusalem and finding no room in the inn, than a
retreat to the hay-loft would be to our farmer's
boys. In fact, such a resting-place is much
more common in Judea than is generally supposed. The cave-country of Palestine is full of
recesses for travelers, who make themselves
comfortable with mats and blankets, every necessary for a journey, which the Oriental carries
with him. Even when seeking permanent
quarters the true son of the East takes his rug
and cushion, his coffee-pot and bag of meal. In
every robber-country men, women, children, and
animals must for safety come within walled in-

closures. In the Rocky Mountains it is a corral shutting out Apaches; in Syria, a caravanserai against the elder brother of the tameless Indian, the Bedouin of the desert. The khan where the Holy Family would rest in journeying was a hotel or inn, without landlord or landlady, clerk, chambermaid, or porter. It was without roof, without rooms, without bed or table; a walled stopping-place, inclosing a fountain, which was free to all. The camels and donkeys are unloaded, and share the rest and protection of their masters. Bread and salt, cucumbers, and olives, may usually be bought, and grapes for the wants of the wayfarer who rejoices in the shade of a canvas, and lies at rest with his domestic animals and servants.

Sometimes there is a division between the guests of the khan and the beasts, a wall a few feet high upholding the raised platform which forms the chamber of the stranger within the gates. Along its edge is a stone trough in which the cattle feed as they stand on the earth below the floor of the guests. Syrian women yet lay their children in this stone manger—a hard cradle without rockers—covered with folded sheep-skins. There the babies sleep well and are safe from accidents of any sort. Of course, when "feeding-time" comes, baby must be taken up to make room for creatures who are tame and as much at home with their masters as our dogs and kittens are. The tourist in Switzerland will remember a like communism, not attractive to parties accustomed to privacy and neatness. The second cradle of the child Christ was probably soft, warm sand, scooped a little below the flat level, and covered with cotton drapery. Thus Egyptian children may be seen lying asleep or gazing sleepily at the lace-like foliage of the restless thin-leaved acacia.

When the sun went down, leaving a glory like the light beyond all lights, the splendor of the throne of God, perhaps, as she pressed the baby to her bosom, Mary thought he was one day nearer the awful sacrifice at Golgotha. She might have caught some notes of the first Christmas hymn sung by the heavenly host, and mingled them with the joyful music of her own hill-country while she cradled the Saviour in her arms. If her lot in exile seems poor and hard, it was softened by precious consolations, memories of transcendent raptures, and prophecies of the beatitudes yet to come. Ah! what pictures of peace and holiness the masters have given of the lovely Boy asleep, the Virgin Mother, with blue veil over her fair auburn tresses, watching beside Him, while angels with flowing locks and wings, each plume the brightness of a star, put aside the branches and smiled down on the beings toward whom they were drawn by mystic kinship.

In the security of unknown poverty in this dreamy Egypt, with few friends and no enemies, they awaited the third coming of the celestial visitant. "Flee into Egypt, and be thou there until I bring thee word," was the command. Thus the years of their banishment wore away. If not in Heliopolis, where I write, near it, they tarried—awaiting necessarily lonely, yet the beautiful Child was a delight new every hour, even as the child of common clay is to the true mother ever since the first baby voice was heard by the outcasts from Eden, and the first mother cried with the thrill which comes but once, " I have gotten a man of the Lord."

The stars which led the Holy Family, if we suppose them not miraculously led, shine down with a spirit-like brilliance unknown in other climes. Did they suggest the light, like an out-glancing of the all-seeing eye, which illumined the dingy khan at Bethlehem, and brought the Magi to the feet of the incarnate God?

In the velvet touch of Jesus's fingers did Mary recognize the miracle-working hand that should heal the sick at its touch and open the eyes of the blind? and, when His hour was come, that the spikes of the Roman would tear through the quivering flesh, and nail them to the cross?

Of the lineage of David, she knew Moses and the prophets, and must have had premonition of the anguish and the glory of Gethsemane and Calvary. Within some leafy tent, if not the " sycamore of Jesus and Mary," then some other low-bending tree, she nursed her baby with yearning and foreshadowing of the cross. And she loved the Child, who grew a fair daily miracle, with a love which was worship and yet not idol-atry, and kissed in adoration the dimpled feet destined to tread the wine-press alone. Could she have known, pondering with silent, solemn mother-heart, that the wondrous Child was fulfilling the prophecy, "Out of Egypt have I called my Son!"

It is difficult for us to realize that He whose kingdom is not of this world was a boy among other children, wiser, sweeter than they, with a boy's wants and temptations, but without sin. Did He romp and play? Did He study in order to learn? Who may guess what intuitions shone in upon Him when He was subject to His parents? There are deeper mysteries in that divinely human nature than have been sounded by the finite mind. We are apt to forget that in His humanity the future Judge of quick and dead knew every pulse of our blood, every need of our bodies; that He was tired, hungry, and thirsty as mortals; loved and suffered; was tempted at all points as we are, and had the same craving for sympathy. In the sorrowful night when He was betrayed, the loneliness of the forsaken man-God burst forth in the exclamation addressed to Peter and the other two who slept while their Lord awaited His doom: "What! could ye not watch with Me one hour?" And when He came the third time He said to them—we may imagine with what gentleness: "Sleep on now, and take your rest."

I linger by the "Tree of Jesus and Mary." Fabulous though they be, the stories which festoon and entwine it are pleasant to my soul. I love all that gives personality to our Saviour, believed in by devout spirits of the mother Church, and not to be despised by ours. They blossom out of the mists and vapors of two thousand years, phantom flowers, yet imperishable as the fabulous amaranth and fadeless asphodel. Let the pretty stories stand. We are not vowed to implicit faith in them, and they have a realism by the Virgin's Well, in this shady garden, in the soft Indian summer air. Golden grains of truth are scattered among the fables. One's faith is strengthened, and dreams come true, as they do not in the fierce light which beats on the New World, lying far away from the chosen land of types and shadows.

XI.

THE FLIGHT INTO EGYPT.

WHEN the warning was given to Joseph in a dream, "Take the young Child and His mother," he arose by night; so the first feeling is, that the flight into Egypt was all made at night.

Few careless readers consider the length of the journey, whether by the caravan route across the desert, taken by Abraham, nearly two thousand years before the Roman road, or through the Land of the Philistines and the Plain of Sharon to Joppa, then skirting the coast southward. Either way is at least four hundred miles, and it must have consumed five or six weeks unless we assume that the whole passage was miraculous. The early Christian fathers taught that the fugitives started at little past sunset, the hour in after ages consecrated by the Ave Maria. To Joseph was confided the care of the Virgin and Child, but the mother was accustomed to the constant ministry of angels, who left the heights above, to have charge concerning Him on whom the salvation of the human race depended. She, too, must have heard the whisper as the vaporous form drew near, " Arise, take the young Child and His mother, and flee into Egypt, and be thou there until I bring thee word ; for Herod will seek the young Child to destroy Him."

Bethlehem was little among the thousands of Judah. About six miles south of Jerusalem, it lies east of the main road to Hebron, covering the upper slope and top of a narrow ridge of limestone. The town is built in square, solid houses, and close under it is the plain, smiling with vineyards and barley fields, where Ruth came to glean in the early days of Israel. The waters go softly in the pretty brook which runs through it yet—a scene fair to the eye, pleasant to memory. There is the Field of the Shepherds where angelic voices, heard but once on earth, sang peace and good will, and there, by the gate, is the well for which the captive David longed.

The long, gray hill, which left no room for travelers in the inn, is bare and burnt now. In Mary's time it was covered with the olive, always like hoary age—the vine, emblem of laughing youth—the fig and the pomegranate, overhanging green terraces, on whose summit, in crescent shape, lay Bethlehem the "City of Bread." At the foot of a neighboring hill was a pillar which marked the tomb of Rachel, the be-

loved for whom Jacob served seven years, and
they seemed unto him but a few days for the
love he had to her. "And as for me," the
pathos of the simple story, "I buried her
there in the way of Ephrah, the same is Bethlehem." In our generation the tomb has been
bought by the Rothschilds— the only shrine of
Palestine belonging to the Hebrews. A rounded
white dome is built over the sepulchre, and once
a week Jews go there to bewail the desolation of
Zion and to burn incense. Eastward the purple
wall of Moab rises against the horizon, and the
modern guide points out the peak where the
hero of the Old Testament, prophet, law-giver,
priest, went up to die. The desolate high-lands
of Judea lie between, stretching far to the south.
Three miles distant Mary could see a sugar-loaf
mountain, lofty and round, with new fortifica-
tions, within which the bloody Herod was soon
to find his tomb. And twenty-five miles off,
through avenues of black and gray mountains,
shining steel-blue, lay the sea which forever
buries the dead Cities of the Plain.

When the Virgin mother looked a farewell
to old Olivet, then crowned with two great
cedars, I wonder if she remembered the mourning procession led by her ancestor, David, weeping over the rebellion of Absolom, as he went
up barefooted and his head covered with his
mantle. Did she have premonition of the sadder lament, mingled with tears of the Child at
her bosom, to be uttered thirty years later from
that summit, "O Jerusalem! Jerusalem! which

THE SPHINX OF THE PYRAMIDS.

killest the prophets and stonest them that are
sent unto thee; how often would I have gathered
thy children together, as a hen doth gather her
brood under her wings, and ye would not!"

She could see in dazzling whiteness the pinnacles of the temple. There she had consecrated
her Son to God and His service, and the
prophecy must have thrilled her soul—"Behold
this Child is set for the fall and rising again of
many in Israel, and for a sign which shall be
spoken against."

Encircling the city of holiness, grim and massive towers rose high in the Syrian blue, symbols
of the brute greatness of Rome. The portal of
Corinthian brass, with a gilded eagle inscribed
with the word Agrippa, gave name to a gate
more precious in its material and make than the
one called Beautiful.

It is recorded that the pillars of the Temple
vibrated like a pulse, as the Virgin passed with
the king-like Child, and the golden gates shook
before the awful solitude of the Holy of Holies.
The veil of Babylonish tapestry, destined to be
rent in twain by the tremble of the crucifixion,
waved its blue and scarlet and purple of matchless beauty, while the pilgrims went out unno-
ticed, bearing the Messiah. And while the
world slept, the sentinels on the gates and the
walls stood moveless—type of the sleepless, omnipresent power of Imperial Rome.

The Mother Church has enriched us with so
many delightful traditions concerning the flight
into Egypt, that I scarcely know which to

choose, or how to reduce them to brief space without robbing them of grace and color.

Among the dangers and perplexities by the way, the Virgin was always serene and fearless. Once the Holy Family entered an untrodden wilderness of trees, and would have been lost, but for the pioneer angel who marched ahead, with a star in his hand for a torch. The birds sang for them with unaccustomed sweetness, the lions left their lairs, the foxes their holes, and bears and panthers came tamely to the forest edge to watch the innocent strangers, and none did them any harm. In the depths of this forest all the trees bowed in devotion and obeisance to the Infant God. Only the aspen, in her exceeding pride and stubbornness, refused to confess him and stood upright. Then the Christ pronounced a curse against her, as he afterward cursed the barren fig-tree, and, at the words, uttered in his mother's arms, the aspen began to tremble through every leaf, and has not ceased to tremble to this day.

This forest wilderness was wide, dark and full of robber paths, and, of all its trees the palms were most intelligent and reverent. They bent to make a bower, a mystical enclosure round the hunted wanderers, and leaned down for them to gather luscious clusters of dates, which had hung high in air. Most honored of trees, for they were strewn before the Saviour on his triumphal entry into the Holy City, and are borne in the hands of the Redeemed in the New Jerusalem. A fountain gushed out of the thirsty ground, and a

babbling stream called to the travelers, Come
and drink of me. Seraphs smoothed their bed
of moss and flowers, and watched with folded
hands and over-shadowing wings while the dove-
like infant slept.

One story runs that they never could have
found their way across the desert but for an accident, which proved a signal blessing. At even-
tide, after a long, hot, dusty day, they overtook
a miserable slave, perishing in the way, abandoned by some caravan. They gave her of their
scant stores, and then she lay down with her
unknown friends to sleep on the flat sand. In
their slumber one of the sleepless angels on
watch blew in the sand, and commanded it to
open. At once a fountain leaped up. Another
ministering spirit brought a slip of acacia and
bade it grow, leave, and blossom. Another
brought a fig and a willow, fragrant balsam, and
almonds, rose and white, and the lesser angels
sowed the border of the fountain with seed of
fine grass, velvety moss, and the royal white
lily, sacred to Mary. Each tree concealed the
nest of a bird; and where they had gone to rest
on the bare earth, they woke in the dewy morning to bird-song and wind-song, palm fruit, and
all the scents and sounds of a blooming oasis.

The wandering tribes gave the spring the
name "Well of Reward," and to this day it remains, and no traveler drinks there without a
prayer of thankfulness and a blessing. The
slave-girl, by signs, made the Virgin understand
that, in a city four days' march southward,

were women wearing veils like hers. For the
favor shown the Jewish race by the Ptolemies,
the Nile valley was peopled with Jews, whom
Herod feared, while he hated; there the fugitives
would be safe among the Israelites, whose women
were veiled like Mary. Led by the slave, they
approached the boundary of Egypt, and a tree
there worshiped as a deity bowed itself to the
earth, and the idols shook and fell, with their
faces in the dust, broken-hearted, acknowledging
the Master, who came to enforce the commandment, "Thou shalt have no other gods before
me."

When the humble wayfarers entered Heliopolis, strange portents drove the priests in affright
to consulting the stars and the augurs; but the
oracles were dumb. No one could imagine the
baby in the arms of the mother of sixteen years
was God incarnate, the son of the Eternal Father.
A few banished Hebrews received the Holy
Family, and conducted them to the Temple of
Jehovah, built on the plan of the one on Mount
Moriah. A lamp of pure gold was suspended
from the ceiling, instead of the seven-branched
candlestick before the Holy of Holies, and on
the dome of the sanctuary was an immense mirror of polished steel, which reflected the rays of
the luminaries of Heaven. With what strange
feeling they must have entered it in the land of
illusion and silence! A majestic mimosa beside
the Temple bowed in salaam to the Divine
Child, and the idols on a pagan altar, tottered,
groaned, and, with lamentations, fell crashing to

the ground. The slave-girl remained the grateful servant of Mary while they abode in Heliopolis, and dwelt in a mohair tent, after the manner of her tribe, close to the habitation of the exiles.

There is a belief among pious souls that the journey to Egypt was miraculously shortened. Time and space were compressed, and on descending the craggy mountain paths and rugged defiles of Syria, the Holy Family entered a delectable plain. It was starred with lilies, cool with streams whose borders were of water-roses, and trees bearing all manner of fruits. Into this charming landscape the old painters have poured their choicest colors. Holy men have given us scenes like revelations from Heaven—ideas which do not enter the mind of the every-day reader running through the record in the Gospels, which is hackneyed to us from childhood.

Those devout artists, with no conscious blasphemy, pictured on canvas the face which no man can see and live; and must have wept as they wrought before easels which they never approached till first purified by prayer. Raphael denied that of his hundred Madonnas any are portraits, but all varied copies, from no earthly face, of the sinless ideal mirrored in his own soul. In his divinest picture, the Mother, the Bride of Heaven, enters the place prepared for her; a tent of leafage in the midst of the pomp of summer. The palm branches bend as though whispering high and holy secrets to the Chosen of God, Blessed among Women. Wishing to

reach a cluster of cherries, the friendly tree
shakes its branches, and the delicious fruit is
showered into her lap. The angelic guard bring
celestial food and minister to her as they afterward ministered to her Son on the Mount of
Temptation. The Virgin appears in close red
tunic, with long sleeves, over it a robe or mantle
like those worn to this day by Bethlehem virgins. Says one quaint chronicler: "Invisible
hands strewed the turf with beds of rose leaves
and pitched the nightly tent." Perhaps he only
meant the blue and glistening canopy overhead,
stretched from the ends of the earth to curtain a
sleeping world.

The artists have been sorely puzzled what to
do with Joseph. He is always represented as a
plain old man with staff and wallet. Usually he
is saddling the ass, and—dare I write?—looking
about as stupid. Once he stands behind the
trunk of a tree, reading something which looks
like a photograph album, while the angels crown
the mother and flutter in the air about her.
Again he lies asleep on his mantle, instead of
appearing the active, ever-watchful guardian of
the young Child and his Mother. In one lovely
picture he helps her over a mountain torrent on
stepping-stones; and in another moonlit scene
he watches while the Mother and Child sleep in
an airy boat steered by an angel and rowed by
winged boatmen, the crescent moon for a head-
light.

I recall one picture in which the Flight into
Egypt is the subject of the tenderest and most

delicate treatment. The Virgin and Child are seated in a flowery meadow of varied landscape, and rings of baby cherubs, holding hands, go dancing round them. There is nothing coarse or familiar in their presence; they are pure as morning dreams, and full of Elysian grace. It appears a sort of rhythmic dance, and you have the impression that it is to no earthly music, but timed to flutings of angels' "golden lutes and silver clarions clear", sounded by unseen musicians close at hand. Other angel babies are hanging garlands on the neck of a snow-white lamb, and are floating gayly, adoring the divine Child, whom they recognize in his twofold nature as akin to themselves. Balmy airs stir the lovely winged creatures, and soft, lithe limbs keep time to the glad harping of the harpers with their harps.

It is the most triumphant thing I have seen on canvas. I wish I could remember the name of the artist, whose fine, forcible hand fashioned those airy shapes, so the reader may find it, some happy morning, in the Museum at Naples. The tranquil face of the Madonna wears a rapt, ex-alted expression, as becomes the priestess and prophetess, and the painter has followed the re-ceived account given of the Virgin in the fourth century, by Epiphanius, derived by him from the Fathers. "She was of middle stature, her face oval and of an olive tint, her hair a pale brown, her complexion fair as wheat." The re-joicing gladness of the scene makes it peculiar among Riposas. The blissful cherubs in rings,

like rosy garlands of flowers, fairly glide before
your eyes, singing as they sang that first Christmas Eve: "I bring you good tidings of great
joy, which shall be to all people."

The day we were there a young peasant
woman—evidently a sorrowing mother—stood
before the picture, and returned, time after time,
to gaze her fill. In some inexpressible way the
Mother of Christ answered the yearning of the
sad heart for the divinest of earthly loves, perfected in Mary, sweetest of all the sweet mothers
in Heaven.

Of the many pretty legends which start into
memory as I write, there is one probably known
to the reader through a familiar engraving. It
runs somewhat on this wise:

One night two wanderers from the roving
tribes of the desert encamped in the lonesome
waste near the deserted tombs of old Memphis.
While folding their turbans about their heads,
when the swift twilight had passed, they noticed
a singular brilliancy in the direction of the
"stone idol," as they name the Sphinx; a pale
light, in tone and tint like the ivory-white of
moonbeams. The night was soundless; still as
before the winds were made. There was no moon,
and the weird spectral glimmer was terrible to
the sight. They thought it must be some foul
demon or djinn, or a ghoul searching the graves
of the long-forgotten dead. To their imagination the sepulchers were peopled with fearful
specters. Awe-struck and perplexed, they could
not sleep. Often as they closed their eyelids the

awakening luster beamed in on them, not by flashes, but steadily shining as the front of Aldebaran or the starry eyes of the seven sisters. Vainly they touched their talismans and called on the name of the Most High, and wildly did they lament having strayed so far from the track of the caravans. "Why tarry here?" said the bravest, "If this thing be evil, prayer will scare it away; if good, we must claim its blessing."

They rose and tremblingly groped through the vast charnel house, once the imperial city of Egypt. Often they stumbled over fragments of temples and palaces, yet constantly were drawn by resistless force toward the fixed white wonder, which illumined a great space with its marvelous splendor. As they neared the gigantic monster, where, between the paws of the lion-body, there was anciently a pagan altar of sacrifice, there appeared a young child and his mother sleeping, with no other canopy than the sheltering stone, which forms the breast of the Sun-God, the type of all kings to its worshipers. "The heathen have lighted their fires again, and have offered these two in sacrifice!" exclaimed the foremost. "Not so," said the other. "It is a Jewish woman in the dress of her people, and a baby. They have a wonderful brightness, like the angels on the ladder of light which Jacob saw. It is a miracle. How else could they reach that high place? They have flown up from the earth or down from Heaven." "Awful is this spot," murmured the more timid Ishmaelite. "Let us make haste and return to

our camels. If we stay, some dreadful **thing**
may happen to us." Then they turned **their**
backs on the mystical radiance, and **as they**
toiled through the sand, strange music filled **the**
stirless solitude, and phantom bells chimed, like
far-off echoes from some viewless temple beyond
the stars.

They told the wondrous tale; but those wild
sons of the Sahara never knew they had been
permitted to behold the aureole above the head
of the Madonna and the Blessed Redeemer, and
to hear the midnight *Gloria* of the invisible
watchers who never slumber nor sleep.

XII.

THE RETURN OF THE HOLY CARPET.

From Cairo the yearly caravan goes out with
the sacred carpet forwarded annually by the
Sultan to "dress" the Black Stone in the mosque
at Mecca. And after a year it is returned to the
same place. Imposing ceremonies accompany
the arrival and departure, and in 1882 was wit-
nessed the singular spectacle of British troops
saluting the holy carpet. There is no act of
more solemn devotion to Islam than this obeisance; and it is a politic stroke to parade victorious troops in honor of the true faith, as elsewhere the red-coats have presented arms before
the Hindu gods of India. These "idolatrous
acts," as the English press has named them, provoked much hostile criticism, and the senior
army chaplains presented a petition to the gen-

eral commanding the army in Egypt, that the men might be released from such a duty. Sir Garnet Wolseley replied, in curt terms, that, as commander-in-chief in Egypt, he issued orders for the public weal. The representations of Col. G. W. Knox, on behalf of the Scots Guards, were more successful, and the presence of that regiment was excused. Debates ran high on the subject, and the apology made in Parliament for such concessions to Moslem faith was, (1) that the religion of Mohammed was not an idolatrous one, and (2) that the ceremony was political and not devotional; but the assertion failed to satisfy the public conscience. An empty litter represented the Sultan at the time, and it was urged the salute was intended for it. The enthusiasm at Cairo was hardly for the imperial litter, and the religious bearing of the rite could not be denied. The salute was not to Ottoman sovereignty, but to the representation of an act of faith in the Mohammedan religion.

The ceremony of receiving the holy carpet on its return from Mecca takes place in front of the palace of Abdin, and you may see it some day, a marvelous pageant of color and an exhibition of fervor such as is never known in the cold races of the North and West. You remember how the Highlanders to the sound of bagpipes. marched up the heights and possessed the citadel of Cairo. You know the earlier historic associations of the place, how Mehemet Ali, having learned that the Mamelukes plotted his destruction, determined to save himself by de-

stroying them. His son, Toossoom Pasha,
commanded the army which was to march into
Arabia, and the august ceremony of investiture
was fixed for the 1st of March, 1811.

All the principal officers attended at the citadel, and the Mamelukes came on invitation of
the bland and polished Turk. As the beys presented themselves where the Viceroy was seated
among the Turkish chiefs, they were received
with Oriental politeness, which is unfailing, and
when the hour passed and they mounted their
horses to return to Cairo they discovered the
citadel gates were closed. The keepers were
not beside them, no sentinel was in sight. Could
there be treachery after an audience conducted
with such exquisite urbanity? A volley of
musketry poured a sheet of flame in answer to
the dreadful suspicions. Some galloped back to
the Divan, hoping to reach the presence of the
Pasha; the flying herds in affright sought the
various gates. But their return had been carefully prepared for. As they neared the closed
doors a well-aimed fire prostrated horse and
rider, and the most desperate valor could not
avail against stone-walls. The palace area was
strewn with corpses and quivering bodies, and
fugitives were picked off by the keen rifles of
Albanian sharp-shooters. Emin Bey, a chief
who had the faculty of quick thought in the
face of danger, remembered that at a certain
place near the wall a mound of wastage had
accumulated. He forced his horse to leap from
the parapet, about one hundred feet high at that

point, and saved from the general doom by the loss of his horse, he fled to the camp of some soldiers on the plain of Bussateen, and was there concealed till he had an opportunity for escape to Constantinople.

The wounded were slain without mercy, about 440 within the walls of the citadel, where traces of blood are still shown. The most partial of historians admit that this bloody and treacherous act was necessary to the peace of Egypt. Mehemet Ali knew the time was come to say, " Your life or mine," and acted according to the received custom of the Turk. He seems to have been humane in his life, and this day of death was but a self-defense. The Mamelukes were like the Janissaries of Constantinople, who turned their camp-kettles upside down once too often for the patience of Mahmood. As constant a plague to the Empire as the Prætorian Guards of Rome, demanding the more, as more and greater privileges were conceded to them; and the wonder is, that they were trapped and outdone in perfidy by the wary Mehemet Ali.

The view from the scene of the tragedy is beautiful exceedingly. Looking from that height a rich haze floats above the Mokateen hills, and a tremulous opaline tinting softens the rough sides of the Pyramids, the sea-like level of the desert, and the Lybian chain of mountain rock. The Nile appears a golden thread strung with palms and feathery foliage. It is bordered by lattices light as lace-work, the ornamental screens for the loveliest palaces.

Not the least of the many beauties of Saracenic architecture is the Cairene minaret, laid in alternate courses of red and yellow brick, and crowned with delicate stone finials pointing skyward. And who may describe the mosque of Mehemet Ali, whose inner walls are of glistening alabaster, with a sheen like satin. There birds nest in the globes of the great chandeliers, and the visitor ponders on the strength of the one-man power even in these latter days.

In the very heart of old Cairo lies, like an oasis, a famous park of several hundred acres, planted with citron, acacia-trees, and tropic plants blooming among tangled vines. It is the daily and nightly resort of natives and foreigners, being the open-air theater, the café, the promenade, the music-hall, the trysting-spot; and there, when the sun goes down, "all Africa dances."

The Grande Place Mehemet Ali is a vast open space below the citadel, and the royal palace of Abdin stands close under the high walls of defense. Toward that center, as by irresistible force, swept a current of humanity, to be found nowhere else in the world, one bright December morning, five years and more ago. It was a gala day, and the city was *en fête*. Business was suspended, for messengers out of the desert brought word days before that the pilgrims were returning from Mecca. The city of victory was in high wrought expectation. The greatest event of the year was about to take place, and in eager expectation a mixed multitude, in vari-

VIEW OF THE GREAT AND SECOND PYRAMIDS.

colored costumes, set steadily toward the citadel.

The Turk is the most tolerant of mortals. Had you started to that festival on all fours, in sheep-skin or in buffalo robes, or had you appeared stark naked, like the Fakirs or saints who dwell in caves, he would merely say it is the custom of their country, and would pass by with lofty indifference, without a second glance. Every shade of complexion was there, from the jet-black Nubian to the fairest Circassian. Every known race was represented except the North American Indian. Conspicuous in the crowd were women in the graceful silken *ferregi*, or sweeping robe like our ulster; sometimes embroidered with silks or bead-work of pearls from the Caspian. Here and there a veil of scarlet gauze betrayed the Arabian bride; the small hands were jeweled, and the almond-shaped eyes strikingly beautiful. "Paradise eyes," as the Faithful call them, are full of witchery, and their mild languor can change instantly to a fierce brightness like flame.

Despite all said about the degradation of Eastern women, they wear an expression of serenity as though living in measureless content; not weighted with cares like the rushing tourist from the North. Theirs is not the radiant loveliness of the vivacious races, but their rare smiles have a magic influence beaming through their white veils, and the indolent lifting of the eyelids has a fine charm for lovers of the beautiful. The day of which I write found the Zuleikas and Zobeidas—veiled beauties of the harems—not so placid as usual. One emotion dominated all minor feeling. The air was filled with excitement, subtle magnetisms possessed the multitude, and the contagion was resistless. The eunuchs in attendance on the great ladies strutted with their usual peacock gait, and held high their threatening whips. The procession of Hadjis or pilgrims was to enter the *Bab-el-Nazr*, or "Gate of Victory," which opens on the Boulak road. They were led by Sheik El Islam, the spiritual chief of the pilgrimage, commander of the guard of two hundred soldiers who had watched with sleepless vigilance the sacred carpet which had lain on the Black Stone one year.

We heard a wild blare of trumpets, a beating of fish-skin drums and cymbals, the clangor of barbaric instruments shrill and sharp. Strange tremors and thrills ran through the masses of humanity. Low, suppressed murmurs were exchanged without the turning of a glance from the direction of the Imperial Gate. Before the French invasion and the so-called reform of Mahmood, the uniforms of the Turkish army were in harmony with the climate and men; now the stiff costume, much like our own soldiers wear, is unsuited to wearers and their surroundings.

The red fez is the last portion of the Moslem dress worn by all Turkish subjects, and law forbids its change or banishment. Still there was rich and exquisite variety of color in the crowd, and the Arnouts or Albanian soldiers wear the most picturesque dress for men—a jacket of pale blue, embroidered with gold, white linen kilted skirt, high-topped boots, spurs, swords, daggers, and jewel-hilted pistols. They tell us that the *Skypetars*, as they call themselves, are more to be dreaded than Turk or Egyptian, but we do not like to believe it. We accept the descendants of the ancient Illyrians as representatives of the symmetrical people who made all fine art before their time an experiment, all that has come after them an imitation.

Troops of cavalry, columns of infantry, and batteries of Krupp's guns were in place. The glinting of the various arms dazzled the sight, and the wind at noon scorched with flaming breath. Those uniforms and arms must be burdensome, and the fez is no protection from heat or dust. The beys and pasha rode splendid mares of the small compact Arabian breeds. They had scarlet velvet saddle-cloths, gilt trappings, and jeweled and fringed head-stalls. The crowd surged and parted as a carriage came whirling with some magnate late at the show, and closed in behind it like waves in the wake of a vessel. As anciently, runners clear the way before Egyptian nobles. Trained to rapid step together, they fly before the horses of the chariots with loud cries of " *Oa! Oa!* "—a warning and a threat in Arabic. Their dress is like that of our circus boys, with plenty of spangles and gilt embroidery, and tall white wands in their hands, borne steadily perpendicular, give an air of authority to their movement. It rather de-

8

tracted from this brave parade to learn that
groups of runners are stationed ready for hire at
the city gates. The stranger may have them,
and enjoy the same style which the proud pashas
have

As the day advanced the interest grew more
intense and the crowd more densely packed.
For half a mile round the castle walls and over
the Grande Place Mehemet Ali human beings
were wedged together, a living mass, not less
than 60,000 souls. There was much patience
and good humor, and a pressure toward the
stately palace Abdin, where the Khedive was to
stand. The foot-soldiers rested on their arms.
There was a sudden movement; a bugle sounded
shrill and sweet. The Khedive was coming. A
squad of Nubian cavalry, gorgeous in arms and
equipment, dashed ahead, clearing the way for
the viceroy. "What are they shouting?" we
inquired of the interpreter. "It is Arabic.
'Allah be praised, the carpet has come back in
safety!'" Thousands on thousands took up the
words, which sounded like an exultant war-cry,
" Allah be praised ; " and all along the line sharp,
fine voices bore the mighty refrain. The carriage was a marvel of splendor, lined with green
—the color of the Prophet—drawn by four
powerful Russian horses white as snow, wearing
jet-black harness mounted with gold. The
head-stalls were burnished brass, and a flying
head-gear of bright ribbons tossed and streamed
on high above the red fezes of the multitude.

The guard closed round the cortege, bowing low in salaam, as the viceroy and his ministers left the carriage and took their stand on the palace stairs. Tewfik Pasha is a handsome man, and would be marked in an assembly of men anywhere in the world. He has clear olive skin, full black beard, which could not conceal the expression of the mouth, that tells without speech of a life of enjoyment after the manner of pleasure-loving Paris, where he was educated. His eyes, long, rather than round, have the peculiar opaque whiteness of Orientals, and are full of expression and intelligence. He wore a superb decoration—the Sultan's Imperial Order—and his general appearance was commanding and kinglike among a group of men strong as lions.

The heat increased, the people grew more excited and anxious. Mounted orderlies galloped hither and thither bearing orders. Is the Khedive impatient? The holy men he waits for have marched in blinding dust and life-withering heat sixty-seven days from the Hill of Arafat, bearing the burden hallowed by contact with the shrine of shrines. They have done gallant deeds in the desert among the wild hordes of the tent who will not endure city walls. Their valor will be sung by the Arabic *Rawis*, or troubadours, and chanted round the evening fires through generations yet to live. Surely the Viceroy, whose life is a long pleasure-party, who steps from velvet carpets to cushioned carriages, can afford to wait one day in the year.

It is not long now; the camels are coming, the

caravan is under the archway of the Bab-el-
Nazr. We see the head of the long procession.
A band of Hadjis, dusty and travel-worn, bearing
banners with strange devices, and chanting texts
from the Koran. Back of them troops, infantry,
artillery, cavalry, and again a long array of dervishes with flags floating on high and bands of
music, the dull, weird, funeral beat of muffled
drums. The men in advance have been purified
by prayer and absolved from sin by penances.
Grim fanatics, with wild, haggard faces, some
half-naked, some in tattered sheep-skins. Their
matted, unkempt locks, sun-scorched and faded,
make them notable even in this motley assem-
blage. They are the dwellers in caves, *Santons*,
or saints. They look like insane wretches without asylum or friends. There are peals of cannon, shrieks of women under the wraith-like
veils, then silence deep as death falls on the multitude. The excitement is extreme, though suppressed. No one abuses his neighbor for being
too late; no one is poked in the ribs for pressing
forward to catch the first sight of the sacred
pageant. And if there was oath or angry gesture we did not know it. The sacred camel
paused under the arched gateway. He was
white as milk, one of the noblest of his kind,
waving his neck with undulating movement as
though in recognition of the homage accorded
him in the consecrated procession. He was
made gallant with lordly trappings; a sort
of turret on his back was overspread with the

hallowed carpet and the holy palms—the *Mahmal.*

A hollow square of Turkish cavalrymen, two hundred in all, surrounded the camel. To them had been given the mighty trust of escorting the outgoing carpet to Mecca, and bringing back the year-old one to Cairo. They were also charged with the defense of pilgrims journeying along the route whose tide has ebbed and flowed more than twelve hundred years, and with money for quieting Bedouins by the way. The desert-born are robbers by profession, and among the laments for the eulogies of the dead the singers chant he was a successful robber. "What do the pilgrims prepare for the journey?" asked the interpreter of a wiry Arab murmuring sympathetically with the emaciated figures more dead than alive. "Nothing," answered the swart Arabian. "They lean upon Allah." Do we believe him? Not quite, for the Hadji considers the earth is the Lord's and the fullness thereof, and might makes right the world over, in the desert or the plain.

Again the Hadjis, with starvation in their eyes, howl and shout. Their filthy rags scarce cover their nakedness, but they are ecstatic in bliss, their demeanor is a delirium of delight. The tumult is almost overpowering even to us who are mere spectators of the strange drama. "What are the wretches saying?" asked an Englishman, near us, of his dragoman. "They are telling of Mecca, the mystic bride, veiled as a virgin, out in the wilderness where there is nothing but God. Of the musky loam of Paradise, where they shall rest on green pillows in the golden pleasure-fields kept for the faithful. They have left their sins with the stones on Mount Arafat, and now, when they die, Lord Mohammed will open the guarded gate and lead them up to dwell by the great white throne." "Bosh!" said the Englishman, peevishly.

But we did not say "Bosh," we were deeply moved. To one used to the scoffs of the disciples of reason and science, the fervor and faith of the Moslem had a certain pathos. "Paradise! Paradise!" they shouted along the line, and far as the outermost circles the choral note was taken up, echoed and re-echoed in the triumphant acclaim and frantic gesticulation. Never, never, have I seen anything among Christians like the devotion of the followers of the Prophet.

The Sheik El Islam is a man of high and princely presence, mounted that day on a gallant steed of the breed of the Neyd. His horse's pedigree is carefully kept, as the Jews keep the records of their tribes. And the documents which he hoards, in proof, are written and sealed by sheiks in the highest authority, and locked in strong chests. The wild tribes call his steed a "wind-drinker," and the minstrels chant how he flings his feet to the breeze and plays with skulls as with balls. Thus mounted any man is a chief in the desert. He may be a brandisher of spears, a cleaver of heads, who can hurl heroes from their saddles like the descent of des-

tiny, and make lions quake with fear. Though
rhapsodists had never sung his prowess, the
Sheik El Islam would be recognized as a king
of men among gentle and courtly embassadors
and crown-princes of Europe. His guardians of
the holy carpet appeared the worse for the hard
journey, but right soldierly yet. Unsubdued by
thirst and exposure, they were true to their com-
mission and ready to do and die for it. The
tapestry, spread out like a canopy, was resplendent with gold, and glowing with crimson—a
gorgeous fabric delighting the eyes of the faithful.

Cheers, yells, shrieks, the wildest uproar,
greeted its appearance; the guard could not
ward off the crowd. They burst the lines and
grasped the *Kiswal*—not to tear it, or mar its
beauty, but to kiss it, to love it, as the children
say, with an ecstasy of delight and admiration
known only to Orientals. The royal dromedary
alone seemed unmoved by the sounds which
stirred horses and mules. The transient storm
passed; the soldiers reformed rapidly, and with
perfect precision, after the break, and advanced
slowly to the steps of the Palace of Abdin. The
Khedive straightened himself—the final, the
supreme moment had come. A silence hushed
the mob, which fell back for the stately animal
to pass. The officer of the guard—a splendid
looking soldier—bows low; the camel is turned
round three times; the bridle handed to the Viceroy, who reverently receives it. The mocking
insouciance of the Parisian-educated Turk gives

place to a solemn sense of the momentous ceremonial. The mission has been accomplished,
the holy carpet is delivered from Mecca.

When Islam was richer, the *Kiswal* was
destroyed to save it from profanation; but in
later times the Sultan has ordered it to be sold,
and the proceeds to be distributed among the
poor who haunt the many mosques of Cairo. It
is valued—I do not know how truly—at £5,000
sterling. Sometimes the pilgrimage is made by
sea as far as Jeddo, but the more devout prefer
the land journey—the desert track where the
sun-heat is fiercest and suffering the most
extreme. Long as I remember anything I shall
remember those half-crazy devotees, wild with
fasting and excitement, yet exalted above measure in their own eyes and the esteem of their
comrades by the Meccan pilgrimage.

XIII.

THE PILGRIMAGE TO MECCA.

THE Arabic word *Hagg* is used to express
aspiration, and among Moslems the noble title of
Hadji, or Pilgrim, is not to be bought with gold or
precious stones or compassed by intrigue. Nor
is that noblest name for any man to be won on
the field of battle. The rank must be earned by
devotions on the sacred spots where the Prophet
(exalted be his name!) stood so long in prayer
that his face began to shine. He has declared
that the one who patiently endures the heat of

Mecca and the cold of Medina merits reward in the highest heaven.

Going on pilgrimage is a concession to feeling which lies deep among the many mysteries of the human heart. The most thoughtless and worldly, who holds in keeping a sentiment of loyalty for any object beloved or sanctified, can understand the strange, gloomy fascination which this act of penance has for the Mohammedans. We call it excess of devotion, fanaticism. Rather let it be written they are believers who live their religion, ready to die in its defense, and holding him deserving of death who forsakes it.

India is chief among the nations who practice pilgrimage. In that seat of awful images, swarming with human life, come devotees from dim and unknown regions, seeking far countries for holy shrines. Still are Hindoos wanderers toward Egypt, to the flaming steppes of Thibet and the snowy peaks of the Cacausus. My readers will remember how the Athenian philosophers visited Alexandria, and the Jews annually flocked to Jerusalem till the city lived on the vast numbers of pilgrims. Old Olivet was then crowded with tents, and booths were erected on housetops to lodge the overflow of visitors. They marched with hymns and with banners and entered the gates to the joyful sound of flutes and the psalm: "I was glad when they said to me, let us go into the house of the Lord. Our feet shall stand within thy gates, O Jerusalem." Tartars, Mongols, Buddhists have their holy

places or *Lamaserais*, and for eighteen centuries
what thousands of Christians have made high
sacrifice to enjoy one view of Mount Zion, and
to kneel at the stone which, tradition says, covers the rock-hewn sepulcher wherein no man lay
till Christ. As the captive Daniel prayed with
window open toward the Holy City, the Moslem
kneels with face toward the sacred city of his
adoration.

In the heart of the desert Mecca lies spotless
as a bride, veiled as a pure virgin, undefiled by
glance of Giaour, unpolluted by touch of unbe-
lieving Jew.

With reverential awe the Hadji ponders the
one hundred thousand mercies which daily descend on the Kaaba. There is not a doubt to
darken his faith. He knows neither variable-
ness nor shadow of turning. His fixedness of
purpose, unswerving and unchanging, is nearest
the eternal sameness of the one God of his worship. Sneers and scoffs of aliens to the true faith
pass him by as the idlest breeze which flutters
the fringes of his *kufiyeh*. Well may our missionaries write, Christianity makes no more impression on Islamism than the winds of the desert make on Mount Sinai. The immovable
fatalist has no concern for the creeds of other
peoples. In 1882 the Sultan of Turkey said to
a party of Americans, with the high behest of
one who is both Pope and Emperor: "I do not
fear your Bible any more than you fear the
Koran."

What to the pilgrim is the scorn of the blas-

phemer? Is it not written by the servant of
Him who spread the earth with carpets of flowers and drew shady trees from dead ground that
they who die on pilgrimage are taken up by
swift-winged camels to the golden pleasure fields
kept for the faithful? There they shall rest on
green pillows beside the happy river and bask
in the light which shines from the great white
throne. Fifty thousand years before the crea-
tion the one God determined and registered every
event, past, present and to come, in the Book of
Destiny. Among the many wonders on its
leaves it was written Mohammed should be the
first and most august of prophets. In the Day
of Judgment the elect will fearlessly range under
the green banner of Him who surely was not
playing the hypocrite when in dying hours He
calmly spoke of Paradise assured and his fellow-
citizens on high.

The tribes of the desert do not strive to rend
the veil which Allah, the All-Wise, has hung
over the face of the unknown. They patiently
bide their hour, knowing that in the good time
decreed the summons will find them waiting
in sure hope and perfect trust. The tradition
runs that Mecca was a holy place before Sirius
was created, therefore should the mightiest yield
it homage. *Om-te-Kora* ("Mother of Cities")
was known to Ptolemy as *Macorabia*, and its
grand mosque, capable of holding 35,000 persons, is on the site of a heathen temple, which
in the times of ignorance, before the coming of
Mohammed, contained 365 idols, one for each

day of the year. The prophet we call False, by
Europe named the Impostor, overthrew the
stones of the desert, hewn into gods, and shattered them to atoms, only saying: "There is no
God but God; and Mohammed is His prophet."

The sacred city has passed through many
changes, and at present is directly dependent on
the Sultan. It is strangely destitute of trees and
verdure of every sort. The falling off in pilgrimage has reduced it from 100,000 to 40,000
inhabitants. Besides the mosque there is no
building of any importance. The narrow valley,
circled by bald, bleak hills and arid plains,
haunts of thirst and starvation, is a great center
in the minds of one-third of the human race;
revered as the holy of holies by forty generations. They say who love it, Mecca is the capital of the world, the center of the universe, and
he who fails to reach it once in holy pilgrimage,
might as well die a Jew or a Christian.

It was a shrine for pilgrimage long before the
advent of Mohammed. After fruitless attempts
to abolish the rite, which possibly had its start
in the roving propensity of the Nomads, he was
compelled to yield to immemorial custom and
confirm it, taking care to annul its idolatry, for
the father of the faithful was an iconoclast and
a hater of idols. One of the latest acts of his
life was to lead 40,000 pilgrims to the shrines of
Mecca. It is said the priests who minister there
number many thousands. The ceremonies prescribed for to-day are probably mixed with
formulas come down from the ancient Sabean

worship, and are too many to be recorded here. The most important are seven times compassing the Kaaba, or House of Allah, seven times treading the stone, worn smooth as glass by reverent feet of the faithful. According to the legends, the earliest worshiper here was the first man. After his banishment from Eden thither he came, repentant, overwhelmed by the burden of sin, sorrowing most of all that he no longer heard the prayers of the angels. Ministering spirits heard his cry and, touched by his woe, let down from heaven to cover his defenseless head a tent with pillars of jasper and ruby roof. At the same time dropped from regions celestial the wondrous Black Stone, now set in the north-eastern corner forming the angle of the oblong building within the grand mosque. This stone of veneration, called the right hand of God on earth, was once (in the centuries numbered only in heaven) a jacinth pure as pearl, glistening as the snow of Mount Ararat. Beholding the sin-laden souls of humanity, it has shed so many silent tears as to become quite black. To press the fevered lip and sun-scorched hand to this miracle stone is to purchase exemption from the hell described in one of the three Suras of Mohammed, well named the Terrific.

The Kaaba is deeply worn with the kisses and touches of millions of lips and hands, through the passing generations. The sentient stone, which can hear and understand and remember, will appear at the Day of Judgment and be a swift witness for all who have laid hand upon it.

The mythic tale of its change of color and its appearance after a thunder-storm are too well known to need repetition. The venturesome Englishmen who entered Mecca in disguise at the peril of life say it is a common aerolite with admixture of nickel and iron, which, in hundreds of years, may have darkened on the surface. The adored relic is banded with a massive arch of gold and silver gilt; prayer may be made in any direction facing it; the *Kibleh*, the center of the universe. And here is the prayer whispered with forehead in the dust in front of the Black Stone: "There is no God but God alone, and His servant is victorious. There is no God but God, without sharer. His is the kingdom. To Him be praise and over all things He is Omnipotent."

The greater the hardship of the pilgrim the richer will be his reward, and at this shrine must he pray for quick and dead, the wife as well as the husband. And angels of Paradise stretch out their arms to anoint Him as He kneels there.

In the Beit Allah, or House of God, the family of Mohammed had for generations been the hereditary guardians, and the fane was a veritable Pantheon of the Orient. Strange to tell, he found there a statue of Abraham, Friend of Guests, and stranger yet, a statue of the Madonna with the Divine Child in her arms.

You remember Paul preached in Arabia, and the Prophet must have heard some hint of the Babe of Bethlehem, the anguish and the glory of Calvary. He doubtless knew something of the Hebrews, how they became a nation of free-men from a rabble of slaves, and how their inspired Lawgiver set up the Tabernacle in the wilderness, and curtained it with purple and blue, scarlet and fine linen. In prehistoric times there was a famous temple in Mecca, and it is recorded its door-veil of silk or linen was offered by the King of the Homerites 700 hundred years before Mohammed.

Thus is the Holy of Holies, the most sacred place of Islam, veiled from profane and vulgar eyes.

Quaint and curious are the rites enjoined by the Prophet. Seven times must the disciple walk round the central mosque, seven times kiss the Black Stone at the corner, and drink of the blackish water of Zem-zem, the fountain which sprang up for the outcast Hagar. To the believer one draught of the miracle spring insures the diamond cup of immortality. This done, he must bury the parings of his nails and the cut-tings of his hair in consecrated ground, with the prayer appointed: "O Allah, this my forelock is in Thy hand; then grant me for every hair a light on Resurrection Day, by Thy mercy, O most merciful of the merciful."

XIV.

MECCA, THE SACRED CITY.

WHEN Burton, in disguise of an Arab, entered the House of Allah, at Mecca, he found it empty as the Holy of Holies in Jerusalem when profaned by the tread of the victorious Pompey. The building has been destroyed by fire and other forces, and rebuilt ten times. Its first plan was made by angelic architects, of what material we do not know. In 1627 it was built as it now appears, with 554 pillars of gray Mecca stone. The floods of previous years had thrown down three sides, and the fourth was removed after the priests decided that mortals might lawfully remove part of the sacred stucture without charge of sacrilege and infidelity.

The present door was brought from Constantinople in the year 1633, and is of silver, burnished with gilt. Every night before it are ranged lighted wax candles and perfume-pans, filled with musk and burning aloe-wood. The drippings of the wax and the ashes of the wood, with dust from the hallowed threshold, are collected by devotees and rubbed on their foreheads as preventives of sickness; and under such treatment invalids regain strength. It is the proud boast of the faithful that at no hour, day or night, throughout the year, is the Kaaba to be seen without its worshipers.

A crowd of idlers, or as we might call them,

loafers, hang about the mosque; conspicuous among them eighty eunuchs, who are in charge of the sanctuary, the mystic bride veiled from the gaze of the vulgar.

All pilgrims do not enter the Holy of Holies, which is a plain cubical building of stone and aloe-wood, perhaps because of the obligations the act imposes. Who steps within the hallowed precinct must never again walk barefooted, nor tell lies, and he must take up fire with his fingers. There is an old, old Oriental myth, that the Israelites who settled at Mecca connected the primitive pagan temple with the Hebrew faith, and the laws of Moses were there expounded.

The veil now curtaining the shrine is of brilliant black, in sharp contrast with the zone or golden band running round the upper portion of the building, and the golden face-veil (*Burka*, or Door Curtain) which are of dazzling brightness. The Prophet preferred a Kiswal (or covering) of fine Yemen cloth, paid for from the public treasury. When it had served its time and was to be removed, Ayesha, the beautiful wife, directed it to be sold and the profit divided among the poor.

The idea about the consecrated drapery was to bury the inestimable relic, that it might not be worn by the impure of heart. At this age the Meccans sell it, but the money is not distributed, as the mother of the Moslems directed. The officers of the mosque keep the proceeds. A jacket of the stuff makes the wearer invul-

9

nerable in battle, and scraps of it are presents fit
for princes and high dignitaries. A small strip
is a precious Koran mark, cherished as a souvenir, and kissed in a passion of adoration when
first grasped by the eager hand of the waiting
pilgrim. Various Kaliphs have changed its
fashion; in the twelfth century it was of black
silk, renewed yearly by the Kaliph of Bagdad.

Again we read it was of fine linen, changed
every year, the old covering being distributed in
shreds among the pilgrims as antidotes to
poison and every sort of unhappiness. Sometimes it was of brocade, and in the ninth century the dress was changed twice a year, then
every two months, and the honor of supplying
it passed alternately from Bagdad to Egypt
and Yemen. When the Holy Land fell under
the power of the Osmanli, Sultan Selim ordered
the Kiswal to be black; later it was a fine Arabian cloak, and then green and gold, the colors
of the prophet.

The privilege of making the holy drapery
is now a hereditary honor, in the keeping of
owners of a cotten factory in Cairo. It is of red
silk and cotton mixed and is lined with white
muslin. The seams are hidden by a broad band
of gold. It is said that formerly the whole
Koran was interwoven there. Now it is inscribed:
" Verily, the first of houses, founded for mankind to worship in is that Bakkah, blessed and
a direction to all creatures." Under this appears
the throne verselet and titles of the reigning Sultan.

Here are a few of his titles: "The Sultan of Sultans, Emperor of Emperors, Brother of the Sun, Shadow of God upon Earth, Dispensor of Crowns to those who sit upon Thrones, Sovereign of the three great cities—Constantinople, the pearl of two seas, Broussa, and Damascus, which is the scent of Paradise, and of Egypt, which is the rarity of the age—King of kings, Commander of the Faithful, whose army is the Asylum of Victory, at the foot of whose throne is Justice and the Refuge of the World." These lines are of gold worked into red silk, like the face veil or door curtain, and this is the hanging which, in the sacred month of Ramazan, rises and falls with the waving wings of the heavenly host, hovering unseen about the mosque.

The huge silver-gilt padlock of the Kaaba is revered, and in the eyes of the devotee almost potent as the key of Paradise. Its hereditary guardians are of the proudest families of Islam, the *sangre azul* of Mecca. The cover of the key is of silk striped red, black and green. Embroidered with gold letters on it are the *Bismillah* (name of God), the name of the reigning Sultan, and "this is the Bag of the Key of the Holy Kaaba."

Let us speak of pilgrim rites with respect. The earnestness of the profession lends dignity to the cause, and it is intolerant to condemn any feeling that is genuine.

The well Zem-zem is in the court about the mosque, the open space called the Harem. The word known to us as a lock-up for women, is

general sense, means any spot peculiarly consecrated and set apart, a delicate and beautiful
meaning to the Oriental. Beside the spring the
kneeling pilgrim repeats this touching prayer
appointed: "O Allah, shadow me in Thy
shadow on that day when there is no shade but
Thy shadow, and cause me to drink from the cup
of Thy prophet Mohammed, (may Allah bless
and preserve him,) that pleasant draught, after
which there is no thirst to all eternity."

If overcome by heat on the way from the holy
spring to Mt. Arafat, three miles distant, the devotee dies apparently without pain, falling as
though shot through the heart, and after a brief
spasm the body is still as marble—the usual
symptoms of sun-stroke, by the pilgrim traveling under his vow regarded as a touch from the
finger of Allah.

On the great day after the assembling of pilgrims, when the sermon is preached on Mt. Arafat, the priests say the number of faithful there
are past counting and not to be remembered. If
less than 600,000 mortals stand on the hill to
hear the sermon, angels descend to complete the
number. There is such a falling off in pilgrimage
that some years myriads of spirits in human
form are obliged to come down in order to make
up the mystic multitude. The change is not
through lack of piety or of inexorable con-
stancy, but because of the excessive poverty of
Islam.

The privations of the pilgrims are unspeakable. To die by the way may come as an acci-

dent, but such martyrdom is not sought except by the reckless, almost insane devotees of India, making expiation for sins which, though scarlet, are thus made white as snow. Ample time does that journey give for reflection and repentance; all sins may thus be wiped away; they will never find the pilgrim out. Those I happened to see were mostly from Russia, and wretched beyond the reach of words to tell. Worn with life-withering marches in haggard lands full of wild beasts. Emaciated by hunger and thirst, without beauty or sanctity were my pilgrims, yet not without a certain dignity, the result of inflexible resolve and self-abnegation.

The Oriental, indifferent in all else, is stern and steadfast in his religion. The belief in an overruling Deity who can do no wrong is a steady guiding light which none may say is not an outshining of the true one. Immovable fatalism sustains its believers in the charges thrust upon them. Unto every man, they say, is appointed a time to die. Though he live in lofty towers, his fate must overtake him. Only God knoweth the place in which he shall die; but we do know the angel Israfil, the black-winged messenger of death, has the most melodious voice of all created things, and that the faithful are predestined to Paradise.

Lofty presences, high over-shadowing wings attend the wayfarer as he marches in the footprints of Abraham, the friend of Allah. Why should we smile at his fond illusions any more

than at the belief of the prince of poets and of
dreamers, who sang :

> " Millions of spiritual creatures walk the earth
> Unseen, both when we wake and when we sleep—

The untamable races, where the old blood-
feuds still rue, are the better for the teachings
of the Prophet.   He made a fierce onslaught on
paganism, and it was a great advance to lift his
people out of the vilest fetishism.   This morning when the sun gilds the exquisite domes of
Damascus, of Cairo, City of Victory, and of
Constantinople, the voice of the Muezzin proclaims from thousands of minarets the unity of
God in the five words embodying the creed of
Islam.   It is a solemn rebuke to the prayerless
Christian, rushing to business without a thought
of thanksgiving or praise, or any recognition of
his dependence on a higher power than himself.

The holy hill Arafat or "Mount of Mercy"
owes its name to a pretty legend which runs
somewhat as follows :—

When our first parents lost their high estate
they fell from heaven like falling stars, without
sound or farewell, through the infinite illumined spaces, through darkness and chaos,
through eternities of twilights, among systems
of worlds, constellations, things unspeakably
glorious.   Solemn and immutable the decree by
which was heaven lost, and to suffer their only
heritage they fell on this dim spot which men
call earth.   Adam on Ceylon, Eve on Arafat,
which overlooks Mecca.   Resolving with high

unquenchable purpose to seek his wife, beloved
alike in sinless bliss and sinning misery, Adam
began a journey to which the world owes its
appearance. Where he set his foot, which was
by no means a small one, a town was founded;
the intervals between strides will always remain
country. Two hundred years he wandered
among the thorns and thistles which his trans-
gression had brought on the peaceful, pleasant
earth. Among sharp peaks and deadly Saharas
he was led by Gabriel, the messenger-angel with
starry eyes and rainbow wings, to the height
where our common mother wailed with strong
crying and tears for the only created being who
could share her sorrow and comprehend her
craving for the forbidden wisdom. Isolated and
despairing, she called his name without ceasing.
Adam heard the voice of his wife, he flew to
her, and their meeting gave the name Arafat,
or recognition, to the mountain. Upon the
highest point the glorious archangel erected a
place of prayer, and in the warm valley below
the reunited pair dwelt in peace till death
dropped the viewless veil of Paradise, and let
them in to enjoy its delights forever.

XV.

PILGRIMAGE.

IN old times, it is said that caravans threaded
the desert like strings of jewels on a tawny
background. In the distance they appeared
movelesss as ropes of bright dyes; and of all
that have traversed the route the Damascus
train was the richest. Under the green banner
of the Prophet, kings and princes set out in
howdahs, hung with scarlet and purple, jeweled
fringes and feathered streamers. Pennons fluttered high in air, and the tall spears of the
desert chiefs were tufted with fluttering ribbons.

Those were the days of the picturesque arms
now found in museums and treasuries; priceless,
for they cannot be reproduced—those ancient
corselets like glittering scales, and swords like
Excalibar. Go to the Imperial Treasury of Old
Stamboul, and see them; the jewels inlaid in
cross-bows and scimiters, the dagger-handles of
solid emerald, sword-hilts crusted with gems,
the profuse and extravagant ornament which
recalls Aladdin's enchanted cavern, and Sinbad's
Valley of Diamonds. Then the horses were
"wind-drinkers," who flung their feet to the
breeze, and sped like the breath of the storm-
fiend, and horse and rider seemed one. Huge
white dromedaries jingled their bells with pride
equal to their master's, litters draperied with
costly stuffs were slung between mules and

camels, and the commoner animals of the rabble
made a picture to stir the dullest imagination.
The camp was lively as the march. Towns of
tents sprung up in an hour. The gilt-topped
pavilions of the nobles were lined with shawls,
and the luxurious harem was always on the
right. The heroes wore vestures of silks and
cloth of gold, fabrics of Yemen and of Bosra,
tissues from Cairo and from Damascus, the
" Eye of the East." Over all, highest in the
eternal blue, were flung the sacred banners of
green, the standards of the Prophet.

The famishing pilgrim of the nineteenth century loves to chant the lost glories of Islam,
when the emperor of emperors, Caliph Haroun-
Al-Raschid, and his wife trod on flowery carpets
of Schiraz and Khorassan, all the way from
Bagdad to Mecca, the shrine of shrines. As
starving men talk of feasts of fat things, so the
wretched beggar, his eyes yellow with hunger,
drones his recitative about the primal splendors
of the founders of the faith. The snows of
Siberia and the burning sands of Africa, floods
and famine, cannot turn the pilgrim from his
inflexible course, nor cool the fervor of his
enthusiasm. About him are hovering troops of
angels, and implicit belief in charms and amulets,
as defenses against Djinn and Afreet, belongs alike
to high and low. Reposing by oases, grave and
reverential men discourse of the supernatural,
and are the ready slaves of its fascinations. The
evil-eye is an omnipresent terror, the "fire in
the eye," for which the best antidote is to burn

alum while reciting the Koran. Cowry shells and turquoises are potent against this spell; but the mysteries of the unknown are best dispelled by prayer to the Most Merciful, Most Compassionate.

We call these weird fancies, superstitions born of fastings and mental derangement. The man who carries a buckeye in his pocket, he who will not sail on Friday, who trembles at the deathlike number thirteen at table, is unhappy over a broken looking-glass, and prefers the moon over his right shoulder, need not sneer at the Oriental.

Untold thousands of low mounds mark the caravan routes—the graves of devotees who perished for the faith; and skeletons of dromedaries whiten in the sun, their flesh devoured by vulture and jackal. Wolves and hyenas prowl down from the mountains after nightfall, and make real the hideous Arabian stories of ghouls who fatten on the flesh of the dead. For more than thirteen centuries the desert track to Mecca has been the highway of death. Close beside the living line marches the specter-caravan, innumerable, invisible. Phantom riders on spectral steeds press close to the affrighted pilgrim, and ghostly garments touch the trembler as they rustle past.

On the Night of Grace, when the angel Gabriel brought to the Prophet the silver roll on which the Koran was written, there is a general uprising of the holy dead. Corpses open their eyes, stir their stiffened limbs, and throw off their grave-clothes. Clouded with misty veils and wraithlike raiment, they make the journey to Mecca and fly back to their graves by daybreak. For in all countries of the world is accepted the legend that ghosts cannot walk abroad after cock-crowing.

The holy city of the Mohammedan is the chosen house of cholera and plague. From its center radiate, in every direction, pestilences bearing death by contagion to remotest bounds of Christendom. In the face of horrors glaring at the pilgrims, with terrors more dreaded than battle or shipwreck, the shrines are visited. Phantoms are realities to them, and their convictions are deep as their heart-blood. Why should we call it all a delusion and a snare?

Devout Christians have trod with naked feet, torn and bleeding, the sharp stones of Bethlehem, and the hills which trembled and quaked under the darkness of Calvary. To visit the spot where the Saviour of the world cried, "It is finished," has been a longing and a desire with multitudes who die without the sight; and soldiers of many creeds have battled for possession of the sepulcher of Christ. It is an established historic fact that, of all the thousands of thousands who made the pilgrimage to the Holy Land before the days of the Crusades, there is not recorded one act of wrong committed on the way, though powerful knights and robber-barons made the pilgrimage with full forces. Many marched with hands stained by crimes to us incredible, too hideous to be recounted. When

the Red Cross was unfurled above the Tower of
David by Godfrey de Bouillon, the bravest warriors fell on each other's necks and wept for joy.
Though the Crusaders boasted of having rode in
Saracen blood to their horses' knees, yet they
marched barefooted and bareheaded, with streaming eyes and folded hands, to the hill Calvary,
and chanted their Psalms in the Church of the
Holy Sepulcher.   Valor and devotion, prayers
and tears, have hallowed its stone floor; and who
does not thrill in the dim, reverential light of
the lamps surrounding the tomb of Christ?
There, every hour, weeping women and adoring
men, foot-worn and exhausted, sink down in sup-
plication and confession, thus hoping to make
less dreary the spot where they are to lay their
tired hearts when their throbbings are stilled
forever.   A continuous living stream of believers sets toward Jerusalem to-day, and the stones
are kissed in an ineffable rapture of worship.
So it has been for centuries.

The inventions of the Moslem are not more
absurd than the multiplied relics of the True
Cross, nor is the adored shred of the Kiswal,
laid in the Koran as a book-mark, a more foolish
relic than Veronica's handkerchief, or the wed-
ding-ring of the Virgin Mary in a church at
Perugia.   There is no imposture given in the
name of Mohammed equal to the fearful jugglery
of the Greek with "the Holy Fire," in the
Church of the Holy Sepulcher.   The high ceremonial begins with the day of the resurrection
of Christ.   Said the dignified and courteous gov-

ernor of Jerusalem to the writer, " Easter morning I march a whole company of soldiers into
the church, to keep you Christians from beating
each other's brains out with the candlesticks before the altar." We bowed and blushed in
answer, for we could think of nothing to say.

Yes, Christians fight each other and the Jew
at the tomb of the Prince of Peace. The placid,
decorous Turk looks on with neither smile nor
sneer, and in his smooth, patient way murmurs,
" How these Nazarenes love!" Grave satire
from the religionist to whom the Christian sects
appeal for defense against each other! There is
no real toleration in the East except among the
Turks. Supreme in authority, they practice the
supremest liberality. The passionate grief of
the Jew at his wailing-place, the various forms
of conflicting sects in their chapels, are protected
by the Mohammedan; and happy is it for us
that the ruling power is of this mind!

By a strange doom, which may well lead the
fatalist to read in it the fiat of destiny, the
shrines of the two great religions of the world
have been controlled by the scimiter more than
a thousand years. It holds the birthplace of
both.

XVI.

THE REPOSE.

IN the river Nile, it matters little where, is a long, narrow island, shaped like an Indian canoe, widest at the center, sharply tapering at the ends.   It was once the resting-place of a deity; the All-powerful who ruled the annual overflow of the river, securing fertility to the land. There is a fable that his body was buried beneath the turbid stream beside this island, and once a year his soul revisits it, rising and troubling the waters till they pass their banks and insure abundant harvests.

In the center, holding their pristine, exquisite grace, amid the desolation of unremembered centuries, are the remains of an ancient temple which was dedicated to one of the many gods of Egypt.   Some majestic and graceful woman, some terrible avenging king, mortal yet divine, —who knows his name and titles may tell.   The forgotten architect had for his model in carving the delicate columns the stem of the lotus.   The flower served for shaping the capital; it was peculiar to Egypt, and the emblem of purity, fertility, and sumptuous state.   The white lily we call lotus grew in bounteous profusion here of old, and though botanists declare it has disappeared, a plant very like its picture floats in the friendly river of the Land of the Pharaohs.

Palms outlined sharply against the ethereal

azure, waved like beckoning hands as we neared
the shore. A few gum-arabic and acacia-trees
straggle about the walls of the temple. Patches
of strange vegetation, and a papyrus-jungle keep
a strip on the main land green and fresh. When
the old deities, whose stony eyes stare blindly
out of the statues on the banks, hovered about
the place it must have been a very Eden. Now
it is beautiful even in decreptitude and death.

It lay so lone, so dim, so dreamlike, that, as
our little boat approached, we with one voice
agreed this is the spot where we may forget the
world. The historian brought his cane down on
the sand which subdued its emphasis, exclaiming with mock-heroic gesture, " Romans, plant
your standards, this is the best place to stay in.
Yet," he added reflectively, with a diminution
of enthusiasm, " we are so cut off from all else
we may be like the two Italian prisoners confined in one cell. The first year they talked up
all they knew, the second was a year of silence,
the third they asked to be separated. I cannot
imagine our talking six months, but it is an interesting experiment, as philosophers say, and
we may never have another chance to come so
near *Nirvana.* As to tiring of each other, we
made that test of friendship long ago, none will
shrink from the trial."

About two hundred yards from the landing
was our camp, in the center of a group of palms,
four in number. It is the magic numeral to the
Moslem, as seven is to the Hebrew. They were
planted in the form of a diamond, and, recurring

to Scott's delicious romance, we named the enclosure, "The Diamond of the Desert." We entered the enchanted lines and established peaceable and undisputed sway. There were two black tents under the feathery fans of green, one for the ladies, one for the gentlemen. A cooking-lodge was made of rice-straw laid on transverse beams which rested on forked poles; the servants slept under the open sky. The speed and noiselessness with which tents are pitched are surprising. Our two men bearing poles on their shoulders were quick in this work as they were slow at all else. Lo! they uprose, "black but comely," the tents of Kedar like the curtains Solomon hung for the daughter of Egypt.

Achmet was man-in-waiting. Hassan was the cook. The former was a pleasant-faced boy of nineteen. He had the Oriental love of high color which blossomed out in a gorgeous turban adorned with a limp tassel of dull gilt, pendant over the left ear. He wore a jacket of scarlet with badly tarnished embroidery, and baggy blue trousers. A variegated sash of many colors held in place a dagger with sheath inlaid with turquoise and coral, and the crooked scimetar of Yemen. Achmet had a glittering eye not unlike a blackbird's, a keen, sharp glance, delicate hands and (must I tell it?) a row of crisp black curls stiffly fringing his turban. These descendants of Ishmael have high notions of rank and family, chiefs and tribes. He boasted pure Arabic blood, but the stiffness of that wiry fringe set me to thinking that Ethiopia borders Egypt; and, plainly speaking, such as Achmet would in the best—or worst?—days of slavery, have been held in the United States of America at a high price for body servants.

Like a friendly hand stretched out from our native land, the American flag floated over the largest tent. I hold up the loose flapping curtain of the bower I've shaded for thee. *Entrez.* No lodge with leaky roof suggesting hardship and exposure. The dark shadow was refreshing to strained and fevered eyes, the luxurious apartment—for such it seemed—was carpeted with over-lapping rugs laid by the unerring instinct for color which distinguishes Orientals.

A table in the center held a virgin's lamp, and copper box of matches, a tiny bell and brass waiter polished like a metal mirror. Against the center-post hung saddle-bags of gay embroidery ready for duty as pockets. A divan, the low, broad seat serving as bed at night, was cushioned and made nice with pillows of striped cotton. The tent-cloth rolled up two feet from the ground to let the wind flit through; two trunks, made gorgeous with arabesque covers, challenged our admiration; and when the festal Achmet bowed himself in, bearing four thimblefuls of coffee in their filagree stands, could anything more delightful be imagined?

As we sipped the rich, strong Mocha he, apologetically, and with many repetitions in the worst of English, stepped to the rear, and returned with his comrade, Hassan. The

10

latter was not trained to reticence, and in
spite of crushing signs and frowns which fell
harmlessly from their mark, as soon as his introduction was given, he with much gesture and
fierce rolling of the eyes, swore by the soul of
his father and the bones of his grandfather, and
by the four archangels nearest the throne he
would live for us and die for us. The sun in his
march across the blue desert of air looked on no
men like the two he had the honor to serve.
The two who in their own country stood on the
right hand of the King of America. Let any
robber dare to molest them, and he would tear
out the robber's eyes, dash his teeth down the
miscreant's throat, break his legs, rip up his
body, and give his flesh to the fowls of the air,
the eagle and the vulture.

The better bred Achmet tried to break in on
the swelling elocution, as well try to stop the
the recitative of the book-agent. He swore to
defend the camp from all enemies whatsoever, by
the God who created the heavens and the earth,
by the Prophet Mohammed, by the seven varia-
tions of the Koran, by the one hundred and
twenty-four prophets, by the soul of his grandfather, by the soul of his father, by his sons and
by his sword. Did he fail, then strike off his
head and plant it on the top of the highest minaret in the City of Victory.

This fervid burst of devotion touched us to
the very core of our hearts, and we refused to believe the quiet remark of Antiquary, as the two

comrades disappeared holding hands: "The men would run like sheep at the first alarm."

We had entered the shady tent with a sense of restfulness most grateful to one ready to exclaim with Portia, "My little body is weary of this great world." Roughing it in camp was an expression foreign to our life there. There was no care of any sort, all so smooth at every turn that content should reign supreme. Our worshiping slave Hassan, and the elegant and polite Achmet had served American princes before, and well knew that dwellers in tabernacles on the Nile do not live on a view, which one must have the jeweled words of Gautier to describe, or must write of in color, as the Greeks wrote music. Nor yet can they live on *Arabian Nights;* (observe the pun if you please!)

Full well that Son of the Desert knew they require plenty of food, sesame-cakes, lamb, dates, pistachio-nuts, and eggs, always eggs.

At once we admitted, to our inmost confidence, the rhetorical cook who was burning to court death for our sakes. We had heard, and credited without question, many tales of Arab fidelity; were nurtured on them, so to speak, in childhood; and the historian tells that in Arabian villages theft is unknown. If any valuable is lost in the road it lies there, every passer-by avoiding to step on it. If not claimed by sunset, it is then picked up, by the proper authority, and hung in the nearest mosque till claimed by the owner.

It may be a coin has dropped from the purse

of the traveler. There goes the bride whose
sole dower is five palm-trees: what tinsel and
glittering nets with pendants for the low brow
would that coin buy! The donkeyman who
who does not know the taste of meat may see,
but not touch the shining temptation. The
water-carrier, whose dinner is a black crust and
an onion, looks a moment, scarcely stops his
slow, steady gait and passes on, maybe murmuring a prayer against the sin; but to pick up a
lost coin—such an act is unknown in Arabia.
If we Christians, were half as faithful to our
beliefs as Musselmen are, the millennium would
be here.

I admit there are fabulous accounts of honesty, but, *en passant*, here is one I know to be
true, told me by an English officer in Alexandria:—A French family fled during the alarm
in 1882, leaving their house and effects in charge
of an Arab servant. Returning after four
months, they found Aladdin, if that was his
name, had pawned his own clothes for food, but
had touched only to protect the property of his
master. Even a bag of silver was found tied;
not one piece used in extremity of need. This
story, fresh in mind, persuaded us to give Achmet and Hassan unquestioning confidence, almost the last grain of the implicit faith which
knowledge of the world tries as by fire. We
had long been stranger to such trust as was
granted by us to the beguiling youths who had
agreed to manage our camp for a moderate compensation.

As I remarked, we consumed a large number
of eggs, having found them a wholesome article
of diet in every country. When, at the end of
three days, Hassan brought in a bill, one item
of table expense twenty dozen eggs, our child-
like trust in Arabian honesty trembled and
turned cold. O, Hassan, Hassan, how could
you, how could you?

The Antiquary, who has the gift of tongues,
mildly observed it was impossible for six persons—two of them delicate ladies—to eat so
many in three days. The suave Hassan smiled
benignly, and began his customary formula, "By
the soul of my grandfather and the bones of my
father, etc., etc., I swear I have not tasted a
morsel of egg, but have served them every one
at the feasts of the Effendi and the Princesses
of America. Then he salaamed with a reverence which would have disarmed any but a har-
dened sword-hand, or still harder, one used to
Oriental rapacity. He gently averred in his
worst English, "Eat, muchee egg," and strode
away to the cooking-lodge with an injured air,
as our cousins across the water say, "all cut up."
Then, after a family council, we decided to have a
daily inspection of supplies and nightly render-
ing of accounts, to the calm disgust of Hassan
and his partner in iniquity, and the lightening
of our expenses.

The Eastern artist, be it remembered, has a
rare skill in the combinations of acid and sweet
which make up sauces. Many a lurking, secret
flavor has the French *chef de cuisine* stolen from

the descendants of cooks who have slept the sleep of the embalmed thousands of years, among the mummies of the Pharaohs. Not algebra and astronomy alone, have we derived from the tribes of the wandering feet and weary breast; dainty viands and savory stews come to us from their slender and pliant fingers, and the delicate banquets of the Greek epicure were not complete without knowledge of Egyptian mysteries.

Achmet was a singer, but his dash of negro blood did not mellow his voice to the softness of the unmixed African. Desert songs are sad— so the poets tell; their inspiration makes them most melancholy, and the strangest sound ever named music, is the shrill falsetto of the Arabs. Naturally they make their audiences sad. Not to mince phrases, the boy Achmet had a dreadful voice. Happily the kitchen-lodge was not near, so we did not go raving crazy.

" A fine musician before tunes were composed," said the laughing Thalia, one evening. " Is it a love song? Listen, my learned friend, and tell me what the lad is saying, sitting there cross-legged like an idol, watching the handful of coal which simmers our dinner."

" Be quiet a moment, please." We listened while our polyglot friend gave his ear to the barbaric strain.

" A tale of war, not love," said he after a few moments' close attention, "of spears and fierce horsemen whose swords are their parentage, whose drink is the blood of slain warriors, and they float in blood like beating human hearts. Now he tells of mountain-fastnesses and plains between, where the Simoon sweeps and caresses you like a lion, with his breath of flame."

He paused and Achmet's doleful train went on.

"Now it is of the Great Desert where voyaging is victory, and if a hostile tribe is met, Paradise is for the slain. The waiting houris stretch their white arms over the battlements of Heaven, and beckon the faithful to their tents of hollow pearls, and jacinths, and emeralds. There in the Pleasure Fields of the Blest, kept safe from the Infidel. In the long and lovely month before us, we shall have many a serenade in tender strain which I shall delight to translate. You should hear the verses of some of the twenty-five thousand Persian bards, and of Mejnoun and Leila, the Romeo and Juliet of the East. This is too exciting for pilgrims entering a *Riposa*."

"Yes; I see we shall have to 'make a business of it,' in the language of our own countrymen, or we shall not be able to achieve the *Riposa*. Shall we have the daily mail? We can arrange for a messenger to bring it?"

Secretly we all longed for the mail, but an open confession of such a positive sensation was hardly in order.

"Good news we shall hear soon enough, bad news always comes too soon. What is the voice of the meeting? I am inclined to the banishment of *all* excitements."

"'That does well for one who has no very strong ties. We would spend more energy conjuring up the possible troubles at home than in running through a newspaper or two. I vote for the mail."

"And I."

"And I," said Thalia, turning the color of a Jaquemine rose. She was thinking of her kriss-kross letters lodged at Alexandria. So the Antiquary was voted down, and we were to have one reminder that we had not swung off on some other planet than the dim orb men call Earth.

The camp-ground was wisely chosen, our order of living arranged. "Now for the sweet pause in the rush of travel." I said it with unwonted emotion; "let us write one chapter unlike all the others of our lives. Let us content ourselves not with doing, but simply to be. Four delightful weeks to loll, to dream, and to rest, no thinking behind screens or over portfolios, and scratch books. Thirty days each day to be lazier and more delicious than all the others. In this glorious Isle of the Lily sacred to silence and idleness we can—"

"Yawn our heads off," said Thalia snappishly. After a brief pause, resumed, "That will probably be our ending. Farewell a long farewell to worry, the *far niente* is ours; we are in the distant Aiden where the blest find surcease from sorrow."

"We must enter the blessed conditions with resolution. Face to face with the solemn loveliness of nature we are to forget the hurry and flurry, in breathless racing after wealth, useless prizes, and accumulated luxuries which go to make up the burden that is named civilization. We must give the future to the winds, and tranquilly sleep; even in broad day be visited with airy and blissful dreams, and become seers of visions better than those which illumine the night."

As the oration ended the orator stretched at length on a carpet, and rested his head on a cushion. "Do what you like," he added, drowsily, "that is my last effort for one month."

Gracious and grateful the palm shade; sweet to the soul of him who seeks to forget the eternal tragedy called living. The stately trunks were like sculptured columns, their tops loaded with ripe luscious dates which hung from the trunk near the root of the lowest green stems, appearing in the fresh foliage like a basket through whose irregular openings the fruit hung down; its amber tint finely contrasting with the dark, shining leaves. The clusters must have weighed seventy pounds; sugary, oily, nourishing, shaded by the plumed head which Moslems say droops like a languid beauty inclining to sleep.

The Antiquary is nothing if not didactic. Enthroned as became the general enlightener of the ignorant, he possessed himself of a camp-stool and spoke his little piece :—

"Let me inform my American Colony we are not far from Arabia, the country laid down in geographies as the anti-industrial center of the world. It is inhabited by the very antipodes of

our serious and struggling race on whom the
curse of work has fallen—a weight to stagger
under. We shall not hear the click of the
telegraph nor the rousing scream of the steam-
engine, nor any sound to remind us of motions
of intellect, unending as movements of the heavenly bodies. There is a stop in the wheel; for
infinite activity infinite repose, a halcyon calm.
Rest for its own sake is almost unknown to our
people. Our holidays take on the activity of an
excursion or some stirring recreation. To be
simply happy by letting go, is not our ideal of
festa days. But," he continued, cheerfully slap-
ping his hands together, " we have changed all
that. Presto! Now we begin."

Easily said, O Antiquary, but not in one day
can travelers from lands where bread is earned
by hard labor and much sweat of the brow enter
the Oriental *kaif*. Fingers busy in the forenoon
are apt to be restless through the afternoon. A
mild languor, a monotonous tranquillity are the
ideal, yes, and the actual life in the East; absolute contrast to life in the West. At first we
did not realize that drowsy indolence is as much
a matter of temperament as of education and
habit. High strung nerves cannot sink to the
joy of calm in one day, any more than the tense
strings of musical instruments can give out the
muffled chords which belong to the slackened
strings, vibrating at a touch, almost at a breath.
When the sun showers down torrents of heat the
true Oriental asks but the shade of his green
tent; the flat sand is his cushion, the cool foun-

tain is his drink, beloved of the Prophet, whose tomb is covered with the splendor of unceasing light. If well to do, a tiny cup of coffee makes the hour festal, and so he sits the day through in happy trance, taking *kaif*—a word impossible to translate into our language. The nearest approach we can make to it is lazing. The effort of conversation is to be avoided. Memories of unpleasant thing are banished, the secret burdens of the heart are dropped into oblivion, the future, ah,—well Allah, (praised be his name!) has appointed all, and we wait for what is decreed. He will send the best, meantime we sit and rest.

Think of a member of the Stock-Board, fresh from the clamor of Wall St. dropping into such quiescence, in a day or a hundred days. His time would be ceaseless *ennui*, insupportable as the level sameness and stillness of the Desert, or I must say it like the unendurable silence of Venice. When the first novelty wears off, anything for variety, even an earthquake would be welcomed just for a change. There is no appeal or suggestion, no stimulus in the Desert monotony. He who is born to it loves it with a perfect love. Men are influenced by their environment, are more like the times they live in than their own fathers, and the fixed sameness of the sand plain passes into their souls.

Give the Bedouin a camel and a carpet, and he is a king of men. That is the nomad or wandering Arab, who despises from the depths of his soul, and treats with withering scorn the

Fellaheen, or slaves of the soil, who cultivate
the ground.

The pride of these people passes belief. Hassan, our cook, regarded that lean, dark figure of
himself in the spring, as the highest type of
created things, and his image is very different
from the harassed faces of the Northern races.
On him, and him alone, he proudly asserts,
Allah has bestowed four privileges, turbans for
diadems, tents for homes, swords for scepters,
and poems for laws. And the final, supreme
boast is they are unconquered. Alexander
dreamed of it, but only in the Valley of Vision
counted himself the conqueror of Arabia.

It is restful to body and spirit to contemplate
the Arab's supreme contentment with his lot,
his carelessness of the future, his ineffable dignity of repose from feverish activity and constant straining after an ideal never satisfied, in
the more active, but hardly more gifted races of
the West. In the enchanting country ruled by
the Kaliphs, it was not without reason they had
engraved on the public seal, "The servant of
the Merciful rests contented in the decrees of
Allah."

In the twilight we arranged the divans and
disrobed before the after-glow had faded.

"How long do you guess we can stand this
sort of thing?" asked Thalia, wide-awake under her gay coverlet.

"Forever. I actually begin to feel a little
rested. How good it is. No sights to see for
thirty days."

" For my part, I think it's rather—well,
slow."

" It's fast enough for me, my Beauty. Good-
night. And now for sleep and waking for no
purpose but to think how sweet it is to sleep
again."

The Faithful were at rest under their spangled
blue tent, without a thought for the morrow;
but we of the far New World could not subdue
ourselves in one day. Thalia softly turned on
her cot, which creaked a little every time; and
I pounded my pillow seeking a sleepy spot in it.
The strangeness of the place brought on the
state known to most women when eyelids will
not close. I stole to the tent-door, and in the
luminous dusk looked up with a sense of near-
ness to the mansions named of old, the Seven
Stars and Orion. How bright they were, how
near they seemed! Not till the night was far
spent did the best blessing rest on our wearied
souls.

XVII.

POETRY AND MUSIC OF THE ARABS.

The Arabian has no soul for music as we
understand it, and the silence habitual to him is
his best condition. Achmet was our chief musician, and when he droned his evening song we
were thankful he was too poor to afford a *rubaba*
—a fearful two-stringed fiddle with which to har-
row up our souls. He had a recitative of verses

which he compared to pearls strung, and another
of prose which he likened to loose ones.

Through the interpreter we learned that his
favorite theme was a legendary chief named
Antar, who flourished in the second century of
the Hegira. He was the son of a Desert king
and a black slave, and of such colossal stature that
on horseback his feet would tear up the ground.
Hence, he was named one of the earth-rakers.
In battle this blood-drinker could put ten thousand to flight. Struck by his sword, heads would
roll in the dust clipped from bodies like reeds,
hands would fly through the air like leaves in
autumn. His voice was as the roaring of a
thousand lions, and it made the tents of the hostile tribes to fall, the dead to rise from their
graves, and infants turn gray in their cradles.
The student of Gibbon will remember that he
quotes Antar as the best record ever given of the
life of the roving tribes of the desert, who look
with haughty scorn on the degraded beings who
labor in green fields. Horses knew the conqueror,
and quaked under their saddles; chiefs knew
him, and fled as from the might of destiny; and
after the battle he would seat himself cross-legged on his horse's neck, and in musical measure
recite his exploits—what might be familiarly
called "blowing his own trumpet." And, says
the Eastern historian, he who can chant these
verses will never require a companion by day or
a friend by night. They are called by the Arabs
"convivial," "social," and are the chosen hymns
of the lords of battle.

One of the poems runs somewhat as follows :—

"I am the son of Shedad, and my lineage is of Absian, known above the brilliant canopy of heaven. I am the knight of noble steeds. In my ambition I exalt myself to the Pleiades by my never-failing fortune and illustrious deeds I have attained honor, glory and fame, by my resolution, so that I am close to Jupiter. Mine is a happy star from God who created all mankind His slaves. Were Death to see me, aye! to see me, he would turn aside from me, in fear of my tempestuous might and power. For I am a stern-faced lion, sublime above all knights in the field of fight, by my intrepidity, by my modesty and forbearance."

The modest, stern-faced lion is madly in love with his cousin Ibla of the coal-black tresses. One night she spread forth three locks of her hair, which were exhibited four nights together. There are objections to their marriage, and the champion of a rival tribe carries her off after the manner of the Homeric heroes. Antar speeds to the rescue. Ibla hears his voice echoing like peals of thunder; cowards gnaw their hands in agony; heroes encounter like mountains; stirrup grates against stirrup; scimetars glitter; spear-blades sparkle; shouts shake the mountains and the valleys, and the swift camels flee in terror away. Weeping Ibla, with the night-black tresses, overlooks the fight, and groans like a mother bereft of her children. Fate was let loose among the enemy. The King of Death grasped at souls and never failed

of his aim. Antar rushed into every peril, for
he felt Ibla was looking at him. With two
blows of his shining steel he cut horse and rider
so they fell apart into four pieces. His steed
Abjer dashed into the *melée* like an outraged
hyena. And thus, while plundering souls from
the bodies they inhabited, Antar gayly sang: "I
am the lover of Ibla, the full moon of full
moons." His tribe lost only twenty men; nine
thousand of the enemy drank of the cup of
death. In abject submission the few survivors
crawled to his feet on the crowns of their heads!
Then the lover sang his lay:

"O Ibla, if the shades of the sable battle dust
conceal from thee my achievements on the day
of conflicts, arise and ask my steed if I ever let
him charge but at the armies, like the gloomy
night. Ask my sword of me, if I ever smote
with it on that dreadful day but the skulls of
kings. Ask my lance of me, if ever I thrust
with it but at the panoplied hero between the
throat and the under jaw. I steep my sword, I
steep my spear, in blood streams. I practice
patience, and fear not hell itself. How many
are the spear-thrusts of which my saddle-bow
and my hip-bone have complained! And were
there not One at whose power even kings tremble, I would make the vault of the firmament
the back of a horse."

He wanders over the desert adoring Ibla,
scattering heads like balls, and hands like leaves
of trees, and dyeing the sand with blood till it is
like crimson cornelian. He releases captive

damsels, and hacks to pieces their captors, and
his wine is the blood of warriors. After each
encounter he seats himself on the neck of his
horse and sings his modest song, with his hand
on the sword which sparkles like shooting stars.
Many adventures the "Brandisher of Spears"
has to recount. Finally the lovers are made
happy, the marriage day, or rather seven days,
are appointed.

I cannot suppress a brief notice of that festival.
Of animals slain there were twenty thousand
dromedaries, twenty thousand sheep, as many
goats and a thousand lions. The bridegroom
himself caught seven hundred lions and two hundred tigers. The tent from Persia, pitched for
Ibla, was the load of forty camels. It was embroidered with fine gold, was studded with
precious stones and diamonds valued at the
maintenance of the world. It was sprinkled with
rubies and emeralds, and there was an awning at
the door of the pavilion under which four thousand horsemen could skirmish. The wedding
guests numbered three hundred thousand. The
presents to Antar were countless slaves, ready
day and night to mount when he mounted, and
halt when he halted, camels, horses, velvets,
jewels, musk, and ambergris, all of which was
returned to the givers except the perfumes, which
the bridegroom gave to Ibla. None but a fool
or a madman would miss that wedding. And
here is the climax: ' Chamberlains spread
carpets that the victuals might not spoil, and
that the guests might eat walking, eat standing,

11

eat on horseback, eat sitting, and *eat in their
sleep!*"

Such is one of the oldest and most celebrated
of Arabic compositions. It is older than the
Arabian Nights, and every evening of the year
portions are recited to entranced listeners in the
cafés of Syria, Persia, Aleppo, and Egypt. From
lethargy and quietism audiences are aroused to
frenzied delight; they clap hands and shout "O,
that we, too, might march to meet the morning!"

You notice the imagery is strangely like that
of the Old Testament. Saul and Jonathan were
swifter than eagles, stronger than lions. In the
battle-song of Deborah and Barak they chant of
kings who took no gain of money. They fought
from heaven; the stars in their courses fought
against Sisera. The Song of Songs is redolent
of myrrh, frankincense, aloes, and the spicery
and balm of the farthest East. "What will ye
see in the Shulamite? As it were the companies
of two armies." "Thy neck is as a tower of
ivory, thine eyes like the fishpools in Heshbon,
thy nose is as the tower of Lebanon which
looketh toward Damascus. Thine head upon
thee is like Carmel, and the hair of thine head
like purple"—Oriental exaggeration which makes
the poetry of our day dull and tame in metaphor.

In the poems, or recitations, having hit a
simile which pleases him, the improvisatore
passes from one image to another, and describes
in detail the scene or object which his imagination conjures up, much after the method of the
singing king at Bethlehem.

Round the little camp fires of the desert, tales from the Arabian Nights are told every night, and the mixture of prose and verse, so popular with them, makes a curious effect in the sing-song narrative. Thus in the familiar story of the Merchant and the Djinn, when the spirit raises its sword to strike, the merchant recites a poem of twelve verses on the varying fates of mankind, which is so affecting that bystanders weep and the wrathful genius stays his hand. Even where reading and writing are known, the taste for listening to poets and story-tellers continues in high favor. Nobles and monarchs of Persia have been so enraptured with recitations that they have been known to give the troubadours a mouthful of gold, or an extravagant sum enriching the singer for life.

The Bedouins of Sinai profess to know the language of beasts, and they translate to the traveler love songs which the uninspired do not understand, sung by the few birds bold enough to haunt the Desert of the Exodus. By the teaching of the Koran this wisdom, the greatest of divine gifts, was expressly vouchsafed to Solomon the Wise, the son of David and the Beautiful One. Let me tell you a fable more than a thousand years old :—

Bahram, King of Persia, was so careless in his administration that half the towns in the kingdom became ruined and deserted. One night, while on a journey with a Magian priest, he passed through a region given up to owls and bats ; and hearing an owl screech and his mate

answer him, "What are the owls saying?"
asked the king of the wise man. The priest,
who knew bird language, replied: "The male
owl is making a proposal of marriage, and the
lady owl replies, 'I shall be most delighted if
you will give me the dowry I require.' 'And
what is that?' says the male owl. 'Twenty
villages,' says she, 'ruined in the reign of our
most gracious sovereign, Bahram.'" "And
what did the male owl promise?" asked Bahram. "O! your Majesty," answered the priest,
"the bird said, 'That is very easy; if his Majesty lives ten years, I will give you a thousand.'"
The lesson of the wise man made such an impression on the king that he reformed his ways.

The adventures of Ulysses run through traditions in various languages, and are the delight
of scholars wide as the world apart. They seem
the property of all people, and, entrusted to the
memories of illiterate tribes, they survive, with
slight modification, the changes of ninety generations of men. The tale of Damon and Pythias
is heard in Arabia, altered to suit its changed
surroundings: —

A young Arab slays an old man for killing
his favorite camel. The heirs of the murdered
man demand vengeance and refuse to accept the
fine which a Mohammedan law allows them to
receive, instead of the life of the criminal. The
youth cheerfully consents to pay the death penalty, but begs for three days' grace, that he may
attend to some secret business in a neighboring
town, and pledges his word that he will return

before that time expires. The Kaliph, before whom he is brought, agrees to allow him to depart on condition that another becomes surety for him, and is willing to suffer death in his stead, in case the offender fails to return. "An old officer of the court who has been a companion of the Prophet—may the peace of Allah be on him, long as the ringdove moans and the pigeon sings!—and whose person was on that account especially sacred, undertakes the office of surety merely because humanity forbids that the prisoner's hopes should perish, and lest it should be said that goodness had fled from among men." Of course the young man is late, and hurriedly arrives at the last instant, just in time to prevent the execution, and has his own life spared, as in the Greek legend. The pressing business, so important, was to provide for a ward of his, and inform some trustworthy guardian of the place in which the child's money was buried; for burying money was from the beginning the only safe mode of investment in the Orient.

Modern investigation, with its perpetual questionings, has spoiled much poetry and the fine boasts of knights of knights, true chevaliers of romance, who despise menial employment, and dedicate themselves to gallant deeds for gentle ladies. By their own testimony, the knight-errant are ready to do and die for the beauty of women with bare and silvery feet, Paradise eyes, and forms waving as the tamarisk when spice winds blow from hills of Araby the Blest.

Some of them beat their breasts, wail, and wander; rejected lovers bemoaning their doom and the cruelty of the obdurate fair. I doubt the whole story. In the Orient, women make no secret of their wish to marry; and fair or dark, the world holds many to be won.

When you see a Bedouin with long pipe, sitting motionless, gazing on vacancy the day through, do not believe he is crossed in love, and pining in dark doom, but be sure he is thinking upon nothing, and enjoying it mightily. The Troubadours—whose Arabic name means an en-enthusiast fired by love of poetry—go on foot from camp to camp challenging rival bards to musical contests in extempore verse. Frequently they are afflicted with blindness, popularly believed to be the result of frenzy to which they are worked up in the composition of poems. Success and the admiration of the audience appear to be their only objects; for unless some high personage happens to be the poet's patron, the contributions are scant—enough, however, for his simple wants. Poverty is his accepted condition, and he may say with the author of the "Ancient Mariner," poetry is to me its own exceeding great reward. What matters it?

> "Clear as amber, fine as musk,
>   Is life to those who, pilgrimwise,
> Move hand in hand, from dawn to dusk,
>   Each morning nearer Paradise.
>
> "O not for them need angels pray!
>   They stand in everlasting light;
> They walk in Allah's smile by day
>   And nestle in his heart at night."

The common people of the East learn from the reciter, of whom our modern lecturer is the dull representative, and the stump-speaker an unpoetic prototype. The language of the Prophet—may he rest in glory!—has a copious fullness of rhyme; rich and varied synonyms which run lightly, trippingly, instead of coming by devious windings, as with us. The vowels are full and liquid, and one anecdote illustrates its redundance:—

The author of one of the seven prize poems written in letters of gold on Egyptian silk, and suspended in the Kaaba at Mecca, walking one day met a market-woman. The illustrious poet asked what she carried in her basket. She answered by a word the scholar had never heard before. The question was repeated, and again followed by a reply unintelligible to the author of the golden verses. And so the old woman went on, giving successively thirty-nine different Arabic names, until at the fortieth, she was understood to mean *onions!* Hence the proverb, " Wisdom has alighted on three things: the brain of the Franks, the hand of the Chinese, the tongue of the Arabs." The charm of the Desert is in the repeated rhymes to stars, the palm, the fountain, the mirage—which allusion is beautifully rendered in the most ancient of languages, "the thirst of the antelope."

They understand the enchantments of distance, and it is always the remote clan, mounted on pawing chargers, which is father of the mighty bard whose sounding numbers charm the ear and ravish the senses.   Here is a mourning-song:

"I am like a wounded camel;
    I grind my teeth in pain;
My load is great and heavy;
    I am tottering again.

"My back is torn and bleeding;
    My wound is past relief;
And what is harder still to bear,
    None other knows my grief!"

This is often quoted as a specimen of the best poetry of the heart. May be when the Asian Romeo chanted it in the ear of the listening night it might have been effective. Transplanted to Western wilds, in the broad glare of day, it would hardly secure a place in the poet's corner of a country newspaper. What does my reader think of a second example of the same sort of verse?

"O handkerchief I send thee off to yonder maid,
    Around thee I my eyelashes will make the fringe of grace.
I will the black point of my eye rub up to paint therewith,
    To you coquettish beauty go—go look thou in her face.

"O handkerchief the loved one's hand take, kiss her lips so sweet,
    Her chin which mocks at apple and at orange, kissing greet.
If sudden any dust should light upon her blessed head,
    Fall down before her, kiss her sandal's sole, beneath her feet.

"A sample of my tears of blood thou handkerchief wilt show.
    Through these, within a moment, would a thousand crimson
        grow.
Thou'lt be in company with her while I am sad with grief;
    To me no longer life may be, if things continue so."

The rhapsodists—dedicated to perpetual poverty, by the blessed law of compensation— console themselves with splendid dreams. They know about sorceries and alchemy, the black art, the

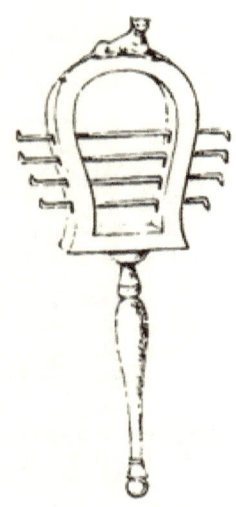

EGYPTIAN SYSTRUM.

BAND OF SIA MUSICIANS.

transmutation of metals in underground caverns, where mighty secrets are kept by a dim-swarming people. Alchemists and their slave Djinns are there at work among grand mysteries, handed down through numberless generations, and furnaces are kept heated so many years that salamanders are born in them.

The supernatural comes readily into lives of loneliness, and in the Desert astrologers, priests, wizards and wonder-workers exhibit jugglery which is old as the Pyramids. The operators in magic are wonderfully earnest, and if a trick fails, they reverently repeat the solemn truth the Kaliphs in their day of pride and power wrote in the lovely mosaics of their palaces: "There is no conqueror but God"—an everlasting admonition to all who seek dominion.

Ask the dozing Achmet why, if lead can be changed into gold by the wise, there is so little current in the tribes, and he answers: "The things belonging to the unseen are not revealed save unto the predestined. All mighty movements are slow; what signifies a thousand years to the soul fated to live forever?"—a mummery which makes us feel like blasphemers and reduces us to silence.

There are delicate measures in Arab verse, and their similes have pretty touches, but as for *music*, it is denied to the Arabian. He is not born or trained to it. One might think in Egypt —land of pleasant groves, dimpling wave and swaying reed—the union of voice and instrument would be perfected. That rhythmic cadence

would come, as Dogberry's reading and writing,
"by nature." Her never-dying melodies bring
endless suggestion to ears attuned aright. But
there is no more music in the war-song and the
love-song of the tribes of the East, than in the
monotonous rub-a-dub of the naked North
American Indian, leaping through the obscene
figures of the Green Corn dance. The Arab's
music is milder, according to his milder environment; and he does not sway violently, as he
sings, so to speak, in the passive voice. The
slow contortions of body accord with the undulating palm leaves overhead, and the restful
scene below. The choice Oriental verses, which
were the delight of my youth, in "Lalla Rookh,"
were the work of a Western minstrel, and set
to melodies wondrous sweet, in the shady bower
of an English garden. They were not born of
the lands they described.

Miriam's timbrel, or tambourine, is the model
of the modern *tar*, found in nearly every Egyptian house. The Eastern voice is extremely
fine, and we can imagine her triumphant burst,
beside the Red Sea, was in high falsetto, vibrating through the pure atmosphere till the waves
of sound touched the outer line of the listening
multitude.

They have modes of time unknown to us, employed in dance-music; alternating bars of various measure. They delight in this mixed time,
which seems to affect them as one of Strauss's
waltzes does an audience familiar with it, making every foot start at the first bar of the orches-

tra. Some strains are like the tremolo of the organ, and no opportunity is lost for gratifying their love of music.

Such as it is, there is a great deal of music in the East; not practiced by professionals alone, but attempted by children, old men and women. and it is held a deplorable calamity yet, in the land where the immortal description of old age was written : " When all the daughters of music are brought low." Christian, Moslem, Jew, chant their services and the congregation accompany with a continuous drone on the keynote. Baptism, marriage, burial, all feasts and solemnities—and they are many—come and go with singing. There is little doubt that the music we hear while journeying through the changeless Orient is the same, and executed on the same instruments and the accompaniment of the same dances—military, social, religious—which pleased the Pharaohs, the Kings of Judah, Assyria, and Babylon.

There is one sound far above singing, heard throughout Islam : the muezzin's call to prayer.

No tolling bell or peal of chimes is like this sound; and after years of residence in the East I never became indifferent to it. Mohammed preferred the human voice to the trumpet of the Israelite or the rattle of the primitive Christian. Had the founder of the fierce faith of Arabia chosen the calls adopted by other religions, the graceful minaret—fairest thing among the manifold beauties of Saracenic architecture—would have been lost to the world.

The Pillar of Victory, as it is sometimes called, answers to the campanile of the Christian cathedral. There is nothing elsewhere to equal it. Even the famous tower in the City of the Red Lily sends out no such thrilling notes, all peace and sweetness though they be. The minaret is a tall, slim, circular tower of marble, white as silver, piercing the eternal sapphire. Within is a winding staircase through which one may reach the balconies. The crowning beauty is an exquisite ornamental finial, tapering to a sharp point like an old-fashioned silver pencil-case. It is impossible to convey in words an idea of such lightness and matchless grace. Icicles turned upside down are nearest minarets in form, and at regular intervals they are ringed with three balconies, which add to rather than take from their aëreal construction.

Punctually, at the same moment, resounding from every minaret of Africa, Asia and Europe, are heard five words, the formula of Islam, chanted to the four points of the compass: "There is no God but God." From the interior glides a ghost-like figure in white turban and long sweeping robes. He pauses a moment in the horseshoe arch, approaches the railing highest of the three galleries circling the tower, and sends a far-reaching note to vast distances, penetrating as the voice of the soul, appealing as the stir of awaking conscience. The tremulous waves of sound float as though in search of hearers yet more remote, who should kindle and glow with the fervor of a devotee at his shrine.

There is a thrill of pathos in the cry when heard by the stranger in dreamful mood, and the stately measure strikes on the heart like vibrant notes of some divine music; like the sound of years and years of departed happiness.

The office of muezzin is usually given to blind men, lest from their lofty elevation they may have too free a view of gardens and harems over the surrounding terraces. And it touches one the more to watch the consecrated servants of God grope their way to the railing. They are selected for their sonorous voices, and the simplicity and solemnity of the appeal make a strangely poetic imprint on the minds of the hearers in day time. Much more touching is it when the sacred chant, with its slow swell and dying fall, resounds through the ivory moonlight of the Oriental night. Then it starts tender memories of lands lying nearer the North Star, of trysting places and summer eves. Phantom faces, long buried, rise again, and accents, long hushed in the everlasting silence, are heard once more. The distant voices seem to meet in the air, greeting and parting in a fineness of sound like the fineness of color in pale shades. When the pathetic music dies, the ear strains after it with a vague sense of repentance for pursuit of the baubles of worldly ambition. The passionate desires, the strivings, the pangs of failure, the exaltations of victory lessen in value and float away with the floating airs. Dim yearnings after a better life haunt the listener and linger in his heart, an inspiration and a desire.

The Arabic language, like the Italian, is marked by such flexibility that it is almost impossible not to rhyme in it. The blind muezzin calls to the dwellers in tabernacles (*i. e.*, in tents), whose greatest luxury is the blessed consolation of sleep:—

> "Come to prayers, come to prayers,
> Come to the temple of salvation,
> Prayer is better than sleep."

And the faithful reply in mutual rhythm:—

> "In the name of Allah, the merciful, the compassionate.
> Praise be to Allah who the three worlds made,
> The merciful, the compassionate,
> The King of the Day of Judgment,
> Thee alone do we worship, and of thee alone do we ask aid.
> Guide us in the path that is strait,
> The path of those for whom thy love is great,
> Not they on whom is hate,
> Or those who deviate,
> Amen. Oh, Lord of Angels, Djinns, and men."

I have seen idlers in green fields, wanderers by the roadside, passengers on the decks of steamers answer the command instantly as it is uttered. Most solemn and inspiring was the sight of a regiment of the Sultan's under the Crescent flag of Islam, responding unitedly. In the dim, blue distance a thousand red turbans went down as one, every face toward the Kaaba, every forehead in the dust. When shall we behold the spectacle of an army of the Cross of Christ reverently kneeling when the summons to prayer is heard? Some such thing might have been in the armies of the Crusaders, or among the troops of Cromwell—that camp where a vulgar jest or a profane word was never spoken—but it is not in our generation of doubters and scoffers at every form of worship.

Let me give from the religious code of the Moslem one passage of peculiar force. It is chanted in the mosques as we repeat the Apostle's Creed: "Allah is sole and Eternal. He lives and is all-powerful. He knows and sees everything, is endowed with volition and action. In him is neither form nor figure, nor bounds nor limits, nor numbers nor parts, nor multiplications nor divisions; because he is neither body nor matter. He has neither beginning nor end, but exists by himself without generation, without an abode, independent of the empire of Time; as incomparable in his nature as in his attributes, which, without being separated from his essence, do not constitute it."

XVIII.

THE FIRST CINDERELLA: A TALE OF THE RED PYRAMID.*

Among the gray pyramids of Egypt stands one that was anciently cased in red granite, and, while resting in its shadow, one day, I heard this tale told of the builder of the Red Pyramid:—

Many and many a hundred years ago, centuries before there was any Christmas, the King of Egypt sat on the ivory throne in his Palace-hall,

* Being the story which the Antiquary wrote in Cairo. For the legend on which it is founded, the reader is referred to the "History of Psammaticus, Fourth Pharaoh of the Twenty-Sixth Dynasty."

guarded by soldiers armed and dumb. At his right hand, a step below him, was the Crown Prince, a beautiful youth of nineteen, the age when the years are all Summers. On the left, two steps lower, sat the wise Counselor, with beard white as frost, and he lived at four-score, when the years are all winters. He was the only subject who sat in presence of the King or dared advise him. Wiser than other men, he could foretell the future, knew the language of beasts, what the stars are made of, and why comets go wandering through the sky. A poet once, now toothless and deaf, he could only mumble scraps of old verses in a voice shrill as a grasshopper's chirp.

It was so hot, one could fairly see the heat. The door-way opened into a court alive with birds and shady with trees, whose leaves hung wilted and curled in the flaming sunshine. Under a pavilion of porphyry and jasper a fountain's plash and gurgle made cooling sounds, very pleasant to hear. It fell into a basin of alabaster bordered with greenery and blue flags, and fed a lake where swans were swimming and a tame ibis sought food.

The sullen King and his gloomy Counselor sat with hands on their knees, their feet close together, like the granite statues of gods on the Nile banks staring eternally at nothing. The Prince was restless as quicksilver, glancing in every direction, talking much and very fast. Suddenly he exclaimed:

THE TWIN COLOSSI OF AMENOPHIS III.

"There is an eagle overhead. I will order my arrows and shoot it."

"No," said the King, languidly, raising his painted eyelids; "that is only a speck of cloud."

"I see it. Look, quick! now he swoops down."

He ran to the lake, but before he reached the bridge spanning it something dropped into the center of the court. He picked up the fallen prey, and was about to fling it into the water, when the King called:

"Bring it here."

The boy returned, holding out a shoe, or, rather, sandal, of very small size.

"What an odd thing for an eagle to carry off. It is foreign."

The King examined it with as much curiosity as he should who is adored as a god by the mere earth-worms called men.

"A pretty thing," he said, weighing it in his immense brown hand. "Some dancer's slipper."

"No; if it had been danced in, the straps would be strained at the holes. It is not the curved and pointed sole of our shoemakers; this is Grecian work."

"Whoever the owner be, she dwells in the Happy Valley of Childhood," chirped the Counselor, briskly. "How delicate the print inside! How tender must be the foot which has pressed it so lightly, for it is not new; the strings are frayed and lining faded. I wonder whose it is? Let us try to imagine her."

"Why not find her? A new idea. Go," said

the King, changing his rigid manner, "take my signet, order heralds and swift ships from the Delta to the Cataract. Proclaim that whoever brings the mate of this shoe, and can wear them both, shall sit on the throne of Rameses and be buried with me in the Red Pyramid. I shall kill my fifty-four Abyssinian queens and have only this one. I swear it by the lotus-bud of my scepter, and make oath by the Nameless Name it is death to utter. For I am Pharaoh Necho."

Then there was tumult throughout Egypt. East, west, north, south sped the runners, and swift camels carried the decree from the Red Sea far as the Mountains of the Moon. The courtiers said the King was so well pleased he was seen to laugh, but that was not believed. It could have been only a mystic half-smile such as the Sphinx wears; for when was a Pharaoh known to laugh? They thought, or would have thought had they dared, that he was crazy, and trembled lest the owner of the slipper should not be found. Who brought such news would have his skull split by a blow of the golden scepter, which was so heavily loaded, one touch would slay the strongest. The death-stroke was on the back of the neck, swift and sure as lightning. There was wailing in the Palace of the Queens.

"Must we die to-day?" was the question of the morning, "and because our royal master has found an old slipper which a bird let fall!"

And their mourning was like the mourning in the days of Rameses, when the first-born were

PHARAOH "NECHO."

smitten. The morning question of the King was, "Is she found who wears the Greek sandal?" And the messengers shivered and shrank as they answered.

Thus three months passed, and the wise Counselor observed, "The girl is dead, and buried to rot as the barbarians bury. She has missed the glory of being embalmed in perfumes and spicery, and lying in the triple coffin in the Red Pyramid."

One morning he and the King sat, as usual, still as ghosts, their feet close together, hands on their knees, staring straight on at nothing. The Prince was tossing up balls of agate, keeping five at a time in the air—the gayest youth, clad in a purple robe, broidered and fringed with gems and belted with netted gold. There was a stir at the gate. The chief of the guard came forward and bowed his forehead to the dust. Without moving, Pharaoh darted a sidelong glance that way.

"O King, live for ever! The lady thou sought is here."

"Bring her."

"O King, pardon the meanest of thy slaves. She is black—black as I am."

"I change not, for I am Pharaoh. If she proves herself the owner of the slipper, she is my elected Queen."

The ostrich plumes of the soldiery nodded and waved a moment, then a solemn hush, while the boldest held his breath. A Nubian woman advanced with uncertain tread. She had jet-black skin, thick, brown lips, and kinky curls smeared with palm-oil. She shaded her oblique eyes and crawled to the foot of the throne, crouching with terror, shaking till the bangles on her ankles jingled.

" Try the slipper!" thundered Pharaoh.

Sitting on the pavement, she loosened the thongs, and fitted it tightly to the small, black foot.

"The Queen is found!" cried the Prince. "She shall sit on the sacred cushion, checkered crimson, black and gold."

"Hold!" said the King, sternly. "Too fast, boy; but one-half the condition is filled. Where is the mate to the shoe?"

The Nubian tried to speak. Words rattled in her throat.

"O King, live for ever! I did not know—" She shuddered.

"Not know!" roared Pharaoh, furious as a tiger. "This may teach thee!"

He gave her a stroke with the terrible whip, never far from his hand; blood gushed from her mouth, one struggle, a gasp, and all was over with poor Neith, who dreamt of reigning in the halls of Rameses.

"Away with the horrible creature!" growled Pharaoh, under his braided beard. "Away with her!—throw her to the crocodiles."

Then there was light in the Palace of the Queens. They wept for joy over their children, thinking their troubles were ended. Two more months dragged into the past, and the dismal

AN EGYPTIAN KING DESTROYING HIS ENEMIES.

King and his Counselor sat, as usual, gloomier
and crosser than ever. Only the handsome
Prince had any pleasure, singing, dancing and
laughing from morning till night—the son of
Pharaoh's old age, and he loved the light-hearted
lad as he loved his own soul—which is saying a
great deal.

It was at the close of a day of splendid ceremonial, and the King wore his double crown.
Again the chief of the guard advanced, pale as
the dead, and fell before the throne, his plumes
sweeping the steps. Pharaoh roused as from
sleep.

"She is found, O King. Give thy slave leave
to bring the lady of the sandal?"

"Go. Beware of another blunder!"

The captain backed out, and soon returned.
Slowly across the wide area marched the officer.
After him, with soundless step, glided a young
girl, slight in shape as a child. White linen,
draped in clinging folds, showed her form of
perfect mould. The robe, caught high on the
shoulders, left her arms bare, and they were pure
as pearl. Her hair, floating like spun gold, was
held by a fillet of scarlet cord, her only ornament, except a necklace of lotus-lilies lying on
her bosom.

"What loveliness!" exclaimed the Prince,
running to meet her. "She, too, wears the
double crown—Youth and Beauty. The marble
is slippery; let me lead thee."

Her modest eyes sought the winsome, eager
face, and in silence she laid her hand in his

strong clasp. Led before Pharaoh, instead of
sinking on the pavement, she looked up at the
tall, high-crowned figure with fearless gaze.
Such eyes, blue as deep-sea water, had never before met that glance unshrinking.

"The sandal," said he, amazed at her boldness.

It was brought. Her bare feet, shaped in
exquisite curves, were scarcely larger than when
a mother's hand held them in her own, and each
toe was separate and perfect as a sculptor's ideal
modeled in wax. One dimpled foot, with skin
fine as white satin, easily slipped into the sandal. She drew the other from her sash, crossed
the thongs on the arching instep, clasped the
buckles of both; then, folding her hands across
the dove-like breast, she stood erect before the
dark, awful form whose voice made men gasp
for breath and women faint with fear.

"What is thy name?" asked Pharaoh,
graciously.

"Rhodope, O King."

"Thou art well named Rosebloom; and thy
nation?"

"I am of Ionia, and a slave."

"Tell me what thou rememberest of that barbarian region."

"Rather ask what I forget. It is ever near
to me," she answered, wistfully, in a tone like
delicate music after the harsh accents of Egypt.
She continued, as one talks in sleep, and the
shining eyes grew dreamy: "I see isles rocked
in a sapphire sea; hills of violet and amber;

cool, green gardens of olives and clustering
vines; altars of carven alabaster with fragrant
fires and garlands. Each tree and rock and rill
is the haunt of some kind nymph or loving god.
I hear bees humming through the wild thyme.
In balmy eves the nightingale sings, and rushing
brooks keep time with flutes and reeds of the
shepherds. No crashing cymbals and fishskin
drums are in my far, sweet land."

"Have you columns like unto mine?" asked
Pharaoh, pointing to a tower built like a stairway up into the sky.

Its wall was painted in vivid color. Giants
with throats circled by asps, gazing with baleful
eyes; crocodiles, snakes, crawling reptiles, hideous past telling—symbols of the brute greatness
of Egypt. And running through all was the
image of Pharaoh, grinding his heel on the foreheads of kings, stamping the breath out of tor-
tured captives, and dragging them, gashed and
mangled, at his chariot-wheels.

"We have nothing like them," she replied,
disgust and horror shadowing the gentle face.
"These monsters must be memories of a fever
dream."

Pharaoh was stunned by her insolence.

"Ahem! She doesn't notice my portrait.
What have you, then?" he sneered.

"We have pictures of women made for love;
godlike men, with ivy and laurel circling their
smooth brows; crowns won in victories where
there is no blood."

This to him whose chief joy was to march on

the necks of the vanquished, to count piles of heads dripping with warm lifeblood, and watch corpses go drifting down the river!

"Her time has come," thought the old Counselor, and covered his face with his hands to shut out the fearful vision.

The Prince stepped quickly to her side. Pharaoh curbed his wrath, and continued: "Wouldst thou return to thy people?"

"A slave can have but one wish."

Sparkling drops gathered under the veined eyelids and fell on the pavement.

"Do not cry, Rhodope," said the Prince; "thy tears fall on my heart."

"I would not grieve thee with my griefs, bright Prince. Thy pity dries my tears," she said, softly.

He wiped her eyes with her hair, smoothed the rippling gold away from her neck, and patted her shoulder as one quiets a baby. A pink flush tinted her brow and faded as it came, while she shyly studied the make of her little shoes. The lotus necklace trembled with the flutter of her breast, and for a time nothing was heard but the splash of falling water and the scream of a cockatoo swinging in his hoop of reed. It was a pretty sight! Two blameless children, heedless of the tyrant who looked over their heads at the outline of the Libyan Hills. Warm winds blowing across the garden wafted a stray ringlet against the Prince's robe. The youth bent low, lifted the bright wonder to his lips one moment, and then went back to his place, but

not with his usual bounding step. The Counselor's dim eyes filled, and the King felt defeated,
he knew not why, nor knew he how to answer
the lofty look and appealing gesture of his
son.

"How long since thou left Ionia?" he inquired, trying to subdue his thundering speech.

"I know not. My father was torn from me.
My six brothers, whom the gods made good as
they were beautiful, were beaten to death. I
was dragged by my hair—"

"Those sunbright tresses," murmured the
Prince.

"Was prisoned in a ship and sold to a noble
lady of Naucratis."

"What misery, father; think of that adorable
form bending under the dreadful water-basket."

"I was not sent to the field," pursued Rhodope,
with a grateful look; "but it was a bitter
change for one who had never heard harsher
sounds than the fishers' chorus answering their
wives out at sea. I had only to arrange the
toilet of my mistress and sing to her."

"Let me hear one of thy native songs, my
Rosebloom," said Pharaoh.

"How can I sing my country's songs in a
strange land, O King?"

Was ever anything like unto it? A slave
refusing to sing for Pharaoh! Why, all the
women of Egypt would give their eyes for such
a chance. But Rhodope was willful as she was
innocent. Fearless and quiet, she stood, neither
willing nor disobedient, only she might not

sing. Never in his reign of forty years had the
monarch such an experience. He was rather
amused, as he had been when a child once
climbed his chariot and pulled his sacred beard.
The mother expected the deathblow for the outlaw, and, instead, he took the boy in his arms
and actually kissed him. There was a warm
spot in his heart, after all.

"Knowest thou, rash girl, thou art in danger
of death? Tangles of yellow hair and eyes like
the shimmer of the sea will not protect thee. I
never strike twice."

His hand sought the dread scepter.

"Canst thou kill that?" retorted the dauntless maid, pointing to a moth sailing by on silky
wing.

Pharaoh struck, missed his aim, and sparkles
of fire followed his blow on the stone. The but-
terfly fluttered to the top of an acacia, and
glowed there like a little lamp. He smothered
his rage.

"Fool!" exclaimed he, grimly; "thou hast
no wings."

"My soul has," she answered; "they are
folded until I shall rise by them to the dear
company of my people."

And this to the King of a Hundred Kings!
Not only she refused to sing, but boldly defied
him to his face. For the first time in his life he
was puzzled. The Rose of the Egean was a
thorny, prickly little thing; but as for letting
her go, no, no. Nor would he beat her brains
out, as he was tempted.

"She is a simpleton," said he, in the language sacred to royalty.

"She is a priestess," piped the Counselor.

"She is a delight," sang the Prince.

"Dost thou know my power?" loudly demanded the despot. "Thousands on thousands of women are this moment dying of love for me. Half the grace I have shown thee would be to them an everlasting glory."

"Thou hast said it," replied Rhodope, simply; in no way moved, except to avert her face from his frown.

"She is tired, my father," said the Prince, coaxingly. "Let her sit on thy footstool. Here, rest thee, Rose-maiden."

"It does not become me to sit in royal presence; thanks for thy courtesy, gentle Prince."

Monstrous, this! King and Prince both baffled and confused by a slave whose life was no more than a bubble of foam broken on the waves of yesterday.

"Ignorant!" said Pharaoh, haughtily, making a last effort to overawe the strange spirit. "Knowest thou why thou art brought to the Lord of the Daybreak, whom the Sun salutes as his brother before he rises?"

"I was told there is a prize waiting for her who can wear my sandals."

"First tell how one was lost?"

"We were bathing in the river. After the bath I hunted it in vain, and supposed it was stolen."

"It was stolen by a bird, Rhodope."

"The King is pleased to jest with his servant."

"No," broke in the Prince; "an eagle carried it off, and let it fall in this very court. I was for throwing it in the lake—"

"Hush, dearest," interrupted Pharaoh. "We must see if the stranger is equal to her destiny. She is—well—unusually dull. What is thy wish? Ask, Rosebloom!"

She scanned the pictured reptiles on the walls, the writhing, twisted asps; then the earnest eyes came back to the colossal statue of the King, created as though to outlast the wear of centuries.

"A slave knows but one wish."

"Thine is granted. Thou art free. Wilt thou return to thy people?"

"My people have crossed the black flowing river, and are in the Fields Elysian. My home is ashes, my city is but dust, her bow is broken. Not a fisher's net is spread on our coast to-day."

The baby mouth trembled.

"Ask; were it half my kingdom, I give it thee. A singular study," said Pharaoh, aside, to the Counselor.

"I know not what to say," rejoined Rhodope, bashful and troubled. She changed eyes with the charming Prince.

"Choose," he insisted, smiling brightly. "The King's son commands it."

She shook her head, and grew red and white by turns.

"I have sworn by Isis and Osiris the wearer of the sandals shall sit on my throne, and bo buried in the Red Pyramid. Cheops and Shofra alone are greater." He proudly looked toward three mighty wedges cleaving the Desert air. "Armies of slaves have toiled on it day and night. My history is painted on the inner chamber. All is ready for our mummies to be laid away in the darkness."

He expected her to swoon with rapture, and kneel at his feet and kiss them. The Counselor shrilly piped, not so low but that all could hear ·

"In the Kingdom of Love, Youth is King."

"I will not lie sealed tight in the Red Pyramid. A mountain of stone on my breast, I could not sleep. Bound in bandages and daubed with bitumen, I should be prisoner even in death!"

The voice, sweet as a Dorian flute, carried a force which abashed the tyrant.

"What is thy teaching and superstition?" he inquired, with freezing coldness.

"Let me rest in the land of my love, under the sentinel cypress-tree, in a pleasant tomb, with a window cut through so I can see the swallows when they come back in the Spring. Or let my body be purified by fire and gathered into a holy urn when my shade has passed the viewless gate."

"Useless to waste words on a silly girl without wit enough to love life or fear death. Only one more question to end the matter: Rose-maiden, what sayst thou to sitting on my throne?"

She surveyed the place princesses would die to possess one hour.

"It is too high for me," she said.

Pharaoh gnashed his teeth, foam gathered on his lips, and they whitened with wrath fearful to behold.

"Now, by all the gods of Egypt," he hissed, "tempt me not, or it may be worse for thee."

"It cannot be worse for the wretched exile. Know, mighty King, I am of a noble line, daughter of a chief." Her voice rang trumpet clear, gaining strength as she continued: "He and my brethren are in the fields of fadeless asphodel, encamped with the heroes. They wear the shining armor of the Immortals. Think you I fear to follow? Break this frail shell. It will be a welcome touch which gives my spirit room to stretch its wings. Happy Lethe will wash away the memories of bondage and the scars of my chains."

She lifted her hands. On each wrist was a ridge where fetters had eaten into the tender flesh.

"Thus I cover them with my own bracelets. None other wears the coiled asps and the sacred beetles."

She drew back.

"The serpent scares me. I would die as I have lived. I go as to a banquet. Now—"

Wild lights blazed in her eyes. They gleamed like dark jewels. One yearning glance for the Prince, one rapt look toward heaven— the mystery so near—and she bowed her head

to the deathstroke, her sunny locks falling round
it in a golden glory. A thrill of admiration
started the pulse of Pharaoh as it had not
throbbed in years, and shook him with strange
power.

"So fragile yet so strong! It is wonderful.
She is upheld by something from the unseen
world playing in this creature to torment me."
His rage passed, and his face resumed its icy
calm. "What is there in thee, what secret
strength I cannot touch?"

"It is the soul of a Grecian. No marvel, O
King; but it is beyond thee. Weak, helpless
as I am, not all the might of all the Pharaohs
can make me blench or quiver."

As she spoke the sinless soul came up to its
windows and looked out without a tremor. And
again the old Grasshopper chirped: "In the
Kingdom of Love Youth is King." The refrain
of a song, mournful as tears, which some lost
love sang long ago. It touched the tiger-heart.

"True, true," muttered Pharaoh, and rising, he
paced the hall alone. "I will not treat her as I
did poor Nini, with the forget-me-not eyes, who
used to sing in the twilight. How her ghost
haunts me now! This foolish child may live,
and so shall my fifty-four Abyssinian queens."
He paused before a vast marble slab, polished
till it reflected his towering person like a mirror.
"The Greeks are a beauty-loving race," he
mused. "This wrinkled, war-worn face is no
mate for yon fresh blossom in the dew of the
morning. Hands which can throttle a wild wolf

are not made to plait flowers, nor are these the
limbs to trip it in gay Greek dances."

Pharaoh had fought many battles; his first
struggle with self was soon over. He re-entered
the court. The sun was setting like a red-hot
ball. In its fiery glow the shape so wondrous
fair stood moveless, lone as some lovely statue
wrought in ivory and gold. She regarded him
listlessly, as if she would say, "What now, my
master?"

The Counselor sat with hands on his knees
staring straight on at nothing. The Prince was
gayly humming a street ballad.

"Son," said Pharaoh, tenderly, "one day my
power almighty will be thine."

"One day, O father; not now," he pleaded,
kissing the extended hand. "The double crown
makes headache, and the scepter is heavy to
bear. Let me enjoy my life while it is May."

"Come nearer, pretty one," Pharaoh continued, with a smile, which became him better than
his crown; "the regal cushion, barred with
black, red and gold, has waited for thee six
months. Thou has seen and rejected it."

"The seat is too high for me," repeated Rhodope, with the stubborn hold of an unreasoning
child.

"Yes, thou art right. Many have fallen in
the attempt to climb this throne, and thy tiny
feet might slip, but no harm can live under the
shadow of my scepter. Come hither, my son,
my darling. Here, on the lower step, beside

thee, I lay the barred cushion of the coming Queen."

Her heart's colors flashed into the flower-like face.

"The blush-rose of the Egean is mine, is mine," sang the Prince. "I gather her home to my breast."

Rhodope gave a glad cry, but stirred not.

"Wait, sit still, my boy. Fair maiden, the beauty of the beautiful race is thine, and a courage which has conquered the world's conqueror. Thus I heal thy scars." Pharaoh brought her slender wrists together, spanned them in one grasp, and drew the milk-white arms over the Prince's head. "Pass under the yoke, Crown Prince of Egypt, captive to the heroic Greek. I set my royal seal on the bonds, and the banner over you is love." He lightly kissed Rhodope's forehead, and pressed it with his signet-ring.

"I yield me prisoner for life and death."

The Prince entwined her in his arms, drew her close, and, as he leaned to the roseleaf cheek, she whispered:

"Thou art my father, my brethren, and my country."

13

XIX.

IN THE ISLE OF THE LILY: THE STORY OF THE THREE KINGS.

It was a breathless morning. The flag hung moveless over our tent, the river ran still as a dream, the palm-leaves were pendant and wilted, waving not a feather of green. There was dead silence in camp; each one self-absorbed and listless. To make conversation, I said, apropos of nothing, "I wonder, Mr. Graham, your long residence in Rome did not make you a lover and member of the True Church."

"My nurse used to be a Catholic," answered the Antiquary, musingly, like one busy with memory. "She told me many stories of the Madonna, and I still repeat the sweet hymn she taught me,

> "Holy Mary, mother mild,
> Deign to hear a little child."

"What is the date?" asked Thalia, carelessly.

He colored slightly through the tan and red scorch of Syrian sun, for his age is his weak point, and slow torture could not extract it from him, "It was in a remote epoch, fair lady, and in a pre-historic era."

"I thought you loved dates," she persisted.

"I do, on occasion, especially those which grow near the sacred city of the Prophet."

"And that far-away dead and gone nurse used

to tell stories of the Madonna; give us one, now."

"With pleasure, if you will settle yourself for the time, and honor me with your undivided attention. You know I do not like straying eyes, and restless fingers."

We disposed ourself comfortably about the story teller, never so happy as when called on to give up his stored treasures. In the sociability of camp, and the absolute security of confidential friends, we were free to yawn, doze, move off, if the tale proved too long for our patience.

"Some of the fables have slipped away," said the old man, shaking his head sadly. "I cannot bring them back. How vivid and real they were to my childish eyes; gone now, with things infinitely dearer." He passed his hand across his forehead. "The thieving years have stolen them; in vain do I try to hunt up their shining trails, they have vanished and forever. As the days are long and time of no value, let us speak first of the three Kings, heroic and gentle, who traveled from afar to worship the Saviour. Do you know the story of the Three Kings of Cologne?"

"No, and I dearly love stories of kings, let us have it at once before you forget it."

"No danger of my forgetting the legends learned in youth. It is the near and recently learned which drop from memory. There are so many tales of the Wise Men I hardly know which to choose. One Arabic tradition runs that in the keeping of their people was a book

which bore the name of Seth, and in it was foretold the appearance of the Star of the Messiah,
and the offering of gifts to Him. The book was
guarded by one family, and handed down from
father to son through unnumbered generations.
Twelve men were chosen to watch for the Star,
and when one died another was elected to his
place.

"These men, in the speech of the land, were
called Magi. They went each year after the wheat-
harvest, to the top of a Mountain named the
Mountain of Victory. It had a cave in it, and
was pleasant with bubbling springs and leafy
trees. At last the Star of Prophesy appeared,
and in it a lovely child, and above him the figure
of a cross; and the voice of the Star was heard
ordering the Magi to go to Judea. They obeyed
the angelic voice, and journeyed northward two
years, and in all that time they lacked nothing.
Neither food nor drink, raiment nor sandals.
At last the Star sank into a spring at Bethlehem,
where it may be seen at this day, but only by
young maidens, young as the Virgin Mother and
pure of heart.

"But to begin at the beginning:—It is written
in the Book of Numbers that when Balaam was
ordered to curse the Israelites he, by divine
inspiration, uttered a blessing instead of a curse.
And he took on the spirit of prophecy and parable, and said, 'I shall see but not now, I shall
behold Him but not nigh. There shall come a
Star out of Jacob and a Scepter shall rise out of
Israel.' And the people of that country, sup-

EGYPTIAN COLUMNS.

posed by some to be Chaldees or Persians, though they were not of the chosen of the Lord, kept this saying as a tradition among their rulers, and waited with trust and hope for its fulfillment.

"Princes of old were students and scholars, and well skilled in astronomy, as the Pyramids prove. They beheld a strange Star unlike its bright brethren within range of their instruments. It moved in unaccustomed spaces and with amazing swiftness, and led by faith they hailed it as the predestined Light which was to guide them to the One which should lighten the Gentiles. They prepared in haste, and at once set out under its nightly guidance. It is said by savans they were nine days on the road to Bethlehem."

"How could calculation be made?" asked the eager listener.

"I do not know. The New Testament record is meager, and the expression from the East might mean a hundred, or it might mean a thousand miles. Who knows, who cares? It matters not."

The Antiquary is one who, in the language of the rural districts, can talk like a book; and having lived much more in libraries than in drawing-rooms, he dropped into quotation naturally as Silas Wegg into poetry. Unconsciously, too, he assumed the air of speech-making. A debator not used to strong opposition, and it was our languid habit to let him run on forever with slight interruption.

"I was saying," he continued, "the Wise Men

came from distant and, perhaps, savage lands. They were of diverse nationalities to indicate the three races of the known world; in that representation accepting the Saviour of all mankind.

"Jaspar, or Caspar, was King of Tarsus, whose merchants are princes. The gift he gave was gold—we may be sure it was much fine gold; the present of an Oriental monarch to a God. Melchior, the King of Arabia, brought a camel-load of precious perfumes, mostly frankincense, (remember I am following the ancient legends); and Balthazar, King of Saba, or Sheba—the land of spices and costly drugs and gums—loaded his white camel with myrrh which means, in Arabic, 'bitter.'

"It is a singular fact," here the Antiquary assumed the didactic and oratorical, "that when the Man of Nazareth was born He was in some vague, indefinite way expected by every race and in every country. Not the Jews only were looking for a Messiah. In India the devotees were waiting for the beloved Buddha to re-appear. The Greeks had long before erected an altar to the Unknown God. The Parsees watched at sunrise for the *Sosiosh* who was to lead men to peace, to call the dead from their graves, and judge the world. And some think it was from the Magian priests the three were sent, by God, to the stable, and found their Sosiosh in the Son of Mary.

"But that was not an exceptional feeling. It is alive and warm, to-day; and humanity is still

stretching out its hands for some Invisible
Power, that shall come to right the wrongs and
heal the sorrows of the whole human family.
It is because we see the great need of a mighty
helper that the prayer goes up in the lodge of
the Rocky Mountain savage, and from the wild
men of the wilderness. An outcry from the
same yearning which moves the second advent-
ists now scattered through the Christian Churches.
The Mongolian, three thousand years ago, felt
the need of the Unseen Man who was to bring
tranquillity, just as the Northmen prayed for
Odin to come in glancing armor, and kill the
Wolf of Evil and give the world eternal summer. Yes, we need him, to-day, as much as ever,"
continued the old man devoutly. "But this is a
digression, as our friends the novelists say. To
resume—

"It had been written, 'The Kings of Tar-
shish and the Isles shall bring presents, and the
Kings of Sheba shall offer gifts.' There is a
picture, little known, in the Belvedere Gallery,
called the 'Astrologers' which is the most satis-
fying of the many I have seen of the Magi. It
shows a blank, wide landscape circled with
mountains, no sign of life except three men.
The first, in Oriental costume, with long, white
beard, stands in the attitude of speech, holding
in his hand an astronomical table; next him one
in the prime of life seems listening to him; the
third, a youth-like Apollo, seated and looking
upward, holds a compass. They are watching
over the Chaldean hills for the miraculous light

whose first ray piercing the far horizon (called in German the 'Rising Sun'), is intended to express the Star of Jacob. They recognize the fulfillment of prophecy, the answer to prayer, and they are not afraid. He was come before whom 'every knee was to bow;' whose name was to be set above the powers of magic, the mighty rites of sorcerers, the secrets of Memphis, the drugs of Thessaly, the silent and mysterious murmurs of the wise Chaldees, and the spells of Zoroaster.

"The night-marches of the Three were mystic, wonderful. Some of the old painters have it they journeyed with barbaric pomp, a caravan with armed followers and banners, long trains of attendants, horses and camels, and surrounded the manger with Asiatic magnificence. The Venetian artists introduce portraits of grand bearded Senators, as the Wise Men, and not unsuitably are they models. Those fine Italian faces deserve such immortality; and sometimes Herod is seen in the background of their pictures, overlooking the strange scene with troubled face and cruel eyes.

"One exquisite painting of the Adoration in Venice, I think, shows camel heads stretching above the slaves in glittering array, who march in with vessels of silver and of gold. They bear vases, ewers, and censers of flaming metal. There are feather fans and gorgeous umbrellas, parrots and peacocks, reminders of tributes offered beforetime at the lion-guarded throne of Solomon. The sweeping robes of silk, brocaded with gold, and ermine mantles of the Kings fairly shine on the canvas, and the diadems sparkle as though set with actual gems. Yet this lavish color and splendor of accessories impress me less than the familiar 'Adoration of the Shepherds,' in their coats of shaggy skins, with unkempt hair and bristling beards, in simple awe and wonder gazing at the Divine Child. All the light in the picture comes from the infant Saviour, and is reflected like fire on the garments and faces of the Shepherds. Mysterious shadows suggesting angel presences, flashing raiment and rainbow pinions. Do you know the significance of the presents?"

"I do," replied Thalia. "When I was in the dismal grind of the Free School, I taught Longfellow's 'Three Kings' to my scholars, as a Christmas Hymn."

"Let us have it, now."

"With all my heart," said Thalia; and she gave it with sweet voice and clear accent. When the recitation ended the party cheered with lazy clapping of hands, and the Antiquary took up his thread again:—

"Yes: the gold meant that Christ was King. The incense that the young Child was a God to be worshiped. The myrrh that He was mortal, also, and doomed to suffer death; it was for the burying. A threefold faith, unerring, for from the beginning he was *the Christ.*

"When the Wise Men had laid their presents at His feet in token of loyalty—for that is the Eastern acceptation of such oblation—they

turned homeward, being warned in a dream to
avoid Herod. They dared not retrace their
steps; they must return by some other route to
avoid the enraged king of Judea, and were at a
loss which way to go. Their wisdom availed
not, and just outside the Joppa Gate of Jerusalem they held council. Their mission had been
accomplished; they had seen the Saviour; they
had declared their allegiance to him born
to be King of the Jews; they had finished
their work and were perplexed. Far from
their own people, and among enemies, they
knew not how to proceed, for the Star
went out at Bethlehem. One of them stooped
to drink of the spring, called to this day the
Well of the Magi, and lo! the miraculous light
mirrored in the pure water. Not then, as now,
a mere puddle by the wayside, but a limpid
fountain.

"They gladly hailed the familiar signal,
moving westward, and with thanksgiving and
courage followed its guidance and were led safely
home. Being eased of their heavy loads, the
white camels traveled fast; they slept by day
in the tranquil shade of oases and journeyed in
the opaline twilight across the desert made fairer
than day. When they reached their own country, wherever that may be, they laid down their
sumptuous state, and in imitation of the lowli-
ness of our Lord, born in a manger, yet who
hath all power in heaven and in earth, they gave
what they had to feed the poor.

"They forsook splendid palaces, fine robes,

and prancing horses, and went about in mean attire; in sheep-skins and goat-skins, teaching and
preaching Him whose kingdom is not of this
world; the Child-king, the Prince of Peace.

"The tale runs that to Balthazar were given
revelations not vouchsafed to the other two. He
lived many years, bearing about him an atmosphere of meekness and holiness, and the freshness of manhood's prime. Age had no power
over him nor time. The other two died before
the crucifixion.

"There is a legend that about forty years later
St. Thomas was preaching in the East Indies, and
there met the three Wise Men; for they were
never separated after they came together as messengers of Christ—an image of the Blessed
Trinity. The Apostle baptized them, and they
in turn, went about baptizing, healing, teaching,
and preaching the Resurrection and the Life;
the finished work of the Babe of Bethlehem.

"They were those of whom this world is not
worthy. The recital of their suffering is, to borrow the Arabian phrase, enough to make the dead
rise in their graves, and children turn gray in
their cradles. In journeyings often, in perils of
robbers, in perils by heathen, in perils in the
city, in the wilderness, in perils among false
brethren. In weariness and painfulness, in
watchings often, in hunger and thirst, in fastings
often, in cold and nakedness. St. Paul's account
of himself well answers for the Magi. In the
farthest East, then named the Ends of the Earth,
they fell among barbarous Gentiles; destitute,

afflicted, tormented, they were scourged, stoned, and put to death. Long afterward—"

"How long?" broke in Thalia.

"In the fourth century, the Empress Helena, who was always on hand to pick up relics, discovered their tombs and brought the remains to Constantinople. During the Crusades, the romantic Red Cross Knights bore their bones with reverence and devotion to Milan. From there, they were carried away by the Emperor Barbarossa, and presented to his friend and ally, the Archbishop of Cologne. The relics were received by the people with great rejoicing. A magnificent shrine for enclosing them was soon manufactured, and it stands to-day in the Cathedral which was made to enrich the world with dream-like shapes of grace and loveliness. And at this shrine, divers glorious miracles have been performed in sight of true believers."

* * * * *

How well I remember that day—that golden day—at Cologne! The print of the Roman yoke is on it yet, for the Church of St. Marie holds the site of the Roman Capitol, and has resounded with the armed tread of the Legions of Trajan.

Of the treasures of the cathedral nothing compares with the shrine of the Magi, the tomb behind the grand altar, where Gothic windows cast varied lights on the tessellated pavement and along the Ionic pillars. The casket is six feet long, modeled as a Roman Basilica, enriched with artistic, sacred figures, carved jewels, and

chased and enameled ornamentation. In the
French Revolution it was injured, and in the
year 1820 a thief secreted himself in the cathedral when it was closed at evening and spent the
night plundering the shrine, escaping in the
morning. It lost about one hundred precious
stones, but, as we say of rich men, it could afford to lose. In the mass of jewels, gems, cameos, a few hundreds are not missed. The carved
stones belong to classic antique art, and the lapi-
dary's work is delicate and marvelously fine. At
the head end of the shrine is a movable panel
which the keeper slips aside, and behold! three
bare skulls, each circled with a diamond crown.

The names are in square letters set with rubies
which flash like flame: Gaspar, Melchior, Balthazar—names as familiar to us as household
words. It was like finding the graves of old
friends in a foreign cemetery. We had pondered over their scant history so long, had seen
the many grand pictures of them, had them in
heart and fancy for years, and now suddenly to
see their names in letters of burning jewels!
What wonder that we started and smiled, saying, Surely those prophets might grant one little
miracle to the worshipers who have loved them
long and well! We lingered about the shrine
as became believing pilgrims; we marked the
scene of the baptism of Jesus in the river Jordan; the panel representing the Redeemer seated
on his throne, with his right hand raised and
holding the Book of Life in his left; the Virgin
and Child, carved by some devout worker who

prayed as he wrought and was blessed in his labors. It is the finest specimen of mediaeval art, and is fitly placed in the first of sanctuaries. Not strange that the making of such a structure is cloudy with myths and traditions. There are the pictured windows of world-wide fame. O, it is a pity to die without seeing them! They were clear glass once; angels brushed them with their wings, and lo! they took on a many-colored radiance like sunset dies. Ethereal hands finished them in a single night, and vainly does mortal artist try to copy tints which were never spread on earthly palette.

And no one knows who designed the famous cathedral. The legend-haunted Rhine abounds in explanations of the matchless work. It was given, so they tell, in a dream of the morning, a trance-like state, to a young architect who sold his soul to the devil in return for superhuman knowledge. Again, they say it was begun by a forgotten architect, who, for some crime, was struck dead, and the work condemned to stand still for centuries.

I like best to think it was conceived in the valley of vision under some divine inspiration. Better to me the tale that an emperor, generous and munificent, long ago summoned his builders together, and promised them eternal fame if they would built a fane which should surpass all other fanes. There should be no limit in design, no bound to expense, no question as to time. Said the monarch to the artisans on bended knees before him: "Let its splendor be like the

EGYPTIAN WAR CHARIOT

first temple on Mount Moriah. What I ask is perfection."

Then there was study and strife among the architects, and who of mortal birth was worthy of such fame as the emperor promised? At the appointed day plans and models were brought, drawings and traceries laid at the foot of the throne. But as one after another was unrolled, the proud emperor said: "They will not do; this cathedral is to keep my name in remembrance while the world remains to let its spires point upward."

The designers left the presence-chamber, their eyes full of rage and tears of disappointment. "Who but the devil can satisfy a king who asks impossibilities?" said they. One workman lingered behind when the train of aspirants had departed. He held no roll of parchment or box of models; he was an old man, bent and weak, wearing a green coat and a gray cap. "Grant me this favor, O king," he demanded, in a shrill, piping voice, "one day more to work at my drawings. I am so near to my ideal, so near. I have sought it through prayers and fastings; and last night I almost touched the plan, the design of a temple which shall eclipse the splendor of others as the sun outshines the small stars. My meditations are nearly ended, but the picture I see with the eye of my soul will not as yet shape itself to my hand. It is very near." He unrolled a slight parchment from his bosom —"Dost thou see aught, O emperor, a shape of beauty on this scroll?"

"I see nothing," said the monarch, coldly, "its blank page has no lines for my sight."

The little old man groaned in anguish and trembled. His hand shook as he refolded the paper. "It is as I feared; the pencil of light was but a snare and a deceit. Only grant one day more, O most merciful, and if I fail, let me go back to my cell, for I have taken Holy Orders, and I will spend the few days left of threescore and ten in repentance that I let ambition lurk under my cowl."

The pious emperor graciously spoke: "One day more, holy man, I give you; and in your prayers forget not the name of your sovereign, who is low as the meanest in the sight of our common Master."

Then the old man kissed the royal hand held out to him, and backed like a courtier out of the chamber.

The monk was devout and humble. "What am I, that I should win a great name?" he asked of himself; "yet the shepherd on the Plain of Midian was no more than the monk vowed to perpetual poverty, resting his naked feet on the bare floor of the cloister. O Blessed Virgin, O Holy Mary," he prayed, "help the weakest of thy children, for my spirit fainteth."

The pale outline of a superb temple floated in the air about him. He snatched his pencil and unrolled his paper, but the vague, formless thing faded like a dissolving view, the dizzy pinnacles floated away. Overcome with the long mental strain, he burst into tears of despair and exclaimed: "Into thy hands, O Mary, I leave it!" Then a sweet peace descended on him like a dove.

He sunk to sleep in his oaken chair, and at the mystic hour of midnight, when the veil between the two worlds, seen and unseen, grows dim, he was roused by an awakening light. It was not like the sun, nor yet of the moon; neither was it a lamp nor the light of tapers. Awe-struck and enraptured, he sat still while his cell filled with the heavenly radiance. His eyes gradually became used to the shining wonder, and he was aware of the presence of four men with starry crowns on their heads.

The first was a grave man with venerable white beard covering his breast; in his hand he held a pair of compasses; the second, more youthful in appearance, carried a mason's square; the third, a strong man with heavy curling beard, held a rule; and the fourth, a handsome lad with light flowing auburn locks, brought a level: thus betokening that they were masters of the sacred art of Freemasonry. They glided in with solemn, soundless tread, and with them, last to come into his dazzled sight, entered the saintly Virgin, clothed with celestial beauty, carrying in her right hand a lily with silver-white flowers.

"I have heard thy prayer, and am here to help thee in thy need," said the Virgin, to the awe-stricken architect. "One penalty I lay upon thee."

" What is it, O Queen of Heaven?'

14

" For wordly ambition, and because thou hast
said in thy heart, Solomon, I will surpass thee,
thy name shall be forgotten among the sons of
men."

" But," cried the disappointed artisan, "it is in
hope of fame I have toiled, prayed, suffered. I
have outwatched Orion, and the sun has looked
down upon me as it rose. The cathedral of my
heart and soul is to be the monument which he
who sees will ask in wonder and amaze, Who
was the architect?"

" There is but one condition," said Mary,
mildly; "choose this instant, the hour passes."

He covered his face with his hands and wept
aloud; a few moments his sobs echoed through
the cell and the struggle was past. He raised
his eyes to the Blessed Virgin in thankfulness,
and exclaimed: " If only my holy work lives
on, I am content that my name is written in
heaven."

" I shall write it with my own hand in the
Book of Remembrance, where the prayers of the
Saints are recorded, for thou art worthy," said the
tender voice. " In six centuries, as men count
time, the cathedral will be finished, hallowed by
the prayers of such disciples as thou, and radiant
with angelic light."

She made a sign of command to the master-
masons, and they sketched with rapid touches a
design which shone like fire on the bare walls of
the cell. The forest of stone pillars shot on
high, the arches curved to meet them, and two
majestic towers, flying-buttresses and pinnacles,

went up higher and higher, like winged things, into the blue of heaven. In silence the old monk (I grieve that his name is lost) contemplated the divine revelation.

When the gray light of dawn stole into his cell the vision softly faded, but the plans drawn by the four masters of the art of architecture under the eye of the Virgin-Mother were burned into his memory. The cool breeze of morning fanned his forehead, and the sun cheerily looked into his narrow window. It was not the fever of a madman nor the delusion of Satan. He rose and whispered, " When I wash my forehead with fresh dew the mists will clear away." He went into the garden and walked an hour, all the while in prayer. He returned to his cell and spread the untouched parchment. An invisible force guided his hand swiftly as light travels. Ground-plan and elevation, longitudinal and transverse sections, delicate detail drawings were made before noon, and when the minster clock struck twelve, the happy architect laid his per-fected sketch at the foot of the throne.

But such a work, firm as adamant, light as lace, lovely as music, is not complete in one, two, or three generations, and after exhausting wars the masons were dismissed by the government. Then at night the ghost of the architect would walk the walls, moaning like the wind in the pines : " I cannot rest till this work goes on ; my bed is hard, it is no place of rest till the men come back to their sheds." He was always dressed in green (for German ghosts are not sworn to white robes), with a gray cap on his head, a measuring rod and pair of compasses in his hand.

Not till the times of the good Emperor William was the finial wreath of stone foliage laid in place, just six hundred and thirty-two years to a day after the laying of the first foundation. And thus was created the fairest temple outside the City of Precious Stones. Fit resting place for the shrine of the Wise Men from the East—the Three Kings of Cologne.

XX.

IN THE ISLE OF THE LILY: THALIA'S STORY.

Breakfast was over. A breakfast of white bread, fresh butter, eggs, and coffee. By some witchcraft Hassan brought luxury into the Isle of the Lily, and we asked no questions about the *menu*. He went to market at unknown hours and in mythical regions; conjured up capital stews and salads, ordered them served in the dining-tent, and waved them off with his hanging sleeves. All with the noiseless movement peculiar to Egyptians who name themselves messengers of the Djinns.

We were under the palms with carpet, cushions, and fans; the gentlemen to smoke, the ladies somewhat conscience-smitten at doing nothing. But ours was a *Riposa*. Avaunt, visions of guides and guide books, of "improved" minds, of culture, and æsthetics. Dinners, Receptions, Clubs, Socials are griefs and cares for far dwellers beyond the seas. We are in the all-golden month of *Rest*.

"This is my time," said Thalia, dropping into an attitude of easy grace on a cushion, and folding her feet under her as though to the manner born. "I am Scherezade, for once. Let us give up useful knowledge through one day" (as though she had ever tried the search), "and quit hunting facts. Your long tale of the Magi, Mr. Graham, excuse me, your short story of the Wise Men, reminds me of something I read in an odd book I had from the Congressional Library."

"What book?" asked the man who loves accurate information from odd books.

"I don't remember the name," answered Thalia, tartly; "don't expect it. It is in one of the two hundred thousand volumes. To begin,"— she softened her tone—" It was when the Holy Family fled from Bethlehem. In the year one, if you are anxious about the date," she darted a quick glance at Antiquary, who nodded approvingly. "The ox and the ass which had stood by the manger went with them, and Mary rode a gentle white mule named some dreadful Hebrew word, I can't remember."

"Perhaps Eleabthona, if you allow a suggestion."

"Like enough that's it, but I can't tell. It was very intelligent, and its name meant 'trust yourself to it.' The baby was in her lap, and Joseph led the kind creature by the bridle."

"There were no bridles, it was a leading strap."

" Well, whatever it was, please don't interrupt
with such trifles, for I shall make worse mis-
takes before I am done. As I was saying, they
went out by night, warned by the voice heard in
Joseph's second vision. An angel marched
ahead, carrying a lantern. I suppose it was
Gabriel, the Messenger. No, it couldn't have
been, either, because he always bears the lily."
She spoke with child-like simplicity and certainty. "Anyhow, it was a brave, strong-winged
angel. There were the poor dead children lying
on the roadside, crying mothers bending over
them, trying to hide their living babies from
the butchers. And they even climbed the hill
Zion to escape the terrible danger.

"Jerusalem was then the joy of the whole
earth, not as we saw it last month. May I
recite the poem of a Jew over the lost glory of
the city of his love?"

" You may if it's not too long. We are too
weak to bear a long poem."

"Only sixteen lines showing the difference
between Mary's time and now. Hear him :—

> " ' On the noble heights of Zion
>   Where were held the golden revels,
>   Whose rare splendor once bore witness
>   To the glory of the monarch.
>
> " ' There by noisome weeds o'ercovered,
>   Now you find gray heaps of rubbish,
>   Of such melancholy aspect,
>   You would fancy they were weeping.
>
> " ' And 'tis said they weep in earnest,
>   Once in every year, upon the
>   Ninth day of the month of Ab.
>   Mine own eyes were overflowing,

> " ' As I saw the heavy tear-drops
> Glittering on the mighty ruins,
> As I heard the lamentation
> Of the broken Temple-columns.'

"To resume," continued Thalia. "The young Child and his mother and St. Joseph went along, guided by the angel. Of all the angels, I love Gabriel best"—she mentioned him as a dear friend—"perhaps because he is so often named, he seems more familiar than the rest."

"Yes," added Antiquary, humoring her mood, "he is a prophet, and explains visions, and he declared to Mary, 'I am Gabriel that stand in the presence of God,' as though he were nearer the throne than other angelic beings. He foretold the birth of Samson, and among Moslem's has the twofold character of Saint and Prophet. Mohammed selected him as his teacher and inspirer, and it was this messenger who gave him the Koran, and though the prophet could not read caused him to understand it."

The scholar continued with gravity and dignity respecting the fancies of the young enthusiast :—

"But the Prince of guardian spirits, the watchful one of all humanity, is Raphael. He is probably the one who guided the pilgrims on their flight from Bethlehem. According to Milton he was sent by the Creator to warn Adam, and he breakfasted with the first pair one forenoon in Eden. The early Christians tell that he appeared to the shepherds by night with good tidings of great joy which shall be for all people.

"In the Pitti is a picture of him, robed in

white, with wings of a deep rose color, and a
casket slung over his shoulder by a golden belt,
to denote that he is a traveler, and the rescuer
of such as lose their path. The friend of the
wayfarer, the young, the straying. His flowing
locks, of deep auburn tint, are wonderfully beautiful, the face serene and seraphic. But I interrupt your story. Pardon."

"Yes, a mere brief parenthesis. As I was
telling, Herod heard of their flight, and sent soldiers after the Holy Family. When they were
some way from the city they came to a field
where a man was sowing wheat.

"Many days passed in a holy manner had
given the Virgin wisdom, and she was at no
loss what to do. She was not as other women,
as her Son was not as other men. So she cried
out to the sower, 'If soldiers come this way and
ask if strangers such as we have passed, and
have ye seen us? you must answer, Such persons have appeared, it was when I was sowing
this grain.' The man was a rough fellow,
dressed in skins, and must have looked fierce
and shaggy in the dark. He saw these were no
common pilgrims, and this mother, calm and
confident among the lamentation and weeping and
great mourning, must have been moving under
some high inspiration."

"You are right there, my dear."

"Thank you," said Thalia gratefully. "I do
not know if the leading angel was visible to his
eyes or not; perhaps he was permitted a glimpse
of glossy wings or a hint of some bright pres-

ence. He bowed low in salutation, saying, 'Peace be unto thee and thine, young Mother; may the son in thy bosom be a wise man and a just, and stand in the gates with the elders of the city.'

"He felt that something strange was going to happen, and was so sure that he determined to sit up and watch. Soon there was a rustling, creeping sound, the ground was moving, not in noise and earthquake, but shaking and stirring. The grains slipped through their husk, the field was alive with growth. By midnight the wheat came up to his knees; the sower was amazed, but not afraid. It grew to his waist. The miracle went on all night: the stalk, the blade, the full ear, and when the sun rose it was on a rich harvest, with ripe yellow grain ready for the reaper.

"The husbandman sent a boy to his hut on the hillside, where a fig-tree shaded the spring, with words to quiet his mother, and directed him to bring his sickle. 'Great things have been done to-night, and I must not leave this post till I deliver the message of the woman with the baby.' He held the message of the Virgin as a sacred command.

"And sure enough in the morning watch came the soldiers—bloody murderers, like ravening wolves—and inquired, 'Have you seen a well-favored young woman, with a child in her arms, traveling this way? She was seated on an ass led by an old man, and they were moving in haste.' The joyful reaper who was reaping his

harvest in great wonder and admiration, waved
his blade high in the air so it a made a circle of
light, and answered, 'Yes, I saw them not very
long ago.'

"'How long since?' asked the head soldier.

"He replied, quietly, 'When I was sowing this
wheat.'

"Then the officers of Herod ordered the soldiers back to Jerusalem, and left off hunting the
Holy Family."

"A pretty fable," said Antiquary "but" (con-
trarily,) "it doesn't hang together well. The historian has not kept up the unities."

"Why not, sir?" said Thalia. She calls him
Sir when she wishes to be crushing.

"The records make it appear that Herod felt
he had destroyed the Child in the murder of the
Innocents at Bethlehem."

"Well, well, I think you might let my story
go without looking into it as a fact. How can
Scherezade continue, if the Caliph bothers her
with suspicious questions?"

And she smiled and pouted her pretty lip a
little. Scherezade herself was not more charming than our spoiled darling. Never did the
Sultana look prettier than she in the muslin
dress dotted with purple, the palm-tree shade
casting restless flecks on her head, making a
glory of her hair.

"Let it pass then. I shall have to ask your
unquestioning faith in the robber-story promised
yesterday."

"No time like the present, let us have it now."

"Yes, I was leading up to that, as the lecturers say. Now for it. At the close of a weary day in the flight when they looked not back, pressing on as fast as the slow-plodding ass could move, the fugitives stopped at the open door, or rather entrance, of a cave, the stronghold of a Bedouin chief, who was, after the manner of his tribe, a thief and a robber. The Arab has not changed since the times of Herod. He welcomes the stranger to his black tent or robber fastness, as one having the right by law to all that is within it. Be the guest his worst enemy, he will slay his best kid and bring forth his choicest stores to treat him; will serve him three days with sacred hospitality, as it is commanded; will set him fairly on his way; and then, by another law equally respected, kill him if he can. Should you plead that you are a harmless, defenceless traveler, his answer is, that you have no business to be unarmed and defenceless; the ancient proverb, ' In the Desert no man meets a friend,' should be known to you, and acted on accordingly. He has a long lance, a swift horse, a keen eye; who has none should stay at home. He looks on books with haughty scorn, and quotes a favorite saying, ' There is more life in one word from the mouth than in one thousand from the pen.'

"The Holy Family did not think to beard the old lion in his den, hard rider and deadly archer as he was; but the descendant of Ishmael happened to be standing in the entrance in the cool of the day, and he beckoned them to stop, and received them into the recess of the mountain which was his present refuge.

"Like all limestone formations the hills of Palestine abound in caves. The remotest histories treat of them as hiding-places and burial-grounds. There is a long line of cave-tombs, partly natural, partly artificial, openings in the rocky walls of Judean valleys, beginning with the cave of Machpelah, and ending with the grave of Lazarus which, in the reading, was a cave, and a stone lay upon it; and the Holy Sepulcher hewn in the rock wherein never man before was laid. They were defences for insurgents and outlaws; and rebel hordes yet fortify themselves in the ancient underground chambers.

"My nurse used to enlarge on the horrors of the sepulchral grotto, where torches flamed with feeble flicker, lighting a little way in with red flame that was soon overcome by the pitch-black darkness. It had awful echoes, too, so that when anyone spoke loudly, the sound would come back like roaring of hungry beasts, or voices of dreadful demons hidden in the dark. I generously spare you the recital of the terrors with which she filled the mountain-side, all seamed with rocky fissures and yawning rents.

"The chief who could ride full-faced against the spear-blades and not blench or quiver, ministered to the dusty, travel-worn pilgrims, with courtesy, gave them of seethed goat's flesh, black bread and dried sugary dates. All he had, the gaunt Arab spread before the unknown wanderers, and the ass was loosed and turned

out to graze on the camel-thorn. The robber's
wife came down from her pride of place as a
chieftainess, saluted the Virgin kindly, and
brought water for her to bathe the child.

"In that thirsty region water is life, and not
the smallest portion of the precious fluid is
wasted. So when Mary had bathed the infant
Jesus, the Bedouin mother used the same water
for her own child, and lo! it took on the brightness of the sun, and for a moment the whole
cavern was illuminated. Then the woman knew
that, like the Friend of Guests in Mamre, they
had entertained angels unawares, and sooner or
later a blessing would descend on the tribe.
They slept in peace and safety; the spear of the
robber, seasoned in many battles, was planted
before the door, and the chief himself went a
day's march, and sent them on their way rejoicing. His eyes were too sinful to see the angel
guard which journeyed in the airs about them,
but the heavenly watchers were on duty, vigilant and well-pleased.

"The robber's boy grew to be a bad man like
his father, only wilder and worse. He scrupled
not to murder the stranger guest as soon as he
passed beyond the shadow of the tent, or the
portal of the cave. The wayfarer in the mountain pass was his prey; unheeded the cry of
children, the prayers of women. A notorious
criminal, he was finally overtaken, brought to
judgment, tried and condemned to death on the
cross at Jerusalem. When the Great Tragedy
was enacted on Calvary, the angel nature which

came to him in the baptismal water was stirred.
His life passed in review before him, as it does
to the eyes of the dying. He remembered his
sinless childhood, and the water made a saving
grace thirty-three years before by the touch of
Mary's Son. He called to the Man of Nazareth
on the cross beside him, 'Lord remember me
when Thou comest into Thy kingdom'—and in
the horror of darkness and the crash of the
earthquake was borne to his ear already dull in
death, the gracious words, 'Verily I say unto
thee, to-day shalt thou be with me in Paradise.'
The robber's child was the penitent thief."

"You tell the story as if you believed it."

"Yes; but not so implicitly as I did when
first heard. The cave was near Ramlah, and is
still in evil repute, a favorite lurk for brigands.
It was the Ramlah of the Lion Heart, and the
Crusaders used to visit the shrine,—for such it
was—with devotion and there renew their vows.
Do you think there is harm in believing these
things, myths though they be?"

"There can be none. Better to trust over-
much, to believe in miracles and dreams, than
drop into the sneer and scoffing which destroy
every sentiment of reverence. Yes, better bow
down to the Sun and Moon, Baal and Ashtaroth,
than crush the sense of worship out of the
heart by neglect of all religion. If only
a plaster-image of Mary by the wayside, to
which the Italian peasant uncovers his head, it
is the sign of a reverence for something dear
and sacred, away down deep in his heart."

XXI.

STILL IN THE ISLE OF THE LILY: THE ANTI-QUARY'S STORY.

THE Turks of Constantinople tell that on Easter mornings, the Faithful at prayer in the Mosque of St. Sophia have heard hymns of Christians who once held the Church of Justinian, and fought and died in its defence. Moslem worshipers, on that day, kneeling with face toward Mecca, are conscious of mystical presences in the high, hollow dome overhead. It is gorgeous in dark color, vast and vague, not silvery like the jewel-glass of the North, and invisible singers fill the space with a delicate music, sweet past telling. Such as we may suppose pale wanderers, spirits freed might breathe in their lost temple of holiness, wrested from them by the conquering sword of Islam.

The Infidel never notes this blissful music. It is only sounded in the ear of the true believer for whom the Blackeyed hold their predestined places in Paradise. Perhaps the musicians are messengers of the strong-winged angel, in imperial purple robe and red shoes, who revealed the plan of St. Sophia to the architect. The happy builder who exclaimed, "Glory to God who has judged me worthy to complete this work. Solomon, I have surpassed thee!" Maybe it is one of the psalms the devout Constantine chanted with the priests, after each twelve layers of Rhodian bricks were laid. The words are unknown, but the true Moslem hears that marvelous music every Easter morning, as something wafted through the open door of Paradise.

And thus, one night, I thought we might almost catch the minstrelsy of the vanished occupants of the Isle of the Lily who sleep in forgotten graves. In dreams and wakeful visions we might hearken to hymns of priestesses, graceful and sweet as the lotus held in their hands, and to the subdued voices of men strong as lions, wearing the ancient stiff head-gear, and bearing incense to the water-god who ruled the Seasons and the harvests. Slow and solemn their steps, low, mysterious their intoning as they worked their miracles of power.

The night I speak of, the moon obscured all but the first stars which shone large and lustrous like clear white lamps. We could see to read by the silver radiance, but we had no wish to read; we were to forget the world. Determined to have absolute rest in that little strip of earth, we found our thoughts concentrated on our past lives and our own experiences, the idleness of introspection.

The Simoom had blown through the day. Puffs of hot air came sighing and sobbing over the blank sand levels, making the air murky with yellow dust carried on the wings of the wind. The Arabs call it Khamseen, a burning breath, often deadly as plague or pestilence. Twilight fell as balm on parched leaf and heated plain; the wind changed, and evening came, with refreshing to withering plant and panting animal.

"I wish," said one, "this was a floating Isle, and that we could waft it away to some other river or sea when the desert wind fans it."

"Yes, or that some miraculous shade might be drawn over the sun, or strange verdure cool and dim the sky, as the green-winged bird came before the eyes of Thalaba and veiled them in the desert."

"While we are at it, we may as well wish for a bracing breeze at once; one of the gracious gales heaven sends to the verdant vales bounded by mountains."

We had noticed that the Antiquary had been restless and moody through the long hours, and supposed it was the quieting effect of the Simoom. We felt the force of Isaiah's texts, and of Job, when he says, "How thy garments are warm, when He quieteth the earth by the south wind." Our garments were not merely warm—they were hot and intolerably heavy and uncomfortable. We were lounging beside the palms, more languid than usual under the influence of the dreaded blast we name Sirocco.

Said Antiquary softly, and with a sense of weariness. "I have been wandering in imagination among mountain airs to-day, and drinking at secret wells of the coldest and brightest of waters."

"At Tivoli, you mean."

15

"No, no, many a hundred miles away from Tivoli. At Monterey in Old Mexico."

"I did not know you had visited that un-happy country."

He rose, shifted his camp-stool, so as to place his profile to the strong moonlight, making his shadow fall, a sharp silhouette on the level ground.

"Would you know me by that?" He pointed to the image, and spoke with a sort of wistful-ness in his tone.

"Never, I should not guess if I had a hundred guesses, who is the substance."

"Yet it is more like me than the man, or rather boy of twenty years, at Monterey. A Lieutenant in the Mexican war, thirty-six years ago."

"You a soldier! I never knew it."

"No; unlike most soldiers, I rarely refer to that passage in my history. We were the First Indiana Volunteers. And while regiment after regiment passed to active service in the field of glory and conquest, ours remained here and there, stationed to guard stores. How we chafed and fretted under orders which kept us idle in the dreary round of camp duty in the enemy's country! Yet we lost more men by sickness than any other regiment did in battle. To re-sist the depressing influence of hospital and sur-geon taxes a man's resources to their utmost. Reckless gambling and hard drinking take the place of wholesome work and recreation fairly won by labor. It is most demoralizing to heart and mind, and the contagion of spirit is deadlier than that of the body."

He paused, and his face changed strangely. His voice sunk to a whisper. "It was in Monterey I had my romance."

We respected his feeling, and for a moment nothing was heard but the low wash of the wavelets and the cry of a jackal from the neighboring Island.

"Mine is but the old, old story—'She was beautiful, and he loved her.' Would you care to hear it?" He spoke modestly, as one not used to intruding the capital *I* on his audience.

"That we should. There is nothing half so interesting as a glimpse of the interior life. It is worth many an hour in the unmeaning round called Society, where we speak in platitudes as though words were indeed made to conceal thoughts."

"You are quite right; but our training makes it a sort of indelicacy to unlock the bridal chambers of the heart. Our English cousins blurt out family histories we would die to hide. I cannot understand Froude holding up the naked soul of Jeannie Carlyle—fondest and proudest of women —to the public gaze; and Bulwer giving us the vices of his nearest of kin, till the relatives of his mother rose in indignation at the shameful exposure. And all for money. Whatever American faults may be, profaning the sanctity of home and making a market of gossip no outer ear should hear are not among them. We guard them like criminal revelations—those fire-

side tragedies—to open them to the world is to
make common a sanctuary."

We disposed ourselves in the attitude of
listeners. Thalia smoothed her cushions. I
wrapped a scarf round my throat; the speaker
bared his head, throwing his palmetto hat on the
ground, his thin gray hair stirring lightly in the
pleasant breeze.

"You would not imagine these the blonde,
wavy locks of a romantic youth." He shook
his head, sadly. "A reader of Moore and of
Byron, whose chief affectation was quoting 'I
have loved the world nor the world me,' and
luxuriating in a soft melancholy."

"Verily, I should not," said Mistress Thalia.

"Only the angels you love, the white-winged
Angel of the Resurrection can smooth these fur-
rows from my forehead, these silver threads out
of my hair. In Monterey there was an old
Spanish Cathedral, crumbling in dimness and
neglect, which has—or rather had forty years
ago—a wonderful chime of bells. When we
were encamped outside the city its peals reached
us at evening, and the *Angelus* was never sweeter,
not even in Florence, sounding from the glorious
tower which Charles the Fifth said should be
kept under glass, and exhibited only on holidays. I never hear it but it makes me a dreamer
of dreams, of what was and what might have
been, but for one old man's stubbornness."

He stopped, hovering about his subject as
though scarcely knowing how to begin.

"The ringing of bells is to many no more

than the breaking of the surf on the shore; with you it is the call of the church to prayer. With me the *Angelus* is a melody which never dies from my heart, for it is forever associated with love."

I started slightly, unconsciously.

" Yes, you may well stir with surprise at the idea. I do not look like a subject for fiery absorbing passion; but," he pointed to the shadow on the ground, " that Shade was once of a different being. I was one of your hand-some men, proud, restless, ambitious, with a poet's heart without his power to sing. That Shadow cannot answer to your ideal of me any more than the bare branches of your beach-trees in winter can give a suggestion of verdure, the smile of spring on every bough."

" Would you mind telling us?"

" With pleasure—and pain. We were a lawless set—we soldiers encamped near Monterey in 1848. Discipline was loose, and some-times under leave, oftener without, I used to frequent a brook not far from camp and add a mess of trout to our dinner of bacon and beans. The brook headed in a delicious spring, shaded by dripping ferns, tangles of wild blue larkspur, and yellow lilies. One of a series of springs which fed the dancing, flashing meadow-brook that gurgled among purple flags and ended in a narrow river.

" I loved the place. Its loneliness was a relief against the ennui of camp, and the coarse games and jests of my messmates. Many a pleasant

hour I spent there alone, hearing friendly mes-
sages, as he who seeks Nature must ever, and so
had solace from much annoyance. Further
away were dark chapparal thickets of thorn and
underbrush, so close set a coyote could not crawl
through them, and beyond the mountains were
flat pastures, measureless as air.

"Beside this spring I met my fate: and never
did destiny come in fairer form. It was at the
close of a summer day, hot but not lifeless, for
the mountain freshness never quite forsakes that
atmosphere. I stood among gray lichens and
water-grass of golden green, arranging the bait
on my hook, when I heard voices speaking
Spanish; not the mixed patois of the Mexican,
but the finer accent of pure Castilian. It was
the first time my solitude had been broken.
Both voices were feminine; one childish in
pitch, the other in the harshness which is one of
the harshest things we submit to from age.
With recollections of College Latin, a gram-
mar, and the help of a priest lean and hungry as
Cassius, I had picked up enough Spanish to comprehend ordinary talk. This ran on a lost bird
which had flown away, and they were pursuing
with the help of a man servant. They came so
near I could hear the crackling twigs snap beneath their tread, but I stood silent in shelter
under the bank which served for a roof.

"I heard them trample in the undergrowth;
cries of delight from the childish voice, cautions
to the man Popo to be careful; the screaming of
the bird captured and put back in his cage with

lavish endearing words of which the Spanish
language is full. The sounds gradually receded,
and I stole from my hiding-place, not feeling
guilty, not I ; but delighted with the adventure
if such it could be called.

"The little mistress of the bird was young,
but not too young for my interest. I determined to see. I struck the blind trail through
the mezquit grove, and saw a fat woman in the
broader path ahead. Boldly but cautiously I
followed, and noted, obscured by the ample
width of the matron, a shape of girlish
slenderness. How young, I could not guess,
but old enough (though for that matter
foreign women are always old enough), to be
watched. Both were dressed in mourning, and
were followed by a man carrying a gilded bird-
cage, and in it a green paroquet. My fishing
came to a conclusion abrupt as the reading of
Dante's lovers. I strolled back to quarters,
feeling sure who the unknown was.

"In a walled garden, about two miles away,
stood a gloomy, tumble-down mansion, ricketty,
with loose lattices, called by the natives, *El Palacio.* It was occupied by a Spaniard who, gos-
sips said, had fled from political storms to the
New World and taken his residence in this castle or country-place which, till then, had long
been desolate and tenantless. I had noticed its
wall of rough stone bristling with cactus-hedges,
behind which bananas waved their green flags,
and oleanders showered pink blossoms in their
season. I had scented magnolia and orange-

bloom in the path, and old rose-vines and ivies
straggled over the wall, and softened the aspect
of the threatening cactus-prickles. The upper
half of the house was visible from the street;
of creamy stucco, originally the tint of Milwau-
kee brick, with colonnade and many columns
round an interior court, the usual design of
Spanish houses. Traditions of by-gone splendor
were not lacking. It had belonged to a Duke
of Albuquerque, of noble and decayed family,
who lost a fortune by gambling, and had returned to Castile. It had been in evil repute
some years, being haunted by the ghost of a lady
who died of a broken heart or of insanity.
Among a superstitious people, idle to the last
degree, the stories gained in credence, and dreadful tales were told in lurid and blood-curdling
exaggeration. *En fin* El Palacio was peopled
with baleful specters.

"The name of the present occupant was Felipe
Velasco, Hidalgo, which title means pure, Catholic, Spanish blood without a taint of Jew or
Moor. I learned by careless inquiry that the
wife died a few months before our army of occupation arrived, leaving one child, a daughter,
doubtless the young girl I had followed through
the forest. She was clad with many graces, and
unconscious witchery thrilled her captive
through and through. That night I had something to think of beside camp duty; the usual
evening lesson of Father Olmedo had a fresh
and vital interest. In my stolen march I had

caught glimpses of an oval olive face with darkest eyes."

"Like those of Oriental women," I interrupted.

"Not at all," rejoined Antiquary, testily. "There are no eyes like the girls of Cadiz; you cannot have forgotten Byron's poem. You must see them to know how lovely human eyes can be. The Señorita Velasco wore a broad straw-hat tied under the chin with a ribbon of lace." He went on, dreamily, as though talking to himself. "I see her yet, I who have forgotten so many things. A trailing vine with blue blossoms twisted round the crown gave a woodland, nymph-like air which suited well my romantic fancy.

"I was dazzled, enchanted. In fancy I scaled the wall of *El Palacio*, traversed the neglected garden, passed the ruined fountain bordered with weeds, to the interior court, where in the lazy afternoons she swung in a hammock like Marjorie Daw. But I forget, this was a generation ago, and Marjorie's father must have been a baby then. I must see this Rose of Castile; dash off with her, the lady of my choice; her father, if he opposed, must be safely lodged in a deep, black dungeon. Through the night, through the day we would gallop away into some fabled field Elysian, I hardly knew where. As I said I was born with the poetic temperament. Do not laugh."

"I was not laughing."

"Not to be blamed if you were, I absolve you.

It does not follow that I was a poet. The faculty is distinct as the faculty of feeling music is distinct from the power of producing it. The hearer who cannot whistle a tune may tremble and turn cold with emotion at the divine symphonies of Beethoven. But this is a parenthesis. I did essay writing verses, that was later. Let us not anticipate.

"The night of my adventure was cloudless, and I lay outside the tent wrapped in my blanket, and looked at the stars which are the poetry of heaven, asking what name had been written for me among those bright leaves of destiny. Absence had weakened the images of sweet girl-graduates in white dresses and blue ribbons. My future was a blank page but for this unknown nymph, this Egeria by the fountain. In the vanity of early youth I supposed myself an object of much consequence to the planets above, and one to tell grandly on the destinies of the orb to which I belong by birthright. I had little money and no fame; but with strength, education, energy, I believed the world was all before me where to choose. I was the peer of any proud Hidalgo in Spain or out of Spain; and I fell to the sound sleep of perfect health counting the shining Pleiades, and trying to trace the figure of the Scorpion.

"I became more solitary than ever. Often as possible I slipped away from camp to pass the Enchanted Palace, watching for the flutter of ribbons and the tread of light steps. It is not too much to say I was richly rewarded. I found my Inamorata was in the habit of making a daily walk with her two attendants. I could not risk a surprise, yet determined to know this Castilian beauty—Andalus all over, from the straight black hair, braided down her back, to the high-heeled shoes of the springing feet. Ah those feet! My heart was under them as she walked.

"I must enter the garden odorous with bloom, but my approach must be delicate, for she was close kept and shy as a humming bird. Daintily, guardedly, must advances be made. Let that aristocratic old father, with his tremendous nose and bald head, look out. I was Lieutenant in the Grand Army of Occupation, and away on the other side of the town from the topmost peak of the Sierra de la Silla our colors were triumphantly waving, planted there after every house was a barricade taken, almost every room a scene of blood. The city in its mountain setting was a jewel bought with a great price, and no holiday soldiering was that which brought its surrender.

"At twenty all things are possible. I determined to put my courage to the test and stake all on one audacious move. The plan was simple enough: to go bravely up in broad daylight, and announce myself an amateur artist, a traveler who begged to look at some fine pictures in *El Palacio*, said to be by Velasquez.

"Fate kindly turned that venture out of **my** hand, and gave me a better part than the masquer's I had thought to play. The old gentleman took a constitutional ride daily, on a skittish little mustang. They are always treacherous, and in one of his rides the vicious beast shied, jumped, unseated the Hidalgo by the roadside, giving him a jar which knocked him senseless."

" You speak of the ancient Hidalgo with a sort of acidity."

" Yes, I hated him because he was father of a peerless maiden, so hard and stern as not to allow unknown Lieutenants in the Grand Army of Occupation the freedom of his house. O dreams of twenty! how vain and foolish, how sweet and strong they are! My heart was rich and full to overflowing. I tell you," repeated the story-teller, vehemently, "I loved that child at once, with devotion entire as though I had known her through years. A treasure wildly wasted."

He paused a moment, a strange bird like a whippoorwill answered its mate in a near marshy thicket. Sad sound as the voices of the night are ever. What with the love-tale, the white moonlight, the dim mystery of Egypt about us almost shaping out a presence from the unseen, we listened *en rapport* with Nature and each other.

" The chances befriended me. When the mustang threw the cruel father, (of course he was cruel,) by the roadside, luckily I was on hand to help pick him up. The groom called some passing porters; a rude litter was improvised, and I marched beside it straight into fairy land. The gate was opened. I must be more prudent than daring, and left my card with the servant and with it dropped the artist scheme.

"My glance at the interior had revealed a tangled, neglected garden, gay with poppies choked in weeds; a shabby mansion, splashed with peeling stucco which betrayed red brick-work beneath. The veranda was bright with clinging vines in masses of bloom. Thus I thought this fresh young vine makes sweet the common air as she twines her life with her father's. The simile is not novel, but was newer to me then than now. It is since hacked to a sickly sentiment. The next day at mess I was startled by a note written in stiff, clerkly hand. The Señor Felipe Velasco had not recovered from his hurt, but wished to thank, in person, Lieutenant Graham, who had saved his life. Would he call.

"My heart had never stirred from its twenty years of steady strong tramp, never till that hour. It beat on my breast like the long roll of the drum. My nerves shook as they never have vibrated to earthquake or battle. I must have turned pale, for my comrades (they all are in their graves, now) rallied me on my letter. No bad news they hoped.

"I answered in a stunned, bewildered way; and in faultless costume soon set out, seeming literally to tread on air. It was morning on mount-ain, river, and plain, and morning in the young man's heart. Visions vivid as sure prophecies uprose before me. I floated my paper-boat on a summer sea, its freightage roses and roselike youth. The hero who saved Hidalgo Velasco from impending death at the heels of a kicking, biting mustang, was chivalrous, adoring as any knight errant of old. A sweet madness was it?"

He stopped abruptly, "Do you know it is near midnight?"

He wound his watch, replaced his palmetto hat, and we went each to his own place in silence, while the Antiquary paced up and down the beach like one in acute pain, now and then looking up to the starry blue as he turned on his heel with the movement which betrays the soldier. I wonder we had not noticed it before, that habit the result of military training.

As we advance in years a certain sentiment which attended early youth comes back with singular force. The circle of existence nearly complete, we look across a narrow gap to the beginning, where the start was made, and feel some portion of the freshness of the morning, when the meads were in bloom.

Several days went by, and the past was plainly the present with our friend the Antiquary. We made no allusion to his sudden opening of the Book of Revelation, but tried, by gentle touches which he was quick to perceive, to assure him that we appreciated his confidence.

Every one knows the subtle power of loneliness to bring out hidden secrets. Many a tale of the agonies, mysteries, battles, loves, and hates of life, is told in the silence of night which would never have been confessed had not the witching hour created the beguiling opportunity. Every woman knows the temptation, and O, how many know the repentance, apt to follow such a trust. The fear it will be told, either in forgetfulness or heedlessness, by the bosom friend, as indeed it usually is, comes with the common light of day. Where there is no crime involved sooner or later there is a betrayal.

In the Isle of the Lily, the unfabled Isle of the Blest, where eternal Summer holds her golden pomp, there was an effort to forget the world. We soon discovered that to loll and to dream were not the surest way. Rushing life in some swift current would drown habitual thought; but oblivion is not in languid airs spicy with scents, that touch the black keys of memory and set its tenderest chords vibrant.

After the fiery day, the mild night is potent as old music to conjure up old faces and places. We knew our Antiquary would give the sequel of his story in good time, and we were sure the good time was near. The next week after the beginning of our chapter, we sat under the palms again, by the waning moon's light, and he took up the thread as though it had not been dropped:—

"I was telling my romance," he began, abruptly, after long silence none cared to break. A simple enjoyment of earth, and sky and river. "Yes, the Sultan has beguiled Scherezade."

"We remember," I said, "and I have had it in mind ever since."

"You thought me a foolish boy, I dare say."

"No, I only thought you—young."

"Ah, yes, young. I left off going to the Palace of the Hidalgo. Happy, O, so happy! I found my natural enemy with his forehead bound in brown paper and aromatic vinegar, lying on a settee in the veranda. Glass doors opened from it into a vast, empty drawing-room cheerless with dark wood-carving, and tarnished gilding. Of the *haut noblesse* he bore an air of faded elegance becoming a man stiff in the knees, surrounded by memorials of better days, when carpets were not threadbare and the house less a crazy barn.

"He thanked me with many a compliment. I, bold as brass, disclaimed everything but ordinary courtesy. Chocolate was served in delicate cups. That rich, sweet chocolate, ambrosia, and nectar in one. I taste it yet a drink for the gods! And as I set down my cup, in came the daughter, crossing the long room, her hat filled with flowers on her arm. Her father treated her as a child, saying when she came to kiss him, 'This is Ninita, my little one,' evidently not thinking her old enough for introduction.

"To the eyes of twenty, seventeen is full maturity. She was older than Juliet when she gave the world its love-idyl, and these passionate Southern women unfold like their own seasons, not in slow, lingering buds, but quick bursting into perfect flower. She was the full-blown rose to Lieutenant John Graham. Winsome and gentle, darting glances of curiosity at me, till taking a spray of white jasmine from her basket, she shyly offered me the fragrant gift, saying, 'I thank you for Papa's escape.' I have the dust of that jasmine yet.

"I was enraptured, and murmured a few words in Spanish (I have since learned how poor they were), at which the merry maiden smiled."

"Was she really beautiful?"

"Undoubtedly. The rich olive complexion Murillo loved to paint, the brightest eyes under long curving lashes, rarely seen except in little children, and a dimple in her chin"—he hesitated—"I would have given kingdoms to plant one kiss there.

"Spanish manner is a glossy veneer which stands the wear of three-score years in any climate. Señor Velasco came down from his high stilts, and challenged me to a game of chess. Though a crack player, I allowed him to beat me, and while the game went on the young enchantress leaned over her father's shoulder, now and then sipped the chocolate, and—stole my heart away. You do not know Monterey?"

"No I have not been further South than New Orleans."

"It is a bit of Spain dropt on the Western Continent. Enclosed on three sides with mountains; sheer cliffs broken by dark defiles and dreary cañons. The changeable colors of the Sierras Madres, 'the mother mountains,' are unspeakably beautiful. They might not look so high and grand since I have crossed the Alps, but they were the first I had lived among, and

16

were robed with peculiar charm to one fresh from
the tameness of the prairie. And the veiling
clouds of these Madres are fine and fleecy as the
mystic veils of gauze which slightly screen the
chosen beauties of the Seraglios. In the heart
of the city is a chain of cool, clear springs which
unite at last in the river. The Plaza is worthy
of Seville. Remember I see it with the eyes of
youth, and so seeing will take off my glasses."

He removed the green goggles, rubbed them
with the scrap of chamois, and returned them to
his vest pocket. Then he brought his slender
finger-tips together, and continued, rather prosily,
if the truth must be told.

"There is a marble fountain in the center,
whose dolphins would not shame a master. The
paths, outlined with wicker work of cane and
shaded by banana and orange-trees, were bordered with violets. Very pleasant to stroll
along those white cemented walks when the
band played at evening, and all Monterey walked
among the blushing alleys of bloom. Yes,
Monterey was an interesting place, and not without historic association, for there was kept the
silken flag of Cortez, the incarnadine banner, a
red trophy faded now to a coffee-color. And
there, anciently, Aztec monarchs in pensive
strain, sung the vanities of life in the depths of
their harems, like the Judean King at Bethlehem. And in that Western Orient came maidens to the springs with water-jars of dull red
pottery on their shoulders, as they do in Syria.
In the Plaza sometimes walked among the

flowers, (herself a fairer flower) my Niñita, attended by her father, oftenest by the fat aunt.

"In a crazy tower, reached by an outer stairway whose stones have been worn into hollows by tramping feet, was the wonderful chime of bells, where the ringers rang with a will and set wild echoes flying. They jarred the windows of Memory; sounded through every hall; and must have reverberated even to the vaults below where they say the Inquisition was once held. I used to sit by the plashing fountain, in airs heavy with orange and citron, and watch my daughter of Castile. A vision of loveliness in that tropic wilderness of sweets. Many expectant watched for their lovers, but she was chiefest among ten thousand.

"Once I saw her marching in a religious procession, after attending a Mass of jubilant music, viol and cornet answering like signals from heaven. It was in May, the Virgin's Month; the Image of the Blessed Mother was born aloft in front of girls in white, wearing wreaths of orange-flowers and flowing veils; in their hands they carried white lilies. Following them, were scarlet-robed boys singing, and priests with tinkling bells and swinging censers; a motley crowd in the rear. They knelt before the altars of various saints; the sacred litter with its Holy Image rested on the lace-covered shrines; and all knelt while hymns were chanted and flowers strewn. A pretty custom. Dared I think of a lay when she should indeed be a bride, not of the

Church, but I beside her, proud and happy, calling her my own?

"Away over the topmost peak of the Sierra
de la Silla streamed our flag, the banner of glory
and beauty, emblem of conquest over an empire
till then the largest in the world after Russia
and China. My country's pride, stars unsullied
as those in the sky, to die for it was no sacrifice.
In patriotic fervor I blest and saluted it. Among
the leaves and the waters the strange clanging
bells rung on, and I vowed a vow that the Rose
of Castile should not droop and perish among
the pale nuns of the ghostly convent, but should
live by my side, with nothing to do but to love
and be loved by me.

"My summer ripened; the visits at *El Palacio*
grew more and more frequent; for Señor Velasco
was badly bored, and chess was a grand resource.
The little maid who unconsciously had bound
me captive, came in regularly with the chocolate, leaned on her father, watching the game;
and my heart like a prisoner pacing drearily his
cell would start at her glance and knock on its
walls till I fancied she *must* hear it.

"I had ventured on a few words, and she met
me half way, naturally, like a fearless child; as
artless as modest. I knew better than to go
beyond the merest commonplace. As to bribing
the duenna, stealing a meeting or smuggling a
note, none of these were to be thought of. I
knew the first hint of admiration would send
her to her chamber under bolt and bar, lost to
me forever. In those days I had not scrupled

to do such deeds, would have gloried in them
had I been sure of success.

"One hot summer day, when the señor had
beaten me, and was in high good humor, we
walked in the perfumed shade of the veranda,
and listened to a song Niñita sung with guitar
accompaniment called the 'Flower of Spain.'
The very cry of the Moor was in the strain, the
burning passion of Othello, and the plaint of the
nightingale breathed in the melody. It swept
through my soul like flame, and I burst into un
controllable words, not to be remembered, nor to
be uttered now if they were. Words which
must have moved the old Hidalgo, for I could
see his lips quiver under the white mustache.

"'Has my child given you cause, by word or
sign, to think your suit would be acceptable?'"

"'Never. I have seen her only in your presence; but I love her as wholly as I could after
years acquaintance. She is transparent as sunlight.' He held up his hand, that lean, wiry,
Spanish hand, slightly waving it in token of
dissent.

"'I know all you would say, young man, and
I like you.' He stopped at the extreme end of
the porch, 'Wait a moment,' he said, hesitating.
The all golden evening was deepening to crimson;
the amber mountain rim changing to royal colors
well named the king's; up the zenith evening's
gray was spreading.

"'I am almost without kin,' he said, laying his
hand on my shoulder; 'as you see, aging fast,
an exile impoverished by the vices of my an-

cestors. My daughter, who is dear to me as the blood-drops in my heart, has been nurtured in luxurious habits, and knows little of money— nothing of the want of it. You have no inherit- ance, you say.'

"'No,' I broke out again; 'but I have what can make fortune—strength, energy, education, incentive, opportunity. Give me a hope I may address your daughter; point a career worthy of me, and I will run the race you set before me or die.'

"'It cannot be,' he answered, quietly and de- terminedly; 'if for no other reason than because your religion divides you.'

"'But I will enter the Roman Church,' I ex- claimed wildly. 'What difference do a few forms make in one's creeds?'

"Velasco must have thought me insane to re- nounce the faith of my fathers for the bare chance of winning a woman, in his sight a school- girl.

"'I have other plans when she is old enough.'

"'May I inquire them?' I asked, with an injured feeling; for no father could love or had loved as I did. His hand slipped down my arm and rested in my hand. How cool it was against my fevered palm. The action meant I must hurt you, but not in hate. 'Youth is headstrong and violent. There is not a throb of your pulse which I have not felt for her mother. It will quiet as mine has. The heyday in your blood will tame and wait upon your judgment, as mine does.'

"'Never, never! while it beats at all—' He did not heed the interruption.

"'I hope to return to Valadolid, next year. Niñita will be thrown with a cousin her equal in rank, heir to an unencumbered estate, something rare in the Castiles. She will have a choice—I will not force her heart—marriage with him or the Church. The Convent is a safe retreat for a fatherless girl, which she must be before a great while.'

" *She* to be walled up in a convent, in gloomy corridors and mouldy, dingy cells! The idea was a bitter blow. From the unseen singer—the subject of our conversation—words like these came, the very voice of the balmy evening.

> "'The night's heart and mine flow together,
> The music is beating for each.
> The moon's gone, the nightingale silent,
> Light and song are both in his speech.
>
> "'A spirit I cannot quiet
> Bids me bow to the unseen rod,
> I dream of a lily transplanted
> To bloom in the garden of God.'

"Then the wild, clanging bells resounded; rising, sinking, trembling, by distance mellow as organ-music in golden tubes. A heart-breaking music that said a thousand things, and seemed to say them all for me. The supreme moment of my life was passing. 'She will be true to the Church,' I murmured. 'That will be her choice.'

"'Why do you think so?'

"'I cannot give a reason. Since my suit is hopeless, let me take my leave. Before quitting this scene forever, may I see her once more as

she sits in the drawing-room? I will not touch
her hand, even, though I would, if you let me,
kiss her shadow.'

"'It is not best,' he replied with hauteur, yet
kindly. And I admitted it was not best. He
resumed with a low voice full of feeling. 'Your
frank engaging manner has won me quite.
Again, I say, how deeply I regret we ever met
or ever parted;' he listened again to the sweet
singer. 'Her fate was fixed before you came.
If either had money how glad I should be to
challenge my young friend to a life-long game of
chess.'

"Niñita never had the disagreeable habit of
striking with the nails, and the soft-troubled
strings of her guitar hummed in perfect time
while she warbled:

"'As the musky shadows that mingle,
    As star shine and flower scent made one,
    Our spirits in gladness and anguish
    Have met. Their waiting is done.'

"I pressed the Señor Velasco's hand; heard
his blessing, as I hurried through the garden,
and the voice of a spirit unknown to sin and
grief followed me."

"You never saw her afterward," said the
sympathetic Thalia, her eyes misty with tears.

"Yes, once, it was in autumn, in one of the
days of October when the earth seems to sleep.
Such days come only to North America and
Egypt. She was lost."

"Not dead!"

"No, but as well be. She was in a nun's bon-

net, calm as a marble statue, marching in line
with clasped, adoring hands. It was All Souls'
Day when the nation prays in the churches, each
for his own dead. In the center of every dark
sanctuary the black funeral dais stands surrounded by flickering candles and grim sugges-
tions. The altars are shrouded in crape and
armorial banners bearing in Spanish the legend,
'Remember the Dead.' On that gloomy fête I
saw her moving toward the cemetery, where the
black-robed crowd brought into sharp whiteness
the monuments and funeral urns. It would have
been less melancholy had I followed her body in
procession to the tolling of the bells for burial.

"I fancied she noticed me among the idlers
of the Plaza; one instant the clasped hands
parted, and she made a gesture of recognition.
The trees shivered to the *Miserere* and the fountains kept time to the mournful music of the
chimes. She was the bride of the Church—no
wedding-seal upon her lips.

"In this affair I had no confidant. I had a
boundless worship and unquestioning belief in
the girl of whom I knew so little. The mould
of each human face is different, and though I
look through varied faces and on all continents I
have met no eyes like hers."

"What was the unique charm?"

"What is the charm of the opal, of the heliotrope's scent, or the secret touch of the nightingale's note? I cannot describe it any more than
I can call back my lost youth and love again. It
does not come at my bidding.

"Soon afterward, our army disbanded. Before leaving Monterey I made a farewell visit to the fountain of my Egeria, where happy phantoms danced with the flashing brook. I knelt among the ferns with hairlike stems and tiny flowers, and the ripples broke on my cheek like a dewy kiss, as I drank my fill. A few tears dropped into the braided stream, and so passed my first deep experience.

"I turned the leaf on that chapter and opened afresh. I studied law; for I was ambitious and it was, and is the path to distinction in the Western States. The law alone should be my mistress. I never learned 'to drink the foam of the moment,' and catch the passing pleasure. I was too earnest and constant. Ever with me was the unsatisfied want, the longing for the unforgotten. It was no boyish illusion, to be dropped with outgrown garments."

"You wrote a successful book," I said, suggestively, "a child of the brain to love."

"My work on the 'Pre-Historic Man.' It cost me a world of absorbing work, went the rounds of the publishers."

"But was finally accepted."

"Yes, on condition that I paid expenses myself. The sale never reached two thousand copies. Iron mines in Pennsylvania lifted me from the compelling labor of poverty; and as to straining after the bubble called fame, who was there to rejoice in my success or lament my failure? I was like Lord Jeffries. Suppose I have rank, admirers, ten thousand a year, who is there to run home to and tell it?

"Quietly I entered the silent castle of Old Bachelorism. Its turrets and towers became possessed of strange enchantment; its dim halls are restful and care-free. But I have had one glimpse through an open door of a prophetic life far different; of a wife and dark-eyed children calling me father. The door then shut will never open again; it closed without one echo. Faint and mistlike grow the dying hues of a pictured fireside, and the craving after the ideal life is not strong now. I have left the whirlpool and the shoals, and rarely stir the bitter waters of memory. Happily for the human family, we can live only one day at a time. One day at a time I seek employment and enjoyment, and I fear no to-morrow though it may be the last."

Again he paused.

"Those nuns are short lived. The bare monotony of their days vibrating between Church and Convent is wearing to the very soul. Had she lived she would now be fifty-five years old. When she let life's flower fall she passed to the kingdom of perpetual youth. In the little cemetery of the convent-garden my first, last, only love has slept well for many and many a year.

"I think it is Chataubriand who says, ' When you have nothing else left in life, go to Rome.' I went, and became the student of Roman history. The Golden milestone has not been set up elsewhere, and Rome is still the center of the world. I grew into a liking for the Imperial city, and lingered over the traces of her footprints, from the *Insula inhospitalibus*, which the Centurion shivered when he named, to the measureless wastes well-named the Ends of the Earth. A girlish shape and flower-like face would illumine my folios sometimes. I cannot realize that the grayhaired matron is what might have been, for where death sets his seal the imprint is eternal and endureth forever. My Niñita is with the saints of her childhood.

"Not often do I summon the ghost of myself before the curtain. Here in the pause of the whirl, among the dead millions, where the dust under our feet was once alive, the temptation to ponder the near kinship of the human family presses on me. Every mummy in yon catacomb has glowed with worship intense as mine, and trembled under the chill of disappointment. 'The thing which hath been is that which shall be and there is nothing new under the sun.'

"This may be called my final flash of sentiment." He spoke with conviction. "And now the last spark is dying. I have little time left, and so—Put out the light, put out the light!"

XXII.

CONCLUSION.

OUR *Riposa* came to a sudden stop. **In the** fourth week the strangest thing happened: a shower fell. Tiny drops came pattering on the tent, and instead of closing curtains against them we ran out to receive the pleasant visitation, and stretched our hands in welcome. The Suez Canal has brought moisture, and this was hailed with delight by the dried-up Islanders. We were so rested, and so bored, that secretly we were counting the days till the thirty were past. Six more, then back to the turmoil we call civilization. Such was the situation when unexpectedly, at least to three of our party, the *Riposa* ended. It was the afternoon we stood enjoying the shower.

"Any one passing might think we haven't sense enough to come in when it rains," I observed.

"Truly, but luckily no one is passing; we are secure."

Antiquary bent his ear to the Earth, Indian fashion, using the aboriginal telephone. "Pardon," he said, "but someone *is* passing. I hear the dip of oars. The servants are in their lodge, we are in danger of invasion by a visitor."

The ladies fled to their hand-mirrors to smooth their limp and clammy dresses, and pick up their hair a little—crimps having been abandoned with other troublesome disguises.

The sound of paddles was soon clear, we heard the keel grate on the sand. Silence all, lo! the apparition of a man. A newcomer into Egypt. From lands lying nearer the North Star he brought that rapid, energetic step, that prosperous and buoyant spirit which carried him along as though he had come to conquer the Isle of the Lily.

Chicago all over, from the natty hat to the

neatly brushed shoe. No nonsense of dragging scarf or flapping tourist handkerchief about him. All was snug and neat, spick-and-span-new. Business, business, was in every line of his face, every button of his ulster.

We knew him afar, not dawdling along the dim path, and the confident manner and cheery voice were like a whiff of Lake breeze. The blood-spots in the cheek of Thalia told the tale even if she had not changed eyes with the stranger. Here was the happy triumphant lover. Our slight acquaintance, begun in London, had been saved from dying by brief letters at long intervals.

He rested his grip-sack on the ground, and shook hands heartily. The rain passed; the ladies—one blushing violently—emerged from their bower. Another hand-shaking, "One more camp-stool, Achmet!" and Allen Cameron was as much at home with us as though we had journeyed without a break since we parted at Havre two years before.

He glanced at river, earth, and sky. "How long have you borne this sort of thing?" he inquired, speaking very fast.

"Twenty-two days."

"Incredible, my friend."

"It is only the incredible which happens. We are in a *Riposa*."

"A rest which none but the dead have leisure to appreciate. I had a time tracing you. I thought to hit you at Alexandria. As well ask the stone Pharaohs as the people along the river, though I had a professional courier and boatmen who knew English. Two words are all, mind you, and they are that deceitful Americanism, 'All right.'"

He laughed, and we laughed with the gay traveler. The Chicagoan was a refreshment, and his air of reserve-force under the light and bloomy manner was irresistible. We lolled no longer on the warm cushions; we braced up and sat each in his own place fairly roused to interest in the world we call our own.

"I give you important news from the interior metropolis. Harrison was beaten. Roache nominated for Mayor on the first ballot. A calamity, a public calamity, but we will recover as we did from the strikes and the great fire. How long did you say you have existed in this old tomb of a place?"

We repeated the date.

"Heroic martyrs, tenacious of life. Do you study the fine arts of Egypt? Drawings with busts in front, heads in profile, eyes full on the side-face, and call it divine?"

"Indeed we find the strange shapes fascinating."

"They told me at Cairo another Rameses has been unwound from his bandages; they know him by his cartouche—the Pharaoh of the Exodus. Always that particular hero done up in spices and a gilded coffin, with endless histories on the lid, rings on his fingers and toes ready for Banbury Cross. I thought he had been lying thousands of years at the bottom of the Red Sea.

There are to be high ceremonies at the opening. Khedive and dignitaries will grace the Boulak Museum with their august presences the day he is unwound from his bandages. This is the third of the Exodus Pharaohs. Maybe they were three twin brothers."

"Maybe they were, but the scientists are not always mistaken."

"Well, well, a living dog is better than a dead lion. They say there's a picture of Cleopatra not far from here on a wall of clouded alabaster."

"We haven't found it—in fact haven't hunted for it."

His restless hazel eyes had taken in all the landscape at first glance, like the prodigies on exhibition by the lecturers about memory.

"Come, Thalia," his voice sunk to a softer tone, "let us make the circuit of this Island. If it's to be found, I'd like to see the picture before I go."

"Not now, Allen," she answered, "it is too hot. We will try it later."

"But we leave in three hours."

"In three hours!"

"In three hours!"

"In three hours. Positively. I am here to rescue you from impending death by boredom. I must be in Alexandria in three days; time and tide, you know."

"We will have sun-stroke to go out now the sun is so high; rest here till sundown, Allen."

"Yes, that is my plan. Is there no shady

walk for us?" he asked, impatiently. "I'm so cramped with sitting in that canoe."

"There is nothing but these palms."

"And these," added Thalia, gently smiling, and extending her upturned hands, delicate as a baby's.

Under our friendly eyes she did not withdraw them when the stranger prest the finger-tips to his lips. Nor did she seek to hide her delight. They were at one, and Allen Cameron had made Egypt dull and faded by his bright presence.

"We must go together, or stay together, Mr. Cameron," I remarked with dignity.

"Of course, that is my plan." He took out his little account book. "We drop down to-night as far as,—let me see—let me see."

We did not wait for the name, but rushed at our trunks and boxes with unwonted activity. Our slight wardrobe was soon gathered together, and before sundown we were ready.

Even Achmet and Hassan roused as with some subtle philter in the tonic atmosphere of the newcomer. They struck up a wild barbaric air, and, keeping time, pulled at the tent-ropes and brought down the "houses of hair" in a twinkling. The cloths were folded, the poles lashed, the boxes packed, and the brown lizards crawled away from under the stones which the cook had made his pillow.

Beyond the river children were playing as if it were midsummer. The sad *Sakia* was creaking in the dreary work of the fields. It is the laziest of machines driven by the laziest of

17

laborers, but it *is* work. Wise for us not to
dash at one bound into the hurry of the West,
but to approach by slow degrees, the *Sakia*
being the mild beginning. We pushed into the
soundless current which hardly stirred the dumb
spell of the Desert.

"There is always an underflow of silence," I
observed, with sentiment.

"Yes, except when it fills up to an overflow,"
retorted the unsparing Cameron.

No use trying to impress him with the tropic
feeling.

"To have seen Egypt is a precious possession."
I added, determined not to let the heretic go
unhurt.

"It is indeed. I shall greatly enjoy the memory in State Street No. 1480, Chicago."

The red gold of sunset melted; crimson or
orange poured over the landscape and gilded the
plumes of the palms, stately and still, never to
be seen again by us.

The frail bark drifted away like a phantom
skiff, a sudden feeling of sadness came over us.
We had been so quiet and in a trance-like state
restful as sleep; now to leave it forever and take
up our weariness again. The two granite
Pharaohs sat on the banks with hands on their
knees, their feet close together, staring straight
on at nothing. Thus they have sat thousands of
years, and thus the stony eyes will be fixed
thousands of years to come. The Resurrection
will find them unchanged, and that Day seems
no further away than the long **yesterdays** rep

resented by the changeless kings. Good bye to the pillared hall where wonderful histories are illumined with vermeil and blue. We shall never see its like again. Good-bye.

The fine gold of sunset became dross; the paling twilight was dull gray; darkness curtained the land after the fiery glow which falls only from a dome of rainless blue.

I sought the hand of Thalia. It was already at home in the clasp of Allen Cameron. Darker grew the sky, deeper the river. Reedy margins echoed the screams of startled night hawks and a jackal robbed of his prey. A gray wolf was a slinking shadow seeking cover in the tangled jungle. Faint the outline of our Isle; a speck, a wavy mote, it sank into the dimness and all was as a dream when one awaketh

THE END.

ALONG THE BOSPHORUS.

ALONG THE BOSPHORUS.

TWO VOYAGES UP THE BOSPHORUS.

I.

THE FIRST VOYAGE: 1390 B.C.

IT was many and many a hundred years ago; how many, who knows? who cares? It was in the morning of time, when the earth was young, that Europe and Asia were one land, and the Black Sea and the Hellespont were great lakes, probably united by a river. In some awful convulsion of Nature—one of those tremendous throes which destroy continents and create new ones—the rocks were rent, hills torn asunder, a chasm opened and the floods of the two lakes rushed together, we can fancy, with a roar which reached to the very stars in their courses and the secret place of the thunder. The rupture left a sort of land-mark in the Cyanean Rocks at the entrance of the Black Sea, against which waves break madly, filling the air with violent noise and darkening foam—the clashing or floating rocks of the poets, destined by the gods to protect the Euxine from the prying eyes of profane curiosity.

In the heroic ages volcanic action had not

ceased; and it is likely such upheavals gave rise to the myths about Jupiter and the giants tearing up mountains and piling them to scale Olympus. Geology, poetry, tradition unite in testimony of the changes wrought by the commotions. The indentations of one shore, thus thrown up, correspond with projections of the other; on one side a bay, on the opposite a jutting point of land with strata identical.

Conflicting currents rush this way and that. A rapid, incessant one from the Black Sea to the Marmora darts from point to point on the shores, like a ball from the sides of a billiard table. The bottom is a succession of descents, over which the water tumbles with the force of a cataract. There is an under-current like that of Gibraltar and other narrow straits, which flows contrary to the upper one. Objects thrown into the Bosphorus at the extreme western end are frequently carried to the other, while at the same moment things floating on the surface are moving in precisely the opposite direction. Its length is about twenty-five miles, its greatest depth sixty fathoms, though poets are in the habit of styling it the fathomless Bosphorus. The cold, transparent stream ever flowing, ever tranquil, makes a silvery link, uniting two seas and two continents. Every line of its shining margin is drawn in graceful, sweeping curves by the Great Master's hand; every hill is a soft picture; and its banks are flowered with lovely legends which enchanted all Greece before the "Odyssey" was written.

The name was given on account of the passage, in the mythic period, of a bull—the word "Bosphorus" meaning "the Passage of the Bull." One day, Europa, daughter of King Agenor, was at play with her maidens in a meadow, such as Pan loved to pipe in, while nymphs and satyrs danced. It was near Scutari, where the heroes of the Crimea lie, the unnamed dead from the bloody field of Inkerman; there, where thirty centuries after King Agenor's time, Florence Nightingale taught us how divine a spirit may wear mortal shape, and minister to men. The story runs that the surpassing loveliness of the princess won the admiration of Jupiter, and he assumed the shape of a bull and mingled with the herds of Agenor. Struck by the gentleness of the snow-white animal, Europa and her maidens caressed it, stroked its flowing mane, hung rosy garlands on its horns, and finally, in fearless frolic, she mounted its back. The god then ran away with his prize, and, in no wise encumbered with his light burden, swam to the Thracian side of the Bosphorus, which has ever since been called Europe, in memory of that day.

The first ship which dared the perilous navigation of the Marmora and the swift-rushing currents of the channel, was the good ship *Argo*. The story takes us back to dim centuries without a date, where the flickering torch men call history gives fitful, transient light, not enough to chase phantoms and shades which haunt the cloudy spaces where dream and fable are eternally at playful war with sober truth: back to the days of the demigods, the beginnings of the glorious myths of classic Greece. An age, compared with which our own time seems the dull gray afternoon of a gold and purple dawn. It was before our British ancestors, dressed in skins of wild beasts and hiding in caves, had learned to tremble at the iron tramp of the Roman legionaries. It was before Carthage existed even in name, before Homer, grand and wise, taught men how long one singer's songs may last.

There are mole-eyed students who see only grotesque fantasies in the noble poems of the ancient minstrels. Others, made wiser by faith, find boundless depths of living glory in the religion whose hymns have become meaningless through lack of worshipers, and have been forgotten. Their last school closed with the tragedy of Hypatia.

It is the class of pleasant scholars who sometimes dream— and every one knows how dreams illumine the understanding —which we invite to a sail in the wake of the *Argo*. The magical vessel could hear and feel, and obeyed its crew as a steed that loves its rider; its lights yet glitter in the blue above, brighter than they shone of old in the broad blue seas which the heroes named as they sailed. The *Argo* was built in the twilight that surrounds the border land of old romance,

> "Magnified by the purple mist
> The dusk of centuries and of song."

There is confusion of date in that remote

epoch. Some historians say it was about the time Gideon delivered Israel from the Midianites, not far from the day when the archers were many on Mount Gilboa, when the shield of the mighty was cast vilely away and the beauty of Israel was slain in her high places. Who knows? Who cares? Where the years run into thousands a few centuries more or less are of small account.

It was the first long ship that ever entered the Bosphorus, was built at the foot of Mount Pelion, and was named for the builder. Athena directed the work, and a speaking branch from the forest of Dodona, the oracle grove, was at the stern. It was but a small vessel compared with the great structures of iron war-ships, with heavy guns, and the mighty armaments which since have swept these waters. Frisian, Thracian, Byzantine, Persian, Samian, Macedonian, Athenian, Gaul, Vandal, Goth, Scythian, Roman, Armenian, Hun, Avar, Russ, Frank, Varangian, Saracen, Venetian, Genoese, English, French, German, have spread their sails as friend or foe to favoring winds. They are forgotten as the waves of yesterday; not one name among them is remembered; but the name of the *Argo* lives forever.

It is said that the merchantmen of the Euxine are modeled after her. They are enormous, unwieldy things, rising to considerable height out of the water, both at the bow and stern, and seem incapable of resisting a gale of moderate force. They have seldom more than one mast with an

immense mainsail, and move with so infirm a
balance that they totter along as if about to up-
set every moment, and are often dashed on the
Cyanean Rocks, which guard, like pitiless sentinels, the entrance of the Black Sea, or are driven
to wreck on the sands. If it be true the *Argo*
was of this shape she was a most ungainly vessel. I refuse to believe those descendants of the
gods, with Minerva at their head, ever directed
such a graceless work. She was pitched coal
black, and painted vermilion at each end.

Fifty oars she carried from the dark pine forests of Pelion; each oarsman was a Greek prince
or a mighty man of valor; for, in those golden
days, the king's sons were the best and bravest,
and the king himself was not ashamed to lead
armies and be their champion. They were hunters who had killed their own game among the
mountains and had cooked it themselves; and
after the feast they lay down to sleep pillowed
on their bucklers, cold and hard. Meads of
asphodel, beds of poppies or flinty rock were the
same to them. They slept like children on the
lap of their mother, and rose in the morning
fresh as youth, wise as age; fathers of the warriors who fought at Troy and made that bare,
empty plain illustrious while this globe remains;
heroes with hair that waved high in air, the race
of the Earth-shakers, whose strength came from
the everlasting hills of the land of perfect beauty.
Jason was commander; and while the centuries
have piled oblivious years like funeral stones
above the grave of myriad captains, fame holds

that one in eternal keeping. Like the Norse king, Olaf, he could run along the bending oars outside the ship, so light of foot was he; light of heart, too, for he had the promise of the crown of Iolcos and a kingdom, if he would capture and bring back from Colchis the Golden Fleece which the king of that country had stolen from one of Jason's relatives and nailed to a beech-tree in the war-god's wood—the all Golden Fleece of the wondrous ram with wings which bore Phreyxus and Helle across the Euxine.

Colchis lay at the foot of icy Caucasus, a far country, where dwelt fair women who belonged to the race of the sun; and to this day the most beautiful men and women in the world are to be found in Circassia, the ancient Colchis, as all know who have visited the harems of the East or who have seen the wild-eyed soldiers who form the body-guard of the Sultan. They were so called, perhaps, from their hair of reddish gold, which is such a delight to the dark races of the Orient.

The fame of Medea, the king's daughter, had spread to the Mediterranean countries; for she was a beauty and a witch, and could throw the thrall of her enchantments over any man who came within the spell of her magic glance. Great was her power. She could unravel the black threads spun in the fates of kings. She knew what plants, gathered under the full moon, had been breathed on by the god of breathless sleep, and she had incantations and talismans for the security of those she loved. In her caul-

dron an old black ram, consumed by fire, became a lamb, and aged, worn-out men came forth
from their own ashes restored to the strength of
manhood's prime. She could become invisible
in a fiery chariot drawn by winged dragons
through the fields of air, and she had a fiery temper, as the reader of Euripides knows, which led
her to destroy her own children and poison with
insidious draught a guest invited to her banquet.
Her love was a consuming passion, her jealousy
a barbarous fury, which demanded the death of
any rival.

When it was known that Jason was to dare the
adventure of the Golden Fleece, the bloom and
flower of Grecian chivalry flocked to his standard. Those youthful princes had no fear of the
unknown; they loved danger for her own sake
and courted her as a bride. Hardships were but
incentives, fairy hands beckoning them on to
daring deed and high enterprise. Chiron was
their teacher, wisest of all men under the sun;
and to souls so brave by birth, so wise by coun-
sel, furies and harpies, dragons and flying serpents with azure eyes, gold-guarding griffins and
death-dealing gorgons, were monsters they loved
to meet. Well might they be bold and venturesome. On board the *Argo* was Esculapius, the
first physician, father of those who study medicine and surgery; and there were the royal twin
brethren, sons of Leda, who alternately lived
and died, and in tempests flames played round
their head, and then storms ceased and the ocean
calmed. There was Orpheus, taught by Apollo,

to whose harp the pine-wood oars kept time.
He had learned by ear and could charm all
spirits of earth and air, Heaven or Hell. When
he played his harp of gold the rivers rolled
backward, wild beasts tamely crawled to his feet,
the mountains stirred and the dead came up from
beneath the sea.

By the old marbles we know those Greeks
were of supreme beauty. The all-beholding sun
sees not their like to-day. Space fails for the
names whose fame fills the world. They had
not adopted the motto of the later Stoics:
" Patriotism is the first delusion of the simpleton
and the last refuge of the knave." They loved
glory, but they loved Greece more; they laid
their trophies at her feet and never swerved
from loyalty to the land of their birth, the violet
vales and rosy hills where their youth had spent
itself in manly games and prince-like learning.
They had cheering responses from the oracle
who knew the number of the sands and the
measure of the seas, who understood the dumb,
could see the invisible and hear him who does
not speak. Neptune, with tumbling hair and
foamlike beard, sat at the door of the Strait of
Helle and refused to give up the key to any new-
comer sailing that way; but among the crew
were men wise in the secrets of the universe,
who could afford to laugh at the sea-god's hoary
head and weak pretense, the senility of age.
They held the clew to the inner shrines of the
winds, and knew what strains from the magic

harp would lull the high flying sons of Boreas to rest.

They were a band of imaginative men steering for the morning twilight, which they believed to be a reflection from the Elysian Fields. To the brilliant fantasies of those early Greeks are due many of the most exquisite conceptions of the human mind. They thought the earth was flat, circularly extended under the blue and starry floor of the Olympian gods, where the highest deity shoots the lightning and rests his many-colored bow, invisible to mortal eye, yet making men tremble by the thunder of his voice. The Mediterranean was the center of the earth, and was filled with floating rocks and rocking islands. In their personified religion no space of earth, sea, or sky was unpeopled. Away to the east were the groves and dancing ground of the sun; beyond them was frosty Caucasus overlooking Colchis. To reach it they must cross the Cimmerian region of perpetual night, where the air is full of feathers, and Boreas, the shivering tyrant, ruled; and they would not stop till they came to the end of the world. When night, which subdues gods and men, received the setting sun into her arms, they had to grapple with mystic shadows, imps with wraith-like veils, supernatural foes which shrink from sunbeams, and to confront mysteries which might make the boldest tremble.

But those royal souls were undaunted. The geography of the wonderful voyage is embellished in a way to rouse the dullest fancy. The

cool chambers of the Mediterranean sheltered
mermaids with golden combs and yellow tresses.
In crystal depths, among the corals and sea-fan,
the palms of the ocean, was heard the laughter
of the daughters of the sea. On its waves naiads
rocked and swam, and halcyon birds sat brooding on their nests, at home and at rest on the
friendly waters. Gliding sirens sung in sunny
bays, tossed their arms on the long wave-tops
which curled in pride to the lovely burdens they
upbore, and sparkled and gleamed with the limbs
of the nymphs, whiter than the foam they scattered. They wooed the heroic sons of an alien
race with softest smiles and dewy kisses. Past
the witching music they safely steered; past
Scylla and Charybdis, past the floating Isle of
Circe, the enchantress, sister of Medea. Two
years they lived in Lemnos, south of the Cy-
clades; they visited Crete and saw where Jove
was cradled among the high peaks of Ida—
many-fountained Ida, mother of wild beasts.
They made friends of the warriors of her hundred cities, leaders, destined to battle on the
ringing plains of windy Troy.

Cretan triremes, manned by corsairs, scoured
the seas, plundering merchant vessels laden with
Tyrian stuffs, jewels of the East, and wheat from
Egypt. The *Argo* promised no such spoil, and
in peace they entered the court of Minos, legis-
lator and king, before whom the dead plead their
cause, and the impartial judge shakes the fatal
urn which is filled with the destinies of mankind.
From the deck of the *Argo* they saw—for they

18

had the far sight of demigods—ancient Troy, overlooking the mouth of the Hellespont, where, a generation later, the Grecian camp stretched twelve miles along the shore, whitening the coast from the Sigean to the Rhaetean promontory. There the flanks of the army were guarded by Achilles and Ajax, bravest chiefs who marched under the banners of Agamemnon. But one of the Argonauts lived to behold the undying glory of that field, old Nestor, the clear-voiced orator of the Pylians.

So they passed the Dardanelles, bound for the limit of the habitable world beyond whose black line were the gates of Tartarus. Those gallant buccaneers did little that was possible; they landed as suited their pleasure, slew men and monsters, and held on their course, even when the Night, her mantle spangled with stars, threw a bewildering shade under which the war of the winds went on. They were ready to do everything a king's son might, and dared even death, to whom it is useless for man to offer oblation, prayer or sacrifice. They passed happy valleys and dark grottoes, fought gigantic beasts with bat-like wings, all manner of horrible prodigies, and, after triumphs, erected votive tablets and holy altars. They stole women when they wanted them, slew giants, sorcerers and wizards, and never lost faith in their power to seize the Fleece of the Speaking Ram.

The pioneer vessel of the Bosphorus made its first landing at Dolma Batché, where the palace of Sultan Aboul Hamid, the Beloved, lifts its

front of marble, and to this day the place is called
Jasminum. A mist hung over the hills, a delicate, evanescent haze, pale rose and silver, shot
with gold. Lightly the morning sun rolled up
the ethereal curtain, as the Eastern lover lifts
the gauzy veil from the blushing face of his
bride betrothed, long promised, now first laid
bare.

The watchers on the stately galley eagerly
gazed on the virgin land, slowly coming to view
as the trailing cloud, a transient garment hiding
the eternal splender, vanished into air. Sky
and sea were speckless sapphire. Nature looked
back at her young lovers, shy and tender, bashful as a bride. I wait for you, she said, in color,
perfume, and melody. The pines, with dim,
aeolian soundings, answered the warm land
breeze. Scented thickets, tangles of resplendent
blooms, echoed and rang with songs of nightingales; butterflies darted, like winged blossoms,
through the air; the cuckoo piped her pretty
note; the sailing sea-birds screamed; the ripples
murmured mellow, musical and low—harmoni-
ous all as the faint, exquisite sights and sounds
of a dream unbroken. It was the supreme moment. Toil and hardship were forgotten, and,
thrilled with rapturous delight, Jason exclaimed :
" Surely this is the dwelling-place of the gods!"

We cannot do more than hint at the perils of
the upper Bosphorus. Pirates pounced on the
regal filibusters, and compelled them to seek refuge in Stenia, where the palace of the Persian
Ambassador now throws its pink shadow in the

glassy bay. Amycus, King of the Bebryces, dared them to mortal combat, and was himself slain by Pollux, brother of beauteous Helen; and again the Argonauts made for the sea of mysteries and fascinations, stopping at Kavake to consult King Phineus as to their course. This miserable man had rested under the anger of the gods, and was blinded, as a punishment for having rashly looked into the future. The avenging deities sent to torture him the Harpies, obscene monsters, with faces of old women, the wings and bodies of vultures, who kept him in constant alarm, and snatched and devoured the meats on his table. The daintiest food was spread before him, and his appetite was keen; but soon as he lifted a morsel to his lips, the Harpies seized and swallowed it. The two sons of Eolus, the wind-god, persuaded Phineus to instruct them in the way to Colchis, on condition that they would deliver him from his tormentors. This was done, and Jason also restored the prophet to sight by the juice of magic herbs. The King gratefully warned his benefactor of the Symplegades at the entrance to the Euxine; two jagged, floating blue rocks, with only twenty furlongs between. They were self-shutting, and closed on objects rashly passing through and crushed them to atoms.

Jason piously sacrificed to the twelve gods, before trying the entrance so like the fatal jaws of death, and, returning to his ship, he sent out a dove to test the narrow opening, shot after it, and safely and hastily pulled into the open sea.

The masts creaked and reeled; every plank and joint screamed and groaned with the dreadful strain, and the ship, in affright, cried aloud, like some despairing swimmer in his agony of fruitless prayer. The cliffs almost entrapped the stern of the vessel, destined by fate, from that portentous moment, never to close again. It is said that on one of the Cyanean Isles, which may be reached on foot in calm weather, is a marble column that once was white, its carvings defaced by long warfare of time and tide, its base defiled with ooze, moss and stain of weed and tangle—by tradition, an altar of Jason, consecrated to the dark and secret powers of Nature which the Argonauts deified and blindly worshiped, with many a weird superstition and incantation.

Says the modern Turk, " We call the Euxine the Black Sea, because it turns men's hearts black with fear." Unceasing winds blew then as now, relentless as the breath of Destiny. Chill mists, like sheeted specters, floated over the cold surface; ghostly phantoms, white and gray, haunted the vast space which stretched away in gloom so vague and undefined it would seem one must sail threescore years to reach its harbor, if it have one, and dying, catch the far-off beating of the surf against the further shore.

The *Argo* was driven on an island; but white-armed Juno loved the heroes, and helped them through this and many other perils, and finally landed the sailor princes at Colchis. Jason explained the purpose of his unexpected visit, and

the king agreed to give up the treasure on condition that the adventurer would tame two bulls
with brazen feet and horns, tie them to a plough
of adamant and plow two acres of ground never
before broken. The savage creatures breathed
flame and smoke, and had never been touched
by the hand of man. After the plowing he was
to sow the teeth of a dragon, from which an
army would spring up to be destroyed by his
hands, then he must kill a sleepless, azure-eyed
snake, which coiled at the roots of the beech-tree
on which the Golden Fleece was nailed; and all
these labors were to be finished in one day, between the rising and the setting of the sun.
They could never have been accomplished had
not Medea, the magician princess, fallen in love
with the warrior, haughtily demanding the prize,
not as a gift or a purchase, but as a right. She
pledged with solemn oaths to deliver the Argonauts from her father's hard terms if Jason
would marry her and take her to Greece—an
easy thing for the Captain of the *Argo* to do; for
the lady of the sun's race was immortally beautiful, with hair like a glory, lustrous, tropical
eyes, and she was wise beyond the privilege of
woman. He swore eternal fidelity, and, by
Medea's sorceries, tamed the fire-breathing oxen,
lulled, with a charmed potion, the scaly serpent
at the roots of a tree, snatched the Golden Fleece
from the limb where it hung blazing in the star-
light, and marched away, leaving the Colchians
stunned with amazement at his audacity.

That was a land of marvels and of mysteries.

Not the least among them was Prometheus, cursed for stealing the holy fire from Heaven, who was chained to a rock above the clouds on Caucasus, the avenging eagle forever hovering, ever devouring his heart. From the mystic ice flower which sprang up in the snow where the blood dripped from his wounds, Medea had distilled the horrid medicine which disarmed the dragon serpent.

Exultantly the Heroes sailed away, away, through hoar vapor, surge, and foam, where the storm spirits ride on the rainbow; and the proud ship felt the added presence of the artful witch-maiden an inspiration which carried them forward with matchless speed. They had passed so many dangers·by flood and field, the men with one· eye, the women with one tooth for three hags, the man-eaters, demons, giants, sorcerers, that Orpheus was moved to finer music than ever before sounded since he strung his harp with poet's heart-strings. And the stars, used only to the wild pæans of the billows, grew brighter as they listened to celestial harmonies, songs of triumphs past and victories yet to come.

How they sailed up the Danube, and out into the circumfluent sea, amid its grand, majestic symphonies, is an old tale and often told. By some miraculous process, not quite clear to mortal vision, they discovered the source of the Nile, carried the sentient ship, which could feel fatigue, on their shoulders, through deceitful mirage and sweltering Lybian deserts, and finally reached Grecian shores. They landed, and drew up into a grotto on the rock the self-acting vessel, which so long had been obedient to the strain and wear of tempestuous years. Shortly afterward she was translated into Heaven. You may see her in Summer nights, shining among the starry host immortal.

Many and sad had been the changes made in Thessaly by the years, whose number is not recorded. The names of the crew of the *Argo* had become part of stories told by gray-haired fathers and mothers in the long wintry evenings —legends of young men sailing off into the unknown darkness of desolate, gloomy seas, seeking far countries and hidden treasure, and never heard from except in airy whispers and uncertain rumors. They shook their heads, and their time-worn eyes filled with tears as they repeated, with moans like the moaning sea, "most likely drowned long ago, long ago, long ago." The Heroes, wofully lessened in numbers, were so haggard, scorched, and weather-beaten that, at first, no one believed these ghastly faces belonged to the beautiful youths who dashed out, fair and free, to fulfill the fate predestined from the foundation of the world, but of which the sagest seer could not forewarn them.

When they were recognized mourning was mingled with rejoicing, and the shouting multitudes crowded round the gallant band, and, in barbaric pomp, preparation for a mighty feast went on. But the king, Æson, father of Jason, was so enfeebled by age as to be unable to iden-

tify his own son, and his cracked, shrill voice
sounded like a grasshopper's chirp. Then Medea,
at the command of her husband, removed the
blood from the old man's veins and filled them
with the juice of certain herbs, restoring to him
the vigor of youth, and the sweet pleasures that
wait on early years and the morning hours.
Capacities for enjoyment, long perished within
him, revived again, and the voice of a singer
came back, with the fresh color in cheek and
eye.

Turn to the poets of the first ages for the story
of Medea's wicked life. One of her crimes was
done the day of the festivities at Iolchos, in
honor of the Argonauts. The daughters of Pelias
begged her to make their father's infirmities van-
ish by the same painless arts she had used on
the king, and she consented, but said she would
employ a different process. By her direction the
dutiful daughters cut their father to pieces and
boiled them in her magic caldron. But there
was no restoration for body or spirit. The
treacherous Medea allowed the flesh of Pelias to
be consumed, and did no miracle. Nothing was
left, not even a handful of ashes to give the holy
rites of sepulture.

It is a sort of surprise to read that she, who
could renew the youth of others, by transform-
ing a perishing body, should allow herself to
suffer death. Perhaps she foresaw higher felicity in the after-life beyond the tomb; for we
read that she waited in hope and eager hero-
worship till the shade of the swift-footed Achilles

reached the underworld; then she crossed the
lonesome Styx, and married him in the Elysian
Fields.

There is a class of disenchanters who maintain
that the superhuman actors and the entire myth
of the Golden Fleece is nothing but a commercial
enterprise idealized. The Greeks, from the beginning, have been a busy race, holding maritime
supremacy. Never at rest, the passion for adventure has been one of their marked character-
istics, and commerce has always been held in
respect among them. The launching of the
Argo, and the roaring monsters by the way opening their abysmal mouths, were only such bulls
and bears as assail the speculator who starts out
to take a flyer in Wall Street. The elements
were personified; divinities to be adored with
fear and propitiated by sacrifice, and the various
forces confronted were, by the poetic Pagans,
given shape and name to suit the brutality opposed to the high courage of the heroes we call
fabulous. Iron will and valor that shrinks from
no enemy, seen or unseen, must win the game
at last, despite tremendous combinations and
powers which, in this story, are but types of
human nature.

Reduced to plain fact, if fact there be, about
thirteen hundred years before our era, some
Grecian sailors started for the Euxine to create
a profitable trade in fish, corn, wool and gold.
They were lawless freebooters, and from various
coasts stole men, women and children, creating
a considerable slave trade, the relic of which

endures to our own time in the traffic for Circassian girls. Various kings have tried to suppress the pirates from that day to this, and the law against it stands in the statutes; but in old Colchis (Circassia) there is yet many a maiden with sun-bright hair waiting to be sought and bought by those who go out seeking brides for such as dwell in kings' palaces.

The disenchanters hold that the harpies, represented as winged old women, were merely locusts devouring the substance of King Phineus; and, stripped of color and poetic drapery, the idea of sending out a dove before the *Argo* was but the advance of a pilot vessel through the dangerous passage to the Euxine. A small craft, bearing the name of another bird, the swallow, is used by Turks at the present time to examine the channel. Both birds are esteemed as omens of good fortune and names appropriate for light boats. When, as tradition runs, the *Argo*, by the separation of the Symplegades, happily passed through, but lost a portion of its end, which the floating rocks, striking together, caught hold of and jammed, the meaning is that the ship, hastening onward, was injured by a rock and lost its rudder.

On the spot made sacred by Jason's sacrifice to the twelve gods, there long endured the remains of a Greek altar to Jupiter and Cybele, of which fragments are still found, shattered and crumbling. It is the highest hill on the Bosphorus, and commands the entrance to the dreaded **Euxine. The** site of the shrine, consecrated

twelve centuries and more before Christ, is now
the hermitage of a holy man, endowed with
oracular wisdom, who is consulted by seamen
before venturing a long voyage into the Black
Sea. Older than history is the legend that the
plain below it is the one where grew the witch's
herbs, gathered in the moonlight, with which
Medea "did renew old .Eson."

Strangely do fact and fable mingle, in many-
colored strand, the threads which lead us. Grop-
ing backward, through the dimness of more than
three thousand years, and peering into the
darkness, we find live truth in the heathen
myths.

I write in a Greek village, called, from the immemorial years, *Therapia*, "the Place of Healing;" and a gentle intervale on the Asian shore
is yet the resort of native women in search of a
plant which they believe prolongs youth, and
robs of his due the common enemy with the
scythe and the hour-glass. Since we have lived
in Turkey I have received more than one letter
from anxious unknown inquirers, asking if the
herb called *serkys* might be transplanted to the
United States, and if I can testify to its delightful effect in restoring a lost youth to faded
faces.

I may be permitted to decorate my page with
a portion of one of these epistles, sent me from
one of the rural districts of the South. After a
few rhetorical flourishes concerning the pleasure
the writer has had in certain printed words of

mine, which I should blush to repeat, she plunges
into the pith of her intent and purpose :

" I have read in the newspapers that there is
a kind of a plant that keeps people young and
handsome, and I have often wished I could get
a holt of some ; and if it isn't too much trouble
and expense, would you mind asking about it,
and send me a few slips by mail, done up in wet
moss, or a paper of the seed, or the dried leaves
or root, with directions how it is to be taken;
or if it is an ointment for external use, a jar or
bottle *C. O. D.*

" I am not very far gone ; have only lost my
complexion and have crow's feet ; you know
American women get old *so* early ; and I am
very thin. I have tried the receipts for fatten-
ing given in the papers, without helping me any,
and would be ever so much obliged if you could
spare time for this. Maybe you wouldn't mind
finding out by some native lady who has tried it
on herself; for I am afraid of poisons or something going wrong, as I nearly ruined my stom-
ach with alkali water when I was in Arizona.
I am now keeping a colored school in Georgia.
You know a single woman naturally wants to
look as well as possible, and I once was not a
very homely girl, if looking glasses are to be
believed. I suppose the beauties of the Orientals know all about this renewer; and as some
great person says—I forget who—beauty is first,
second and third to a woman. You know the

first question about a man is, what did he say?
about a woman, how did she look?

"A prompt answer will much oblige your
friend and well wisher always,

"LUCINDA BEASLEY.

"P. S. Please send a few used postage stamps.
I am making a collection, and have none of
Persia or Egypt."

Oh! my Lucinda! You have ventured on a
sadder search than Ponce de Leon made when
he went wandering up and down the Everglades
of Florida. I have inquired diligently of the
wise, and learn that nothing made by mortal
wisdom and skill can banish the crow's feet or
bring back the vanished bloom to brighten your
maiden cheek. Among the unalterable decrees
it is written; the decision can never be re-
versed. In the sear and yellow you must abide.

Revenons à nos moutons. Now comes the
worst the disenchanters have to tell of the poetic
myth of the Golden Fleece. From the side of
frosty Caucasus there runs a river with gold-
bearing sand, once a very Pactolus for wealth to
its owners. It lies on the southern coast of the
desolate rainy sea, which was the terror and
despair of primitive navigators. The country
of old was subject to depredations of covetous
princes and barbarian hordes, and the famous
water-course, glowing with grains of gold, was
guarded well for its inestimable treasure. So
rich a mine, not in narrow fissures, but a sparkling flood, naturally became the resort of specu-

lators by land and sea. Its value was noised abroad through the length of the Mediterranean countries, and its possession was the subject of many a bloody struggle. Anciently, and even in historic times, the unskilled miners of Colchis, shepherds through many generations, used to lay a skeepskin in the bed of the shallow stream, which we would hardly call a river. The wool caught and held the shining sand in its thick mat; it was then hung upon a tree, and, when dried, the particles of precious dust were shaken out; and lo! you have the whole fable of the Golden Fleece

II.

THE SECOND VOYAGE, A. D. 1884.

THE reader, dear to heart and fancy, who has kindly followed the sail of the first long boat which entered the Bosphorus, may perhaps accompany me on one of the present day—not a frail sail-boat, but a handsome steamer. Many such ply, from sunrise to sunset, along the shores and touch at the principal villages which dot both sides of the strait. They are well-built, clean, and so admirably managed accidents are almost unknown; and it is a pleasant thing to watch the passengers come and go. To reach the landing one must cross Galata Bridge, where the Orient meets and mingles with the West. This pontoon spans the Golden Horn and unites Stamboul, under whose dark cypresses, hung with aerial traditions, the scent of human blood still lingers, and Pera, the noisy, modern city, a cheap imitation of Paris. Streaming across the bridge, at the rate of a hundred thousand a day, is a ceaseless procession of people of every nation, tongue, dress, religion; and in the tideless, landlocked harbor floats every sort of ship from the heaviest ironclads—the great war vessels of the Sultan—to the light caique, the airiest, most graceful craft ever shaped by builder of boats.

Strange and curious are the studies on Galata

(288)

Bridge. Such flashing color, outlandish costume, grotesque shape, such exhaustless varieties of the human face, starting far-reaching associations in the remote past, are to be found nowhere on the globe as in this narrow pass. Here, conspicuous among the complex multitude, beggars most do congregate. They crowd, in picturesque rags, exhibiting disease and deformities unutterably disgusting. Children plead with professional whine, and gypsies follow and besiege your carriage till you are glad to throw out a coin to get rid of them.

Nearly one-third of the human race hold the fierce faith of Arabia, praying five times with face toward Mecca to-day, and all the days; and this night, in the streets of Stamboul, when the watchman cries: "Who goes?" he hears from the Mohammedan, along with his answer, "There is no God but God." Well is the Moslem named the Faithful. In the sacred month of Ramazan, from sunrise to sunset, no true believer touches food or water. It is the holy month of Predestination, kept in memory of the revelation of the Koran, by the Archangel Israfel, the word of the uncreated God which descended in leaves from Heaven, verse by verse, to his prophet. When the weary thirty days of self-denial are ended, comes the grand fête of Bairam; three days of feasting and revel. At night the six thousand lamps of St. Sophia are kindled, the many minarets are ringed with lights, showing in the darkness like glittering crowns let down from Heaven. Texts from the

19

Koran burst in illumination from slender tower
to tower; the mosques, rounded domes and taper
spires are festooned with ropes of lamps; the
Bosphorus reflects trembling ribbons of flame
from the palaces on its shores; and blazing
globes on high flaunt in the face of the stars,
seeming close under the sky; the guns of the
forts thunder; echo answering echo from the
girdling towers of the city of many fames, and
Olympus, "high and hoar," watches the scene
which poet has never sung and artist can never
picture.

And yet, compared with its ancient splendors,
Constantinople is but the reflected ray from a
fading sunset. Once the fitful winds of the Marmora brought gems, spices, myrrh, balsam of
furthest India. Ivory, gold-dust, silks, carpets,
perfumes, came by caravan from Persia and
Arabia. Every luxury poured into the lap of
the most voluptuous of cities, which disputed
with Rome pre-eminence of riches and numbers.
It had been swept by tempests of armies before
it fell under the scimetar of the Turk. The
conquerors of the world all came this way, Persian, Macedonian, Carthagenian, Roman, Genoese
Venetian; and the walls which circled Byzantium like a regal diadem were gashed and scarred by catapult and battering-ram ages before
gun-powder was dreamed of. We can see the
breach over which the last of the Constantines
looked out, and, foreseeing his destiny, asked
forgiveness of his friends, and with the courage
of a Christian, serenely put off the imperial **pur-**

ple, that no man might recognize his corpse, and fearlessly went forth to meet the coming doom.

Seraglio Point is the fairest spot in this historic region; and, whatever view is taken of the matchless panorama, that promontory dominates and draws the eye, even from the myriad ships, lying, like birds, afloat on the flushed water. It is unspeakably beautiful, and has no peer for situation. In its treasury, palaces, temples, the pride and accumulated wealth of centuries culminated, and in its libraries the science and learning of olden time were hoarded. After the Asian conquest the Emperors adopted the magnificence of the Persians. Not Pharaoh, not Ahab in his ivory house, Nero on his golden throne, Indian Mogul, Mexican monarch, or Peruvian Inca ever beheld such pomp and dazzling state as were enthroned in the court of Constantinople when it was capital of the Roman Empire of the East.

In later ages the delicious gardens of Seraglio Point shadowed veiled and delicate beauties, of the royal harem. Musky odalisques, soft Circassians, sweetest and daintiest, pelted each other with flowers, and, under the snowing roses, waited in unsunned loveliness for the coming of the one man who was their sole communication with the outside world. Deep and singular emotion follows the track of memory; for this was once the center of the brain and heart of Islam, where twenty-five sultans held their court. It is said servants lived and died without knowing all the devious windings, recesses, and secret chambers in this scene of imperial wars and loves. Then every class, down to the scullions, wore a distinctive uniform; and, in the time of Murad Fourth, nine hundred horses were led to silver mangers by Bulgarian grooms. The "*slipper* money" of the Sultana was the revenue of a province. The favorite odalisque was the owner of one hundred silver carriages, and the treasury was rich enough to build fleets with silver anchors and silken cordage. Ambassadors were received in stately, sumptuous ceremony, between two walls of silk and gold. The ancient chroniclers repeat, till it becomes a proverb, learning for the Frank, money for the Jew, pomp for the Osmanli.

In rooms lined with bright marbles the Padishas went to hear aged dervishes read the *Thousand-and-One Nights*; thirty-two muezzins, with solemn, far-reaching voices, called the hours of prayer from the minarets; and the father of a hundred sons, the man before whom all other men are but as dust, knelt at the cry "There is no God but God." With his forehead bowed to the earth, he repeated the ninety-nine beautiful names of Allah, and thought on the Golden Garden, kept for the faithful,

"And of the hourls, pleasure's perfect daughters."

Among the buildings grouped on Seraglio Point is a small octagonal palace, of Saracenic architecture, called the Bagdad Kiosk. They tell us the material for its composition was brought by caravan from Persia, and it is elegantly wrought, as some airy toy; exquisitely finished as a lady's jewel-case. And a jewel-case it was, when whatever was most sacred and most precious was hidden from vulgar eyes beyond its silver door. The pearls of the East sparkled in the screened apartments, which are lined with jasper, lapis lazuli, alabaster, and tortoise-shell, cushioned with eider down and stuffs now named with the lost arts. It is lovely as the enchanted fabric with which Aladdin surprised his father-in-law. It has no unfinished window, and the very touch of the Arabian is in the bright blues and reds of the ceiling, and the wonderful figures of its geometrical lines.

Of the images of breathing, smiling life in the jeweled rooms, we can but dimly guess. They were forbidden to the eyes and thoughts of all save one, and imagination falters before the hangings, rich and rare, which curtained the most holy place. The august center of Ottoman greatness, home of heroes, " with bodies of iron, souls of steel," is lonesome and melancholy now; gone to decay and neglect. The long swell of the Summer sea breaks into sweet rhythms of sound on many a pearly beach and rock-bound shore; but nowhere is that musical cadence so suggestive as here. The palaces on the water's edge have been destroyed by fire, and the seraglio, with its inmates fair and faithful, is removed to the heights of Yildiz, beyond Pera; but the fountain which bubbled with crimson foam—poetry, romance, history, tragedy have here an abiding place and cannot be transferred nor burned away.

One day, when I sat on the deck of a steamer, enjoying the tranquil, drowsy air, thinking of the venerable past and watching the languid wavelets pulsing against the loose stones, I was roused from reverie by a party of tourists coming up the stairs. There is a peculiar, penetrative quality belonging to the voice of my country, making it easily distinguishable. Not that it is pitched so very high ; but from some cause to me unknown, it has a certain tension which compels hearing. (I use the word tension applied to the violin string, rather than the sewing machine.) It does not caress the ear, as Charlotte Brontë exquisitely expressed the charm of the voice best loved by her, but rather goes into it and humming through the head, sharply, incisively, and always unmistakably.

Well I knew them as they crossed the plank and filed up the gangway, that party of American tourists. First came the courier—a lank, vicious-looking Greek—leading his train, then four or five gentlemen, with white scarfs dangling down their hat brims, a little tarnished embroidery and scant fringe at the ends, identifying the pilgrim from the farthest East; a Professor in gold spectacles, from Andover, I think, general answerer of questions ; an ancient maiden carrying the usual red-backed Murray, reticule, and opera-glass. She wore a Saratoga wave, which weakly broke over her forehead, and a

hat with narrow brim, turned up by a rosette
which might have been coquettish in its day,
but that day was in a far country and some pre-
historic epoch.

My attention was caught by a weather-beaten
old lady in a tattered and distracted bonnet and
suit of rusty alpaca. She looked tired to death,
yet anxious to see and eager to spend the expir-
ing struggle in pursuit of knowledge. Holding
her hand was a blush-rose young girl, the tenderest, loveliest thing, who addressed her as
Grandma, with a smile whose bright warmth
could be almost felt, like sunshine. They
scuffled noisily about, and after considerable
racket were quieted and snugly settled. My
seat happened to be near two young gentlemen,
who had reached the weary point in life where
man delights not—No, nor woman neither; the
juice was gone; only the dry rind remained;
and this when, by appearance, they could not
have worn away more than twenty-four tiresome
years on this dull planet. I could not choose
but hear, and, in fact, did not, as they went on
somewhat after this wise:

"Jo, what are you eyeing down there in the
deep water?"

Jo, without stirring or looking up:

"A possible President, my Thomas."

"A harmless lunacy, Joseph. By way of
amendment, let me say an impossible one."

"And what do you see?" cuttingly retorted
the unabashed Jo.

"See! Gulls!" observed Thomas, with the

significant self-conscious air of the habitual
punster.

"A blighting sarcasm. Any idiots about?"

"No. Why? Do you feel lonesome?"

"Not while you exist," responded the satiric
Joseph; and with dreary intervals of rest, after
such blistering wit, the young men leaned over
the rail and stole glances at the blush rose. In
loud whispers they irreverently spoke of the
mateless bird, meaning the maiden in pursuit
of knowledge, and she, in return, took no pains
to conceal her aversion to what she styled
"those reptiles!"

(N. B. It is difficult for tourists to avoid hat-
ing each other.)

A youth with attenuated mustache, who had
spent a year in England, gave variety to the conversation by delivering his convictions on the
subject of privileged and middle classes and
vested rights, ending many sentences with "Be
Jove!" We secretly took his measure and
rated the counterfeit at what he was worth.
The first two *blasé* companions called him
"smarty."

One very noticeable figure sat in the best
chair, apart from her fellow travelers. A woman
in rich belongings, with a haughty manner,
which plainly said: "I am among Cook's
tourists, but not to be classed with them."
About thirty years of age, she would have been
a superb beauty, but for the cold expression of
contempt (perhaps at herself in her present
position), a scowl that came and went, marring

the statuesque features. Occasionally she glanced over her shoulder, like one pursued. Was she a fugitive traveling with these people for protection, or was it only a pursuing memory which hovered at her back? A woman with a history not written on the imperious brow too deep for a surface reading.

The old lady clung helplessly to the grand-daughter, who was all sweetness and color, the rare tints in her cheek, fleeting as the vanishing hues of the rainbow, but for her brief season of bloom a radiant apparition that illumined the whole deck. Her grandmother called her Pussy; and the grave, dignified Turks gazed fixedly at her in their solemn fashion, as if thinking she should be veiled and locked in.

·The tourists were from Palestine, the usual route toward Constantinople. That was plain by the olive-wood cuff buttons of the gentlemen, the Bethlehem cross of Pussy and a pair of Cairene ear-rings, which betrayed Egypt.

"Well, I *do* declare, this *is* comfortable!" said the old lady. "After the dreadful donkeys and the sea-sickness, jest to set and take it all in without stirring a step!"

"Did not your experiences amply repay you?" asked the New Englander, reprovingly. "This is an educational tour. The opportunity for such self-culture doesn't come every day. Oh!" she went on, ardently, her Saratoga wave back-sliding in a bias line to the crown of the hat, "what a privilege! what a privilege!"

"No; it doesn't pay *me!*" returned the old

lady with emphasis. "Nothing *can* pay for
thirty days on a horrible horse and that dreadful
one in the Valley of Fire. Mr. Cook!" she
called out to the courier, who glared at her like
a tiger.

"Not Mr. Cook, Grandma," said Pussy, taking
a card from her pocket. "Let me spell it. Pap-
parigopoulo. These Greek names are so hard."

"Well, Pussy, I don't care. He's Cook's
agent, and I should go crazy trying to remember
Pop—what's his name? Mr. Cook, what's this
place we're comin' to?"

The noble Greek almost foamed at the mouth
while he rattled off the speech prepared for the
point where the sweet waters of Asia meet the
rapid currents of the Bosphorus.

And here I pause a moment to say, would
you have one day like the stuff which dreams
are made of, an idyllic day, that will stand apart
from other pictured memories far and near, go to
the Valley of Sweet Waters, the beauty-spot of
the Bosphorus. In the lazy afternoons it is the
resort of lovely ladies, pallid as lilies, robed in
vaporous draperies of snow-drift and thistle-
down, scented with rose and musk. White
veils, dim, mysterious, hide their faces, all but
the swimming, lustrous eyes. Oh! what eyes
they have! Bright as stars, black as death.
Dreamy pictures they make, reclining on the
crimson cushions of the rocking caique, which is
draped with India shawl or Persian hangings.
The armed slave in the stern is clad in barbaric
splendor, the rowers in wide white trousers and

scarlet jackets stiff with gold embroidery—
Greek boatmen, bearing the old names that can
never die.

It would hardly be a surprise should visible
Loves and Graces start from the azure overhead
to shower roses on the warm, rippling sea, to
twine the gay vessels with garlands and drop a
flowery wreath on the head of some uncrowned
princess. Out of the swift currents they glide,
silent as ghosts, past the grim towers, hoary summits scarred and seamed, venerable with age, and
float the light craft without the dip of an oar in
the lace-like shadows of the chestnut leaves
which bend to kiss them. Among the ferns on
the reedy margin an enchantress is waiting, ah!
for whom? Under a parasol of fleecy mist,
waiting, waiting till the watchers are asleep, till
the nightingale pours out its plaint to the rose,
till evening unfurls her waveless banner of amber,
pink and violet, fringed with gold, and the silver
horse-shoe of the waning moon leaves its track
on the lulling waters. This enchantress has no
secrets hidden in witches' caldron, nor invisible
tangling nets spread for unwary feet, to catch
helpless prisoners. Her marvelous charm is beyond the reach of words. A witchery, lies in
the depths of those unfathomable eyes, compelling mortals who come within their subtle magic
to fall down and worship forever.

Let us watch in the twilight; for a messenger
will bring a love letter from shore, and, kneeling,
offer it, in a dainty basket lined with satin and
covered with cloth of gold and crimson. It con-

tains hieroglyphs not of Egypt. The paling afterglow reveals an ivory fan, a bouquet of jasmine and heliotrope, a silken tassel, some sugar candy, and a piece of trailing vine. One by one the love-signs are lifted by jeweled fingers and carefully scanned; and this is the reading of the symbolic writing: The fan is a wish to pay an evening visit; the flowers that they shall walk in the garden under the trailing vines; the sweets, they shall have refreshments; and the tassel, being called *shubarrch*, means *shareb*, the sound of the word signifying wine.

The answer returned is a leaf of aloe-plant, several black cummin-seeds, a scrap of gauze, and a string of a musical instrument, which, being interpreted, mean: The aloe, patience, because it will live months without rain; the lover must wait; the black cummin-seeds, so many evenings hence; the scrap of gauze, that she will be dressed in evening costume and ready to receive visitors; and the guitar-string gives a promise that the night shall be filled with music. The loveliest of our love letters cannot equal this message, expressed in bloom and perfume. No, not though it be written from the golden inkstand incrusted with diamonds which Mahmoud the Second left in the imperial treasury, as a testimonial that his victories were not exclusively in the field of battle and of blood.

The long, lustrous Asiatic eyes, " the Paradise eyes," are wonderfully magnetic, shining languidly beneath the jet black lashes, drawing us, even against our will. Under their compelling charm we are in danger of forgetting our own tourists. Let us return to the steamer.

They listened intently to the guide's explanation—all except a pair under one umbrella—a homely man of middle age and a plain-faced girl, a teacher, I should guess. Rapt and self-absorbed, they gazed at each other admiringly and, through the long recitation, kept up a murmurous whispering. No need to tell those words which seemed to separate them from their fellow-travelers; for they were lovers, within and around them a new heaven and a new earth. Even this elder world appeared fresh and unworn to them, as it was to the first and fairest of lovers when the evening and the morning were the seventh day.

Not for them the song—

> " O Paradise, O Paradise,
> The world is growing old."

Under the dingy umbrella—cotton, at that—on the deck of "Steamer Number 64," lay the last boundary of the Garden of Eden.

Said the blonde cynic, sneeringly: "The spoons don't seem to know there is anything worth seeing but themselves. However," he added, consolingly, "it's a comfort to know it won't last long. Now, if it was Pussy, I could stand it better."

"Wasn't it somewhere along here that Andromeda was chained to the rocks?" asked the old lady.

"No; that was at Joppa, Grandma."

"Sure enough, Pussy, so it was. I get things so mixed."

"At Joppa," said the Scholar, kindly, beaming on the poor old creature, as he picked up her parasol and raised it to screen her from the freshening breeze. "That was a deep myth. She was probably a Canaanite, an offering to the forces of Nature. You remember the fearful surf at the harbor and the narrow way through the rocks?"

"That I do!" said Grandma.

"And the Greeks made a sacrifice of the beautiful virgin as their most precious possession"—he looked at the pretty face of Pussy—"an offering to the winds and waves in the times of fear which died out before the higher, sunnier faith in human gods."

He turned to the book again, which he shared with a clear-eyed boy, evidently his son; a promise of bright manhood: a youth glad to learn, willing to work, not thirsting to snatch the prize of glory without the dust of the race; one of whom any father might be proud.

"What else did the old heathens do along here, Pussy?" broke in the high, shrill voice. "You know this is an educational tour and we must study as we go."

"I can't think of all, or of half what I" said the artless girl, fumbling the leaves of the guide-book.

"Well, well; read something. I don't like Mr. Cook's speeches. He runs his words together so."

She read, and then explained:

"There's the Giant's Mountain. In the time of the Argonauts, Pollux killed the king of the country, and erected his monument here, and planted it with a laurel tree."

"You don't say that's the highest point on the Bosphorus! It seems rather small to a woman raised in the White Mountains. Why"—her voice flew up to the ledger lines above—"'taint no higher'n the Palisades of the Hudson. Looks like 'em, too!"

"That is what every traveler says," observed the thoughtful Professor.

"The enchanted herbs which renew youth grew on the hill yonder," continued Pussy. "The old witches used to gather them in the full of the moon."

"I wish I had some of that 'erb now!" groaned out Grandma.

"The blessed law of compensations holds yet!" whispered the blonde cynic to his two compatriots. "She can't get it. Let us be thankful."

There were three widows in the party whereof I write, and they clung together not so much to enliven each other as to club their loneliness. The dusty and mournful veils, which should have hung down their backs, fluttered, like black flags, in the breeze, and their spirits had profited little by the tour of Europe the American prescription for sorrow. They were no longer young, and had the worn look of women whose introspective life is one of self-denial; hungry minds in tired bodies. I saw it plainly, as one endowed with the vision and faculty divine looks into the hearts of suffering humanity. Grief had fallen on them like frost; their holiday was sad; still they kept a keen lookout; nothing of importance escaped their notice; and one was working at a diary—doubtless a melancholy record, a long contrast between these days and the blessed time when a dear presence was a lovely light in the past. Could I look over her shoulder I might read of a voice that was sweeter than the ring-dove's, now lost in the everlasting silence; of star-shine and flower scent; of the joy of meeting, the pain of parting, in another phase of existence so foreign to this it might indeed be in another world.

My three widows (called Three Black Crows by the blonde cynic) watched the veiled Oriental ladies coming and going at the various towns.

"Are they all widows?" asked one.

"No," replied the patient, answering Professor. "A Turk never appears in public with his wife. It would be a deadly insult to ask after the health of one, or even to know of her existence. Among the higher class, you notice, each has her jet black Negro attendant. Spruce, tall fellows, in no wise bowed down by their own position. Well do the Arabs say the children of Shem are prophets, of Japheth, kings, of Ham, slaves."

A country clergyman and wife were of the party which interested me. His people had given him a long vacation, allowed his salary to go on as usual, and, at the last moment, the pastor had been enriched by a handsome donation from a wealthy member of the church. You know that odd communicant, who saves in dimes and quarters, and then, suddenly and unexpectedly, does such a generous act, you wonder why you ever called the old man " close." The minister is easily identified by the white (not very) neck-tie, and the worn black suit. His wife had had the transient prettiness of the village beauty, and firmly clung to a fond superstition that curls behind the ears are becoming ; otherwise she was dressed in accordance with the prejudices of civilization.

This was a long dreamed-of holiday ; and now it was come, she had a scared look, as though bewildered at finding herself so far from her own cooking-stove.

I noticed, and was very pleased to do so, that he touched her hand, now and then, as if to reassure the timid, startled thing, who blushed scarlet when she saw I was looking. Easy to see, he had profited by the chances of self-culture, while her day-dreams and air-castles had been flying up the kitchen chimney. But he did not despise her, though, mentally, and in all outward graces, he had outgrown the wife of his youth. When he mildly smiled on her sallow face it brightened for a moment ; but her eyes had a faraway look, thinking of the children at home, borrowing trouble, as my countrywomen are wont to. This is her ideal man—wiser, better than other men ; she worships accordingly,

20

and fully believes (fond, faithful heart!) if he only had the opportunity, he would make his mark in New York, or Brooklyn, City of Churches. Under the sustaining belief, she does not sigh in discontent over her belongings, nor covet many talents. He is all—self nothing— in the sum of her life. Hers is the duty of ironing the napkin in which one talent is hidden, and she secretly thinks the world knows nothing of its greatest men. She would color to the roots of her hair at a hint of such pride; but you and I know her, my reader.

She looks over his shoulder at the copious notes in his scratch-book. What fine writing she thinks it! Plain as day another book of travels is to be dropped on a patient, long-suffering public. Some heavy columns offered to, possibly accepted by their own religious newspaper and gathered manna for his hungry flock in the old meeting-house—all garnered up in that scratch-book.

The three widows hovered about this pair. Such a gentle disciple, moving in a halo of peace, attracts sorrowing souls, naturally, as amber draws straw, to borrow the comparison of poor Jeannie —heroine of the pathetic Carlyle tragedy. These observations flash through the mind like electric light; but it requires some minutes to read them. The courier illustrates the saying, "The worst objection to the modern Greek is that he makes you forget his ancestors." Sulky to the travelers he conducts, he chatters glibly to a woman of his own nationality; a

wild creature, bare-headed, except for her own
jetty braids of hair, shot through with a sharp
gilt arrow. She does not remind you of Helen,
or Sappho, or Phryne; by no means; but there
is a dangerous look in her bearing, as of a fierce
dog chained; and on occasion she might spring
into the sparkling water, or stab you in your
sleep, if baffled or bitterly wronged. Strangers
in modern Athens say the old Greek fire lives
even in the ashes of the violet-crowned city.

Such are some of the voyagers on the Bosphorus in the nineteenth century. And, after
the fashion of those who believe human nature
is the only thing which never changes, I ask,
What material is here for romance to build
upon? The fabled streams have all been
sounded, and there is no new Atlantis to be discovered, no empires to be conquered or founded,
no dragons to be slain in the pleasant land, so
placid it seems always afternoon. Are these
the race of beings from whom the royal poets
created demigods, and the Pagans formed their
living models? These the women, tender and
strong, who taught and guided their visions?
The Yankee shamming the Englishman might
possibly be a perfumed, flying Paris, in disguise;
and there cannot be two opinions as to who
would win the golden apple inscribed "To the
Fairest," could it be rolled along the dingy table-
cloth at the *table d'hote* this evening.

Blasé New Yorkers are not the scions Nature
chooses for her great men. By no stretch of
poetic fiction can they be called god-like, wise-

hearted, or even like Telamonian Ajax, the defiant.   I rather fancy heroic stuff rests, a power
unused, in the person of the mild country parson.   He may lack the brute courage of Grecian
youth, born in the purple and trained to battle,
with far-shadowing spears; but he has a force
at heart which teaches how to die nobly.   If I
read him aright, some day, when the yellow
fever is raging in the South and there is a cry
for help, he is the sort of man to say, " Here is
my opportunity for good," and to go out, not
with martial music and shouts of applauding
multitudes, like the heroes marching in valor
and splendor through the ages long gone.   He
forsakes his adoring wife, whom he entirely
loves, and rushes away in the night express to
meet an enemy more deadly and poisonous than
the great scaly dragon beyond the sea of dread
and terror; he returns in the long black box to
which we give the kindly name of casket, and
is the hero, not of the passing hour, but of
eternity.   That last parting—a fireside tragedy
—has none of the elements of the picturesque.
The armor of the earth-shakers, horse-hair crest
glancing helm, bossy shield, belt bright with
purple, and shining sword, are not for our hero,
ready to do and die.

The short man, in ready-made clothes, cheap
for cash, would cut a sorry figure on a background of variegated marble.   When he takes
his life in his hand, the farewell is made in the
library of the parsonage.   The name suggests a
well-ordered, ample room, holding a slight scent

of Russian leather, luxurious arm-chairs, sumptuous volumes in carved cases, hangings that subdue sound and light, neither gloom nor glare in the atmosphere of seclusion and refinement. No such thing. The country parson's library is the reception room. In it he listens to stories of sorrow and of spite, which troubled members of his congregation—mainly women—pour into his patient ear. Here the bashful young bridegroom comes to arrange for the happy day, slowly nearing ; mourners stray in from the streets, asking, Is there no balm in Gilead, is there no physician there ; and husband and wife —I have known more than one such instance— bring their quarrel and seek the minister's mediation. On birthdays it is open to the children, and is the scene of the festive donation party and the Dorcas Sisterhood meetings.

The book-shelves suggest work. Concordance, Cyclopedia, Josephus, Travels, Sermons ; solid old blocks, out of which modern discourses are hewed. Piles of newspapers lie on the inky desk, under the student's lamp, which has been the only witness of many a midnight wrestling in prayer, in weariness, and despondency—straits to which the wisest sooner or later sink, happy if they do not reach the desparing wail of the Judean preacher : "All is vanity." Secret longings are to be subdued. His is the office of the faithful, the hopeful, the helpful.

Above the door is the motto, "God Bless our Home." Several feverish chromos, or "chromios," as they are called in the pokeberry districts,

adorn the walls; embroidered slippers rest on
the rug, where the pattern in hectic worsted,
bears slight proportion to the brown-holland
ground. A small mirror, much tilted forward,
is above the mantel. It reflects a vase of pam-
pas-grass, on which dried butterflies are glued.
The shelf is further embellished with a black
panel picture of a one-legged stork, and plaques,
gray and brown, with pansies and wild roses,
photographs of brides in wedding dress, and
first babies, white and flabby. These holiday
trifles are presents from loyal, admiring parish-
ioners. Nor does their generosity stop suddenly. The slippery hair-cloth sofa is gay with
tidies of riotous color, and is ornamented by a
unique cushion of moderate softness, singular
fabric, and lurid tint, called a crazy pillow. The
struggle after the beautiful appears in the pine-
bur frame surrounding the certificate of life
membership in the Foreign Missionary Society,
presented by his Bible-class; and a china dove,
hung by invisible thread from the ceiling, is a
poor type of the spirit of peace brooding over
the parsonage, her white wings folded.

The angel of the house, in brown gingham
dress, does not dream she is a heroine. Her path
is regulated by the hard, strait line of duty, and
to shirk or to shrink is not in her plan of life.
There are neighbors, to whom the environment
of this pair appears the "soft spot to drop into;"
and when our hero, unsung in epic, goes from it
unsustained by applause or publicity, they think
it's no more than a preacher ought to do.

Though when he pays the last full measure of devotion, they start up in plaintive obituary and head subscription papers for a highly respectable tombstone.

Do you suspect that Andromache is one of our widows, and Penelope, and Laodamia? Broken lives, moving in minor key, like sad, unwritten hymns; psalms of love and death, and life undying? Such they are, though they are neither gifted nor celebrated; though their main study has been to make a little butter spread over a large slice of bread; and they know how to turn dresses, cut down stockings, sew carpet-rags, can peaches, and make pickles.

On second thought, I am not quite clear that the youngest one, who, in a faded way, hints of by-gone beauty, would spend ten years weaving a shroud for her father-in-law, if hard beset by suitors young and gay. Not quite sure, I say; but may be she would wait so long for Ulysses. In this age of steam, one goes from Troy to Ithaca in three days. She would run no risk of an Enoch Arden affair, if she married in two years; and I, for one, would fully justify her in it. But he must be a man in his prime who would woo her; not one of those two bald elder-lies, sitting with the toes of their boots dug in the deck, like Bill Nye.

And the pale professor, in the gold spectacles, if I mistake not, has in his soul the elements of heroism. There are no distressed virgins chained to rocks for sea-monsters to devour. If there were, Perseus would not be lacking.

Grandma and the flowerlike child go about the world collecting much good advice, still too ignorant to be conscious of danger. Should they need it, the every-day man, in a plain business suit, would strike a blow for them, be mighty in courage as the blameless knight whose

> "Strength was as the strength of ten,
> Because his heart was pure."

The last glimpse I had of them, the Professor was carring the straggling old lady's shawl, and the school-teacher's riticule; and again I said, this man is chivalrous as any knight-errant in the dim realm of the *Fairy Queen*. No; the age of chivalry is not past so long as strength upholds weakness, and good men are to be found ready to resent insult and right a wrong, though it be only an insolent official cheating an acrid, withered old woman, who had better be at home. The age of Fable, the Kingdom of the Beautiful Myths, have passed. Those years have run out to the last golden grain of their sands. Summer sun or wintry moon will never shine on revel of monster, dragon, or giant more. In their graves they lie, well laid to rest; and they have left no ghosts to haunt these classic shores. Phantoms, vast and wan, no longer troop under night's blue and starry pennon, but spirits of evil, cruelty and meanness stalk abroad, and confront the wanderers on sea and land. The same heavenly voices which urged on the adventurers building the *Argo* are thrilling high souls with the sense of great things, visible and invisible, to be struggled for. The same worthless prizes are offered for low natures to spend the energies of three-score years upon. The same mighty impulses stir in hearts ready for awful deeds of good or ill, that throbbed in the breasts of men before the first Pharaohs watched for Sirius to rise and put on the glory of the sun and order the swellings of the Nile.

My tourists vanished like shades filing off in the dusk. Their voices lingered a moment under the seven antique plane-trees of Buyak-dere, where Godfrey de Bouillon planted his standards and encamped his army of Crusaders, and Gypsies now swarm and tent. Then they mingled with the dash of the black Sea surf and were lost as the Pilgrims went on their way, and I saw them no more.

＊　　＊　　＊　　＊　　＊

There is an Arabic tradition that a wayfaring son of Ishmael once bought a seal, and found that, by some mistake, it was without a motto. He went to Solomon the Wise, and asked of him what legend he should have engraved on the blank chrysolite. The prophet, after a moment's silence, answered: "Write on your seal, and on all the seals, *This, too, shall pass away.*"

ONE WOMAN: A TRUE ROMANCE.

I.

DURING a three years' residence in the East, I heard personal histories so much wilder than fiction, that any attempt to color and embellish them would take from their seeming unreality. Under this feeling, I now tell the tale which follows as 'twas told to me. First, I had it from one of our missionaries, resident in Palestine; later by an English teacher in Athens, who had known my heroine in the beauty of her earliest youth, before the bright and morning star shot from its sphere. I violate no confidence. This revelation would not be given to the public did it profane the sanctity of home. Since her death, some years ago, the details of her reckless career were printed in French and English newspapers, with names, dates, places, exact as statistics of a Cyclopædia. There may be living one who can yet be pained by mention of the name blazoned throughout Europe; now passed beyond our judgments to the bar of the Judge who can do no wrong.

We will call her Lady Ellen—for she was born to the title; of a line honorable and ancient, illustrious through generations, especially distinguished in the reign of the most unhappy king of the unhappy house of Stuart. Her ancestor

of that stormy period did the state good service,
and for daring deeds was recognized and rewarded as a faithful servant of the First Charles.
The name is usually mentioned when my tale is
told, but we will not record it now. This daugh-
er received the education common to children
of her rank, where one of the first considerations,
if not the very first, is health. She was trained
to walk, to run, to drive, to go through audacious feats on horseback, fearlessly as the startling gymnast who holds breathless the lovers of
the gay circus ring. Excelling in out-door
sports and exercises she had a well-knit, compact frame, a springing step of bounding elas-
ticity, and grew to womanhood slowly ripening,
maturing a strong, rich beauty, which the fever
and fret of half a century could not dim. Such
education of the physique, under the veiling
skies and soft, moist airs of the Gulf Stream, de-
velops full, fine contours; and the pure tints,
perishable with us, bloom on in England like
Autumn roses.

An English girl associates the idea of freedom
with marriage. Then her horizon enlarges and
brightens, and then begins her chance of shining
in society. Till that time she is limited in
pleasures; at home or abroad, always under the
watchful eye of a chaperone, till she looks to
marriage as an escape from restraint, and usually
accepts, unquestioning, the hand accepted for her
by her parents. Arranging a marriage is an expression unheard on this side of the sea; we

thinking the high contracting parties competent to arrange for themselves.

At the age of eighteen, the Lady Ellen was betrothed to one she did not love; but she acquiesced without demur, and settlements were made in due form, contingencies in the future provided for, and the wedding was all that wealth and position could make brilliant. Her husband was high-born, a leader in Parliament. At once their house became a fashionable social center, and their country-place was second only to Holland House, as a resort for literary men and women, wits and poets. Those the world called famous were delighted to share the table-talk, which never sank to the level of the mediocre. Her consummate tact harmonized representatives of discordant parties, and captivated the guests trooped about her. The pride of her noble husband, who loved her with a great love, the ambition of her haughty father were fully satisfied. But the Lady Ellen—was she content?

Said a gentleman who knew her well: "She had in one, the elements which go to make up many women. She should have been named *Pandora*, 'the All-Gifted.'"

Various herself, all varieties pleased her. She had a full mind, and pliant as oil, knew every secret conveyed by the word adaptation. Whoever came before her was made to feel that for the moment her entire interest centred in that person who absorbed, or seemed to absorb, her whole attention.

A ruling trait of her character was boldness, and in her shining circle she was ambitious as Cæsar, while apparently actuated only by graceful kindness, a cordial interest toward the courtiers who kissed the small, white hand. Bright and winsome, healthful as Hebe and seemingly as happy, who could guess that under the urbane sweetness called high-breeding, she carried resolve unquenchable; a soul of hidden fire, false as Hell; her purpose to sweep over Europe, dazzling the sight; in the face of society, defiant of law and public opinion?

Her daily walk was among fair women and brave men. About her were arms and coronets, stars, badges, orders, ambassadorial furniture, hereditary plate, historic pictures; baubles men strive for, women live for and die for; symbols of the rank and power of the patricians of England and of the world. But they paled before the Lady Ellen, whose majestic presence made such trifles valueless as the gewgaws of a country fair. No one could believe that in this meridian height she was plotting escape from the showy thralldom she deemed insufferable, about to break the marriage bond, which has been likened to a rope of diamonds or a garland of morning roses. She had two children, but they did not satisfy her heart, if she had a heart. Her husband she did not profess to love. She wanted power. Had she been born a man she would have had opportunity to rule in cabinets, or would have made a career in the army. Such tireless energy and longing for the foremost place has quick response in the restless changing movements of camps, the swift coming and going, the pomp of parades, the hot fierce combat, the mingling of anxiety and animation, which make every vocation tasteless and colorless after one has been a soldier. She would have said, "I will be celebrated or die;" for she was dauntless and ruthless, ready to go to death herself, and deal it to others, without remorse. She was endowed with what our French cousins call the genius for command; but being woman, there was no need of the rich inheritance, no outlet for it; she might only intrigue.

One day she fled to Italy, and after years of reckless living, thence to Greece. The House of Lords easily granted divorce to her husband, and the children remained with him. It was given out that the fair lady's mind was as wandering as her feet, that she was partially, if not wholly insane. By the terms of the divorce, a large income was allotted her, and she set up the standard of wit and beauty, and to it flocked genius and valor. A woman so calculating would not dissolve her pearl of life and toss it off at one delicious, maddening draught. She sipped it slowly, with deliberation, not to reach the dregs at the bottom of the cup. What thoughts went through Lady Ellen's mind only the recording angel can tell. If there was remorse for abandonment of her husband and desertion of her innocent children, for her lawless life, it did not appear in the Priestess of the

Beautiful, dwelling in the famous city of Aspasia.

She married again—a nobleman in the service of the King. This was in the days of Otho. The Queen was displeased, and censured him without avail, for he was bewitched; and finally, her Majesty gave him notice to quit her service, or that English woman he named his wife. His place in the King's retinue was for life, that of husband of Lady Ellen might not be. To give up her wealth with such a sum of loveliness was hard indeed, but that was the alternative. He hesitated, tried to conciliate and compromise, but there were no terms to be made. The Count must go. And he did go, and left the lady fetterless once more.

Among the versatile accomplishments of this singular creature, unique in my knowledge of women, was the gift of tongues. Travelers from all the Mediterranean countries meet in Athens, and in its streets are heard many languages.

She was fond of Oriental life; and, familiar with the career of Lady Hester Stanhope, and Lady Mary Montague, of whom much was then written and said by travelers from the East, she seemed fired with the idea of emulating their example. She would be queen again in another empire, a Zenobia, a ruler in the desert, and her willing subjects should be the untamed and untamable Bedouins; among the tribes who, from the remote times of Job and Sesostris, have been a nation of outlaws and rebels, whom Cyrus, Pompey, and Trajan could not subdue, and whom the weeping Alexander might have found in a peninsula yet to conquer. To fit herself for fresh adventure and sway this imaginary scepter, Lady Ellen studied Arabic.

Determined to rival Chatham's eccentric granddaughter, she sailed away from Greece to see what the gorgeous East is made of. She had entered the violet-crowned city without affections, she probably waved adieu without regrets. Her ample income gave means of gratifying a taste exquisite as it was luxurious; servants, carriages, furniture, plate, linen, a French maid, the companion of her changeful moods, even her little lap-dog went with her. There are old citizens of Beyrût who remember the stir among an idle populace when the great English lady landed at the seaport and, uncrowned yet a queen, set out for the shadowy realm where she should rule by divine right, "*La reine aux yeux bleus.*" That city is to Damascus what Tyre was to it in the times of Ezekiel, and there the tourist has his first taste of the true Orient, for there the palm-orchards grow. When the old Greek and Roman colonists first saw this lovely tree they named the country *Phœnicia*, "The Land of the Palm;" and in like feeling, Vespasian, when he conquered Jerusalem, struck a coin representing a woman weeping, sitting under a palm tree, with the inscription, "*Judæa capta.*"

You have not felt the Orient till the leaf of the date-palm fans your forehead. There is no more delightful drive in the world than the eleven hours in a French *diligence*, which runs daily between Beyrût and Damascus. The road was made by a French company, and is as good as any in France or Switzerland. The coach is the ancient pattern with postilion and guard, the whip constantly cracked over three mules, harnessed abreast, to do the pulling, behind three horses who furnish the *élan* and the dash. The gradents are long and steep, crossing the two chains of the Lebanon, but the plains of Cœlo-Syria are smooth as water. The stages are eight miles each, and fresh relays are prompt and ready.

When this road, through scenes of matchless beauty and undying historic interest, was complete, it was thought there would be an end of transportation by camel. A mistake; the varied product of the interior still comes to the coast by caravan, and European goods are carried back by the same transport. Whirling along very much at our ease in the comfortable *diligence*, we understand in what state Lady Ellen went forth to see and conquer. The camels go in strings of six, each led by a donkey, who gives a sharp hitch to the rope when his subordinates sway out of line. On these ungainly brutes the brown bales and big boxes are girded, and so she sent her French furniture and English comforts across to Damascus. She did not perch on a bale, or rest on the airy height of a curtained howdah, made a place of soft ease with cushions and pillows, rugs and awning. She rode a prancing, milk-white Arabian of the Khamsa. The Arabs name it a moon-colored horse, and breezes from

the snowy summits of the Lebanon must have lent
a fresher glow to her cheek. The gardens, enclosed in cactus hedges, scented the summer air;
and the olive, the cane, the mulberry, pomegranate, and the vine gave out their perfume, each
after its kind, for this Frankish princess from a
remote barbarian isle. The natives watched in
admiring wonder as she passed, and she gazed on
the new and delightful landscape with eyes of
untroubled azure.

Soon as you set foot on Syrian soil your Bible
readings, forgotten or overlaid, so as to be
crowded out of memory, come back again with
the same force they held in childhood. You see
Abigail, wife of Nabal, astride a white mule
driving other mules; those are the bells of
Eleazar's camels, tinkling by the fountains at
evening. Blind Bartimeus begs by the wayside,
and green and fresh are the gourds of swift
growth, such as shaded the Prophet of Nineveh,
and solitary lodges in the gardens of cucumbers.
From tombs and dens in naked rocks rush weird
shapes like fabled ghouls, or searchers of graves,
hideous with knotted hair and cancerous faces.
They cry for help, holding up hands with fingers
rotted away and skin-like scales of fishes. Fling
a coin before they get nearer, for they are lepers.
These sights the fair lady saw, and profuse in
in charities, doubtless she showered on the plague-
smitten the small white coin called asper.

A gaunt figure, with sunburnt hair, wearing
raiment of camel's hair, and a leathern girdle
about his loins, might pose for Raphael's picture

of one crying in the wilderness, "Prepare ye the way of the Lord, make his paths straight.' Yonder, among the mountain intervals, Joseph, in every-day suit of sheep-skin, feeds his flocks with his brethren; his coat of many colors you may see in the bazar. The low-browed, sullen-faced Ishmaelites yet travel from Gilead, with camels bearing spicery and balm and myrrh, going to carry it down to Egypt. Judging by appearance, these remote descendants of the ancient slaveholders would buy Joseph if they dared, and his brethren would sell him cheap.

Well has it been written, "The hills of Judea are a fifth gospel." Lady Ellen's guide was not an agent of Cook, but even as they who lead Pashas. He was mounted on a Meccan drome-dary, with splendid trappings, a saddle with bur-nished metal peaks before and behind, covered with a huge robe of fur-dyed crimson, and girthed over with voluminous saddle-bags, whose flowing tassels hung almost to the ground. They were of gorgeous color and diverse; stiff with silk needlework embroidery, such as ladies from far countries pay twenty prices for, and make into eider-down cushions for their boudoirs. These things we see just as they were thousands of years ago, when this fine French road was un dreamed of. To the Oriental mind a good road is a perilous experiment and mighty temptation. "Why smooth the rocks from Jaffa to Jerusa-lem," asks the courteous Governor, "that the Russians may bring their siege guns to bear on Mount Zion?"

II.

LADY ELLEN was not disposed to isolation
from her kind, like Lady Hester Stanhope, nor
was she severe as that priestess, who, in the ful-
ness of her self-won power in the Lebanon, anni-
hilated a village for disobedience, and burnt a
mountain chalêt, with all its inhabitants, for the
murder of a traveler. With her faithful friends
Miladi tasted the matchless *vino d'oro*, the golden
wine of the Lebanon, which makes of common glass a cup of amber; and through a field-
glass she discerned, against the intense blue
columns pure as sculptured snow, which mark
the site of Baalbec, the supposed Baal-gad of
the Old Testament. There they stand, like
monarchs in exile, despoiled, but not fallen;
mournful and majestic as the imperial marbles
of the Acropolis.

She saw, my heroine, the same varied landscape we see to-day. She recalled the renowned
warriors who have fought their way through
these defiles, perhaps not Saul and Gideon, but
Tancred, Saladin, the romances of the Lion-
Heart, and tales of the kings of Persia, Egypt
and Rome. Every step of her steed had been
trodden by the feet of a chief, a prophet, a hero;
has rung with the clash of steel and glistened
with the curving scimetar, in whose shadow
Paradise is prefigured for the Faithful. The
tradition runs that the lone city of the wilderness was built by Djinns, for the purpose of hid-

ing in subterranean caverns immense treasure,
which still lies buried there. Those wondrous
columns are haunts for blue lizards, which the
Turks kill because, they say, by bending its
head it mimics them at prayers ; and near them
Moore's Peri caught the precious tear of the
repentant sinner, which bought her admission
into Heaven's gate.

At nightfall, Miladi, with her prince-like
retinue, encamped by the wayside near a fountain, and slept, nestled in downy silken cushions.
Perhaps for supper she ate a cake of *sesame*, to
remind her of Ali Baba, and had a glass of
sherbet made of violets and sugar. From the
draperied doorway of her shawl-lined tent, she
could watch the western sky flush with a red
like the redness of roses, and almost scent its
fragrance. She could understand the rhapsodies
of the native dwellers in tents ; their chanting
of the golden prime of Haroun Al Raschid ;
their rhyming to all sorts of tender remem-
brances, and chiming to the stars of Heaven, and
to the sun, grandest of sheiks, lord of the blue
desert of air. Dearest to the Desert wanderers
is a familiar idyl, sung in slow, soft strains,
about a Fountain of Youth, hid in some dim
region untrodden save by the angels. It lies
away in the far East. History, poetry, fable,
hold here eternal and undisputed sway, and Lady
Ellen was not insensible to their sweet influences.
What she saw was unfamiliar, except the birds ;
for of the three hundred and twenty-two varieties
of Palestine, one hundred and seventy are

English. The timid lark starts out from her
nest on the ground, and goes singing up to
Heaven's gate, circling the sky with waves of
melody. The hedge-sparrow twitters tamely
about to pick up scattered grain, reminder of the
care of the All-Seeing One. Swallows skim the
sky at twilight, and gentle are the notes of coo-
ing doves and tame pigeons on the roofs, as they
twine their silver beaks, repeating the old, old
story, new every morning and fresh every evening. The titmouse flits unresting as the birds
of the Bosphorus, which never alight, *les âmes
damné*, and the carrier-bird scatters cinnamon-
seed into fresh fields. Sweeter than these is the
nightingale in the pomegranate-tree, wooing,
with ravishing note, the rosebud and the rose to
rend their thin veils and lay the soul of their
beauty and love all bare. Sing the poets, You
may place a hundred handfuls of fragrant herbs
before the nightingale, yet he wishes not in his
constant heart for more than the sweet breath of
his beloved rose.

In her guarded tent the Lady of the wandering heart, perhaps, had fleeting dreams of cool,
gray English skies, green lawns, and parks, and
meadows dotted with sheep; but she was not
beset with morbid fancies, though the vesper-
song of the Syrian bulbul is the saddest, tenderest sound ear ever heard. Somehow it always
reminded of young mothers hushing their sick
babies to sleep; plaintive and tired the lullaby,
while the rest of the world is putting on evening beauty and mirth.

Thirty years ago the country was more unsafe than now, and even to-day, the *fellaheen*, except close to towns, must sow and plow with muskets at their backs. Along stupendous cliffs of Hermon and Lebanon are fissures offering in their recesses shelter for banditti, and organized raids of a thousand men sally out in forays, almost to the gates of Damascus. Miladi must not trust to the prestige of a name, nor rely on the charm of her presence to quell a mob; she must travel with a strong escort, though her fame had preceded her, and from the villages crowds flocked to see her go by on her way to the City of Delight.

Syrian villages are much alike, low, mud houses, bare of ornament, a plaster floor, a flat roof, laid with lime and sand, where the family may sleep, where maize is spread to dry, and pigeons flock and feed. An outer stair leads to this useful roof; the doorway is a great arch covered with a hanging mat, answering to the Arab tent, just as the fathers of these people in the wilderness closed the Tabernacle entrance with a veil. At sunset, as of yore, men and women gather about the wells and gossip. None but the rich can afford to sink a shaft through solid limestone a hundred and fifty feet, and once made, the spring is a precious heritage, belonging forever to one family and his tribe; no law or combination can wrest it from him; and it is the saying when Bedawin are hard pressed: " We can stop the wells. Water is life ; how, then, can the horsemen follow ? "

The villages are picturesque in the distance; at near view filthy and poverty-stricken past telling. In the narrow streets, roofed to keep off the sun, among famished beasts, squat worn-out women, with diseased children, who are taught before they can speak, to put out hands for alms to the traveler. Beggars, in every stage of sickness and deformity, miserable dogs quarreling over dry bones, the blind, the lame, the mixed multitude which followed the Master, beseeching that they might touch if it were but the border of his garment; and as many as touched Him were made whole. As you advance into Holy Land, at every turn is new and startling evidence of the truth of sacred history, and forgotten texts start into remembrance with vivid meaning. In the midst of this squalor and misery a shining minaret points with slender finger to the one God; a square of green turf is nicely kept about it; and a prayer stone shows the direction of the Kaaba, the center of the world to the Faithful. A few plane trees—which are our sycamore—with dangling balls, fringed the place of prayer and the fountains. Without this oasis are heated rock and scorching sand, bare except for a shrub, like sage bush the food of the camel.

Circling waves of mountains bound the horizon. One pleasant spot in these forlorn towns is the burial place; not sequestered and forgotten, but a sort of park, where Moslems, old and young, hesitate not to stray; where children play hide-and-seek, black goats browse, and the

dead seem in a sort of fearless companionship
with the living. Once a week, on Friday, the
Mohammedan Sunday, ladies picnic among the
tombs, carrying white umbrellas, lined with
green (a sign of rank), and lay on the graves an
herb called *rihan*, which is our sweet basil. In
dreamy quietude they sit beside the turbaned
headstones, motionless almost as the still sleepers
below. Many other sights, worth traveling far
to see, our traveler, the Lady Ellen, beheld on
her triumphal march toward the city of delight.

I am not here to prose, guide-book in hand,
on the Pearl of the Orient, the most ancient city
on this planet, which has survived every Empire
since the Flood, and under every change of
dynasty—Assyrian, Persian, Macedonian, Roman,
Saracen—has kept its loveliness and prosperity.
For more than four thousand years it has risen
from its green sea of verdure in bright buildings,
airy, ethereal, as some deceitful mirage which
looms up to the vision of the traveler, maddened
with thirst in waterless wastes. The vale in
which Damascus lies was in the forgotten centuries named *Beit Eden,* "the Abode of the
Blest," where are fountains enough to slake the
thirst of ten armies. Every one knows the
story of Mohammed's refusing to enter its walls,
saying it was "too delicious." The enjoyment
of that Paradise would make him forget the
Eternal One, on the shores of the quadrangular
lake where stand one thousand goblets made of
stars, out of which spirits predestined to felicity
drink of the crystal wave. The spot where the

Prophet resisted the fascinations of the tempter is consecrated by a mosque resplendent with green tiles. After the pitiless, blinding glare of white rock and arid gray sand, you feel the unspeakable beauty of this luxuriant valley—really an oasis—and the force of the Arab saying, " The mere sight of Damascus is food for vision, and pure water to the parched throat." It lies like some enchanted city of rounded domes, towers, and minarets, with shining crescents close below the speckless sapphire. Here are the shady rose-gardens where the shrubs are trees, and all of the kind we call damask, loading the air with wholesome perfume ; here are the rushing waters Barrada (the Abana of Naaman's time), and the Thege (the Pharpar), better than all the waters of Israel. Yonder is dewy Hermon, and this wall of amethyst and beryl, edged with pearl, is snowy Anti-Libanus.

But why try to describe the indescribable? One glance is to thrill the coldest nature, and bring tears to your eyes with the mere sense of the beautiful.

Within the decayed and decaying walls of the city, not far from the silver waters of the Barrada, is a private place, hidden from passers-by with a high stone wall. It allows a view of the streets from overhanging balconies, projecting above the dead, blank masonry, which is pierced with one barred gate. About it is a garden freshed with greenery, much water and many fountains; a grateful shelter from sunglare and street-dust. In their season there

bloom the apricot and oleander, carnation, tulip
and lily, poppy and lavender, the never-failing
sweet basil " for remembrance," to go with the
dead to their graves, and the rose, always the
rose.

Lady Ellen bought this palace. For dwellers
in houses of the East the first ideas of living are
plenty of light and space. Many apartments
with multiplied windows, suites of rooms in
ample vistas, or a great hall surrounded by bed-
rooms or boudoirs, and never without a central
court open to heaven. Our lady had wide scope
for elegant tastes. Some rooms she furnished in
French style. The grand *salon* of reception was
carpeted with costly fabric from Persian looms,
the hangings of damask silk shot with gold. In
the boudoir, her special retreat, she gathered
(what contradiction) home treasures, and on
strange altars set up the household gods of her
youth.

There were miniatures of her children, dead
years before this apartment became a show place :
the portrait of her father, whose crest she had
dragged to the dust, painted in his knightly
uniform, looking with unseeing eyes on his
daughter's disobedience. There, too, was a portrait of herself, framed as became her imperious
beauty, in velvet and gold, a bride among the
foremost at the proudest court in the Christian
world. The artist was no common painter, he
caught the very turn of the regal head crowned
with braids of abundant hair, the delicate aristocratic features, the magic of the witching eyes,

blue as the blue of deep sea water—lodestone
eyes, from which none might turn away. On a
table of fragrant woods from India, lay superb
portfolios filled with drawings of Lady Ellen's
own work—home scenes of England, Swiss land-
scapes and original designs—and a piano with
the hushed music of buried years. I did not
see these rooms, but have the account from one
who did.

The English Colony then numbered perhaps
twenty souls. The Britons flocked round the
new-comer and were fascinated. The Pashalic
of Damascus is the most important of the Ottoman Empire, and Orientals felt the charm of the
enchantress, for her languages gave the broadest
range of acquaintance, and she had a genius for
friendships. Officials of rank crowded the *salon*,
a throne room where she spoke, in one evening,
French, Italian, Slav, German, Spanish, Arabic,
Turkish, Greek, readily as her native tongue.

She had a liking for country as well as city
life, and looked after her poultry, stables, flowers,
planned improvements in buildings, and excelled
in music and sculpture as well. Said one of her
country-women, resident at Damascus, She was
always the perfect lady in sentiment, voice,
manners, speech; for those who enjoyed her confidence it was a treat to pass hours in her society.
Idolizing friends never dropped from their allegiance to her, some subtle quality in her composition enforced remembrance; she captivated
women thoroughly, as men, and they worshiped
with unswerving devotion. A caprice of this

wayward woman was to attend service in our missionary chapel; she asked with apparent sincerity and simplicity to be allowed the privilege, knowing well (the artful siren!) the missionaries would be only too glad of her presence and influence.

Meanwhile it was announced in London that Lady Ellen was dead; and in her boudoir, odorous with rose-oil, cedar, and musk, she had the unusual pleasure of reading her own obituary, and smiling over the charitable mention given by common impulse of humanity to the defenseless dead.

What with myriad lights streaming from latticed windows of rooms heavy with languid narcotics, lute and zither resounding through hall and bower, gay voices in court and balcony, the Palace, once the harem of a dismal Pacha, became a notable edifice. But the sound of revelry under the myrtle blooms was within the limits of becoming mirth, noise and uproar were foreign to the *grande dame*, flexile and fair, accustomed to the atmosphere of courts, now queening it to her heart's content. It is said her low laugh was cheering as the matin-hymn of the meadow lark, winsome of the wooing of the cushat in her nest. Still it was a decided change of occupancy from the beauties whose henna-stained fingers drew close their envious veils while they sat in the gardens, ever silent, ever sad, whose gayety was at prayer time, to answer the blind muezzins' cry, in a chorus called *Zira-leet*; whose utmost stretch of freedom was a

slow walk or drive under the eye of the black
guardsman.   The story went abroad that in the
Palace of the Pacha dwelt a foreign princess,
with eyes like stars in the middle watch; allur-
ing as a Peri, the link between men and angels.
She wore a saffron shawl, and was wise as Bal
kis, Queen of Arabia, who went from the south
to hear the wisdom and admire the glory of Solomon.   The witch-woman's veins ran wine, she
knew how to enchant men with cunning sorceries, and could game away the sun before it rises.

III.

CAIRO has been named the heart of the Orient,
but since the changes there by Isamail Pacha,
and the advent of the locomotive, Damascus is
the best place for the coloring of Haroun Al
Raschid.   The Orientals have a saying, "Who
commands iron will soon command gold."
The blades of matchless temper, worth a king's
ransom, have vanished from her markets; but
two of ancient work, wrought to such perfection
they bend like thin whalebone, remain for the
wonderment of the stranger.

The wealth of Damascus is immense, and there
are hundreds of khans for merchandise, built
round a large covered court, where kneeling and
groaning camels deposit their loads.   Two galleries run round this space into which store-
rooms, hardly larger than presses, open.   The
merchants who sit cross-legged in front of the
meager shops, and smoke and wait for customers,
are dignified and reverend as patriarchs.   "Pa-

tience," they say; " by patience the mulberry
leaf becomes satin." One might suppose in the
small stock of goods there is hardly enough
profit to make both ends meet, even with Oriental frugality. Yet those silent, grave shopmen,
seemingly so poor, are worth their millions, and
could you visit them you would see palaces
which make real the visions of Aladdin.

The houses of the city are alike; plastered
with yellow stucco, a dead wall to the street,
giving a dreary and forbidding aspect. Enter
the carven doorway into the court with tessellated pavement, a mosaic of bright marbles,
where fountains laugh and sing to overhanging
vines and blossoms, and the peculiar figs which
made the Roman epicure rejoice that ever he was
born. One such house (not Lady Ellen's, for
there were bounds to her extravagance,) was
built of Italian marble, brought from the coast
on mules. It had balconies despoiled from Saracenic carvings of Egypt, and was hung with
shawls of Hindostan. But this does not interest the stranger like the bazars, shadowy, arched,
and picturesque. When you become used to
dim lights and the gay confusion of colors, discordant voices of men and animals, you will be
delighted with them.

As the great English Lady, with armed attendant, approached, the turbaned Moslems
would start to their feet, and show her the small
cupboards and stalls; in dirty alleys were
precious magazines. One Persian, low salaaming at her lustrous glance, murmured under his

beard, " But for the eyes of sapphire, an Houri
escaped from Paradise ; " and when she passed he
shaded his eyes as from the glinting of the sun.
She did not think it flattery ; she was well-used
to open admiration of the crowd, and accepted it
as she accepted the radiant image in her mirror,
of which none might say aught, except that it
was beautiful. Not in a week, or a month can you
explore the recesses where are gathered quaint
rarities, new and old, exquisitely finished, dazzling the sight. Uninviting and evil-smelling
though they be, here are heaped the spoils of
the East. Amber from the Baltic Sea, coral
from the Caspian, shell and gold work from
Cairo, filagree carvings in ivory and jade from
China, coffee cups of native work crusted with
precious gems, chains and suits of armor inlaid
with jewels. And there are spices from Arabia
Felix, ointments from Moab, and alabaster boxes
from the country of its name. And such amulets
of opal, iridescent and glimmering, talismans of
moonstone, and turquoises of the mines of the
Pharaohs, warranted to keep off the evil eye ;
wonderful caskets hinting of inestimable treasure,
and ivory chests, delicate as frost work.

In the dark, crowded chambers of the Turk,
are rugs soft as down, changeable like the
feathers of tropic birds, with tints toned com-
pletely as the hues of the rainbow ; scarfs stained
with sea-purple, barred and brocaded with gold ;
vari-colored stuffs which always harmonize. No
magenta-reds and sunflower-yellows in the Damascus bazars. They would strike the eye as
sharp discords pain the ear attuned to music.

There is the Koran-stand, where only the holy volume may lie, the uncreated, the Eternal Word, subsisting on the essence of Deity, and inscribed with a pencil of Light on the table of His everlasting decrees. The consecrated stands are shaped like the letter X, and are made of cedar and mother-of-pearl. Hanging overhead, in dust and gloom, are ostrich eggs, quaintly ornamented, and ringed with hoops of gold and gems, to be suspended in sacred places—symbols of the resurrection. There are skins of the spotted leopard, of the black-maned lion from reedy coverts along the banks of the Euphrates, and superb tiger-robes from the Ganges, to be thrown on divans or consecrated as prayer-carpets.

How can I tell of the Indian work of screens and cabinets; fans, and of ancient arms, the mere mention of which stirs the ghosts of dead and gone crusaders and Paladins? Here are wonderful peacocks with enameled breasts, and jewels for the argus-eyes of the sweeping tail; coffee-services of brass and silver, set with diamonds, in trays arabesque, old Moorish work; nargilehs with long ropes for smoking through water, amber mouthed chibouks, every conceivable shape of pipe; meerschaum and ambergris, rose-oil and musk, shawls, silks, table-covers, fabrics of soft wool, furs, and leather work pliant as silk. The experienced and enthusiastic shopper goes mad with delight in Damascus. And after the slow day's bargaining, comes the pure, sensuous enjoyment of cooling breeze from snowy mount-

22

ain tops, the pomp of sunset, the glow of starry
skies, and the chirp of insect life in restful uni-
son. All is poetry, picture, romance, appeals to
memory and imagination such as are never
found in the raw newness of western cities without a history.

Many days the Lady of whom I write, spent
pleasantly in the magnificent fatiguing bazars.
She bought much and she bought well. The
shopmen knew her, and the pedlars who prey on
the stranger and the pilgrim respected the great
lady, who could address them in their own
tongue, and offered them fair price and no more
for their wares.

Her fame went abroad in the regions round
about, and it spread through the Hill country
that there was a foreign woman, a Giaour in the
City of Delight, beautiful as the father of Mohammed, who was so beautiful that the night he
was married two hundred virgins died of jealousy and despair.

The vari-colored shows of Damascus had a
strong hold on Lady Ellen, and they amused her
for a time, but the trail of the serpent is over
them all, and she tired of the splendor and the
squalor of street and khan. Her palace was
done; filled and finished, wanting nothing but
the roe's egg under the central dome. The
placid indolence of the place was too monotonous for the unquiet soul of the Queen of the
Blue Eyes.

Her chief amusement, not very amusing, was
the Bazar of the farthest East, after the prayer

Has-arr at three P. M., when the galleries are the theatre of auction sales, and shifting shapes and colors are most vivid and complex. In one of these idle saunterings she espied in a draped archway, a man unlike Turk or Persian, standing behind a glass box of trinkets. He was short, swart, with oblique eyes, and curly hair fringing a black turban. When she approached his magazine of merchandise the seller bowed to her with sullen and gloomy indifference. Unused to such scant courtesy Lady Ellen, somewhat piqued, advanced to the stranger and asked indifferently: "What have you that is new to me?" She addressed him in Arabic, and the man replied in the same language, first saluting her with deep salaam :—

"I have such jewels as have never been seen in Damascus. Will the Princess honor the poorest of her slaves by looking at them?"

"Yes. But looking does not always mean buying with me."

"Certainly not. Still it will please the Princess to see the gems, so far from their happy home on the White Nile."

Fumbling the ample folds of his robe, the man drew from his bosom a package covered with black woolen cloth. "This," he said, explanatorily, with a forbidding and sinister smile, "is their cloak, manufactured in Djerid, the country of golden dates and silky sheep."

He laid the black cloth in the bottom of a deep, narrow box, and slid down his flowing sleeve a coiled belt of spun gold, with bright

clasps on top. Then he shaded it with his dark
burnous, and said: "Will the Princess look
down the tube, and tell what the jewels are
like."

She bent over the black box, and, with sudden, rousing interest, exclaimed: "Like two
flaming coals of fire at the bottom of a well.
They are the famous twin topazes of Ethiopia."

"A good guess for a stranger," said the man,
his dark face brightening, "but, pardon, they
are not topazes."

"Ah! carbuncles, then," said the Lady, gaily,
now fairly awake to the strangeness of the fanci-
ful ornament.

"No," said the trader, artfully shaking the
tube to give best effects. "Those glancing
lights, *reflets* the French call them, are not the
property of carbuncles. The Princess is a con-
noisseur, but she must guess again."

"Mohammed was a merchant and commended
commerce to his disciples; you have profited by
his teaching."

"Pardon again, oh, Princess; I am not among
the followers of the camel-driver of Mecca. I
come from the most ancient of Christians, the
Copts of the first Cataract of the Nile. I swear
not by the Prophet; I swear by the Lion of St.
Mark, these clasps are older than the seal-ring
of Rameses."

"I will examine them a moment to pass the
time," said Lady Ellen, with a charming animation.

The merchant drew the belt out of its hiding-place and laid a band of sunlight—the very cestus of Cytherea—on the delicate wrist extended to receive the coil.

"Pliant gold," she said, "that is modern work."

"It is," the merchant reluctantly admitted, "but the clasps, that ancient setting, is from the mines of the Pharaohs. The jewels have a history."

"The design is unique; more curious than beautiful," said the buyer, examining the jeweler's work; "but you have not told me the name of the stones."

"They are rubies of the Redeemer."

"Unknown to me. What a singular name!"

"And so is the quality, oh, Princess. These are glistening blood-drops, rimmed in black onyx, reminders of Calvary and the Holy City of David." He went on pleadingly: "You like them because they are so old. They are older than this world, and potent as Solomon's signet."

"You will persuade me this is the belt of Orion, dropped from the clouds. A talisman, too valuable for every-day mortals," said Lady Ellen, lifting her even brows.

"The princess has clear vision. They are magical amulets of Egypt."

"Suppose I buy one jewel, what will it protect me from?"

"From the curse *Nazar*, or evil-eye, mentioned in the Koran, and believed in by Moslems and many who are not Mussulmans. The fire in the eye."

"How did you come by a thing so precious as these clasps studded with rubies," she spoke imperiously. "Tell me the truth."

"I will, oh, Princess. I love the truth," said the jeweler, mysteriously lowering his voice. "Should you not please to buy the burning belt, for that is its name, will you hold the legend I tell you with seal unbroken?" He spoke reverentially, and feigned anxiety for her answer.

"I shall never think of it again," was the careless rejoinder, for the man was growing too confidential.

"Pardon. I am sure nothing will be done to mar the fortune or dull the luster of my costly jewels."

"Certainly not. Proceed with your story."

"Will the Princess be seated?" He threw a coverlet of velvet, embroidered with gold, on a cushioned seat.

"A moment only," said Lady Ellen, to humor his whim. "Be brief."

"I will. It is a short story the Princess graciously deigns to hear. Last year I was in my reed-hut on the upper Nile, when a party of Englishmen came to dig among the tombs. The sheik of our village is jealous of the Northerns and has spies to follow them, listen to what they say, and secretly report on them. I was honored with his confidence, and because I understood their language he gave me a handsome sum to serve them and him at the same moment."

"Do you mean to say you understand English,"

asked the Lady in her native tongue. "Now I am surprised."

"The praise of a Frankish Princess is worth years of happy life to her servant. I am no scholar but can make myself understood," said the Copt in tolerable English, "but it is not easy for me, and if the Princess please, I will return to the language of the false Prophet. May his name be confounded!"

Lady Ellen nodded indifferently, and the Copt with hands crossed on his breast stood behind his glass box of wares and continued:—

"These Englishmen discovered the tomb of a king, they said, which had never been broken into or touched. They are full of precious things, a fortune to the finders, for my ancestors buried valuables with their dead so that when they rise again they may not be poor and miserable. They hired me to go with them, and promised to kill me if I told of this sealed tomb, in the rock. I worked for them faithfully, and went with them through dismal caverns in the heart of catacombs. We found two coffins lying side by side."

"A king and his queen."

"The same, O Princess. Their painted portraits were on the lid, and their history, which I read at a glance. We bursted them open, we raised the lid by the light of torches, and in the terrible heat, and there was nothing, nothing, not even a bone. Other Englishmen had been there before them; for wherever wood will float, there is the Englishman."

"What has that to do with these clasps?"

asked Lady Ellen, impatiently; "I should like
to know."

"All to do, Princess. The coffins had been
robbed hundreds of years ago. The torchlight
is dim in the stone caves; my sight is better than
that of the bald-headed Englishmen, and as we
turned to go back, (how they did curse!) I saw,
like fiery eyes, these jewels flashing in the mum-
my-dust and sand on the floor of the king's
chamber. They had been dropped when the
tombs were first robbed. I set my foot softly on
the king's girdle, and beg the English gentlemen
to bear my torch ahead one moment, while I
tighten my sandal. They obligingly do so. I
slip the prize into my bosom. I hold these gems
there. Ever since that day they have been worn
under my burnous or my turban. Behold my
story! It is ended."

The lady was gazing absently at the mountains, now putting on crowns of gold, and made
no sign, except a balancing of the belt as though
weighing it in her hand—an affectation which
dashed the confidence of the Copt a little. He
waited in disappointed silence, eyeing her eagerly.
She appeared to have forgotten him.

"What is the name of the star of war and of
blood?" he asked, when the pause became unendurable to the hopeful vender of antiques.

"Mars," said Lady Ellen, recalling her wandering attention, and wondering what the man would
make out of that. "It is a red planet, and keeps
the first watch of evening." She relapsed into the
bored expression which made the Egyptian

desperate. His face flushed, he continued: "I am charmed to know the English name of the star of the heroes. Deign to hear your slave, O Princess, and believe, for I swear by the law given on Sinai—"

"Do not fatigue yourself with oaths; they do not impress me," said the listener, making a gesture of dissent.

"Pardon, pardon, fair Princess; I love the truth, and will tell it, as a Christian should. My treasure is not of this earth, and there is but one lady living worthy to wear it."

The speaker drew a long breath as though about to make a plunge into deep water, and nervously twisted his fingers together, his voice thrilling with excitement :—

"These blazing jewels come from the War Star. They fell away from it in the ages of the forgotten. Soon as I touched them, I knew they were enchanted stones from the regions of upper air, under the silver ceiling to which Moslems say the stars are strung by strong chains. When one shoots from its place, flying flakes like sparkles of fire trail after it through the sky. Only once in ten thousand thousand years do they reach the earth, instead of burning out like lamps."

The man had touched his climax; there was nothing more to tell. His peculiar eyes gleamed with hope.

"Suppose I buy one ruby, from what will it protect me?"

"The marvels of flame are useless apart and

alone, O Princess; but the gems in a circle make
the wearer proof against magic and sorcery.
They are stronger than the mystical sapphire
engraved in letters of light with *the Nameless
Name*, on the hand of Solomon the Wise. The
silken girdle of the mummied king was dropping
to pieces with age, then I had this belt from a
holy dervise of Assouan. It is, as you see,
modern; but its metal makes the electric circle
complete, and whoever wears it may command,
enchain, and hold spell-bound Demon and Giant,
Afreet, Dives, and Djinn."

"Anything else?" asked the lady, with satire,
lost on the dull wits of the seller.

"Yes, fair Princess, I repeat, the burning belt
will keep off the evil-eye, the *Nazar*, named in
the Koran, and plague, ship-wreck, nightmare,
and fire."

"What price do you ask for the pretty belt,
which insures long and peaceful life?"

He named a moderate sum, for he knew the
Princess was familiar with Oriental prices; and
she laughed as she snapped the strange lock,
inscribed with miraculous signs and cabalistic
devices.

"It is mine," she said, "and now I am safe
from the monsters."

They were nearer than she knew.

Perhaps a tinge of superstition had touched
Lady Ellen's imagination by residence in the
Orient, or maybe a mere caprice led the wayward
woman to wear the mystic zone ever after it came
into her possession. The girlish waist, set off by

the close clasp of glittering buckles, made a
conspicuous ornament for one whose quiet costumes were not often noticeable. Her condescen-
sion made the Copt her bond-slave for life, but
she waved him away when he approached with
more wonderful gems and still stranger histories.
She had all good things within the ring of starry
gold, nothing remained to be wished for.

IV.

It is a law of psychological mathematics,
that the immovable force of dullness will, in
the end, overcome any varying and irregular
force resisting it. In the third year of the
undisputed reign of the Queen of Blue Eyes
she began to feel the strength of opposing
natures unlike her own. One morning she
abruptly announced to her worshipers that she
was tired of Damascus. (The word environment
has not effected a lodgment in Asia.) She was
sated, *ennuyé*, bored with the insipid legend of
the "Seven Sleepers" and forever recurring
traditions of the "Father of the Faithful." She
longed for a glimpse of Bagdad, ancient of days,
the seat of the Vicars of the Prophet. Suppose
there was a sandstorm or an attack by robbers;
it would give her something to think about.
She had purchased what choice things, large and
small, she cared for; she had lolled and dreamed
in her fountained court long enough; had dashed
over the hills and far away on the moon-colored
horse—an apparition calculated to make the

dull, irrational Turkish women start with
horror.

That peerless animal was a small, compact
Arabian, with mild eyes and familiar, loving
ways, like a house-dog. She could leap like a
gazelle, with no fear of her groom, whom she
used as a rubbing-post; was never intimidated
by lifting up of sticks or hands; for she had
never been struck, and did not know the meaning of such gesture. Arab mares are stanch
friends and laborious slaves, and so fleet and
steady that a chief of Circassia, mounted on one,
galloping at full speed, has been known to shoot
a crow on the wing with his rifle; and they can
travel two hundred miles under the saddle in
three consecutive days. Ambling is the favorite
gait in the East; and for that reason Lady Ellen
chose the long, low gallop, where the true
Arabian, even on the roughest, rockiest hills,
never makes a false step. She could not ride
forever, and she tired of sunny days, which lazy
Turks use for taking *kief* in their kiosks on the
banks of the Barrada or Pharpar. She had
enough of the venders of curios and Damas
blades. They were impostors, and their arms
were counterfeits, every one.

She was tired of the ladies with the Paradise eyes (ah, those eyes!) who own the cash-
meres, and never wear them, but go about in
balloon-like draperies and shuffling slippers; in
their movement graceless as water-birds on land.
She had climbed the walls of the old castle,
which looms up in the pictorial city, and looked

back over the valley enclosed in bloom, and idly
watched the silver flow of the rivers eastward
to the great marshy lakes which lie twelve miles
beyond the gates, and are there lost in the sand.
She had haunted the ruinous mosques, a mingling of Gothic and Saracenic architecture, and
pondered and mused over the fantastic, incongruous mixture of magnificence and misery, filth
and luxury, which goes to make up the Oriental
City. Yes, she was tired of Beit Eden: its
languor and repose. It was tedious and humdrum in spite of her troops of friends. She
knew herself in a favorite stronghold of fanatics.
The lover of facts (not you nor I, my reader)
will remember that, in 1861, over twenty-five
thousand Christians were massacred in and
about Hermon and Anti-Lebanon. They hate
Jews and Christians; but there is no reason to
believe the Moslems hated my Queen of the
Blue Eyes. She knew their ways, good and
bad, and gave much backsheesh. Why should
they hate her?

Damascus still retains its elliptical form; and
its walls, pierced with seven gates, doubtless
occupy their first foundations. It was once
threaded from east to west by a street called
Straight—a noble thoroughfare, a hundred feet
in breadth, divided by Corinthian colonnades
into three avenues, of which the central was
used by footmen, the other two traversed by
horsemen, chariots and beasts of burden. Thus
were built Bozrah and Samaria, and thus
Palmyra, as proved by its four long rows of

columns, sixty feet high, beginning in a majestic, triumphal arch. Round about Damascus are mountains sterile as Sinai, which glow at evening like the very splendor of the Eternal Throne. Lady Ellen surveyed them as the barrier of the desert which lies on the other side; a level of yellow sand, smooth as a floor, soft as a tufted carpet, where run lines representing roads, and creeping specks, like ants, which are men and animals. Deep in it, fiery leagues away, is Tadmor in the Wilderness, the city builded of Solomon, girdled by the desert, as other cities in pleasant isles are girdled with the sea. She would cross that mountain wall, and seek the city named Palmyra by the all-conquering Roman. There, at least, she would have some sort of change from this *triste* valley, ruled by endless quietude.

What if it was like a sweet dream to sit in the roses and hear the birds sing? to be awakened by the lark and lulled by falling waters? Enough of that sort of thing. Time to ring down the curtain on Damascus. Good-night to the Eye of the East.

Across the graves of forty centuries she would march—Miladi, in search of novelty. The resplendent, rose-strewn palace chambers were too narrow, this kingdom too small, the wearisome Turks too stolid and staring. She would get out of their sight, and throw off the trammels of civilization. She had worn those bonds lightly enough, to be sure; but the leopardess must be loosed again. Her English friends opened the book of lamentations; they could not let her go; she took their daylight with her. Vainly they pleaded danger. She answered:—

" Did not Lady Hester Stanhope live, the only woman among thirty-seven serving men, in her convent palace? And did not Madame de la Tourelle live for years on the top of an exceeding high mountain, in peace and safety?"

She would travel the road of old Phœnician adventurers, of mailed knights and crusaders, where many lances have been shivered, and many a hero who used to prance in the tilt yard, in the sheen of bright eyes and bright armor, has bitten the dust. Why should she be cooped up in stone walls when the free desert was wooing her as the lion woos his bride? As well be locked in a harem at once. The ruins of Tadmor, or Tudmur, as the Arabs call it, are not imposing, they urged; the low, mean, mud-built modern village is the home of plague and fever; of jackals, masterless dogs; a decrepit and dying place, hardly a camel to be seen in the streets; the Desert glows like a furnace; and your only thought, after getting in, is how to get out. The towers are used as stables for miserable, mangy donkeys of the lowest tribes, who rob and strip the wayfarer.

Lady Ellen was never listless; so her friends tell me. She heard each argument with infinite and gracious gentleness, and smilingly did as she pleased. And it pleased the lady to set her fair face eastward; to tempt fortune outside the Happy.Valley. There is a true saying: " In the

Desert no man meets a friend." Take protection of the caravan, or have a strong guard, as our heroine did, departing in state with a party of Anazees, under Antar, an inferior sheik, a Bedouin. Tents, baggage, maid—every equipment for comfort went with her.

The Desert, forbidding to our imagination, has its own charm, which it keeps for its lovers. There are secret waters in the sand if you choose to dig for them, and hidden pleasure found by search. You must, along with food and water, shelter and steed, take an atmosphere with you. Lady Ellen took hers. They say her glance was like a saber in the air the morning she started, in eager delight. Good-by to flashing streams of lucent waters. The liquid music will not stay her step, nor shady garden, nor balcony with striped awning, where friends crowd, with waving hands and scarfs. Good-by to verdant leafage and tropic blossom, summer house of marble and gold, gilded kiosk, and cool pavilion. Hail to the Desert chief who escorts the incoming queen to the storied realm of Zenobia.

Though your lips parch in the Desert, you do not feel oppressed. The senses are sharpened acutely, and the constant presence of danger keeps one on the lookout, and at his highest spirit; the air is tonic as spiced wine. Evening mild is pleasant past telling, the bivouac delicious. Tents are pitched silently, rapidly; carpets are spread; the grunting camels ungirded; the supper eaten heartily.

The stars flash out at a breath; not slowly as

with us; and then is the witching time. While
dim Æolian soundings haunt your ear, look
toward the North Star, and sing the tender
evening strain from the Koran:

> " Have we not given you the earth for a bed,
> And made you husband and wife,
> And given you sleep for rest,
> And made you a mantle of night?"

When the lights are out, and all else is
hushed, some Arab will tune his two-stringed
guitar. His boundless tent is the infinite
spangled arch which upholds the Throne of God.
Mingling with your dreams are his soft chants of
bubbling fountains, waving palms, leafy oases,
white arms, and the ba'my breath of the Black-
eyed (always the Black-eyed!) whose tresses
are as midnight shades, whose form is like the
tamarisk when the warm wind blows. Or he
may chant the thousand and one verses of the
Persian Poet, Nizami's Lay of the Frantic Lover
and the Night-black Beauty who died of love.
Or he may drowsily thrum and sing of Borak,
the milk-white steed, swifter than lightning, who
bore Lord Mohammed beyond the Seventh
Sphere. Up he flew, up the path of purple
glass, to the light which hath not any name on
earth. Up to the dim " Region of the Veils,"
where ten thousand thousand bars of flame,
lambent with loveliness and mystery, shut all
times off from eternity, and guard the Everlasting City of Precious Stones.

With such fervid enthusiasm did Lady Ellen
set out for the City of Palms that she declared

she would love to push on to Aleppo and Bag
dad, to Shiraz and Persepolis—last stronghold
of the Magian—the hills of the fire-worshipers
and the glorious region where the sun rises.
Useless to oppose the whims of the spoilt beauty;
to threaten her with plagues, the "Aleppo button," the "Bagdad date-mark," the evil-eye.
She clasped the burning jewels of her belt, and
laughingly said she wore talisman and amulet,
and could more easily cast a spell than submit to
one.   In pleasant Eastern fashion, friends,
mounted on goodly steeds, escorted her half-a-
day's march into the wilderness, and, after much
salaaming and salutation and fine compliment.
consigned her to the guidance and guardianship
of a squad of Anazees, under Sheik Antar.
That is not his name, you know; it is best not
to tell names and tales together.

At once, my reader pictures him an emir of
emirs, a supreme, haughty leader, of dauntless
bravery, who sways his tribe as one man, though
his power is a splendid weakness; for the order
of succession to the first place is loose and pre-
carious.   But his desert brethren and followers
worship him, and are ready to do and die with
him and for him.   His banner, displayed at the
head of the column, deserves the honors of a
kingly name.   He (this ideal sheik) wears a turban with tremendous diamonds, and lives in the
saddle. His horse's neck is clothed with thunder;
the glory of his nostrils is terrible; and he
smelleth the battle afar off, the thunder of the
captains and the shouting. The **monarch of**

the illimitable desert has the eye of a falcon, the brow of a conqueror, is wiry and agile, and his heart is filled with a sad unrest. Though his people keep the roads, they scorn to attack parties with women, and are actuated by high and generous impulse. He tosses a javelin, decorated with tufts and flying streamers, wears a murderous yatagan and cimeter of crescent shape, and is forever swearing by the law and the prophet and the soul of his grandfather. On the march he is foremost, a guiding light amid the shine of lances. In camp his is the central tent of striped scarlet and white, with mighty standard of green, the color of the flag of the Prophet (he rests in glory!). His spear before the door, like Saul's, is a terror to evil-doers; and, when provoked to wrath, he is a lion come up from swellings of Jordan.

Such is our ideal sheikh. I saw him in the area about the mosque of Omar at Jerusalem, and again escorting a party from the Holy City to Hebron. Many times have I seen the real sheikh, much more easily discovered. Especially do I recall one who cheats travelers by selling counterfeit antiques and false coins in the shadow of the Pyramids; a hungry-looking rascal, followed by a dozen or so beggars; the pettiest of petty chiefs, the small head of the smallest of clans; a robber by profession and practice, not of the Paul Clifford school, but a savage, skulking behind rocks and in gorges. And of such, in all probability, were the ancient "kings" who held Canaan in Joshua's time.

Dare I whisper to you, dearly beloved, that the vast majority of the unconquered Bedouins, when stripped of romance and glamour, clad only in their homespun rags, resemble, very nearly, those gentle wards of the Government, our own Digger Indians, and their sheikh is the sachem of the tribe?

Just here let me snatch one moment to say, when you *do* find he be t Oriental, the exquisite grace of his bearing the smooth, patient, courteous dignity of his manner, surpass the highest breeding of Christian courts. At the risk of rousing my reader's indignation I repeat the remark of one long resident in Persia: "The further east you go, the finer the manner. First among the sons of men for polish and urbanity is the Arabian; ext him the Turk; then comes the Italian; the the Spaniard, Frenchman; then the cold, stiff Englishman and lastly the helter-skelter American; and I presume, California is worse than Chicago, though I have never been there." Remember, this is not my assertion, nor dare I confess to endorsing it.

As to the glittering arms and blood-curdling prowess of the Desert kings they are things to be laughed at. A band of tourists can chase a thousand brigands, and a very small army can put ten thousand to flight. The wonderful mares sung in song and famous in story are the property of princes. Occasionally the average Bedouin owns a scraggy, famished beast, badly pounded with sticks, which we call a donkey.

V.

Inhabitants of the Desert are easily recognizable by a network of wrinkles in the skin round their eyes, the result of half closing them to avoid the intense sunbeat. This was a peculiarity of the face of Sheik Antar, and, like like many of his nation, he had visible front teeth. At a distance, before the features are discernable, either a short upper lip, or some way of holding it, reveals the ivory-white in the dusky setting. I have not been able to learn any characteristic by which he was distinguished above his fellow Anazees, and the many descriptions which have come to me represent him as the ordinary Bedouin—swart, keen-eyed, straight-haired, somber. And now my story has two branches. I give both; and my precious reader may take his choice :—

One is that Antar was ugly, dull and dirty—a poor outlaw, who, if found on the Lebanon by the Maronites, would be shot at sight, and his flesh be given to the fowls of the air, meat for the eagles if the jackals did not rob them. The other version is that he was gallant and noble, tender, chivalrous and very young. All agree that, when two days' journey toward Palmyra they were attacked by a wandering horde of Ishmaelites, the youth was intrepid and wary, and after a sharp skirmish, brought off his charge, camels, mules, baggage, princess, maid, dog, safely within the gates of Damascus.

Here is the testimonial made by Lady Ellen's own fair hand, in the grimy, well-thumbed register of the Hotel d'Etranger, dated at Damascus, June 13, 1853. You need not waste valuable time hunting for the record. Years and years ago the leaf went to the portion of weeds and worn-out faces: "*Je prends cette occasion de recommender le Scheik Antar, chef des Anazzés, à tout voyageur que desire entreprendre le voyage de Palmyre; l'ayant trouvé parfaitement capable, et digne de confiance, sous tous les rapports.*"

Undoubtedly this electric woman, whose study was to attract, by resistless force, every person who came within her orbit, had qualities which fire the Arab imagination, and Sheikh Antar very naturally fell in love with the unveiled Giaour. He lingered in and about Damascus, haunting its environs, and became a visitor to the *grand dame* whom he had rescued. In the lofty salon, entrancing with vivid lights, languid perfumes, dreamy narcotics, waltz-music, and the indescribable elegance of perfect taste and wealth, the son of the Desert met—his destiny. He was welcome, as all were, to that open house; and in the sultry, balmy eves, after the day's burning glow, he went mooning about under the citron trees, we may fancy, trying to get his own consent to make an audacious move, which would shock even the meanest of his tribe. Finally he proposed to divorce his Moslem wives and marry Lady Ellen; to give up many in order to become the husband of one; to pass one-half the year in Damascus for *her* pleasure, and one-half with his tribe for *his*, in order still to live his natural life, according to his religion and traditions. That is the prettiest version, and not improbable. Grievous is it to write the other, because I have a sort of liking for this soft, tame leopardess, full of tiger-blood. I hesitate to repeat the truth; but stern are the duties of the historian.

After her safe home-coming, one day she astounded Sheik Antar by telling him she wished to become his wife. He was scared, so the legend runs, and fled to his defenses—the Desert and the bosom of his tribe, whose range was on the ancient plain of the Sun-god. The Queen was imperative, and not used to denial or opposition. She did not pursue him with dainty three-cornered notes, perfumed with strange odors, and dispatched by trusty hands. She sent beguiling embassies, under strict orders, who persuaded him to return; and he consented.

When a Moslem woman marries a Giaour, or Christian, it is the duty of the Faithful to track her, catch her, make an example of her apostasy. She is "caused to disappear." With a man the authorities interfere to prevent, if possible, such an outrage on Mohammedan religion. The Turkish Governor at Damascus took the matter in hand, and made the breach of faith such a heinous crime before Sheik Antar that again the chief, in affright, took to the sands and disappeared. Again the lady sent for him; but he came not. He did not fancy stifling airs in city walls, still less the threats of the Turkish *Serail*.

At last she sought him herself, and—Oh! dear, dear!—proposed to marry him. We may well ask, with Brabantio, "What foul charms, what drugs, what conjuration, and what mighty magic had he to cast such a spell over the daughter of an alien race?" Antar had been a silent visitor in the Palace. No feats of broil or battle had he to boast, nor tales of rash adventure, moving accidents by flood or field: a plain man at his best, yet able to bind her in chains of subtle sorcery. Or did some malicious elf touch with a love-philter the veined eyelids of this Queen, so she exclaimed "Thou art wise as thou art beautiful!" and followed the monster to stick musk-roses in his sleek, smooth head?

It would be grotesque, if it were not painful; and there is no solution for the killing mystery.

In his black tent, with his small tribe, she found the little man, and (sorry to relate!) there they were married by the Bedouin ceremony, with no witnesses but his Anazee companions. No matter how the offer was made, certain it is the marriage was consummated in that place and way. Under the ever-burning stars she vowed her vow and sealed her *kismet*.

A friend who knew her well, one of her countrywomen at Alexandria, wrote me: "Lady Ellen's romantic desire of becoming Queen of the Desert did not greatly startle us who are used to her eccentric fancies. In spite of determined opposition, and the protest of the British Consul, she was married by Moslem law, and her name changed to Madame Antar, wife of the

Sheik of the Anazees. Too late, too late, she learned, and was aghast with horror, to know, that, by the act, she had lost her nationality, and had become a Turkish subject. She gave the world for love, and thought it well lost. Verily, there is no mystery like the human heart; or is it true that the days of witchcraft are not ended?"

After it was over and the fact established that she *was* the Bedouin chieftainess, the infatuated lady appeared, like Desdemona, subdued unto the very quality of her lord. Repent? Not she. No! No! No! She made over to him her palace and gardens at Damascus, being there part of the year, and in his tent the rest of the time. For one of the conditions exacted when he yielded to her suit (!) was a written contract that she should never require him to go west of the City of Delight.

Yes, she the high-born, the all-gifted, crowned by the Graces with garlands to make life lovely, stooped from her place to become the lawful wife of the head of a wretched tribe of wanderers in the Desert. Among old letters, which furnish material for this strange, eventful history, I copy one which has survived much that is more valuable, written by the wife of a British Consul —an answer to the question was not *la reine aux beaux yeux bleus* acting under some unrecognized form of insanity:

—"the malady which slays
More than are numbered in the lists of Fate,
Taking all shapes, and bearing many names."

She wrote: "Lady Ellen's head was clear and cool, and her personal charm beyond compare. Even at forty she was more attractive than half the young girls of her time. We thought that, when the delusion died and the wizard spell dissolved, she would behold in Antar a creature even more repulsive than the one the Queen of the Fairies chased through Athenian groves; but she did not tire of her bargain, though formerly fickle in attachments. The halo of a dream—if dream there be in this waking existence—was round him to the last, and she never woke from the marvelous illusion. There was no masque or claptrap in the conduct of the Sheikh, and if there was deceit, she but practiced it on herself; if repulsion, we never found it out."

Unchangeable is custom in the East, binding as the sternest decrees of the Kaliph. The Mohammedan passionately cherishes the legends and traditions of the fathers, and admits no innovation. I have said the marriage was according to the laws of Islam, which ceremony is, to say the least, extremely simple, consisting of a written contract, if the bride has a dower of palm-trees, camels, or a donkey, and a few words spoken by the woman, equivalent to I take thee, or wed thee, or give myself up to thee.

When they were absent in Palmyra, the show-rooms of the pretty house in Damascus were exhibited by the French maid, who talked volubly of Madame Antar's habits since her last marriage, and showed how she sat on the floor, opposite her **Arab**, and how they ate from the same platter. She paraded—not without Miladi's consent, of course—the sad souvenirs of her early life, reminiscences of the sinless girlhood and triumphal career in society at the Court of St. James.

The feminine reader, who has graciously followed my rambling story, now nearing its end, may ask, "How *did* Lady Ellen live out there in the Desert?" The tone of society in Oriental cities is French; but the most ingenious and versatile cannot carry that tone into the "houses of hair," which, from the beginning, have been the shelter of the nomads.

The **Arab** tent is not like our Sibley or Rhodes tent. It is made exactly as it was in the time of **Abraham**, of goat's hair-cloth, brown, and, in the distance of the shimmering plain, looks black. Thus the poet-king of the Israelites sang: "I am black, but comely, **O** ye daughters of Jerusalem, as the tents of Kedar, as the curtains of Solomon." It is shaped like a parallelogram, the door at one of the long sides. The cloth is water-proof, and the dark color absorbs the sun's rays, making them much cooler than the glaring white tents of civilization. The cloth is raised to a considerable height above the ground, with a loose, flapping drapery below, to allow free circulation of air. The interior is divided by a curtain, the harem, or woman's apartment, being on the right. Cushioned divans, rugs and shawls make seats by day and beds by night. Mats are there, and the consecrated prayer-carpet. After

all, not so bad a lodge in a vast wilderness, in
which to sing, "I am my Beloved's, and he is
mine."

The scriptural narrative of Abraham, Friend
of Allah, sitting in the tent-door to catch the
breeze in the heat of the day, and hastening to
invite the passing stranger, still has its counterpart in the Plain of Mamre. Still do men, rich
in cattle, sit in the tent, a refuge from noonday
sun, and run to meet the stranger. (Few angels
pass that way, now.) They salute him, and
offer him the hospitality of the shade, water to
wash his feet, and a hasty meal. The wife
kneads the cakes in the same kneading-trough
that the Israelites used, and bakes them on the
hearth on hot stones ; and the calf, " tender and
good," dressed with butter and milk, is a dish
fit to set before the king. The scorching sun
makes haste as urgent, and the Bedouin is ready
now, as he was three thousand years ago, to
stand in the shade of the tree and wait on the
visitor as he eats.

The tent of the ancient Friend of Guests, as
the Arab names the first patriarch, was probably
under a great oak ; and one of the descendants
of that ancient forest king cast the acorn which
lies on the table where I write. While the
host attended his angelic visitants, in accord
with universal Oriental custom, Sarah, though
invisible, was close by, peeping through the
tent-curtain and overhearing what was said. So
the women hide, and catch furtive glimpses from

behind draperies, and laugh if there is any absurdity in speech or manner of the stranger.

The visitor washes his hands, exclaiming, *B'smillah!* ("in the name of God"), and repeats one of the ninety-nine beautiful names of Allah. A piece of bread is dipped in salt as a pledge for unbroken hospitality, and used as a spoon to scoop up meat and vegetables, if such be the feast; and, lastly, the spoon itself is eaten. The wife waits on her husband, calling him lord, even as Sarah did Abraham; and he eats alone, or with his eldest son, and the women have their meals by themselves. Hands are washed again at the end of the repast; but dishwashing is dispensed with in the dry and thirsty land, and so clean is Desert sand that rubbing the brass platters with it polishes them brightly.

There was a concession to civilization in the Arab Antar when he and his Queen sat on cushions, beside a tray of food placed on a table about eighteen inches high; presumably, the *pièce de résistance* was *pilaf*, a dreadful mixture of rice and stewed meats, and after the banquet they had pipes and coffee. Lady Ellen suppressed the flute-like music of her voice, and probably ate in solemn silence, beloved of the Oriental. On the most ancient of Arabic houses is inscribed, as a text, our familiar proverb: "Speech is silver, silence is golden."

Thus *la reine aux yeux bleus* lived in camp—she, the peerless, the adorable daughter of Britain, called by her subjects the "Northern Panther," because of her tender grace and leon-

ine courage; for she was brave as the soldier
who lives but to die. What was her compensation? If Damascus was monotonous, the Desert
was weariness intensified. The great sand-levels
are solemn as the sea. Was its stillness haunted
by bitter memories, thoughts of better days in
other years? It would seem her vision was not
retrospective, and the free life of untrammeled
roving seemed to suit her restless spirit.

Among a degraded people there was small
opportunity for using the power which goes
with the fair and gracious gifts her good genius
laid in her cradle. The nomadic instinct, born
of every descendant of Adam, once wakened,
never sleeps again. It is old as the first wanderers from Eden, and there is no credible testimony to show distaste of Lady Ellen's marvelous choice. She was loyal and loving, and
abided by him till the fever called living was
past.

A letter from an English woman at Jaffa, an-
nounces in the London newspapers the death of
the chieftainess Antar: "For fifteen years she
lived as she died, the faithful and affectionate
wife of the Sheik, to whom she was devotedly
attached. Half the year was spent by the
couple in a pretty house in Damascus, just
within the gates of the city, and the other half
was spent according to *his* nature in the Desert
among the Bedouin tents of the tribe. In spite
of this hard life, necessitated by accommodating
herself to his habits —for they were never apart
—she never lost anything of the English lady,

nor the softness of a woman. She kept her husband's respect, and was mother and queen of his tribe; the natives flocked around her with affection and friendship. To the last she was fresh and young, brave, refined, and delicate. In the Desert stillness to-night the singers are singing to the low beat of the cymbal and the mournful two-stringed guitar their hymn of the Chief-queen, whose hair was of amber, whose eye was like Sirius, when the Nile begins to swell. She wore a wonderful belt of burning jewels, and gave much gold with her white-rose hands, and was worshiped by the tribe Anazee. Her grave is a beautiful shrine. Though a Giaour, her soul is at rest with the blest on green pillows by the Happy River, where the great light shines from the Throne. The river is wide, like the wideness of the sea. It is sweeter than honey, whiter than milk, cooler than snow, smoother than cream. Its banks are of chrysolites, and they who drink of it shall never thirst again. In a shady pavilion of rosy-veined marble, pillared with silver and pearl, and ceiled vermilion and blue, she is waiting, waiting for Antar, in the Golden Pleasure Fields kept for the Faithful."

Under the palms, one summer night (O happy night!) I heard the low, slow song of an Anazee, and from his strings of rhymes gathered the few tender threads woven into this *True Romance*.

IN THE HAREM.

SLAVERY is nominally abolished in the Ottoman empire, but it is said—I know not how truly—that 10,000 slaves are annually bought, the larger portion women who become inmates of Turkish harems; and this mingling with the fairest race has subdued the original ugliness of the Tartar.

There are boundless possibilities in their exchange of circumstance. Each may become an odalisque, the mother of princes, even a Sultana. For, by the strange code of the Moslem, the Sultan must marry a slave, one who has been bought and sold, and the lowest on whom he casts a passing look has hope of such high destiny. The Turk can have four lawful wives, though few have more than one. We copy Father Jacob, they plead, and if you hint at forbidden numbers, we are like Solomon, the wise, and Jacob, his father. No Oriental woman makes secret her wish to marry, any more than the widow of Moab in the barley-fields among the gleaners at Bethlehem, and her prayer is yet the prayer of Rachael—"Give me children, else I die."

With this underflow of feeling, Caucasian women willingly leave their wretched homes

and, when ships touch at the coasts, come to the
travelers and implore them to carry them away
as servants. They have seen their brothers—
handsome and fearless as leopards--marched off
to service in foreign armies. Their costume of
Persian embroideries, belted with silken girdles;
their sharp scimeters, enameled with gold, dazzling the sight. The women long to follow and
tempt fate in the city which they have heard
lies like a bird afloat on the waters of the
Golden Horn. Those young girls have little
tenderness to remember. In one garment they
have herded sheep and carried water jars on
bruised shoulders in the fierce sun heat of the
summer; and rolled in skins, on the mud floor
of a smoky den, they have shivered in the biting winds blowing across glaciers which never
melt. They do not sigh for freedom; they have
had freedom in their own native hills; they
want to thrust their bare feet into velvet slippers
spangled with gold, and loll on soft divans in
rooms lined with bright marbles.

The trade is carried on by Jews and is a
necessary part of polygamy. The slaves enter
better conditions than they leave, are usually
kindly treated and by law are free at the end of
seven years. The whole system is patriarchal,
and was ancient before the coming of the Father
of the Faithful. Contracts for marriage are
oftenest made by the mother of the bride, who
sometimes does not see her fiance till she is
robed for the ceremony; and old maids are un-

24

known in the empire where maids are marriage-
able at sixteen or younger.

Wedding festivities sometimes last a whole
week. The men, in their rooms, smoke sol-
emnly and sip coffee. "Laughter," says their
proverb, "is for women and children." And
merrily laughter rings through the screened
doors before the apartments of the women. Their
gaiety overflows in jests and playful tricks, triv-
ial and meaningless to us, but delightful to them.
Charms are practiced, fortunes foretold and
dreams, in which they have childlike faith, are
related. Sometimes a marriage is delayed on
account of a bad omen or unlucky dream.

The presents of the wealthy are jewels, furs,
and embroideries, shawls from the goats of
Thibet, silks of Indian dyes, rich as coronation
robes, scarfs of Mecca, woven of pure, white silk
shot with silver. The larger garments are
strung on cords stretched against the walls of
the bridal chamber. A wreath of artificial
flowers borders its ceiling and the draperies
below make a vari-colored lining, gay as the
shawl-lined tent of Haroun Al Raschid. All is
arranged with the unerring eye for color which
distinguishes the Oriental, and the work goes on
with intervals of feasting, eating sugar-plums,
and wild fantastic music, at once harsh and sorrowful. The bride is radiant in white or rose
pink, wrought with gold; her nails and finger
tips are dyed with henna, and an amulet of cornelian, inscribed with a verse from the Koran, is

hung round her neck—a defense against the evil eye.

When the hour comes for the betrothed strangers to see each other face to face for the first time, her best friend kisses the bride between the eyebrows, removes her veil and spreads it on the floor. The bridegroom kneels upon it and offers the touching prayer appointed by Lord Mohammed, regarded as the most acceptable that can be addressed to the Deity on this occasion.

The word harem means " the Holy or Sanctified," and in general sense is given to any spot peculiarly hallowed. I was a long while learning that the name applies to the spacious enclosed court about mosques; not a barred prison, but consecrated ground, revered as a sanctuary. However blank and bare the remainder of the house may be—and usually is—the forbidden rooms are well furnished according to Moslem fancy, in which is copied, nearly as possible, their ideal Paradise; an adorable palace with a thousand windows, and before every window a sparkling fountain. Free light, abundant space, shady gardens, where the nightingale sings among the roses, and rushing waters cool the air. These are the luxuries dearest to the Oriental. The women, old and young, assemble in the sacred rooms with their children and attendants, and they are the center of the world to the home-keeping Turk, who cares nothing for travel and never emigrates. His spare time and money are spent there, and the

wife is in the tender Arabian **phrase**, "the
keeper of her husband's soul."

Turkish houses are much **alike**. The entrance is through a double door large enough for
horses and carriage. Beyond it is a swing-
screen suspended like a gate, and hides the ves-
tibule, or court, when the street door opens.
Two outside staircases appear, one leading to
the men's apartments, the other to the women's.
At the first landing the visitor finds the black
Aga on guard before the door, to which only
one man is admitted, and which is forbidden to
the sight and thought of all men save that one.

There is no special place to eat or sleep in.
A low divan running round the wall of each
room is made a bed by night, the clothes being
kept in presses by day. In imperial palaces the
coverlets are of Lahore stuffs embroidered with
colored silks interwoven with pearls and turquoises, the sheets are of fine cotton, barred with
stripes of silk like satin ribbon. The pillows have
silk and gold covers, and during summer, mosquito
nets of Tripoli gauze, spotted with gold, are suspended by gilt hoops over the sleeper. Nothing gayer or daintier can be imagined. Formerly cashmere shawls served as "spreads" for
the beds of the rich. The small round mirror,
framed in velvet, is always at hand for toilet
use, and the laying on of cosmetics is so deep
that it is named "face-writing." Turkish
women understand the arts of repairing the rav-
ages of time, and their toilet service is varied
and effective. Meals are served on bright brass

trays of various sizes, and a piece of bread serves
as spoon, knife and fork, so deftly used that
there is neither spilling nor crumbling about the
low table, beside which cushions are ranged
instead of chairs. Exquisite neatness prevails
and many attendants are in waiting.

Every Turkish harem has its bath-rooms,
three in number, if the owner is well to do.
The first is square, chiefly of marble, (in the
Sultan's palace of Egyptian alabaster), lighted
from a glass dome. A large reservoir, built
against the outer wall, with an opening into the
bath, contains the water, half of which is heated
by a furnace below it. Hot air pipes throw
intense heat into the room, fountains lead the
water from the reservoir and here the rubbing
process is conducted. The second room is less
and furnished only with a marble platform holding mattresses and cushions, where the bathers
repose after the fatigue of ablutions too many
for description. Here they smoke cigarettes, eat
fruits and sweets, and finally wrap themselves in
soft burnouses, and pass to the outer chamber
where they drowse and doze on downy couches
till they recover from the steaming heat and the
languor that follows a long warm bath. Besides
these, there are public baths where women
spend many hours in gossip and the passive enjoyment of being thoroughly rubbed, brushed,
combed and perfumed.

I once met a famous lady, bought with a great
price by a high official of Stamboul. She was
a Georgian, I think, with hair of reddish gold—

the sun-bright tresses of Medea—ivory white
skin, eyes black as death—the antelope eyes of
the poets. The faintest line of antimony drawn
on the lids at the root of the long lashes added
to their luster and the witchery of her glance.
She wore the *yashmak*, and as only ladies were
present I begged her to remove it, so I might
see her unveiled loveliness. She complied
without affectation of timidity or blushing and
returned my gaze with smiling serenity, too
well used to open admiration for embarrassment.
I cannot recall her name; it was something
which, being interpreted, might mean Tulip
Cheek. A *rivèrire* of pearls lay on her neck—
snow on snow—and the exquisite mouth was a
very Cupid's bow. My princess must have been
a peerless maiden ten years before, now, unhap-
pily, growing stout, as Eastern women usually
do; the result of luxurious living and much
eating of sweets. Her manner was soft and
gracious, her aspect the repose of supreme content.

Ladies of rank are now struggling into the
miseries of French toilet, but the old Turkish
dress is much prettier. A loose, flowing robe
of silk or crêpe wrought with gold and silks,
without belt or tightness to limit its comfort.
Nothing better adapted to their climate can be
imagined. The white veil, prescribed by law,
without which no one may appear in street or
presence of man, is thin gauze, folded bias and
placed over the head, coming down near the
eyebrows. A larger piece covers the lower half

of the face and is secured to the back hair by
jeweled pins. It makes a light, pretty turban
which is a merciful charity to the homely, and
enhances the grace of the graceful; not hiding the
Paradise eyes—ah, those eyes! Well may the
minstrels liken their liquid splendor to the reflection of midnight stars at the bottom of a well.
And the veils grow thinner and thinner in spite
of firmans, issued by the sultan and read in all
the mosques, calling attention of heads of families to this back-sliding and violation of the law
of the prophet.

Often have I been asked how do Constantinople ladies employ themselves. Like others
who love leisure, in visiting, promenading, dress
and shopping. Their chief joy is to float in a
caique to the valley of Sweet Waters. On Friday—the Mohammedan Sunday—hundreds glide
by, dressed in brilliant color, mist-like veils
faintly shading their faces. The rowers wear
jackets of scarlet, stiff with shining broidery,
an armed slave is on duty clad in barbaric stuffs,
Cushions of eider-down, crimson hangings touching the blue water make the enchanting picture.
O, how its beauty comes back to me now!

Their talk with each other is of their children, the changes and intrigues of the palace,
and of dress. The Turkish woman does not
know the word responsibility. She has undisputed control of her property and time, is able
to take her own part, and by finesse and perse-
verance manages to have her own way.

Speaking through an interpreter dulls the

edge of conversation and the merest trifles suf-
fice. Yet on thinking over our talk it does not
seem greatly inferior to the average morning
visit in the land we love to call our own. The
seclusion of the harem gives much time for discussion and many a question of grave import is
there debated. The women are well informed
in politics, fond of intrigue, and so artful that
our missionary, Dr. Dwight, of Constantinople,
writes: " Any one who has a private scheme to
advance, a policy to develop, an office to gain or
to keep, a boy to provide for, or an enemy to
crush, sends his wife to the harem of a grandee.
Women here bring about the most astounding
results."

Their manner is ceremonious during formal
calls, and they still kiss the hem of the garment
in deference to age or superior. In familiar
places, they have a sweet frankness, like un-
trained young girls, and listen with interest to
accounts of our ways of living, how we keep
house, do great charities, manage the churches,
etc., etc. " How hard," they say in tender pity ;
"that life may be good for you but would not be
good at all for us. You are made for work, we
are made for love ; this suits us best." So they
lean back on the silky cushions, taste the con-
serve of rose and of quince, light their cigarettes
and are happy.

WEDDING CUSTOMS IN THE EAST.

The house rests not on the earth, but on the wife.—Oriental Proverb.

AMONG Oriental nations of unmixed blood, marriage ceremonies are almost the same as in patriarchal days. Negotiations are begun by parents or near relatives of the bridegroom and the bride, who have no voice in the matter. Settlements, all preliminaries, are conducted by guardians of those we call the high contracting parties; and love must come, if it come at all, after marriage. Compensation to the parents, for the loss of a daughter, is made. Still do Uncle Labans drive sharp bargains with those who must work for a wife, and practice deceits disappointing as that one revealed in the sorry morning when Jacob awoke and behold it was Leah. After betrothal there is an exchange of presents; from the beginning a sign of loyalty. The reader remembers how Abraham's servant sought a wife for Isaac, and, not content with giving her a golden ear-ring of half a shekel weight, and bracelets of ten shekels' weight of gold, he enriched her family with jewels of silver and jewels of gold, raiment, and precious things.

Sometimes a bride's whole fortune is in her trinkets—an inalienable dowry. One Sunday, while returning to Jerusalem from the Mount of

Olives, by way of the King's Dale, we followed
the dry bed of the Kedron to where the waters
of Siloa go softly, now, as in the age of miracles, an intermittent fountain. A Syrian woman
was drawing water in an earthen jar. Dressed
in the poor cotton gown of the peasant of Judea,
it was surprising to see a chain of valuable coin
pendant across her forehead, and white metal
bracelets, heavy almost as horseshoes, and not
unlike them in appearance, on her wrists.
Thinking to secure a souvenir of the day the
interpreter asked the price of her jewelries.
She named a sum ridiculously high, at which I
shook my head, and inquired if nothing less
would do. She smiled, showing teeth like hail-
stones, and said in Arabic, "They are my marriage portion; the Frankish lady has not money
enough to buy them."

In districts remote from cities, where ancient
customs rule, the Jewish ceremonies are length-
ened with a disregard of time not known to the
restless sons of Japhet. The festival may last
seven, ten, fifteen days, and, in comparison, any
merry-making in our domestic life is tame and
dull. Distant friends come with their families,
the ox and the fatling are killed, hundreds are
bidden to a mighty feast, and the rich man dis-
tributes wedding garments to those not able to
buy.

Before the happy hour when the bridal pair
may sing "I am my beloved's, and he is mine,"
there are protracted shows, games, jugglery,
rope-walking, and strange pastimes unknown to

us. The last day the bride, with her attendants, goes to the bath. Her nails are stained "like branches of coral" with henna, a powder made of leaves of camphire dried and pounded. Her eyelids are blackened with a fine line of antimony; and, while her maidens lay on thick cosmetics, red and white, she surveys herself in a small round mirror. She uses a perfume of ambergris and musk-paste called seraglio pastilles, and chews a white gum named mastic to sweeten her breath. Her dress is rose-pink embroidered with gold thread, and over the many plaited dark hair is thrown a gauzy veil which makes the air balmy with heavy odors. Then come plaintive songs, farewells full of tears, and the final benediction given to Rebekah, "Be thou the mother of millions."

Meanwhile the bridegroom, with his comrades, has spent the morning in the bath, where he is anointed with oil, scented with myrrh, and robed in vestments, purple and scarlet, costly as his purse will bear. Says the Oriental lover, "In the night, the jealous night which drops a veil over all else, we lift the bridal veil." When the midnight stars arise, he marches away in gay and noisy procession to a swell of drums and sounding pipes and cornets. There are flaring torches, waving scarfs, flowery garlands on horse and rider, dances, songs; and the rabble of the street—always a ready concourse—are free to join the wedding march and add wild shouts to the revelry.

Virgin's lamps are little terra-cotta things

made to hold about a half-pint of oil, and are
found in profusion about ruined cities of Judea.
They should be trimmed and ready for use when
the procession comes; but after two weeks of
continuous festivity it is not strange that some
of the bride-maidens forget to fill their lamps.
In fact, the wedding-guests are pretty well worn
out at the last hour, and drop to sleep—the children on the floor, the bride in her appointed
corner, the visitors on divans and cushions.
Finally, the watcher on duty—usually an elderly
matron—hears the sound of advancing music,
lute, cornet, and cymbal. She rouses the sleepers. The bride adjusts her dress, (can the maid
forget her ornaments or the bride her attire?)
and, at midnight, the joyful shout resounds.
"Behold, the bridegroom cometh, go ye out to
meet him." There is a sudden start for lights,
and ranging in line to receive him. When he
passes in with his train, the door is bolted
against the throng of the street, eager to crowd
the house, and rob, if possible. In the parable,
mixed with the mob were foolish virgins who
started at the last minute to buy oil, finding they
could not beg of the wise. Too late for explanation. Naturally, the bridegroom supposed
their loud knocking was the clamor of the multitude, and called out, " Verily I say unto you, I
know you not."

It is told that the janissaries of the Turkish
army once broke into a house, and, not satisfied
with stealing the wedding presents, carried off
the bride herself, and held her, in honor and

safety, till a heavy ransom was paid for her release.

Autre pays, autres mœurs. The Turkish wedding is on Monday, and among the poor the ceremony is merely the sentence, spoken by the woman, "I give myself up to thee," and there need be no witnesses. The ceremonials of the well-to-do are so long and elaborate, space forbids a description here. Divorce is equally easy. The Mohammedan can put away his wife at pleasure, and without cause, by simply saying, "I divorce thee;" but he must pay her dowry —which law is the check on the husband's caprice and tyranny.

With Circassians and tribes of the Caucasus we call heathen, after a bargain is made with the parents, the bridegroom carries off the daughter, a willing captive; and the bride is at home in a wretched hut, soon as a few incantations against evil spirits are practiced.

The prettiest wedding procession I have seen was in Constantinople—a stately and rejoicing march, though without music. Fancy a narrow street of high stone houses with projecting balconies, latticed with slats so close together that persons within can see without being seen. A long line of sedan chairs, cushioned and curtained with satin, each borne by two men holding poles, and keeping step together like trained horses; their uniform braided jackets, baggy trowsers, and scarlet fez made festal by a bunch of lilacs on the bosom—for it was rejoicing

Spring, and the gardens of the Bosphorus were radiant with color and bloom.

At the head of the column, an armed attendant, in gorgeous costume, with whip in hand, cleared away dogs and gaping idlers. They were *en route* for the Greek Church outside Pera, and the beauty of the beautiful race was on the bride. The shining face at the window was like some lovely human flower, too tender for exposure, blossoming under glass. On the classic head a wreath of orange-flowers, to be laid away on the morrow, and carefully kept for her burial.

As they near the church-door, a bridal chorus rules the slow steps of the carriers; and when the bride, lovely as a lily all white and gold, steps from the silken seat, bonbons are showered on her by waiting friends. The bridegroom, also crowned with a wreath, joins her; and they stand with clasped hands at the altar while the long ritual is read by the priest. Three times the wreaths are interchanged by the priest, in the name of the Father, Son, and Holy Ghost. Three times the pair are led by him round the altar; a glass of consecrated wine is offered first to the bridegroom, then to the bride, afterward to the best man and first bridesmaid, whose duty it is to be godfather and godmother to the children. The ceremony ends with kisses, congratulations, and leave-takings. much the same as in our own country.

AT YILDIZ PALACE.

THROUGH four hundred years the Turkish house-royal has had unbroken lineal male descent without a lateral branch. At Old Seraglio Point thirty successive Sultans held their sumptuous state till about forty years ago, when the chain of palaces bordering the Marmora was burned, and the court was removed to Yildiz, on the heights beyond Pera.

Beautiful for situation is Yildiz, Palace of the Star. Built nobly in a park of many hundred acres, it overlooks an amphitheater of stately cities with domes, towers, minarets, castles, islands, seas, fleets, and in the farness of the distance the Mysian Olympus—a panorama of vivid color and varied movement without a peer on the globe. What St. James Palace is to London is Yildiz to the Turk—the center of interest in Constantinople, the well-guarded, " the enchantress of many lovers."

Barracks have been added till it is in reality a citadel, and there beats the heart and plots the brain of Islam. Within the walled enclosure are kiosks of marble and gold, outbuildings, stables, a military camp and parade-grounds, cypress groves, unshorn forests, gardens with every kind of singing bird; a miniature city with the delights of the country as well—a fortress and a sanctuary. The least attempt of an unauthorized person to enter the buildings appropriated to men is punishable by death. It would come as a lightning stroke should any try to approach the forbidden rooms into which one man enters; the uncontrolled, irresponsible master of hundreds of women.

Among them are no family distinctions, no records, no questions of ancestry, hereditary titles or names. All have started from the same level, each one has been a slave bought by the mother or sisters of the Sultan, educated to her position, and presented to him on the third day of the Feast of Bairam, "the Night of Destiny." Nor are they married to him. The Padisha, being above law, cannot submit to matrimonial bondage. Since Othman, illustrious founder of the empire bearing his name, girded on the sword, which is the imperial scepter, but two Ottoman Sultans have married. Of the mates we call wives only four hold the highest rank. All have been chosen for personal charm, and are in the bloom of youth; by far the larger number are from Circassia, the ancient Colchis, from whose palace gardens Grecian heroes stole their brides in the dim centuries before the Iliad was written.

Imagination is bewildered by thoughts of such an array of beauties set in palatial splendors. They live for one sole purpose—the study of pleasing him who has lifted the silvery feet of these Daughters of Love from the mire and rested them on cushions of rose leaves and eider-down. Instead of grinding toil, they enjoy the

sweetness of rest ; one cotton gown is exchanged
for bright raiment and jewels rare ; for black
bread and goat's milk, they have suppers for
Sybarites, honey of orange-flowers, and sherbet
of violets and sugar. Each odalisque has her
kiosk, her court, grand officials, boats lined with
satin, gilded carriages and trained servants shod
with slippers of silence, who minister to them in
cool, perfumed chambers. Their career depends
on their own tact and grace. By these gifts the
ragged beggar may succeed to the highest rank,
and compel princesses to kiss the hem of her
garment.

One will in the harem is supreme as a Provi-
dence or a Destiny. To this power, before
which great and small are but dust, is yielded
absolute submission. Says Janilla, the Exalted,
teaching the newly arrived Laleli (Pink Tulip)
and Benefish (White Violet): "Should the
Prince at noonday say it is night, declare your
feet are wet with dew, and that you behold the
moon and the stars."

In February a new palace was ordered. In
June it was completed and furnished, fountains
playing, cascades dashing, nightingales nesting
among roses in bloom. We know how the
Turks furnish. In the Summer-Palace one room
is hung with pale blue silk, another with
Broussa satin, tapestries of India and broideries
of Persia. There are no pictures—they encour-
age profanity ; no statues—they lead to idolatry.
The Prophet (he rests in glory !) was a hater of
idols. In the day of judgment pictures and

25

statues will rise and flock round the artists who produced them, and call on the unhappy makers to supply their creatures with souls.

Humanity is unchangeable; the king of a hundred kings, the shadow of God upon earth, must have his preferences, and naturally the reigning favorite makes the most of her brief season of command. Doubtless tears, clamors, poutings, work the same results in Constantinople that they do in Washington, and the luxurious harem may have some dull corner where the discarded favorite may weep neglected while her victorious rival sweeps by in triumph.

The Turks are tender in the extreme to animals and children, and we must believe they are also gentle toward women. Sometimes the caprices of wives have been costly as the Sultan to the Empire. Sultan Ibrahim allowed his to take what they pleased from shops and bazars without payment. One houri complained she did not like shopping by daylight; and at once the sovereign issued an order requiring merchants to keep their shops open all night, and to have enough torches burning to exhibit goods to advantage. Another, whose name means Little Bit of Sugar, whispered to Ibrahim that she wanted to see him with his beard fringed with gems. The Lord of Lords was adorned accordingly, and made a spectacle of himself thus tricked out. Enormous treasures were lavished on a chariot, and, as in the days of Solomon, silver was nothing accounted of. But these whims are in the records of two hundred years ago, when the milk-white hand of a queen tightened the bow-string for the Grand Vizier, the Cadin of two thousand and seven hundred shawls reigned over two continents and two seas, and the odalisque of a hundred silver carriages ruled the imperial Divans.

A conspicuous person about the palace is the Bairam Aga, Keeper of the Maidens, a jet black Nubian, probably from the Soudan. He wears a gorgeous uniform of scarlet and gold, has the air of authority, and on his ample breast displays a dozen Imperial, Royal and Christian orders of which he is knight. He ranks with prime ministers and field marshals; disputes precedence with ambassadors, and is courted for his influence. A genuine African, he loves jewels, and on the hand graciously extended for kisses of the Faithful there glitters a ruby second only to the one for which Kubla Khan offered a city and was refused. From the savings of his income the Guardian of the Lilies has built a mosque for his lordly sepulcher when his term of vigilant service is ended.

The true Oriental is unsurpassed in secrecy, and there is a fascination in his silence which moves the gossip to insatiate curiosity. The foreigner must stop at the carved and gilded portal of the consecrated place. Even Bairam Aga does not pass it. Ambassadors have petitioned and princesses sued in vain for entrance into the Gate of Felicity. The outside world hears not the faintest echo of the strange, adventurous life of women whose loves, hates, spites, intrigues, are plays played out with neither audience nor spectator to report. If Bairam Aga knows more than we do, he makes no sign; he is secret as the grave.

It is said that harem etiquette was regulated ages ago by laws that change not, and is observed with rigid exactness and minute observance of detail. The mothers of children have apartments separate as families in flats, and visit with the grave ceremonials by which Orientals salute strangers. What jealousies may flash in the languishing dark eyes, whose witchery has made their fortune, who knows may tell.

At the Bairam feast the rose door of Paradise opens, and the ladies of the seraglio take place in the long procession of carriages. Their unsunned loveliness is closely veiled, and there is something delicate and sweet in that modest veiling, like the consecration implied in the pure white bonnet of the nun. Children's faces crowd the carriage-windows, heads lovely as seraph or cherub crowned with lilies and jasmine.

Here is a constant recurrence in mind to the court of Solomon and the Old Testament women. Could we lift the draperies which shadow the sanctuary we might find childless women mourning over their curse, and young mothers exulting, like Leah, at the birth of Reuben, when she says: "Now, therefore, my husband will love me." Vashti and Queen Esther after her may enjoy a transient season, but the mother of his

sons alone has the lasting affection of the Eastern monarch. And this brings us to the second person in rank of the Ottoman Empire, the mother of the first born prince. When her son comes to the throne she has the title *Sultana Valide* (Queen Mother). She enjoys an immense income, called slipper-money, a separate court and palace, with one hundred and fifty servants. When she drives her suit is thirty girls and from ten to fifteen black Agas mounted on Arab horses. No other lady moves in such pomp. When she takes her pleasure on the Bosphorus, it is in the imperial caique, the most exquisite boat since Cleopatra's barge floated on the Cydnus. It is painted pure white, with traceries of gold and pink, and under the perfect stroke of twelve pairs of oars darts like a winged thing across the waves. The rowers, dressed in white silk shirts, white trousers, and red fez, make a stroke with absolute precision, as one man, every thirty seconds. A crimson canopy of velvet, bordered with gold, is upheld by four gilt columns, and in its shade reclines the Sultana Valide on cushions of down and velvet carpets fringed with gold. A retinue of five caiques filled with maids of honor attend her. They are guarded by black slaves, whose duty it is to hold umbrellas over the young heads screened by the white turbans. The little fleet on the shining water is a most picturesque sight.

The Sultana Valide is the only inmate of the royal harem who is privileged to receive visits from foreigners. Under a manner of quiet dig-

nity she carries determination which makes
high officials dread her influence and seek her
favor. In time of peril and distress she may
admit deputations from the army and people;
her judgment in affairs is acknowledged, and she
has been known to plead for her son with eloquence and pathos. At the festival of Bairam,
celebrated by the departure of pilgrims for Mecca,
she joins the highest dignitaries and ministers,
officers civil and martial, in kissing the hem of
the Sultan's robe.

By court etiquette he must stand in her
presence, sitting at her request; in return the
place at his right hand, given by Solomon to his
mother, is still the reserved seat for the mother
of the Padisha. The pontoon bridge spanning
the Golden Horn, crossed daily by one hundred
thousand men, is called the bridge of the Sultana
Valide, and leads to a mosque of the same name.

Seven female officers preside over the *harem-
lik*. Each has her slaves and establishment, and
may be often seen shopping in the city, attended
by the Imperial servants. Seven thousand
persons daily eat the bread and salt of the Grand
Seignor. My brief space forbids enumeration of
service or wages. A few items are: three
hundred cooks, four hundred musicians, two
hundred men in charge of menageries and
aviaries, twelve hundred female slaves. Properly
speaking, there is no civil list, and accurate
figures are not easily reached. The ladies, veiled
and attended, visit in their walled gardens and
palaces, hired musicians play on lutes, and almehs

dance for their amusement. Donizetti, brother
of the famous composer, was at one time direc-
tor-in-chief of the Sultan's music. Story-telling
is in favor, and a good reciter is in high request.
Happy the Scherezade who knows the tales of
the genii and can amuse the Kaliph who has
gone through all the pleasures described by the
singing king at Bethlehem: "And whatsoever
mine eyes desired I kept not from them; I
withheld not my heart from any joy."

THE END.